An Undefended Heart

An Undefended Heart

a novel

Danielle Hering

DEDICATIONS

To David Elliott,
Thank you for shining the light so brightly.
This book only exists because of your
constant encouragement.

To Mother Earth,
may this help your children remember.

Contents

An Undefended Heart

Prologue

———

She leapt, knowing she had no choice and that this was her destiny, something to which she had agreed several lifetimes ago. None of that made it any easier, however, as she felt herself falling through time and space. Several others had taken this same journey before her and moved humanity along, and now, it was her turn, and time for the Goddess to be resurrected.

It was her mission to embody the Goddess in human form.

By now, the world was at the point of destruction. With pollution, wars, greed, violence, and abuse of power, Earth was crying out for help.

The people on the planet had become so polarized that Mother Earth was continually having to shake off toxic energy, seeking to regain Her balance by creating cataclysmic natural disasters.

In short, the planet's inhabitants needed the Goddess in order to survive.

In actuality, the Goddess had never left them, not even for the briefest of moments; on the contrary, she had been present all the time, and had merely transmuted into Earth, existing beneath their feet and in the air they breathed, in the water sustaining their life, and in the fire's dancing flames keeping them warm. But it was sad that they knew none of this.

They could not see Her because their hearts had grown closed, their eyes unwilling to see.

Someone needed to help them remember the Goddess before they destroyed themselves.

Sophia was eager to take on this challenge as her greatest act of service to date, fulfilling the reason for which she had been created. She had been cut from the same cloth as Athena, Mary Magdalena, Mother Mary, Kuan Yin, Tara, Vesta, Durga, and many others who served the Cosmic Mother, and in this way, she had already succeeded in liberating planet after planet.

The catch—and the tragedy—was that this time, she could not use her powers to transform Earth, nor could she be born awake as she had been in her other lifetimes. This time, she had to be born as a mere mortal, embedded deep in forgetting, susceptible to all the planet's density.

It meant that she had to embody all of humanity's wounds, only healing and reawakening alongside the rest of humanity. Everything she would heal via her body would create an opening in the planetary grid, a path for others to follow. No one had ever succeeded in this before.

Only those born remembering who they were or carrying some of their gifts had been able to accomplish anything. These Great Ones had incarnated multiple times with the specific aim of trying to teach humanity to open their hearts. *Trying* would be the correct description, however, since each time they departed, those in power would twist the teachings and corrupt the messages until the Truth became lost once again, setting everything back to how it had been before.

Watching what had happened with the Crusades, the Inquisition, the Conquest, the genocide of Natives, the ongoing oppression of women, and the destruction of the natural world—men marching for millennia to their deaths in senseless wars, slavery, and the Holocaust—the Galactic Council had determined there was no point in sending yet another Savior to the planet.

Messages of peace and love would never be enough to heal the wounds from which this world was suffering. The Council had to address it all from a different angle—or with a different angel.

"We can't just keep sending more light to the planet. We need to bring the darkness to the light; the Goddess must rise before the planet explodes," they concluded.

When humanity forgot about the Goddess, they lost their connection to their divinity as she was the container that could hold the light of the Divine. Without Her, humanity could only remember the Divine's male aspect, a memory that came only through their crown chakras.

God existed only in the heavens, within the realm of their thoughts.

They could think about the light, but they did not know how to bring it all the way into their bodies; this was why they had never felt safe in their bodies, with the result that they persisted in fighting with one another. To remember who they were, they needed the other half of the Divine to return. And to embody the Goddess, their bodies had to be made sacred.

The wounds they were holding within the darkness and density of their bodies would have to be brought to the light, to be delivered there and rendered whole.

Yet before the Goddess could return, all the damage done to the feminine needed to be healed.

Sophia knew she would not remember any of this once she was in a physical body because her human self would have no access to Sophia's wisdom until they reconnected. Until then, she would experience life on Earth just like everyone else.

She tried to focus on the benefits that would come about as a result of this endeavor. *I will save the world*, she tried to tell herself...but first, it would destroy her.

She had been traveling through the outer dimensions when she'd first received the call to help humankind, and this news was not what she had wanted to hear.

It meant that she had argued with the Council extensively, but all the seers had insisted on this route, asserting this was the only way for Earth and humanity to survive.

There were also those on the Council who had been wanting to pull the plug on the humans a long time ago, declaring themselves more than ready to give up and start over elsewhere.

The planet's density had grown so thick with fear that it seemed improbable for the light to ever manage to break through, and all earlier attempts to save Earth had been undermined by parasitic entities—minions of their dark-force-energy overlords—that had come to live off of fearful energy emitted by humans. Though a considerable and sustained effort had been made to eliminate the parasites, they were spreading faster than they could be contained.

It was a losing fight, bringing a stark sense of urgency to the mission now.

This was humankind's last chance.

"The tighter we make the contraction, the greater the catapult into expansion," the Council had said to her. "Yes, Sophia, it will without doubt prove to be the hardest thing you have ever done, but that is the point of it. Your journey will exist within the paradox of being both impossible to achieve *and* destined to succeed. Through the greatest wound, you will discover healing.

"In the darkness, you will find the light, and in surrender, you will find victory. In duality, you will find Oneness. As you succeed in opening your heart and reuniting the sacred love of the masculine and feminine energies within one physical body, seven billion souls will remember."

As she approached the gravitational pull of the Earth, her descent accelerated.

Everything became blurry after that, making her see flashes of light and feel the extreme cold of the atmosphere, growing nauseated as gravity continued to accelerate her fall.

She heard the whispers of the wind constantly reassuring her that she would never be alone.

I will always be here with you, breath by breath, were words that soothed her.

The comet in which she was traveling burned brighter as it approached its destination, its speed and momentum bringing her to and through the ground. Since she didn't have a physical body yet, there was no experience of pain, only a sense of entering Earth's denseness.

I will always be here to provide you with whatever you need, she heard the ground say to her.

She then plunged through water, instantly feeling the nourishment it promised to provide. Next, she fell through the fire, seeing with her mind's eye its promise to always light her way.

As she connected with each of the elements, they all placed their activation codes within her. She now had almost everything she needed to start her human journey.

She had landed in a cavern deep inside the center of the Earth, a place consumed by a green mist filling the space, making it hard to see clearly.

"I have been waiting a long time for you," she heard a voice say. "I know you are probably tired from your journey, but we have no time to waste. We have only a few minutes before your essence must be placed inside your human mother's womb."

She couldn't see who was speaking, but the voice seemed to be coming from the green mist.

"Thank you for coming. Thank you for saying yes," it added.

The green mist began swirling around her, merging with her spirit.

"Breathe me in, and I will anchor myself inside the physical body's heart as it is created; I will be her compass. Once she is born and her mind takes over, her chakras will close down, and she won't remember anything. She won't be able to see, hear, or feel me for a long time, but I will always be there, waiting for her to remember. Have you chosen a name for her, your body?"

"Yes, she will be called Mia," Sophia said quietly.

Taking in as deep a breath as she could, she filled her lungs with the life force energy of Mother Earth. Then everything went black.

1

John, the Mystic Healer

After crossing the Sierra Nevada mountains, Mia dropped into the Imperial Valley where she could see the heat rising off the road ahead, feeling grateful she wouldn't have to stop for gas anytime soon. Mexico was just a few miles to the south. She had driven through the desert many times before, each time wondering why people would choose to live in such a hot place.

This arid and barren landscape reminded her of how she had been feeling inside, her heart overcome with numbness since the breakup. It wasn't the typical heartache one would feel after the ending of a relationship; this was something different. She wasn't grieving the end of the relationship per se, not missing Richard or wanting him back.

No, what she felt was even scarier to her.

It was an inner questioning, a sense of confusion. How could she have been so wrong?

She had been so certain that what had burgeoned between

them was true love, so solid a love she would have bet her life on it. She almost had done so, too.

Yet her intuition had proven to be a hundred percent wrong. Everything in her had told her to run full speed ahead into this, yet it had still failed. The devastation inside of Mia wasn't from losing Richard; rather, it was from losing herself. How could she trust herself after this?

And how could she live without having that sense of trust in herself?

Dammit! I don't want to think about him anymore. I came on this trip to clear my mind.

She decided to distract herself with Dr. Wayne Dyer's audiobook, *Manifest Your Destiny*, to help pass the time. *Come on, Wayne! Tell me how to manifest a better life!*

She crossed into Arizona, then decided to bypass driving through Phoenix; she'd take the scenic route instead, heading north through Prescott and then east to Jerome, an abandoned mining town that had been brought back to life with art galleries and restaurants.

The two-lane road was winding but well worth the extra time. *Northern Arizona's so beautiful! Why doesn't everyone in the state live up here where it's lush and green?* she wondered. *People just don't make any sense to me.*

It was dark when she arrived in Sedona, so she couldn't see the red rocks, but boy could she feel them! A spinning sensation whirled in her chest as if her heart was doing flip-flops, her body vibrating. *Whoa! How do people function here with all this energy?*

She made it to the hotel, checking in at the front desk.

"My heart's spinning for some reason," she said to the clerk.

He gave her a knowing smile. Once in her room, she didn't think she'd be able to sleep but drifted off before she knew it, the night's slumber bringing vivid dreams of aliens and starships, of long slithering snakes, and of a strange talking owl that lived down by the river.

What a weird night, she thought as she woke up. *Maybe it's part of the Sedona effect. I'd better get out here anyway and see what this place is all about.*

As she stepped outside her hotel room and gazed upon the red rock formations for the first time, the sight filled her with awe. They were mesmerizing—their deep red color, their height and mysterious shapes, all looking so magical. No, it was more than that; they looked majestic and powerful, her body becoming energized by her heart's joy.

It had been a long time since she'd felt anything like this, and it was beautiful.

She was surprised to find the same clerk at the front desk again this morning.

"I'm looking for suggestions on where to go and what to see," she told him with a smile. "I've been hearing about these vortex tours—are they worth the money, or should I go explore on my own?" She paused, thinking it over. "I'm not sure I even know what a vortex is."

"Yeah, not a lot of people do. They're just locations on Earth where you can feel the energy spiraling down into the ground or spiraling upward. Think of a vortex as a concentrated dose of Mother Earth's energy that some people think can help with healing, meditation, or self-exploration. Some people even believe they can help you contact aliens!"

Mia laughed. "I could probably use the help of a few aliens to get over my ex. Is there a specific vortex for that kind of healing?"

"The vortex energy's so strong in Sedona that you don't have to go to the exact location to experience it," the clerk continued. "Personally, my favorite hike is Cathedral Rock, especially early in the morning while it's still cool. The view up there's spectacular.

"You'll be able to see Oak Creek down below. Plan on spending the afternoon there so you can cool off in the water. I can show you a spot on the map that only the locals know about, so it won't be crowded with tourists." He smiled.

"That's great. Thanks for the advice!" she enthused and headed off on her adventure.

She quickly arrived in the parking lot below Cathedral Rock and got out of the car.

The energy here was alive, her being filled with a sense of overwhelming awe and gratitude that she would be spending her morning climbing up this colossal red rock.

Thank you, she whispered out loud.

She wasn't sure why she did, but it felt right for some reason.

This hike—more of a climb, in fact—was easy, yet others were so challenging she had no idea how she could make it up. At only three-quarters of a mile to the summit, it held a gain in elevation of 650 feet. "But if all those other people can do it, I can too," she said aloud, pushing through her fear.

It really did feel impossible at some sections, however. They were so steep that people had carved notches in the rocks where a climber could place a hand or foot. It was *not* impossible, of course. Taking it literally step by step, foothold by foothold, she slowly ascended.

Her mind flashed to a scene in which she was climbing a pyramid in ancient Egypt.

That's weird, she thought. *Why is this making me think about Egypt? I don't even know if Egyptians ever climbed the pyramids...*She giggled. *Ha! Maybe I helped build one in a past life.*

She laughed again at the thought and just kept climbing.

By the time she reached the top, she was out of breath, sweaty, and covered in red dust.

Her breaths were hard, struggling to get oxygen to her now aching head, gasping as she looked out at the valley far below; the contrast of the red earth and the sea of green treetops was unlike anything she had ever seen before, especially with the deep red rock spires framing the view on either side, and the bright blue sky sprinkled with fluffy white clouds.

She felt like a kid again, climbing and clambering around the rocks.

And it was more than that, far more. Yes, it was as if the rock called her to specific places. *Come look over here! Climb down here!*

She crawled around the top for a while, exploring all the sections she could reach. She had never experienced anything as beautiful as this rock, anything as enigmatic.

"You are so beautiful! I love you!" she called out, unable to contain her emotions.

Now and then, her legs got wobbly, or she became a little dizzy, a sensation she erroneously attributed to the altitude. She didn't realize that it was the vortex energy already working on her, peeling away her resistance and fear so she could feel her heart.

After an hour at the top, Mia was sweating and overheated, her lips cracked, mouth dry.

She looked down, seeing Oak Creek wasn't too far away and it seemed as though the water was calling out to her now. She headed back down in the general direction of the parking lot.

The hike down felt a lot easier; she was feeling lighter, freer than in a long time.

Even the sections of the hike that before had seemed so steep and indomitable now appeared much simpler to navigate. *Why didn't I realize how much I loved hiking? It's so much fun!*

I need to do this more often. The way my body feels climbing on the earth... it's amazing.

Following the clerk's directions on the map, Mia made her way to a quiet spot on the creek. The only sounds were the water flowing over the rocks and the birds chirping in the trees.

Cathedral Rock stood to the east in the distance. It seemed hard to believe that less than an hour ago, she had been standing on top of it, looking down at precisely where she was now.

She took off her shoes, finding a rock to sit on while she cooled off her feet in the water.

"Watch out for that snake," she heard someone say from behind a tree.

"Where?" she exclaimed, pulling her legs up out of the water so quickly she almost lost her balance. It would have sent her tumbling in. Luckily, she managed to steady herself in time.

"I'm kidding; there aren't any snakes here...not right now anyways," a man said, chuckling.

Mia scowled at him, wondering why he thought it was funny to scare her.

"Well, there was one here earlier, but I sent it on its way. It might have been your snake, probably the one from your dream."

He inspected his soapstone pipe before wrapping it up in a piece of deerskin.

Mia's jaw dropped. *What did he just say? How does he know about the snake in my dream?*

"Well, how else were you supposed to know who I was if I didn't tell you about the snake?" the man answered as if she had spoken the question aloud.

This was crazy; apparently, this guy was a mind reader.

Mia wanted to think that this man was just insane and she wanted to get out of there, but she was also incredibly curious about how he could perform such a feat of knowing what was in her head. *I...how do you do that? You preempt what I'm thinking. Good guesses, I suppose.*

"No. Guesses they are not. Your thoughts are very loud," he said, again answering her silent question. "Mia, my name is John, and we have a lot of work to do."

"How do you know my name?" she asked, finally able to speak again.

"The owl told me," he said, chuckling. "It also told me it was time for you to heal your heart."

Is this a joke? Am I being punked? What an idiot he is!

She looked around to see if there was a hidden camera somewhere.

But I never even told anybody about my dream, so that explanation makes no sense either.

Then she looked back at John, still sitting on a log in the shade. His expression told her he found her bewilderment humorous.

"What makes you think my heart needs healing?" Mia finally said.

"Because I heard some *Dick* broke it," John said, chuckling again. "And I don't *think* it needs healing; I can *feel* that it does. I felt your sadness the moment you stepped on the trail. I may even have felt it when you were standing up there on top of Cathedral Rock. But the main reason I know is that if it were already healed, you'd remember me. You would know who I am."

Mia's mind was racing. *He knows about my dream. He knows about Richard. He knows I was just on top of Cathedral Rock ... Is this some sort of weird Sedona hallucination? Maybe he's the alien in my dream, and that's why he can read my mind.*

John started laughing again.

"Well, you may be more correct than I'm willing to admit right now, but I don't think we need to bring extraterrestrials into it just yet. But no, you're not hallucinating."

He stood up and walked toward her.

Mia didn't feel she was in any danger, so she stayed put. John was a nice-looking man, maybe a little over six feet tall and weighing around 185 pounds. He had brown hair and was probably in his fifties…no, maybe his forties—she couldn't tell. He had a little gray in his hair, and smile lines around his eyes. He 'felt' younger than he looked, she decided.

As he got closer, she noticed he had kind eyes, bright blue. He was dressed in a spring green T-shirt, long cargo shorts, and sturdy leather walking sandals and spoke in a southern lilt that she imagined must be from the mountains of Virginia or North Carolina.

"It's nice to see you again," he said as he reached out to shake her hand. "Or I can say 'meet' you if you're more comfortable with that. And I usually hug people instead of shaking hands, but I'll give you a chance to warm up to me first."

When Mia shook his hand, a spark of energy traveled up her arm.

Now, there was something remarkably familiar about him as if he were an actor she had seen in a movie, or maybe in one of her dreams. *I suppose I'll have to let down my guard and see what this trippy experience has in store.* At that moment, a hummingbird flew up and darted around them, hovering in front of Mia's face for a moment before flying off again.

"Nature will come close and dance for you whenever your heart is open. That was a ruby-throated hummingbird that just visited us, a favorite of mine. Did you notice how it connected with you before darting along? That was a validation of your decision to let your guard down.

"I know all of this seems strange, but I promise if you give me a chance, it will make sense in the end. Come, let's sit in the shade. It's going to take me a while to explain everything to you."

He led the way back over to the log on which he'd been sitting and offered her a seat.

"And the way I see it, since the way you've been living your life hasn't really worked, why not try something new? What I have to say to you is so simple that most people miss it altogether.

"Mia, you're looking for something outside of yourself to fix what feels broken inside. You're waiting until you've got your life together before you start to love yourself. But have you noticed how no matter how much you achieve, there's always something else that needs to be fixed before you can accept yourself? You're spending all your time trying to get other people to love and to validate you. And if they don't, you blame them for your pain. The solution is as simple as loving yourself, but most people have no idea how to do that."

John paused to see if Mia was keeping up with him.

"Did you love yourself when you lost that extra weight you were carrying, or did you just find something else that was wrong with your body? Were you at peace with yourself when you got your dream job, or were you still trying to prove that you were good enough? Do you tell people what you think and feel, or do you hold back because you're afraid they won't like you? Do you really have any idea who you are?"

Mia's brow furrowed, John's words hitting home.

"Now, before you start to think there's something extra wrong with you, this is a problem affecting everyone on the planet. It's not just you, Mia. This is why people aren't happy. The mind keeps everyone trapped into thinking they can't love or accept themselves yet, all waiting for someone else to give them permission to be here."

"Be where?" she asked.

"To be here on the planet, to be living their lives, to be in their bodies," John said emphatically.

Mia wanted to object, but deep down, knew he was right.

She had never felt good enough, no matter how hard she worked at it.

But what John was proposing felt impossible to do, especially after the hellish mess she had somehow created while dating Richard. The thought of always expressing her feelings or opinions made her feel nauseous. And how could she love all the things that were wrong with her? How could she love this body of hers with all its flaws? She started to feel dizzy.

"That dizziness you feel is your thoughts starting to unravel. The nausea is because your identity has been created around these beliefs, the ones you're holding in your solar plexus.

"And I'm going to add more fuel to the fire, Mia, because I know you're up for it: that feeling of powerlessness is because you still think you're a victim. You think that if your parents had loved you more or seen exactly who you are, you wouldn't be in so much pain."

Mia glared at him, starting to get pissed off. *That wound is real, and I'm willing to defend it. My parents should have done a better job of loving me,* her mind insisted. *It's a simple fact.*

"How could they, Mia?" John said, listening to her thoughts. "They don't love or accept themselves, so they had no way of giving or teaching you that. This wound has existed for ages; feel into it. What do you know about your grandparents, your great-grandparents?

"They've all been trying to earn their value, to be good enough to be loved. But can't you see, Mia, that no one is ever good enough? Unconditional love hasn't existed in your lineage for millennia. So how long are you going to keep blaming them for your pain? Aren't you bored with telling yourself that story yet? Are you ready to forgive them and set them free? As long as you're blaming them, you're going to be stuck in this cycle of self-pity.

Find compassion and understanding for why they were the way they were…and get on with loving yourself."

Mia's head was spinning even faster than ever.

"The pain feels really big—and even though you say it's affecting everyone on the planet, it doesn't seem that way to me. It feels like it's affected me more than other people," Mia said.

She was finally acknowledging her profound sadness.

"That's because you're empathic, Mia. The sadness you're feeling isn't just yours. It's the sadness that's been carried in your lineage forever. You took on your parents' pain as a child.

"When we are dependent on someone else for our survival, we take on their pain, trying to process it for them to ensure they'll be strong enough to continue to care for us.

"Your body is full of energy from so many other people that it's hard for you to distinguish what's yours and what isn't. That makes it hard to know who you are and what you think, want, and need—which can make expressing yourself really difficult. Are you starting to see how it's all connected?"

Mia looked down, not wanting John to see her tears.

"Yes, I do; I feel the truth in what you're telling me. And on the one hand, I feel relieved that I'm not crazy and it's not my fault, but on the other, how can I fix any of this?

"It feels kind of hopeless, as if I'm screwed. I don't know how to stop feeling other people's feelings or how to fix something that's been in my lineage forever. And my mind's still insisting that despite what my parents went through, they could have loved me more. I can see how lovable I was as a little girl, but can't figure out how to convince my mind I'm lovable now.

"Because as stupid as I know it sounds, I really believe that if my body were perfect, I could love myself, or if I hadn't made so many mistakes, or if my last relationship had worked out …"

Mia instantly regretted having brought up her last relationship.

She was suddenly flooded with all the pain and sadness she had been suppressing for months.

John let Mia cry until it seemed she was done.

"That's why I'm here, Mia; I came into your life to help you fix it. This conversation was to help you to recognize where you're stuck and to get you to feel your feelings. Feel it to heal it."

"Why me, though?" Mia asked. "Why come into *my* life? Why do you seem able to read my mind and know about my dreams? Who are you, and why even care whether I manage to heal or not?"

John smiled as if he'd been waiting for this part of the conversation.

"Are you ready for it to get weirder, Mia? I can answer your questions, but you need to listen with your heart, not your mind. Because what I'm going to say won't make sense to your mind."

"Go for it," Mia said. "*None* of what's happened today makes sense to my mind. And how much weirder can this day really get?"

"You and I have known each other for an inordinately long time. Since the beginning of time, in fact. We come from the same..." John hesitated for a moment. "Well, think of it as though our souls are cousins," he said, cocking his head. "And realize that I agreed to help you remember who you are in this lifetime. I came to you to fulfill this task."

"So, who am I then?" Mia asked. *And why is he staring at me with glazed eyes as if he's really looking at—or thinking of—something else? Weird!*

"I can't tell you who you are; you have to remember that for yourself for it to feel real. But don't worry. I am going to help you do that," John said.

"Okay, that all sounds good in theory but how exactly will you do it? You'll help me remember? Are you going to hypnotize me or something?"

Her tone of urgency seemed to say, *let's get on with it already.*

"I'm going to teach you how to find yourself in the breath, a type of breathing meditation that will allow you to heal yourself and remember the truth. It will release all that sadness you're carrying, along with everybody else's energy you've long since been absorbing into your body."

"Sounds good to me," Mia said.

John seemed relieved. "I'm going to have you lie down on the grass, and you are going to breathe through your mouth, two breaths in and one breath out. The first inhalation will fill your lower belly, and the second will fill the upper chest, and then you will make a gentle exhale. Like this," John said, demonstrating the breathing pattern he wanted her to follow.

"Hold these stones while you breathe," he said, handing her two gray rocks. "They're ocean stones. Keep your eyes closed. There's nothing to think about; stay focused on the breathing."

Mia lay down on the cool ground and noticed how good her body felt, finally getting to relax after all her hiking this morning. The stones he had given her were smooth against her palms.

She closed her eyes and started breathing the way John had shown and described to her. It felt awkward. *I won't be able to keep going for very long, will I?* she thought.

"It'll get easier in a few minutes, Mia; we just have to get you through your resistance. Keep breathing," John said, watching her struggle with the rhythm of the breath.

Mia started to feel dizzy and her body, which moments ago had been so relaxed, was now hurting.

"Breathe into the pain, Mia. If you're ready to heal your life, then breathe as if your life depends upon it," John said, smiling at his own humor as if he had an audience.

Mia pushed through the pain and willed herself to breathe harder. The dizziness got worse, and then…it stopped. Mia was breathing rhythmically without even thinking about it.

Her body began to vibrate and tingle, and then her hands started to cramp, her fingers tightening around the stones in her palms as it intensified.

The next thing she knew, she was flooded with sadness.

"Let your emotions move, Mia—open your heart," John encouraged.

Mia breathed into the sadness, a terrible sobbing overtaking her, racking her upper body as she fought to breathe and to see. Tears were pouring free as she struggled to keep taking in the life-giving air. But it was so difficult, such an overwhelming and seemingly never-ending sadness, as if it would drown her. It seemed as if there was no point in trying to do anything about it because this sadness was going to consume her no matter what, and she would be powerless to stop it.

What was the sense in fighting against it?

One painful memory after another flooded into her, making her heart break over and over as she remembered every rejection, every abandonment, every time she hadn't been seen or understood, every time she had felt unloved and unworthy, undervalued, and dismissed.

Lost in a sea of sadness, Mia barely heard John say, "Ask Mother Earth to help you now, Mia. Call upon Earth's energy, Mia."

Desperate to stop the pain, Mia did exactly that in her next breath.

"Please help me," she cried out.

As if she had been hit by lightning, an electrical surge moved through her body, opening her heart chakra. Instantly, both the pain and sadness were gone.

It was suddenly easier for her to allow these breaths into her body, and Mia breathed deeply, steady in the rhythm as her inhalations and exhalations gained momentum.

The breath seemed to take on a life of its own until it felt as though it was breathing her. She lost all awareness of where she was, only experiencing herself as the breath.

She was now vibrating high enough that her spirit, Sophia, could begin to interact with her body. Mia saw a golden light in front of her, soft and iridescent, like a cloud of golden energy. It expanded all around her, filling her with more love than she had ever experienced.

She wanted that golden light more than she had ever wanted anything.

Take me, she said in her mind to the golden light surrounding her.

No, you take me! Sophia responded as she entered her body. Sophia had been waiting over thirty years for this moment.

In an instant, every need she'd ever known became satiated, every desire fulfilled. Everything was in the breath, making her whole and complete, infinite and eternal.

Each breath was more delicious than the last, deeper and yet more fulfilling, the sensation of air moving past her lips exquisite. Mia felt as though there was nothing else she needed from this life; all was complete, beautiful air reaching down to the bottom of her lungs and into her heart.

She felt never-ending and everlasting, as if she had always existed in every place and across all time. She experienced her body being seventeen feet tall, no—wait—it was taller, going on forever in every direction. She realized there was nothing to heal as nothing of her had ever been damaged. She realized there was no one to forgive as no one had ever done anything bad to her.

All she could feel was love, unconditional, and for everyone and everything.

The next awareness was that of being pulled inside Mother Earth, into the heart of the planet, her awareness now inside a green cavern deep within Earth. She felt she belonged here, that this was her home. Everything was green, even the air; she breathed it in, merging with it.

"You've a lot of work to do, Mia," she heard Sophia say. "And it's time for you to get started. You are going to help in the healing of the surface of the planet and all the people who are suffering. Trust John and do as he says, even when it makes no sense. He is here to assist you."

Mia was filled with love and adoration for this voice, feeling humbled in its presence.

She understood that the green energy was the key, and that she was here to help bring it to the surface of the planet. This was her mission, and nothing else mattered. As Mia agreed to dedicate her life in service to this energy, she felt herself fall the rest of the way through the earth.

Suddenly, Mia was floating in the Universe—finding it was made of love, of feminine energy.

The tiny part of Mia's mind that was witnessing this experience felt as though it was jumping up and down with excitement at this revelation.

The Universe is female, and everything within it is made from green goddess energy, pure feminine love; it's inside Earth, then drops through, out into the Universe!

Every time Mia's mind tried to conceptualize what was happening, her vision expanded.

I am infinite, beyond all understanding...I am you. You are me. We are one and the same.

Mia could feel the truth of this, allowing her definition of herself to expand until she experienced herself as all of life, as all of existence.

She could have remained in this state all day, but a growing sense of urgency brought her back to the present. She opened her eyes and found herself back in her body, lying on the grass in Sedona. She looked around for John, finding him sitting on the log, carving his pipe as if just contentedly enjoying a peaceful day out in the countryside.

She sat up and looked at him with her eyes wide, not yet able to speak.

John chuckled and nodded, anticipating every thought inside her mind. Knowing it.

"You were shown more than I expected for your first time. They must have moved up the timeline. We're going to have to work hard to get you ready."

"Was that real? It did feel imminent, like I needed to get to work right away—although I've no idea what it is I'm supposed to do."

Mia was trying to understand in practical terms how she might go about getting the green energy from inside the planet onto the surface.

"Is it symbolic?" she asked John. "This is real, right? It *feels* real—more real than anything I've ever experienced. My body's still vibrating. Everything I look at is vibrating. And you, you're glowing, and you have a purple halo."

Mia cocked her head the way John had been doing when he'd looked at her earlier.

"Yes, it's real, probably more real than anything else in your life. That vibration that you feel, that's your spirit, your higher self. The breathwork raises your vibrational frequency so that your spirit can start to interact with your nervous system. The moment you feel the tingling begin in your hands, that's the indication that your heart is opening."

"What do you mean by my heart opening?"

"Each time we experience fear and pain in our lives, our hearts begin to close down. It's a reflexive measure initiated by the mind in an attempt to protect us. Just know for now that the mind was never meant to be in charge; the heart was always meant to lead. The breathwork helps relax your mind, making it easier for your heart to open."

John leaned back against an outcropping of rock, giving Mia a chance to take it all in.

"John," she said. "I don't quite understand what you're saying, and yet it just seems right. I feel so amazing! Can I stay like this? I don't want to go back to how I was. I want to feel this way forever, feeling connected, like I'm finally me. I feel love for myself… for the first time ever."

With those words, she appeared radiant, as if a door to a divine secret had suddenly opened, truths appearing before her. She loved herself and was aware of it. It felt amazing.

Mia held her hands in front of her at eye level, looking at the backs of her hands, then turning them slowly to see her palms. They were still vibrating from all the energy moving through them. She wasn't sure if it was possible, yet it seemed as if light was shining right through them.

"You feel this way because your heart is open and you are connected to your spirit, the eternal, broader, and wiser part of you. Your heart will stay open as long as you stay grounded in love. When your mind starts to judge something, it will block your love.

"But don't worry about that, Mia. The breathwork will always open your heart back up, and in time, you'll be able to keep it open." John smiled at Mia. "It's always a treat to see the wonder shining through when someone's heart opens again. It's amazing to see it happen."

"So, it isn't just happening because we're in Sedona, then? The breathwork will open my heart no matter where I am? When I first drove into Sedona, I felt something spinning in my chest..."

John chuckled. "Yes, the breathwork will open your heart no matter where you are. The Sedona vortex energy does add in a boost. It can heighten experiences, and it also amplifies whatever you're feeling to help bring to the surface anything that needs to be addressed. You'd shut your heart down tightly after the breakup, and the spinning you felt was your heart chakra starting to move again, allowing the heartache to come up for healing."

"So, what now? What do I do next?" Mia asked.

"Go back to your hotel, get something to eat, and have a good night's rest. Maybe do some journaling about your experience today. Meet me tomorrow morning at the Boynton Canyon trailhead at sunrise. How does that sound?"

"Sunrise?" Mia asked. *I sure hope he's joking again.*

"Yes, we want to get in and out before the tourists start showing up. Trust me; you're going to be ready for sleep sooner than usual tonight. Besides, it'll be good for you." He turned his attention back to his pipe, carefully wrapping it in a deerskin hide.

Mia went back to her hotel just as John had said, and decided she'd better order room service since she hadn't eaten all day. She wrote down everything she could remember in her journal while waiting for her food to arrive. It seemed as if there weren't enough words in the English language to describe her experience accurately, but she did the best she could.

Just as she finished writing, there was a knock at her door.

"Room service," she heard a familiar voice say. She opened the door, surprised to see the kindly desk clerk carrying a tray with her dinner.

"You're still working?" Mia asked.

"Just came back in for the night shift. I left right after you went on your hike this morning. How was it, by the way? You look so different from when I first met you; you're glowing!"

"Well, I *feel* like a different person!" Mia responded without taking a breath. "It was amazing. I went to that spot you told me about down by Oak Creek after hiking up Cathedral Rock. And I met this man—well, at least I *think* he was a man, although he could've been an alien for all I know—and he could read my mind! Oh, and he was glowing as well, you know…And I mean it literally! Like one of those aura thingies. And he showed me this breathing meditation, then I went inside the earth, and…Well, it's kind of hard to explain what happened after that…

"To be honest, it's hard to explain *all* of it."

She said it all without drawing breath.

The clerk laughed heartily. "Well, it sounds like you probably had an encounter with the Mystic Healer." He set the tray of food down on the table.

"The mystic who? He just said his name was John. You know him?" Mia asked.

"Yes, John, the Mystic Healer—that's the guy. He's sort of a local legend, kind of like our version of Bigfoot. Many people have heard about him, but very few have had the chance to interact with him, so consider yourself lucky. And you may be right about the alien thing! The way he appears then disappears without a trace, they say he's an elemental alchemist."

"What's an elemental alchemist?" Mia asked.

"Someone who can control the elements—earth, fire, water, and wind. He works with them to change things, like changing fear into love. He can help people heal, but doesn't like to be around them much, so he keeps to himself, far preferring the company of nature."

"Oh! Well, actually, that sounds about right. He was magical, and I have to say, I feel amazing; my body's still vibrating. I can't thank you enough for suggesting I head down there."

She signed the check, giving the clerk a fifty-dollar tip.

She decided not to share the part about the Universe being female or any more details about John, figuring there must be a good reason for John not interacting much with the locals.

I don't want to create a Bigfoot-sighting frenzy!

"I had a feeling the vortex had something special in mind for you when you came in last night. Well, I'll let you eat your dinner before it gets cold. Have a good night."

"Thanks again."

She closed the door behind him, yet her thoughts caught on his words.

Wonder how he knew the vortex would have something special for me? I'll bet John the Mystic might have a thing or two to say about that. Must remember to ask him tomorrow.

She sat down at the table, taking the lid off her plate. She was happy she had ordered dinner because now she was ravenous. The bacon avocado cheeseburger was the best she had ever tasted. And the French fries were crispy, with just the right amount of salt.

So I've been to Earth's center, and now I'm having bacon and French fries! A perfect day!

Mia giggled.

She showered after dinner, having finally noticed she was still covered in red rock dirt.

The hot water felt good on her tired body, and soon, she slipped in between the cool sheets of the bed, thinking she would write some more in her journal.

But she did not, *could* not, her eyelids suddenly heavy and her mind exhausted.

As she lay down, she thought she heard coyotes howling in the distance. It was not sufficient to keep her awake a moment longer.

Within minutes of her head hitting the pillow, she was sound asleep.

She dreamt about Richard, a peculiar reverie in which he came sneaking into her hotel room and began trying to seduce her. She told him to leave, emphatic that she didn't love him anymore.

But he would not listen and didn't care because to him, it did not matter what she wanted or said she did not want. He pinned her up against the wall and pressed his body hard into hers, regardless. "Come on, you know you want me," he said, insisting she was powerless to resist, pressing forcefully against her and persisting in kissing her neck. She wanted to—intended to—push him away. Yet for some reason, she did not do it.

It was as though her body wasn't her own.

Mia could feel the sexual desire in her, and it was overwhelming, feeling as if her inner compulsions were betraying her, melting into his, accepting and welcoming him.

It turned out he had been correct, then; she was powerless to resist him and was about to give in when suddenly, an inner strength appeared, and she yelled out, "No!"

It took all her effort to pull away from him, and she didn't think it would be enough. When she finally broke free, she woke up. She was breathing hard, her body feeling as if she had just had sex. She was sweating, even though the air conditioner was still blowing cold air into the room.

Dammit! she thought. *Why the hell am I still dreaming about him?*

It disturbed her how strong the feeling had been in the dream.

In fact, she could still feel him in the room, so she turned on the light and got up, splashing cold water onto her face. She decided to write down the dream and ask John about it when she saw him, thinking that he would have the answer. That thought helped her relax.

It was already five o'clock, so she'd get ready to make it to the trailhead before sunrise.

2

The Cave

———

John was waiting for her in the parking lot when she pulled in. They walked in silence as they started down the trail. Not being a morning person, she didn't have much to say yet, so she was simply grateful to enjoy the quiet. *The birds aren't even awake,* she thought, the only sounds being their footsteps on the red Sedona sand.

After they had walked for twenty minutes, John stopped and looked at her.

"We are entering into an area that Native Americans consider sacred. They teach that you need to ask Mother Earth permission to be here and walk with reverence for the land," he instructed.

Mia smiled and nodded. Remembering her vision from yesterday, she felt that all of Earth was sacred. But she was happy to ask permission and show respect for this special place. As they walked, she noticed John kept reaching into a bag and dropping stuff on the ground. Mia knew by now she could just ask him in her mind what he was doing, and he would hear her.

"I'm making an offering to the land. This bag's filled with to-bacco and corn I've grown. Many Native Americans use tobacco as an offering, and they use the smoke in ceremonial pipes to send their prayers to the Creator. Then the corn, that's an offering to the little critters that live on this land as a way of saying thank you for letting us be in their home.

"There are also some sage leaves, pine tree clippings, rose pet-als; basically, whatever feels right to me when I'm making up a batch of offerings goes into the mix. Here," John said, holding out the bag to her. "Why don't you take a handful and offer it to Mother Earth?"

Mia grabbed a handful, holding her fist to her heart. She in-fused the offering with her gratitude and love and then let it sprinkle in the wind.

John turned off the trail and headed through the bushes.

There was a slightly worn pathway, but not one that you would notice if you hadn't already known it was there. Mia fol-lowed John up the side of the red rock canyon.

"Watch out for the cactus—they'll kiss you if you're not paying attention!"

They made it up to a cave that John told her had been used for ceremonies by the early Yavapai people. The sun was just barely high enough in the sky to start lighting up the canyon.

"Catch your breath and have a drink of water. We're not staying here; there's a second cave farther on that we're going to," John said as he pulled an apple from his backpack. "Want one?"

"Yes, thank you. I'd love one. I didn't have time to eat this morning," Mia said, catching the apple as he tossed it to her. She sat down and admired the view, the red rocks looking pink to her now in the early morning sunlight. She looked around, wonder-ing where the second cave was.

There didn't seem to be any way to go but back down the same way they had come up.

That's strange, she thought. *I wonder what the point was in coming up to the first cave if we have to go back down the rock to get to the second...*

She decided John had his reasons, and she didn't need to worry about it. John seemed so wise, so knowledgeable, and it was not for her to wonder about anything he might be doing.

"Did the Native Americans consider this area sacred because of the vortex energy?" she asked.

John smiled, his warm eyes crinkling.

He said, "I appreciate your curiosity and interest in the people who lived here in harmony with the land. There are many reasons, but yes, that's one of them. This is also where their story of creation took place. The Yavapai, which means 'People of the Sun,' were the first known inhabitants of the area. According to their creation story, the Lady of the Pearl was sealed in a log and sent from Montezuma Well, about thirty miles south of here, to prepare for a great flood.

"It rained nonstop for forty days and nights, the floodwaters rising so high they covered every landform on Earth. After the waters receded, the log came to rest on Thunder Mountain, just five miles south of here. A woodpecker freed the woman from the log and guided her to the top of Mingus Mountain where she met the sun, who fell in love with and impregnated her. She then came here to Boynton Canyon, where she bathed in an enchanted pool. She gave birth to a daughter who lived in these caves and became the mother to all the Yavapai people."

"Umm...that sounds a lot like one of the stories from the Bible," Mia commented.

John nodded but didn't acknowledge her comment directly.

"The Yavapai settled in the surrounding areas and came here

to these caves to do their spiritual ceremonies and perform healing rituals. This area was so sacred to them that they didn't actually live here. For them, this was where the Goddess, who had birthed them, resided. Others came here as well—the Hopi from the south, the Athabascans from the north, the Apache from the east. These lands were cared for, prayed for, and inhabited with great regard and reciprocity by ones who still hold that energy today for us all, many of them in spirit or guardian presence."

John finished his apple and tossed the core over the edge of the cave. "For the critters to finish off. You ready?" he asked, picking up his backpack.

She was so entranced by his story that his sudden readiness to get going startled her.

"Oh, uh, yeah," Mia said as she got up.

John walked over to the cave's eastern side, then across the face of the rock.

"Are you serious?" Mia couldn't imagine how it would be physically possible to walk along the nearly vertical surface ahead of them.

"Trust me, Mia, there's a wide enough ledge here to walk across. You'll be fine."

John continued walking across the rock.

Not wanting to get left behind, Mia followed him with trembling legs. She moved slowly and cautiously, leaning into the rock as much as possible.

This man's crazy, she thought as she looked at the ground a couple of hundred feet below, all covered in cactus. She looked at John, and it seemed he was skipping across the narrow ledge. *He must have done this many times before. If he can do it, surely, I can, too.*

She tried to convince herself, but her trembling legs weren't buying it.

"Oh yeah, remember to ask the Guardian's permission to

cross," John yelled back at her. "You'll sense him standing in the place where you'll feel the most fear."

Within a couple of steps, it seemed the narrow ledge had all but disappeared.

Mia was terrified, her body frozen with fear.

Damn him, she murmured, thinking that he could have better prepared her for this.

"I humbly and respectfully ask permission to cross," she said, hoping this was the worst her fear would get. In an instant, it was gone, and the ledge expanded to a comfortable three-foot width. Feeling confident now, Mia hurried to catch up with John, who was already climbing down over a ledge filled with cacti. She followed in his every footstep to avoid being poked.

Then John climbed up a slope of rocks to a tiny cliff opening.

There, he had to take off his backpack so he could slide his body through the gap.

Mia handed the backpack to him once he made it through, giving him hers before she also clambered through what felt like the eye of a needle. After a few more minutes' hiking, they had made it up to the second cave, both taking off their shoes before entering.

"Is this where the Goddess lives? Am I going to do the breathing thing in here?" Mia asked.

"I don't know yet. We'll see what happens after I smudge you."

Smudge? she thought.

Mia wasn't sure what he meant by that, so she just watched him open his backpack.

He pulled out a large abalone shell filled with sage leaves, as well as what looked like a bird's wing, and a piece of deerskin on which he placed a crystal and several other small objects.

She couldn't quite see everything.

He seemed to be saying something, maybe a prayer, she thought as it was so quiet.

"Okay, come stand over here and place your hands above your head on the roof of the cave. And tell me all about the man of your dreams," he said, chuckling.

Mia looked at him with confusion on her face.

"The man you dreamt about last night," John clarified with a grin.

"Ugh! How do you already know about my dream?" Mia replied. "Where do I begin? How much do you need to know?"

"Give me the short version," he said as he lit the sage in the abalone shell.

"Well, I thought he was my soulmate. There was something magical about him at first, a magnetic quality that I couldn't resist. My body got all tingly around him. When he touched me, it felt as though we were the only two people in the Universe. I trusted him, thinking we were meant to be together. Turns out I was completely wrong, and he was a lying, cheating asshole.

"Oh, and I should probably mention that he was also married."

Mia tried to stay focused on her anger instead of feeling sadness.

"Mmm-hmm." John used the wing to move the sage smoke around her body. "And why do you think he was able to fool you so easily?"

"Uh, because the entire Universe conspired to trick me!" Mia answered, becoming annoyed.

"And why would your spirit want you to have this experience?" He set down the sage and wing.

"I don't know—maybe because my spirit's also an asshole," Mia said, clenching her jaw.

"Hmm…Is that what you really think of your spirit? Sure didn't seem like it yesterday during the breathing."

Mia sighed. "I don't know why my spirit would want me to have that experience. I don't know why my spirit lied to me. I felt like I'd been divinely guided to be with him. My dreams told me we'd get married and I thought my intuition was telling me to wait and be patient. It wasn't fair. I did everything I thought I was supposed to. 'Leap, and the net will appear,' that's what people say. Well, I leapt, and there was no fucking net, was there? I just crashed and burned."

Mia was quiet for a moment as she reflected on John's question.

Then she asked, "Why? Do you think there's a reason my soul wanted me to have this experience? Do you think this experience has benefited me in some way? I lost all trust in myself. How can there be any good in that?"

"Mia, sometimes we have to learn what love isn't before we can learn what it is. And I think that relationship was a PhD-level course in what love is *not*. Now, I want you to let out a really loud yell," John instructed.

Mia screamed.

"Louder," John instructed.

Mia screamed louder than she ever had in her life, sending the sound carrying through the canyon on the wind. It startled some nearby birds, making them take off in flight.

"Again," said John.

Mia started to scream again, but only got half of it out when she began to sob, her body convulsing as she let the sadness pour from the depth of her being. All the heartache, betrayal, lies, cheating, disappointment—the rejection of herself, self-doubt, self-loathing, and her fear of never being loved came out in an ugly cry with tears so heavy that she couldn't see.

"He never was going to rescue you, Mia," John said.

Mia nodded, feeling better, thinking that John was telling her it wasn't 'meant to be' with Richard—but that she would find her knight in shining armor when the time was right.

"No one is ever going to rescue you, Mia," John said emphatically.

Her face fell. No one? Not ever? That was frightening.

As the words sank in, Mia's legs became wobbly.

Then I'm screwed, she thought, *because I can't do this on my own.*

"Let out another yell, Mia, and claim your power. Claim your right to be here!"

Mia yelled through the fear, through the sadness, through the pain, shattering the silence of the shame she had been keeping inside of her.

To her surprise, her body started vibrating and tingling as if electricity was running through it, coursing up her legs from the bottom of the cave, and through her hands, which were still above her head on the ceiling of the cave. Her spine shook in rhythmic waves.

If she hadn't been bracing herself on the cave ceiling, she might have fallen over.

John placed one hand below her belly button on the front of her second chakra and one on the back. Mia felt as though light was pouring out of his hands into her body, casting out a black worm-like energy that had been wrapped around her ovaries.

"Mia, you have been carrying abuse and addiction energy, which is what has caused all the confusion around relationships, love, and sex. This was the reason Richard was able to seduce you and also the reason he still has access to you through your dream state.

"The abuse and addiction energy connected you both at a psychic level. It is also how Richard has known exactly what to say to keep you addicted to his energy for so long.

"I can see the original lifetime in which you and Richard met. Your connection is a combination of some of the 'soul imprints' your spirit picked up and the wounds inherited from your family.

You incarnated into a family carrying the wound of adultery, your grandfather and great-grandfather both having many mistresses. Because of this, your grandmothers believed that love couldn't be trusted, while your grandfathers confused love with sexual attention, becoming addicted to obtaining it, using their position as powerful men to assure their desires were met."

Mia knew the stories about her ancestors so that didn't surprise her.

"What are soul imprints and why did my spirit pick those up?"

"Your spirit picked a selection of soul imprints that were all connected to Richard. The lifetimes of one of his concubines, his mistress, his courtesan, his lover, his geisha, and his hetaera were all combined into you. Therefore, you carry the energy of every woman Richard seduced or possessed sexually during his many past lives, and this explains why you mistook Richard for your soulmate, why he felt so familiar, and why your attraction to each other felt so powerful and magnetic. But it was abuse and addiction energy, not to be confused with love.

"Richard, of course, loved the strength of the power he had over you, your addiction to him allowing him to drain you. Taking your life force energy made him feel more powerful—it was his high—and he craved your light to feed the insatiable emptiness inside him."

"Are you saying he's a vampire? And why the hell would my spirit do that to me?"

"Look inside your body to find the answers," John encouraged.

Mia saw that the black worm-like entity energy inside her—that the light from John's hands was illuminating—had been feeding off her life force energy in the same way that Richard had.

"What are those black worms?"

"That's the entity, the parasite that is draining your life force energy."

"Did Richard infect me with that?" she asked, starting to freak out.

"Again, ask your spirit to show you how the energy got in. Look inside you for the answer."

Mia focused inside, realizing this entity must have come into her as a little girl when she had erroneously believed she was unlovable. It started as a thought form, continuing to grow every time she felt hurt or rejected, eventually gaining a stronghold in her chest at age eleven when it told her it would protect her from any more pain if she would only close her heart to her family.

It fed off of her loneliness, leading her to partying and drinking to excess, becoming woven into her depression and suicidal thoughts. It had continued to grow more powerful until, eventually, it had led her to Richard. And even though she had grown stronger and changed in so many ways, this entity's hold on her was tenacious. Like all entities, it survived as a parasitic presence, hiding within Mia's body and surviving by threading its way through her so completely that Mia thought the negative thoughts it emitted were her own.

She believed deep down inside that she wasn't good enough, that she wasn't powerful, and that she needed someone to save her from herself—someone to complete her.

She saw how Richard carried perpetrator energy, giving him the ability to identify women who would be easy prey. And because of the past-life karma forged between them through the lifetimes of soul imprints her spirit had taken on, she had been left almost devoid of any defenses against him. Her nervous system experienced his energy as love, the entity energy thriving through Richard's presence in her life and increasing its stronghold over her. And even though she had ended her relationship with Richard, this parasitic energy had still refused to leave her.

Now that the entity was being threatened with eviction, it was fighting back, enjoying having her energy as a free lunch, and it wasn't about to let go without a fight.

The entity flooded her mind with memories of Richard's strong arms around her, the way his lips felt pressed up against hers, how her body felt when he was inside her.

She knew every inch of his body, the way he felt, the way he smelled, the feel of his touch.

Around him, Mia felt as though she was drunk since he had worked himself into every small fiber of her being, and she had known nothing about it. As much as she hated Richard for hurting her, a part of her still wanted him, yearned for him. She would always remember how much fun they had together and how she could just sit and listen to him telling stories to her for hours. She adored him, idolized him even. He was so strong and handsome and charming, and—

Mia's mind was spinning her deeper and deeper into the tangled web of the illusion.

"I knew this energy would put up a fight, which was why I brought you to the cave for this healing session. We need the extra support from Mother Earth and the power of this land to help set you free. I can feel the battle happening inside of you. On one side, the unconditional love of your spirit is waiting for you. On the other, the insatiable, power-sucking entity is flooding your nervous system with what feels like love yet is really nothing more than the seductive darkness of predatory addiction energy. This wound is deep, and this energy we're dealing with is very tricky. Mia, you need to master this energy if you're going to fulfill your mission."

Mia couldn't feel the unconditional love of Sophia; all she could feel was her desire for Richard coursing through her body.

"Mother Earth, we need your help. I give you back your child. I know she has the free will to choose, but also know how ready you are to have her on the team, helping you, fulfilling her mission," John yelled as the wind picked up outside the cave.

Mia could feel the force of gravity starting to pull that parasitic energy out of her, the wind blowing through the cave, counteracting the spin of the illusion of Richard's so-called 'love.'

There came the piercing screech of a red-tailed hawk flying by, bringing the flood of memories to a halt as its shrillness permeated everything around.

"Remember the truth, Mia—the energy is trying to confuse you. You know Richard never chose you. He lied to you, cheated on you, broke every promise he ever made to you. What you had with him wasn't love; you were addicted to his sexual energy. You choose, Mia.

"What do you want? Do you want the love of your soul that will fulfill you and be eternally yours, or the sexual addiction energy that is insatiable, that will never fulfill you, and will always keep you chasing after it for more?"

Mia tried to say she wanted her spirit, but the words wouldn't come out, her voice gone. The black entity worms had wrapped themselves around her vocal cords, preventing her from speaking.

"Mia, I'm going to have you lie down now and do the breathwork."

He placed his hands on her waist to steady her as he helped her lie down.

"Just close your eyes and start breathing. You remember how to do it, right? Inhale into your lower belly, then your chest, and then exhale. Two breaths in, one breath out. Good."

It felt as if her lungs were full of dust and that she was going to choke. Her gut hurt, her ovaries were cramping, and her lower back ached. She knew that if John hadn't already done so much work on her, it would have been impossible to continue.

"Keep breathing, Mia," he encouraged. "You're doing great. Keep reaching for the light. I'm going to burn some sage to help pull the entity into another dimension."

Mia kept forcing herself to breathe. John then placed his hands on her hips and pressed slightly into her psoas muscle. She let out a gasp as if he had gouged her with a stake.

"The psoas holds the memories of all the attempts to hijack your power. Breathe through the pain. I'll speak directly to this entity, and want you to respond on its behalf. Is that okay?"

Mia wanted to scream out, "You're killing me!" as her body contracted in pain, but her voice made no sound. She continued to breathe.

Why does it feel so much harder today than yesterday?

"Mia, can you hear me?"

"Yes," she managed to get out in between breaths.

"I claim this body for the light," John said to the entity. "You are no longer welcome here and must leave immediately."

In response, Mia felt the entity getting bigger and darker.

"You have no power here," it said through her voice. "I own her, and I also own this planet. The humans will never get rid of me; they are too weak and pathetic, loving the distraction I provide them from their miserable lives. They need me."

Mia felt the entity uploading a huge dose of energy into her nervous system.

She felt aroused, powerful, invincible, desirable. She wanted sex, money, food, alcohol, drugs—all of it. She felt she was on the biggest high of her life, the flood of all these desires overwhelming her senses. She remembered the feeling of Richard's energy all over her.

Exhilarated, Mia thought, *Yes! Give me more of this!*

She heard the entity laugh at how easy that was.

"See how much she loves me? She's never going to tell me to

leave. I give her what she needs, and she's going to keep begging me to give her more, no matter what the cost."

"No, you can't have her. I command you to leave, terminating any contracts or agreements she made with you," John said.

The entity laughed.

"She will die for me; she will willingly give me all of her life force in exchange for the pleasure I provide to her." The entity doubled and then tripled the energy of desire it was pumping through Mia's nervous system.

At first, Mia felt she was riding the wave of this desire energy, as if she was on top of the world and floating in a sea of pleasure. When the energy tripled, Mia's system overloaded.

She suddenly realized the energy was insatiable, that she wasn't in control of the wave, and couldn't get off. She started to panic, realizing this energy would consume all of her, making her void. It didn't give a shit about her, only intent on using her up and tossing her to the side.

Nothing would ever manage to satisfy this energy.

It didn't matter how much sex or money or power it had, it would always want more. She saw her own addiction to it, seeing Richard's face and how he had used this weakness in her to control her. At this realization, Mia was suddenly full of fear.

What do I do? she screamed silently inside her mind.

A white light flashed through her body.

BECOME...THAT...WHICH...HOLDS...ALL...DESIRE echoed loudly in her mind.

It was the same feminine voice she had heard yesterday during the breathwork. In an instant, Mia fell into the earth, seeing herself become the Grand Canyon.

The entity's energy rushed through the canyon but couldn't touch her. She was impervious to its effect because the second she became the earth, every need was satiated.

As Mia opened into her trust of Mother Earth, she heard her own thoughts answering a question she hadn't quite been able to form.

In this place of connection, separation disappears. And separation is what allows addiction energy to think we need something outside of ourselves to be complete. We are Earth's children, and when we merge back in with Her, we are made whole.

Mia felt the energies of Sophia and Mother Earth come rushing into her body like a tsunami of love. In this wave of purest light, the parasitic energies were washed away and transmuted into love. The lead entity attempted to escape once it realized what was happening, but it wasn't fast enough. This energy of the Goddess converted everything in her path, all resistance futile.

All that was not love inside Mia's second chakra moments ago had now become love.

John burned some sweetgrass over her to cleanse the debris out of her energy field.

"Ask your spirit to show you how you allowed this to happen, Mia," he whispered in her ear.

Mia saw herself as a young woman enjoying the sexual attention she was receiving from men.

It amused her, considering all the things these men would do to get her attention.

Hearing how beautiful and sexy she was made her feel special, and getting attention from men in this way made her feel valuable, powerful even. Mother Earth showed her the vibration and frequency of the sexual attention she was receiving, and Mia saw how her body would misinterpret that vibration as love. There was no substance or depth to this kind of energy, so it didn't fulfill her, only making her need more of it to feel good about herself.

The energy convinced her that the more desirable she was, the more valuable she was. Sophia showed her how this energy was transmitted through the second chakra instead of through the heart chakra, the way love was. She showed her how the men who were giving her this attention weren't interested in her heart or commitment or partnership; they wanted to possess her, to have her, to pleasure themselves with her body, and that was all they desired.

To them, she was nothing more than a conquest, something to be taken, exploited, and then discarded when they moved on to seek and to claim their next conquest.

Mia was connecting the dots, seeing her part in it and her confusion around the attention she enjoyed getting. And she felt compassion for her younger self.

"Ask your spirit to show you why this benefited you," John said.

He was wanting her to get the whole picture.

Like a glitch in the matrix, the images that Mia was seeing grew fuzzy and disappeared.

She experienced herself falling deeper into Earth before finding herself inside a dark cave in which she witnessed all of the decisions she had made not to trust love, and how, as a little girl, she had closed off her heart a little more every time she had been hurt.

By the time she had finished high school, she'd built a fortress around her heart.

Finally, Mia was now seeing how she was the one who had been avoiding intimacy, connection, and commitment. Sexual attention was all she was willing to allow herself to experience. While she knew it was true, there was still a voice inside her head.

It was screaming, *Wait! What the fuck? This isn't possible!*

I've always wanted commitment and intimacy, and true love. Haven't I?

Mia was so confused, unwilling to argue with the evidence she was being shown, yet her experience of herself was so different from what Sophia was telling her. Then she saw it, the whisper of a voice arising from a nest of dark energy, telling her things: if she stayed quiet, no one would hurt her; if she closed her heart, she wouldn't feel pain; if she just agreed with what they wanted, they would not attack her. As she had agreed to each element of the purported 'protection' this voice offered, the entities had been allowed in.

After this, they had moved through her mind, creating a network of false beliefs fortified by the fear already existing in her lineage. Many of her female ancestors had given up their voices and opinions in exchange for being accepted and taken care of.

It felt as if these decisions had been protecting her, but in reality, they had merely functioned like magnets for the very circumstances from which she was trying to escape.

It proved to be a self-perpetuating cycle.

The more she closed her heart, the stronger the magnets became at attracting painful experiences. The more she kept quiet, the more she attracted people who would try to control her. The more she pulled away from people, the more they judged her.

The more she tried to protect herself, the more she attracted situations and people that made her feel so unsafe. Her so-called "protection" was the very thing keeping her in danger.

She could see how this system was operating inside everyone on the planet, everyone being controlled by fear, everyone trapped. This was why change was so hard to create and why generation after generation of humans were continuing this victim/perpetrator destructive cycle.

As she saw the magnets for what they were, the system started to collapse within her. She felt forgiveness for everyone who had ever "harmed" her, seeing now that the entity magnets had elicited that behavior from them. Everyone was innocent, even Richard.

Mia was still deep inside Earth, watching the patterns fall away.

"You needed to experience all of this to understand how to heal it; this is why you came here," she heard Sophia say.

Mia was unsure if the voice was referring to her coming to Sedona or something bigger, but she did have a sense that her entire existence was about to change.

Another surge of green energy pulsed through her nervous system. She felt strong, supported, nurtured, and loved. A red-tailed hawk flew by the cave and let out a screech, bringing Mia's attention back to her present moment. Mia started laughing and sat up.

The feeling of the power of love running through her body was beyond anything she could imagine. It was absolute and impenetrable, and nothing could affect it.

John handed Mia her water bottle and a small bag of trail mix.

Mia drank slowly, savoring the cool water that seemed to dance across her lips and tongue, swirling, delicious, and alive. As Mia looked around the cave, she was surprised by the vibrancy of the red, orange, and copper rocks, their layers of color mesmerizing. As she enjoyed the sweetness of the fruit and nuts, she looked over at John. How was he glowing even more now?

A breeze picked up, and the sensation on her skin was pure ecstasy.

The red rock of the cave vibrated with energy. The Ponderosa pines in the canyon below were a sea of deep greens. Mia could see their life force energy shining and feel the joy of their spirits as they danced with the wind, sensing the earthy stillness in the aged and twisted junipers and the distinct personalities of the scrub oak and yucca, all so vibrant and alive.

"Everything you're experiencing now feels different because of the changes in you, because your heart is open, and you've released a lot of the fear and addiction energy that was controlling you. You're evolving. With an open heart, you'll be able to interact with the world more deeply, especially with nature and the elements."

Mia nodded.

Everything in that moment felt so clear, knowing herself in connection to all of life.

"I want to show you what's possible...how magical life really can be. See those dark clouds in the sky headed this way?" John asked.

She nodded as she looked to where he was pointing.

"Do you want it to rain, Mia, or do you want it to stay dry?"

Mia contemplated this for a moment, deciding the moisture from the rain would feel delicious on this hot, dry morning. "I want it to rain!" she exclaimed.

"Then make it happen," he said, offering no other instructions.

Mia instinctively walked over to the edge of the cave and held her vibrating palms out to the clouds. "I want it to rain!" she said again, willing it so with all of her being.

The clouds looked at her.

"I humbly and respectfully ask for rain," she corrected herself, opening her heart wider.

She connected her essence with the clouds, becoming one with them. She felt love and excitement for each raindrop before the clouds released any water.

The wind picked up and blew her hair behind her as the clouds rolled in her direction.

"Good, now offer gratitude for all that you have received," John said.

"THANK YOU, MOTHER EARTH!" Mia yelled.

Her heart was overflowing with love and gratitude. She had never imagined that life could be this magical, that she could feel this connected and alive. As the raindrops started falling, tears of joy rolled down her cheeks. The canyon had filled with the music of the rain, its sweet scent flooding the cave. She could feel Earth's joy as it welcomed the moisture from above.

The red rocks, the canyon below, the vibrant life around them in its variety of expression, all were washed clean, their colors shining even brighter.

"Thank you, Mother Earth," Mia whispered over and over.

She turned and walked over to John standing at the cave's edge, watching the rain.

Mia wrapped her arms around him.

"Thank you, John; a million times, thank you!"

"You're welcome, Mia. You are worth it. Remember that."

He patted her on the back of her heart. They ate more trail mix as they sat and watched the rain come down. It seemed as if every dark cloud in the sky had made its way over to them. It rained so hard that it created a waterfall in front of the cave's entrance.

"Wow, I've never seen the rain do that here before. Maybe you could turn it down a little, so we can make it back down the trail?" John asked, smiling.

Mia grinned, delighted by the force of the rain.

Did I really do this, or is he just playing with me? Did he already know it was going to rain and timed it so that I'd have this experience?

She held her arms up to the sky.

"I humbly and respectfully ask that the rain stop. Please make it stop, Mother Earth."

Within minutes, the downpour stopped and the sun came shining through the clouds.

"Looks as if we can make it out now." John picked up his backpack, ignoring the look of surprise and delight on Mia's face.

As they headed down the rocks, John noticed a rainbow and pointed it out to Mia.

"Mother Earth's pulling out all the stops for you today. Ask the rainbow to bless you, Mia; as you exchange love and gratitude with it, let the rainbow's colors merge with your being."

Mia did as he instructed, in awe of all the magic John had brought into her life in just two short days. She had always enjoyed rainbows but had never known she could interact with them. She sent love to the rainbow and complimented its beauty, thanking it for appearing and humbly asking it to bless her. She felt its colors move in answer through her chakras.

The walk across the face of the rock was effortless on the way back as Mia had opened her heart even wider, delighting in the way nature danced around her and John as they walked back to the parking lot. A bright red cardinal followed them along the path, butterflies appearing every few minutes, floating around them. A couple of hummingbirds buzzed nearby, and Mia and John even came face to face with a small gathering of deer. Mia felt as though she was in a Disney movie.

"Is it always like this for you?"

"Nature loves an open heart, so yes, this is a pretty typical experience for me," John replied.

Mia delighted in every step of the hike back to the car. She was so full of love, she didn't even notice how quickly it had gotten hot after the rain stopped or how hungry her body was after all that work. She now found she loved everything with which she came in contact as she experienced the world through her open heart.

"What's that smell?" she asked John as she took a deep breath of a sweetness in the air.

"Those are the juniper trees loving you back," he said, chuckling.

They made it back to the parking lot, which was now full of cars.

Mia was still smiling from ear to ear, taking it all in.

"Go get something to eat and relax. I'll pick you up at your hotel tonight just after sunset."

"Okay," Mia responded. "Where are we going?"

"Hot Spring!"

3

Hot Spring

Mia walked out of her hotel just as the sun was setting and saw John waiting for her in his truck. She waved, quickly walking over and getting in, excited for whatever he had in store for tonight.

She told him about the rest of her day as he drove toward Oak Creek Canyon.

After several miles, he turned off on a private dirt road that had a locked gate at the entrance. John handed Mia a key. "Open the gate, and after I drive through, pull it closed."

Mia did as he instructed and got back in the truck.

"Where are we?"

"There's a hot spring a few miles this way that's pretty secluded. Mother Earth has cloaked it so very few people know it exists. If She hadn't, it would have been packed with people as everyone's naturally drawn to soak in Her healing waters. But most people don't take care of Her, so She's reserved some places for those who are here to help Her.

"That's who you're going to meet tonight, some of the other members of the team. Like you, they all have a special mission to help heal the planet," John said.

After a few miles, they arrived at the hot spring. Mia could see the light of a campfire, three figures standing around it. She got out and followed John as he made his way toward the group.

"Hey boss," said a slim man with a mohawk and a big smile.

He walked over and hugged John.

"Good to see you, my friend," the man said as he patted John on the back. "Really fucking good to see you, man!"

"Good to see you too, Nick. You been keeping out of trouble?" John asked playfully.

"Ha! Never!" Nick responded. "What would be the fun in that?"

"Well, who is this pretty lady behind you?" Nick asked, noticing Mia.

"Mia, I'd like to introduce you to Nick."

"Actually, it's Nicholas and it's a pleasure to meet you."

"Nice to meet you, Nicholas," Mia said, shaking his hand.

"First time we meet is the only time you'll get a handshake. After that, it's all hugs in this family," Nick said with a wink.

"Allow me to introduce you to the others."

He signaled for Mia to join him as he walked toward the fire.

John was already giving hugs to the two women standing by the campfire.

"You won't find them nearly as charming as I am, but they're pretty friendly," Nick added.

"Mia, meet Dominique and Lori. Dominique is…"

Nick stopped himself, looking at John inquisitively.

"What's her clearance level? I'm assuming since you brought her here, she's all good?"

John smiled and nodded. "Yep, Mother Earth's given her the highest security clearance."

Nick continued, extending his hand, indicating the tall black woman with big brown eyes.

"Dominique is our multi-dimensional seer and vortex traveler. And Lori," he said as he pointed to the slim Asian woman, "is in charge of keeping order in time and space."

"Oh please!" said Dominique. "Quit being such a dork. Hi Mia, I'm Dominique. And feel free to just ignore Nick. He gets carried away with himself."

Lori laughed and smiled at Nick.

"I think he's funny! Welcome, Mia; it's nice to have you here."

Nick leaned in and whispered to Mia, "As you can see, this one gets irritated easily, so feel free to keep your distance."

Mia could feel an easy camaraderie between the three. She didn't understand any of what Nick had said in regard to what Dominique and Lori did but decided to play along.

"And what is it that you do, Nicholas?" Mia asked.

"I, my lady, am a demon slayer," he said with a bow.

"Dear Lord Nickle-Ass," Dominique said. "Are you trying to flirt with her, or scare her away?"

Lori elbowed Dominique, saying, "Be nice! I swear you two act like brother and sister."

"All right, enough you three," John said, taking off his flannel shirt. "How about we all get in the hot spring before your bickering heats up the water even more?"

The air outside was surprisingly cool given how hot it had been during the day. The thought of getting into the hot spring was appealing.

"This way, my lady," Nick said, motioning toward the path to the hot spring a few feet away.

Mia wondered what Nick had meant by "demon slayer." Was he just kidding or was that a real thing? She also tried to remember what he had said about Dominique and Lori—dimensional vortex-something, and space traveler. Given what she'd experienced in the breathwork the last couple of days, she figured he probably wasn't kidding.

The hot spring was large enough to fit at least twelve people. Mia took off her T-shirt and jeans and put them on the rock where the others had also left their clothes.

The water was warm against her skin as she slid into the pool. She felt a little light-headed once she was all the way in, and her skin was tingling and vibrating. She could see the campfire out of the corner of her eye, yet there seemed to be a green light glowing in the center of the hot spring. Perplexed, Mia looked over at John for an explanation.

The four of them were standing in the warm waters, watching her.

"You're right, John," Nick said. "She's got pretty high security clearance, seeing how she just made the emerald light turn on!"

"She also made it rain today," John said, smiling at Mia.

Mia laughed, realizing she felt as if she was drunk.

"Is this feeling I'm having normal?" she asked. "Or is it out of the ordinary?"

"Didn't John tell you? You can forget about anything ever being normal again," responded Dominique.

"Yes, Mia," Lori said, wading past Dominique and heading over to Mia to help her. "The energy of Mother Earth is really pure in this spring, and it can take a while to get used to it. That drunk feeling is your mind loosening up. The water's dissolving the control the dark-force energies have had over you."

Mia looked confused. "The control what?"

Lori looked over at John.

"I take it you haven't told her everything yet?"

"I only just met her a couple of days ago," John said. "There hasn't been time to get her fully up to speed. I haven't even asked her if she wants to join us."

"Asked her? Ha!" Dominique laughed. "Did you ask any of us? Was it ever a choice?"

Mia started to lose her balance and Lori reached out to support her.

"Just let it release—don't fight it. Are we going to float her?" Lori asked, looking over at John.

"Maybe in a little while," he responded.

"Well, if you think she can stay vertical for that long," Lori said, looking at Mia's body wobbling.

"Yeah, you're probably right. Judging from what I've seen Mother Earth do with her so far, she's probably not going to last too long in these waters."

John made his way over to Lori and Mia.

Mia's legs completely gave out and she slipped under the water, Lori still holding onto her arm. John reached under the water and scooped her up.

As he and Lori supported her body, allowing her face to remain above water, Mia's consciousness traveled down into the shining emerald-green light.

A translucent humanoid being made of water met Mia there.

Welcome Mia, we have been waiting for you, said the Water Being.

Who are you? Mia wondered.

We are your family, the Water Being responded.

What do you mean? Mia asked.

The Water Being didn't answer, instead taking Mia by the hand, swimming with her through the emerald light. The feeling was familiar, as if Mia had known the Water Being all along.

In fact, she could feel herself in every drop of water on the planet in that moment, knowing herself as water, able to flow and move in any direction; it was as natural to her as breathing.

As she began to lose all sense of her own body, she heard the green light speak gently into her heart. *Focus here, my child.* As Mia held focus within her heart, she was able to gather herself back. This way of moving between forms was also familiar, the waters holding her in a depth of timelessness. She felt embraced in the stillness in their fluidity, feeling the strength in their softness and a presence of love beyond words.

The Water Being rested her hand on Mia's shoulder.

Mia opened her eyes to realize she was standing in an underwater cavern, the warm waters reaching her belly as a soft, gentle flow of air moved around her. A shimmering green glow illuminated a circle of iridescent Water Beings who were standing and watching as Mia came more wholly into the moment. Mia's gaze took in their shimmering forms, reflecting the cavern's gray rock, and emanating a pulsing sphere of deep emerald-green from each of their hearts.

Her eyes widened in surprise to see her own heart alight in response. Their faces radiated happiness at her recognition and Mia sensed their love washing through her in gentle waves.

Her eyes brimmed with tears as she sought out her guide.

Still standing by Mia's side, the Water Being nodded in understanding.

Mia wondered if she had died.

Am I in heaven? Surely this must be what heaven feels like. She vaguely remembered entering the hot spring. *I must have drowned,* she decided, yet she felt no sense of loss, filled only with a completeness of love and belonging. She had imagined there would be angels with wings, not translucent beings made of water and shining emerald hearts.

Oh well, she thought. *I don't need there to be wings; everything here is more amazing than I could ever have imagined.*

Sweet child, Mia heard in her thoughts, coming from another being. *You have not died. If anything, it would be more accurate to say that you are fully alive. You are not IN heaven—you ARE heaven, Mia. You have returned here to the heart of Mother Earth to remember. You are of us, and this love that you feel is the truth of who you are. Welcome home, dear one.*

This state of love and interconnectedness that you are experiencing is the natural state of Mother Earth. Humanity once lived in reciprocity and balance with Her, moving with awareness in the flow of life. All beings have known themselves as one life, individual and together, yet they are never separate from the All. Yet humans have become lost to their knowing, leaving Mother Earth to carry all of life while their hearts sleep. They have forgotten that they are of Her and that all they do—or do not do—affects all life. And so arises great suffering.

The fighting, the greed and belief in scarcity, the love of power, control, and domination—all of these strain Her. The depletion of Her veins of carbon, Her minerals and soils destabilizes Her. She has to create bigger and bigger natural disasters to shift Her energy back into balance.

Her waters mirror the tormented emotional state of those on the planet.

Her winds express the imbalance in mental energy.

Earth shakes and erupts as She continues to try to wake Her children. She loves you dearly, but She will not continue to sacrifice Herself for those refusing to change.

The time is now, Mia, and you are a part of the solution, the one to help the others on the planet remember, to help them find their way back to their hearts, back to love.

Humans have been lost in their minds for too long.

The mind was never meant to lead; it was meant to follow the heart, to be in service to love. Only when the heart leads can your planet heal.

The words seemed to come from all of them. As the beings spoke, Mia saw images of hurricanes, earthquakes, fires, floods, and volcanoes erupting, all reclaiming the planet.

She sensed in what she was being shown an awareness of the devastation to arise, yet also that there was a fierce love creating it all.

What am I supposed to do? Mia asked. *What contribution can I possibly make?*

You are to be the eye of the storm, a force of light and peace. Do your work and forgive everyone your mind tells you has hurt you in some way.

Come back to center every time you feel yourself getting pulled into discord or fear. Dissolve your judgments of others by finding all the places within yourself that still need your love. As you purify your heart and mind by loving yourself more, you will become the light that the world needs, a lighthouse showing others how to find their way through the dark.

Mia couldn't connect with any thoughts of judgment or fear at the moment; all she could feel was love and acceptance.

Isn't it already done? she asked. *All I feel is love. I can feel the truth of what you are saying, and see that there is nothing more important than this. This truth is so vast, everything else seems inconsequential. It doesn't feel as if anything could pull me back into separation.*

The beings said, *That is because you are inside the heart of the Goddess right now. You are home and once again in your pure essence energy. This love that you feel is who you are.*

When you return to the surface of the planet, you will again be exposed to polarity. Your work is to take this knowing—of the love you are—back with you, finding it again and again every time you forget. Finding it will be the hardest thing you have ever done, yet every time you do it, it will get easier. And we will be all around you, helping you remember.

Anytime you need us, find a body of water to swim in and you will feel us nearby. Our connection to one another here has awakened your heart, so it will be easier for us to communicate now. You are not in this

alone. You have all the support you need, and you are destined to suc-
ceed. Failure is not an option, Mia; the fate of the world rests in your
heart.

As Mia tried to soak it all in, a part of her wanted to just stay here in the heart of planet Earth, basking in the love. Yet she knew she also wanted to share this feeling with everyone and everything on the planet. Was she really a part of bringing love to humanity?

She imagined what the world would be like as people began to remember themselves as love, how it would feel as more and more people trusted living through their hearts, knowing themselves each as a part of the whole, living together harmoniously in a spirit of cooperation instead of competition. A humanity choosing to live through their hearts, knowing how truly they were always supported, and that everything they could ever need was already provided.

Mia could see so clearly that there would be no limit to what they could create.

She saw images of human potential at its best, societies where no one was struggling to survive. People were not working all day to pay their bills; they were working to create the gift of expression that was inside them, this freedom of being contributing to the well-being of all and growing exponentially. Human beings once again were full of love, not fear.

The world was compassionate and kind, and life thrived in response.

There was again a deep regard for Earth and a reciprocity of heart. Knowing that she could be a part of this arrival filled Mia with delight and purpose.

Suddenly, her consciousness shot back up through the water into her body.

Nick, who had taken over for John, was startled as Mia went

from being limp and relaxed to fully engaged, arms and legs moving wildly.

"Whoa Nelly, easy does it there!" he exclaimed as her body's undulations sent waves throughout the hot spring.

John chuckled, watching Nick try to manage Mia's reentry. Her body was gasping for air, suddenly remembering it needed oxygen to exist in physical form.

"What? Did you forget how this works?" Dominique asked. "I thought this wasn't your first rodeo, Nick."

Nick was too busy trying to keep from getting hit by Mia's flailing arms and legs to respond to Dominique. Lori went over to help him by grabbing hold of Mia's legs.

"We've got you, Mia; you're safe. Just keep breathing. Open your eyes. You're back with us now," Lori said calmly.

John went over to assist with Mia's return to her body.

As he helped her stand in the water, he placed a hand on her heart chakra, helping her consciousness regain its balance inside her.

"Welcome back, Mia. How was your trip to the Heart of Gaia?" John asked, smiling.

Mia stared at him with eyes wide, attempting to open her mouth to speak. But her verbal skills weren't back online yet. So instead, she telepathically transmitted what she had experienced and the information with which she had returned to the surface.

John laughed, feeling the burst of love energetically washing over him.

The bubble of love energy Mia emitted was so big that everyone felt it, and they all started laughing with delight. All of the nearby critters in the area clearly felt it too, venturing a little closer to the hot spring to soak in the love. Getting a boost of pure love from Earth's center revitalized the life force energy in all of them.

When the laughter finally settled down, John said telepathically to Mia, *Well done.*

She realized she knew what he was saying even though he hadn't spoken aloud.

John smiled, continuing to communicate, *Yes, the Water Beings activated your ability to expand your energy like water. By tuning in to me, you can hear what I'm thinking or feel what I'm feeling. You can do it with anyone now, but only use it when you need to.*

You don't want to unintentionally tune in to people. Use your focus to guide you and keep your awareness contained around you until you feel it's necessary or important to tune in to someone. You'll find that most people's thoughts are quite amusing but not all that interesting.

"Hey! Do you think we can get out of the water now? I look like a raisin," Nick said, staring at his hands. "I've had about all the love I can handle for one night."

He instantly regretted it as he looked up at Dominique, knowing he had just walked right into one of her smart-ass remarks.

"It's no fun for me when you make it that easy, Nick," Dominique said. "And I actually agree with you. I'd like to dry off and go sit by the fire. I'll spare you my witty comeback if you'd be a dear, Nick, and go put some more wood on the fire."

"It would be my pleasure to stoke the fire," Nick said, quickly jumping out of the water before Dominique changed her mind.

It wasn't like her not to take a jab at him. He was impressed.

Mia's love bubble packs a powerful punch if it's capable of softening Dominique's sharp tongue, Nick thought, placing a few more logs on the fire.

Mia looked at John in surprise, realizing she had just unintentionally heard Nick's thoughts. *Use your focus,* John reminded her. *It'll get easier with time.*

Soon, they were all sitting around the fire, wrapped in cozy soft towels and enjoying the sliced fruit Lori had brought for them to eat.

"Thank you, Lori! This is the best pineapple I've had on the mainland, and pineapple's my favorite," gushed Mia, finally regaining the use of her language center.

"Yeah," Nick chimed in. "Where did you find such sweet strawberries this time of year? They're usually only this sweet at the beginning of the season."

John's mouth was full of watermelon, so he just nodded as he held up the rind and gave her a thumbs up.

"Lori loves to nurture others and make everything more beautiful, softer, sweeter, and gentler. She brings a graceful feminine energy to our group that we all appreciate," said Dominique.

"Aw, thanks, you guys. I figured we'd be hungry at some point and there was so much beautiful fruit at the market, I had to buy a little bit of everything. It's so hard to resist. My guess is that the love blessing we got from Mother Earth is what's made it all taste so amazing. So, thank you, Mia for bringing that back with you," Lori said, smiling sweetly.

"My pleasure!" Mia smiled. "So, the green vortex portal thing—you've all been through it?"

"Sort of," John answered. "She takes people wherever they need to go, to wherever and whatever it is that they specifically need to experience. We've all been through it, but the information you got tonight was for your piece of the puzzle."

"So what do I do with the information?" Mia asked. "I mean, it all made perfect sense while I was down there, but I'm not really sure what I'm supposed to do now. It feels like...a lot."

"What did they tell you?" Nick asked.

"It's hard to put into words exactly," Mia said, hesitating at how grandiose the information now sounded in her head.

"Don't be shy, Mia," Nick offered. "They told me I'm more

Archangel than human, which is why I'm so good at performing exorcisms. Whatever you were told, repeat it freely and we will understand and accept it. Then we can help you to know what to do with the information."

He playfully held his palms out to the fire as if he were casting out the demons.

"Yeah Mia, you're not going to sound crazy to this bunch. Go ahead and tell us," John said.

"Well, okay. They said I was here to bring heaven to Earth and that I was going to help to balance the energies on the planet. They showed me all these natural disasters that will happen as Earth mirrors our energy, telling me to become the eye of the storm, to be a lighthouse of peace to help others navigate their way in the darkness." Mia lifted her gaze from the fire, taking a deep breath as she looked at the group. "They told me I was here to save the planet. It sounds crazy, I know…I have no idea what you must think of me now."

No one said a word, each looking from one to the other.

Mia turned to John, waiting for some encouragement, as did the rest of the group.

Finally, John nodded. "Sounds about right to me," he said nonchalantly.

No one seemed to flinch at the words after all. They merely pondered on them.

Mia let out a breath she hadn't realized she'd been holding. Her face softened.

"Really?" Dominique asked. "They're putting all that on this one? She doesn't even seem to know what she's doing. No offense, Mia, I'm just curious is all. Who is she, John? What Order is she from?"

"Aw, who gives a shit what her galactic pedigree is, Dominique?" Nick said. "Good for you, Mia! You go for it!" Nick got up and started pacing.

Mia tuned in to Nick and heard his thoughts.

Holy shit! Really? I work my ass off for You and she's the one You pick to save the world? Why require an exorcist if this one's going to heal the whole fucking planet?

Mia flinched and looked over at John, tuning in to him for help.

John smiled. *It's a blessing and a curse, Mia. Sometimes, it's better not to know exactly what people are thinking. Give them some time to process this; they'll be fine. You've done nothing wrong. We all knew help was coming, we just didn't know it was coming in the form of one person who doesn't have fully developed gifts yet. They've been working a long time on sharpening their skills. They just had some expectations of what the help would look like; they'll sort it out.*

Mia tuned in to Lori to see what she was thinking. *Seriously? Barbie here's supposed to be the Second Coming? This is our new savior? Lord help us! We're doomed.*

Mia slumped down. *Maybe they're right; it can't be true. Who am I to be able to help anyone, let alone the entire planet?* Mia allowed her mind to be flooded with doubt, causing her heart to close. There was just no way she could be some sort of savior.

A coyote howled in the distance as a log on the fire crackled, making a loud popping sound, sending sparks flying high into the air.

John tried to help Mia understand.

I know this hurts, Mia, but try to let it go and forgive them. The light coming through your heart can create a backlash in everyone around you. It's the pure green ray of the Goddess.

It will pull the darkness to it so that it can transmute it with love.

Mia, you need to learn how to keep your heart open when the energy comes at you. It's going to be really challenging for you because you're so sensitive and because this is all so new to you.

It will find the darkness in even the purest of beings because all that is unconscious must be brought to the light. *Any negative or judgmental thoughts that someone has within them, no matter how small and seemingly insignificant to them, will rise to the surface.*

This is the most important part of your mission.

I will help you, Mia. I will help you keep opening your heart up every time it closes. It will be exhausting, and we will probably fail a thousand times before you finally get it. But once you do, Mia, it will pierce through the darkness like a bolt of lightning.

Mia, are you listening to me? I know your feelings are hurt, but you can't let the doubt win.

You know what you heard. You know what you saw, he offered softly.

Mia wiped the tears from her eyes. *No, they're right. I don't know what I'm doing. How can I? This is all new to me, and nothing makes sense. I don't have the right training for this. I don't have any special galactic gifts. I'm sure I don't even belong here.*

Mia's shoulders slumped, but then came John's reply. As ever, he had so much to say, so much that made sense on the one hand, yet made none whatsoever on the other because Mia was sure she was nothing special and believed she possessed no powers, no gifts to help even herself.

Oh, I'd say your galactic gifts are coming on line just fine, seeing how we're having this conversation without any spoken words. And you wouldn't be as upset as you are if you hadn't heard what Nick and Lori were thinking. At least Dominique was blunt enough to speak her mind out loud. This is where the work comes in, Mia. This is the hard part.

Hearing their judgments of you has activated all your self-doubt. But don't be afraid of it; this is hard, I know, but it's something we all encounter, and all must pass through.

Their reaction to you isn't even about you, Mia. It's about them and the places they still have left to heal, the places where they still lack self-

love. Self-love is a practice. You have to decide to love yourself, no matter what. You have to believe in yourself.

You have to choose self-love, especially when it's hard. You have to make the choice not to let anyone or anything cause your heart to close.

Mia's mind was spinning with stories of not fitting in, not being loved, and not being wanted. Her body contracted, and her chest began to ache. She needed to get out of there. She wanted to run but was barefoot and still wearing her bathing suit.

I'm so stupid for thinking I'd finally found a group of people who would accept me. But how can I blame them? Clearly, this is my fault for having such ridiculous, grandiose thoughts.

Maybe I'm manic or schizophrenic. I should probably be on medication.

In fact, I should have been on it long ago.

The wind picked up and it felt as if the temperature had dropped a few degrees.

Mia scrambled to get her T-shirt on to cover herself.

Please take me back to the hotel, she pleaded.

"Well, I think it's time we called it a night," John finally said. "We'll meet at the river's edge at daybreak. Nick, you're in charge of putting out the fire. And Lori, thanks again for the fruit. I'll see you all tomorrow."

John walked over to the truck, motioning to Mia to climb in.

"Let's get you back to your hotel. You've had a long day, and I don't think we're going to get anywhere with this tonight."

They drove back to the hotel without talking, John filling the silence with country music from the radio. He pulled up in front of her hotel, bringing the vehicle to what felt like a slow and hesitant stop. He sighed, a long exhalation.

As she was getting out of the truck, he reached over and touched her arm.

"Mia, I know you're hurting. But please don't give up. Just get some rest. I promise this will feel different tomorrow. It takes time, all right? That's all. Like I said, we all—"

"Yes, I know," she said quietly. "We all have to go through it."

She seemed slightly short-tempered but was only tired. John said nothing more.

Mia nodded and got out of the truck. She made it up to her room and crawled into bed, so exhausted from her rollercoaster ride of a day that she fell asleep the moment her head hit the pillow. The pack of coyotes howling on the hill outside her window didn't even wake her.

But it was not a restful night, Mia tossing and turning in her sleep as she dreamt about being on trial for all her myriad mistakes and failures.

In each case, she was the plaintiff, the attorney, and the judge, and she found herself guilty on all charges, sentencing herself to a lifetime of loneliness.

And the worst part of it all was that she knew she was culpable.

4

The Creek

Mia woke up to the sound of someone knocking on her door, not even a soft knock; this was persistent, the knocking of a person determined not to go away until they had spoken to her.

When she looked through the peephole, she was surprised to see John's face, peering close to the door. "Rise and shine," he said, sensing her on the other side.

Damn, she thought, remembering that her last thought before sleep had been to drive home first thing in the morning and not meet up with the others.

"I know, that's why I'm here. I couldn't have you sneaking off before we have a chance to set things right," he responded. "I had to come find you, talk to you."

Ugh, Mia thought. *Sometimes, this telepathic thing's a real pain in the ass.*

"Well, are you going to open the door? Or do you need to dress first?" John chuckled, amusing himself.

"Give me a few minutes and I'll come out," Mia said, sighing hard, knowing it was pointless to try to get rid of him. And she actually did believe he could fix things.

If anyone could, he could.

And she certainly didn't want to live a life sentence of loneliness but still, the awful dreams burned in her psyche, the ones in which she was *guilty, guilty, guilty!*

John handed her a cup of coffee once she got into the truck, for which she was grateful because she still didn't feel fully awake. She stared out the window, grateful again that John wasn't the talkative type as she really didn't have much to say to him either.

Her chest still ached when she thought about what had happened the night before, her mind vacillating between believing the others were right and that she had no right to be here, to feeling mad about them being mean to her. She didn't ask for any of this. She hadn't made it up.

Well, she wasn't totally sure on that one, but still, she was just telling them what she had understood, and they had acted like jerks about it.

Her mind wouldn't leave her alone about it now anyway, even making her suffer in her dream, the one place she should have felt safe. No matter how many times she thought the same thought and tried to dismiss it, it persisted in coming back, troubling and insistent.

John even turned up the radio so that he wouldn't have to hear all of Mia's thoughts circling around, reaching out twice to crank the volume higher. He chuckled as he heard Johnny Lee's song, "Looking for Love in all the Wrong Places" streaming from the radio.

Nick, Dominique, and Lori were already at the river when they arrived, Dominique sitting by herself under a tree near the water's edge.

Nick and Lori had been quietly talking until they saw John and Mia walk up.

"Let's not waste any more time," John said. "Come on over here and let's sit together."

Everyone slowly made their way over and sat down.

"Hold hands and feel the energy moving around the circle."

Everyone reached out a bit stiffly to hold their neighbors' hands.

John walked around the circle with a few pieces of lit white sage. "Good to get a start on the clearing. I have a feeling this circle's going to bring up a lot of issues for everyone to clear."

He acknowledged the directions, also sun, earth, wind, and water, and the love he knew was supporting the group through the presence of so many beings dedicated to humanity finding its way forward. As he returned to his place in the circle, grabbing ahold of Mia and Dominique's hands, he gave a half-smile and shook his head ever so slightly. "Here we go," he mused.

"All right, now let's close our eyes. Feel the tension in your body—the sadness, the anger, all of it. Acknowledge what you're feeling. And imagine that you have roots growing out of the base of your tailbone and can send your energy deep into Mother Earth.

"Ask Her permission as you gently send your energy down into Her, and as triggered as you guys are, you'd better make those roots as thick and sturdy as those of a mighty oak! Let Mother Earth know what you're feeling and thinking. Give Her the story activated in your mind.

"And tell Her, how old do you feel right now? The place this has activated in all of you is very young. This whole thing isn't at all about what happened last night. This is about all the places you don't have self-love. Now everybody, take a nice deep breath and focus on your heart."

After everyone had taken a few more breaths, John continued, "Go ahead and release those sweaty palms you're holding. You can rub your hands together a bit and then place them over your heart."

Mia was trying to pay attention, but her body was aching from tension, and half of what John was saying seemed to make no sense to her.

She just knew she felt really, really sad and that it was too hard to try to hold back tears.

"The hot spring last night activated the places where you are still unconscious, which is a good thing. We need to know the places we are still blocked so we can heal ourselves. I'm going to have you all lie down and do some breathwork so we can clear out that stuck energy," John said.

Dominique was about to protest.

"And yes, Dominique, you need to breathe too," he said before she could get the words out.

"But why?" she said. "I'm not triggered; I just like to get my information from a higher source. There's nothing wrong with that."

"That's exactly why," John offered. "You don't trust people and you use your galactic communication connection as a way to keep people at a distance, and also to avoid feeling."

John lit some prayer mix before continuing. "Who does that remind you of, Dominique? Who didn't believe you when you were a child?"

"Oh fine!" Dominique responded, annoyed that John had brought up her daddy issues.

Did he really have to say something like this in front of everyone?

They all lay down, closing their eyes as they began to breathe. Two breaths in, one breath out. Tears streamed down Mia's face as sadness poured out of her. She felt rejected, as though she didn't belong. *They don't like me; they don't want me here,* her mind insisted.

As she continued to breathe, she traveled deeper down the stream of thoughts. *I don't want to be here. I don't like myself. I don't belong. I'm not good enough. This is all my fault...*

She kept following the trail on which Sophia was leading, finally seeing that she was the one keeping herself separate from the others. She could see how throughout her whole life, she had been waiting for others to include her, to accept her, and yet she had never accepted herself.

Her self-doubt was the perfect hiding place. If she wasn't good enough, then she never had to try. She could keep acting small and hide from her life while never taking responsibility for any of it. She could see that she had been waiting to live her life, waiting until someone gave her permission. And she saw that no matter how many hoops she jumped through, her mind was never satisfied. Ultimately, she realized it was a trap; there was no one outside of her who could grant her permission to live her life, and her mind on its own would never be at ease.

Suddenly, it made sense why John kept telling her, *Claim your right to be here!* It was a decision only she could make. She had to choose herself through the love in her heart. *I was looking for love in all the wrong places; it's been inside me all along.*

Mia breathed harder as Sophia continued to make things clearer.

She saw that her self-doubt kept her from trying, which "protected" her from failing because if she failed, she believed she would be rejected. And yet she could see that she had never rejected anyone for failing. If anything, she only admired them more for trying to do something challenging, especially admiring those who continued to take risks.

She could see that everyone was infected with these doubts to some degree, and that the people she most enjoyed being around were the ones who had just decided they were good enough, the ones who had stopped trying to jump through hoops.

The breath showed her how much cleaner and lighter it felt to be around them.

They didn't pull on her energy the way someone who was insecure and needy of approval did. Mia knew down deep inside that she was a good person and that her experience was just as valid as anyone else's. *Why shouldn't I be the one to save the world? Clearly, someone has to!*

And with that thought, she let out a loud laugh.

Her breathing got faster. Now that she had cleared away that old, stuck belief, her energy was able to move unimpeded throughout her body. She was vibrating and tingling all over. It felt as though the ground was shaking beneath her and moving her along with it. She wasn't sure what was happening; the breath seemed to be breathing her, and she couldn't stop it.

I'm right here, Mia, John said as he watched her closely. *It's not unusual for the breath to spontaneously pop people's bodies into yoga poses. You're okay; just keep breathing.*

Her spine arched and she ended up in "fish pose" up on her elbows with the top of her head arched so far back it connected with the earth. John could hear that her thoughts had switched from not belonging, to, *I claim my right to be here!*

"Say it aloud, Mia," he encouraged.

"I claim my right to be here," she stammered in between breaths.

As the energy shifted in her, it helped the rest of the group. Like kernels of corn sitting in hot oil, each of their hearts popped open once their minds quieted down.

Mia's body caught John's attention again as he watched her

extend her arms in front of her. The energy coming out of her palms was so strong that her arms, bending at the elbow, moved back and forth faster than he thought humanly possible.

He saw a vortex being created between her arms, fueled by the masculine, positive polarity energy in her right hand and the feminine, negative polarity energy in her left hand.

"What are you doing, Mia?" he finally asked.

"I...don't...know!" she managed to get out, finding it hard to talk while her body was shaking so violently. The energy was beginning to make a toroidal field, a doughnut-shaped energy field folding in upon itself.

Mia's arms were moving so quickly she wondered how long she would be able to keep this up. Her breathing pattern had shifted to a rapid single inhale and exhale, so much energy moving through her that she half-expected to launch like a rocket ship.

"Ask! Ask for clarity, ask for answers, ask for instructions," John insisted.

Mia wasn't sure whom she was supposed to ask as there didn't seem to be anyone there. She just felt as though an earthquake was happening inside her body.

Hearing her confusion, John said, "Just ask and the answer will appear—and if it doesn't, keep asking until it does."

Mia asked, *What's happening to me? Why am I moving like this? What do I do?*

She didn't sense any response.

Mother Earth! Mia screamed in her mind, *Help me! What's happening to me?*

In that moment, Mia felt her body become a tree, her legs turning into roots extending deep into the earth. As they grounded her body, her arms became branches and her fingers turned into leaves waving in the wind moving around her.

Green life force energy traveled from deep in the earth up through her roots, moving up her trunk and through her branches, its radiant light shining from her vibrant leaves.

The green energy was emanating from Mia's fingers, traveling around the circle touching Nick, Lori, and Dominique.

As they breathed in the green mist, they exhaled a black, smoke-like energy.

"Well, I'll be damned," John said. "This is going to be very helpful."

The green energy was love, and inhaling it caused any fear-based energies to be expelled from the body effortlessly.

This is how you will heal the world, Mia, Mother Earth said to her. *I need you to bathe the planet in this green life force energy to heal the planet's surface and everyone on it.*

Mia, I need you to be my vortex. The trees will help you; embody their strength. At any time, you can connect to their underground root systems to steady you. The trees live always from their center through their deep-rootedness, and from there, they connect all life on Earth.

Mia saw the Goddess's plan and a network of resources available to her. This didn't seem so challenging anymore. In fact, it felt as if everything made sense now. And while the task felt urgent, there was also a strong feeling of success, as though it was already completed. Mia was filled with so much love, it was hard to remember great suffering existed on the planet.

The fear and hatred felt inconsequential compared to the vast quantity of love there was.

So, while Mia was happy to assist in whatever she needed to do, she also felt as if she was floating away in a sea of bliss.

"Keep grounding, Mia!" John yelled.

There was so much energy moving through her, he could tell her body wouldn't be able to hold it for much longer. He leaned down, pressing his thumbs into the arches of her feet to help open up the channels. "Dammit, Mia! Ground! Can you hear me? You need stronger roots; send your energy down through your feet," John instructed firmly.

Mia was so blissed out, she didn't want to listen to John, but when he dug his thumbs into the soles of her feet, the sharp sensation of pain got her attention.

Mia poured herself back down into the earth as deep as she could reach, going all the way through the center of the planet to find herself inside the green crystal caves again. A bright shimmering Light Being appeared to her there, bringing with it a message.

Your body is going to have to carry new clear energy. You must train and prepare for this, or it will overload you and your physical body will no longer exist.

Oh, was all Mia could say.

She was still so blissed out that she had no attachment to whether she even had a body or not. She was floating, soaring as if she had departed her flesh-and-blood self.

You have to have a body to complete your mission, Mia, the Light Being responded.

Oh, okay. Mia felt a spark of memory. Through it, she could feel her desire to serve Mother Earth and the importance of her mission.

It is within the paradox that you will always find the answer. Stay focused, Mia. It's only going to get bumpier from here. The Light Being reached out and touched Mia on the chest. *Remember to always keep your heart open.*

Mia heard John's voice again.

"Come on back Mia, that's enough for one day. I don't like your complexion just now; you're bright red. The energy is too much for your body to handle and you need to slow down, or it will fry your nervous system. Take slow, deep breaths through your nose. Let your body relax."

John got her to wiggle her fingers and toes and roll onto her side.

"Open your eyes slowly and look out at the creek. Take your time. Just be real gentle with yourself right now."

John finally relaxed when Mia was able to open her eyes.

She tried to talk, but her mind couldn't engage to create language. She could see the others sitting up, watching her with concern.

"What's going on John, is she okay? What was that green light coming out of her? Did everybody see that?" Lori asked.

"Yeah. I've never heard you cuss during a healing session or pull somebody out of their breathwork experience before. You always take everything in stride and act like nothing's a big deal," Dominique said. "This was a new experience, slightly worrisome."

"I didn't mean to alarm you. She's going to be fine. Lori, did you happen to bring any fruit along today?"

"Why yes, I did." Lori reached over for her backpack and pulled out a banana.

She brought it over to Mia, but Mia wasn't even able to raise her hand to take it.

"Just set it in front of her. She'll regain the use of her body in a few minutes."

"Are you sure?" Lori asked. "She's still really flushed with color. I think I should help her get a bite in her mouth." She peeled the banana and held it so that Mia could easily manage a bite.

Not able to wait any longer either, Nick spoke up.

"Hey Mia, I want to apologize for what happened last night. I realized after you left that I responded the way I did out of jealousy. And really, underneath that jealousy was my own insecurity. It all hit that tender place in me, a place of feeling like after all I've done, I'm still not important to Mother Earth. It brought back childhood memories of never feeling I was good enough for my dad's approval. I've worked my ass off to heal that wound and I thought I had.

"So, I'm actually really grateful that, through you, I got to see that I still need to love myself more, 'cause it's not my dad's acceptance that I really need. It's my own."

Mia smiled and winked at Nick, letting him know she accepted his apology.

"I owe you an apology too," Lori said. "As much as I want to believe I'm a feminist and that a woman can be more powerful than a man, my mind instantly judged you as not being capable of doing the job because of the way you look—which is totally my issue.

"How you look has nothing to do with how capable you are. But you know, I've felt judged based on my appearance my whole life and that's where my own insecurities and my own bias come from. It got pretty bad, trying to control how others would see me. I've healed most of my eating disorder issues but there are still voices in my head, projecting any self-judgment that flares up in me onto others. I really do know my value isn't at all determined by the way I look, and neither is yours. I'm sorry for putting that on you last night. And like Nick said, I am truly grateful to have found within myself this place that needs more love. You helped me see it."

"Well, look at that!" John said, smiling. "Hearts are open, and love abounds. You all must have really been doing some breathing."

Nick looked over at Dominique.

"What about you? You ready to own *your* bullshit yet?" Nick asked.

"Of course I am. I'm always willing to admit it when I'm wrong, especially since it happens so rarely. It's not a daily practice for me like it is for you," Dominique said, smirking at Nick, knowing she was winning their little war of words. Then she turned to Mia.

"Mia, I too was projecting my unresolved 'daddy issues' onto you. I can see now that needing to get everything validated by the Galactic Council has been a form of overprotecting myself and keeping others at a distance. It can get quite lonely at times, so I'm actually happy to welcome you to our group."

Having finished the banana, Mia finally had regained enough strength to sit up and speak.

"I appreciate the apologies, and you are all very kind, but you have nothing whatsoever to be sorry for. I only responded the way I did because of my own rejection issues, so truly you are not to blame. Thank you, John, for helping all of us to heal ourselves," she said, smiling at him.

"It's all part of the grand master plan," John said laughingly. "How are you feeling? That was a lot of energy moving through you!"

"Emotionally, I feel amazing. Physically, everything hurts! Mentally, I don't know...doesn't seem like my mind has much to say at the moment."

Mia tried to move her body enough to stretch but found it too painful.

"Let's get in the creek. I think the water will help wash away the pain," John said.

Mia tried to get up but found she still wasn't able to move on her own. John and Nick helped her to her feet, taking her weight between them as they carried her over to the river.

"Should we just toss her in?" Nick teased.

"Yes, on the count of three," John responded playfully.

"Whoa! No! I don't think I can swim," Mia protested, grabbing onto their arms.

"Aw, we're just kidding, Mia," Nick smiled as they sat her down at the bank of the creek.

The water felt good against her legs, and she welcomed the idea of having her body fully submerged in the water. The guys took off their shirts and emptied their pockets before they helped Mia make it the rest of the way into the water.

The mushy red clay felt good as it squished between her toes.

"Ask the water to wash away the pain," John instructed. "Ask it to soothe your nervous system; I dare say it got a little fried with all that power running through you."

"Yeah, what the heck *was* that?" Nick asked, "I've never seen anything like it!"

"Me neither," John said. "Did you get any answer to what it was?"

"Yes, but neither of you has clearance to hear the information."

Mia tried to keep a straight face, but her laughter gave her away.

Nick let go of Mia's arm, letting her body submerge almost all the way underwater before he picked her back up.

"Hey, it's not wise to tease the ones keeping you upright!" Nick said playfully. "Now spill it! What was it?"

Mia told them everything she could remember.

"I traveled back down into the green caves, and this time, there was a Light Being there. It said something a little weird...that I would be running nuclear energy through my body and that I needed to prepare for it, or it would kill me, and that this energy is what will heal the planet.

"I don't know how nuclear energy could be healing, though. Oh, and the first thing that happened was that my body became a tree, which is how the green energy moved through me.

"The Light Being told me that the actual trees are supposed to help me, but I wasn't given the specifics on that yet, well, aside from being told to ground into their root systems. I was told my success was guaranteed but that I could die, so I need to train so I can complete the mission...and then there was something about the answer being in the paradox."

Mia stopped speaking, her brows knitting as she tried to work out the message.

"That sounds about right," John said. "But I think the Light Being you saw meant 'new clear' energy rather than what we think of as 'nuclear' energy. New clear energy is healing."

"Really?" Nick interjected. "So, you know what she's talking about? How do you know about this? And why haven't you told us about it? A nuclear reactor is a part of the team, and she might blow herself up in the process?"

"I didn't know about this before she showed up," John clarified. "What I meant was, what she just said matches what I was seeing and hearing while she was breathing. I could tell the powerful flow of the green crystalline energy was going to take her out if I didn't stop her, which is why I forced her to ground. My sense was that it felt so good for her to be in that place that she wouldn't have shut it off on her own. Am I right?" he asked, looking at Mia.

"Yup. I didn't want to come back, and was annoyed with you for making me do it. However, I'm so grateful now. I'm also incredibly grateful for this creek. The water really is washing away the pain just like you said it would."

"Did the Light Being tell you how to train or what to do to prepare your body?" Nick asked.

Mia reflected on Nick's question for a moment before speaking.

"Not that I can remember. It does seem as if it would be useful to know," Mia said, laughing.

"The beings that arrive as our guides usually only answer questions…that's why I was telling you to ask," John said. "My sense is that today was just a demonstration, so there will be plenty of time to get the information you need. Just make it a habit to always ask questions. That's the only way to lead the conversation."

"How is it guidance if we have to know how to draw out the answers?" Nick grumbled.

"Well," John offered, "I think there is some sort of prime directive to only offer assistance if it's asked for, in order not to violate our free will. It could be that your guide let you have the experience you did today to help you stop doubting yourself and your mission, not to mention helping get all these other jokers on board." John looked at Nick.

"Nick, were you aware of inhaling green energy and exhaling the black smoke?" John asked.

"Oh wow, you could see that?" Nick said, surprised. "It was a trip! My mind had quieted down enough that my heart was starting to open when all of a sudden, I was inhaling this green mist.

"It felt like pure love energy filling me up on the inside. All the traces of darkness within me started retreating as if they were terrified of the green stuff touching them, so they bolted as fast as they could. The darkness that didn't escape in time just dissolved when the mist reached it."

"Well, you can thank Mia for the entity flush. That green energy shot out of her and flowed right into the rest of you," John said.

"Cool, thanks, Mia," Nick said.

"You're welcome, anytime!" Mia laughed. "Hey, I think I can stand on my own now."

Both John and Nick loosened their grip on Mia's arms but quickly grabbed hold again as her legs gave way.

"Okay, maybe not yet," she said as they all laughed.

Mia noticed the look of concern Nick and John were exchanging. She could hear their thoughts. Both had expected her to have regained the use of her body by now.

She wasn't worried, however; she felt protected and knew she wouldn't be incapacitated by Mother Earth before the mission.

"Strength comes from the four elements balancing within the body," John said. "The green energy was too much for her body, so it overloaded her nervous system. Let's walk Mia over to that rock in the middle of the creek so she can ask it to replenish her strength. She can soak up some sunlight while enjoying the breeze and dip her hands and feet in the water as she rests."

"I've got more food too," Lori offered from the shore. "And let's get Mia some water with a little sea salt and minerals. We need to get her depleted electrolytes balanced again."

Nick went back to get the snacks and water from Lori while John got Mia settled on the rock. It was warmed from the sun and had a divot, a perfect spot for Mia to sit comfortably supported.

"Ask all the elements to help your body regain its strength," John said. "Tell them you did a lot today and need their help. It's good to begin cultivating these connections. You've got a big mission ahead and you'll need a lot of support. Let them know it all and keep offering gratitude."

Mia relaxed into her seat in the rock, letting her legs dangle in the flowing water as it gently caressed them. She felt the warmth of the sun on her face, and a gentle breeze lifting her hair.

It felt so natural to just be, her gratitude instinctual as she let her heart communicate with the elements. Soon, Mia felt the water that was flowing around her legs begin to swirl in the opposite direction, a chill tainting the air as a cloud had moved across the sun. Her body reached for the warmth and the gentle breeze grew into a wind that carried the cloud away.

Mia's body opened even more deeply to the sun's healing rays.

The rock on which she was sitting seemed to soften, holding her so perfectly that she found herself relaxing into a dreamlike state, a symphony of birds singing sweetly in the nearby trees.

A dragonfly landed right next to her and Mia allowed herself to receive all the love and support being given to her, letting her gratitude flow in return.

Nick brought over some food and climbed onto the rock with Mia.

"Those two will join us after they've been back to the car and changed into their swimsuits," he said to Mia and John. "They didn't want to get their fancy clothes wet like we did."

He gave John a nod as he handed him an apple. "John, are you still fine in the water? There's enough room up here on this rock if you want to warm up a bit."

"I'm good," John replied. "How is it that Lori always thinks to bring food with her? I'm always grateful for her. Every time, I think I'll bring food and never do. But Lori never forgets."

"Yup, she's a keeper that one, but maybe we could trade in Dominique for a less grouchy model," Nick joked.

"Oh, she's worth her weight in gold as well," John replied. "We've just got to help her let her guard down so that big heart of hers can open. Dominique's the most sensitive one of the bunch, and she needed that shield of detachment for a long time in order to function. Since she came from a different Universe, it's incredibly challenging for her to be in a body while Earth's still in the third dimension. You teasing her all the time isn't helping, you know."

"Ugh! All right, I'll try, but it might take me a while to break the habit!"

"Do, or do not. There is no *try*," Mia said in her best Yoda impression, causing the three of them to break out into laughter.

"You said she was a vortex traveler and multidimensional seer the night we met. What does that mean exactly?" Mia asked Nick.

He answered, "It means that Dominique has the ability to communicate and see things happening in other dimensions. So she's often looking at multiple realities all at once. She'll be able to tell you more about it as you get to know her better."

John said, "You won't hear her thoughts, or if you do, they might not make a lot of sense to you. Sometimes there are multiple languages happening at once and not all from this planet!"

"I didn't even know you were clairaudient, Mia," said Nick.

"It just started happening last night," Mia responded. "But I'm not quite sure how or when to use it. It still catches me off guard too…Like I find myself thinking, *how is this possible?*"

Lori and Dominique eventually joined them in the creek. They all spent the next few hours laughing, playing, relaxing, and enjoying nature. By the time they were done, they all felt renewed, including Mia, whose body had finally come back around.

They hugged goodbye when it was time for them to leave.

Their bond had strengthened through the green life force energy moving between them.

All except Mia had been through these road trips many times so they knew there was no need to make future plans; when they were needed again, they would simply know it.

As John drove Mia back to the hotel, she reflected on all that had happened in the last few days. "So now what do I do?" she asked, as if expecting John to know the answer.

He smiled at that. "I suggest taking it easy and having a good dinner, maybe getting another one of those burgers you ate a few nights ago. Your body will need the iron and the calories."

"No, I mean the bigger picture stuff! What do I do tomorrow? I'm supposed to go back home."

"Mia, I've never seen anyone being brought into the fold this quickly. It usually takes a few years for someone to get all the information they gave you these past few days.

"I wasn't sure why until this morning. I think the reason they want you up to speed so expeditiously is pretty clear to all of us now." John paused. "I'm going to be direct, Mia. It looks like you'd better go home and get your affairs in order so you can work on this full-time.

"Get rid of everything you don't need—give it away or put it in storage. Quit your job and tell your friends and family you're going away for a while. *That* is what you need to do next. Is that enough big-picture stuff?"

He looked over as Mia took in a deep breath, and he knew the answer already.

Mia was quiet, as if struck dumb by his response. Perhaps she was.

"That part of your life is over now, Mia," he added softly, looking over at her as if assessing her ability to cope with what he was telling her. "There isn't anything there for you anymore. Mia. You realize that, don't you? And the sooner you quit eating sugar and drinking alcohol, the better. Your body's going to have to be able to carry that new clear energy, and sugar and alcohol will only make it a lot more painful for you physically. Heck, look how hard today was, and you haven't been drinking at all since you've been here, right?"

Mia nodded as she let his words soak in. She didn't need him to tell her twice; the mere thought of trying to meld her old lifestyle with this new energy was already draining.

He added, "Meet me back here in a few weeks once you've gotten everything taken care of. This plan can't happen without you. The team needs you—heck, the whole planet needs you."

Mia's mind was spinning.

"Quit my job? I'd love to, but how am I supposed to pay my bills?"

John laughed. "You don't need to worry about money. Mother Earth will support you. She needs you and you work for Her now. I'll teach you how to get clear on exchange, the flow of consciousness given and received as energy, respect, value, appreciation, and love. It's the key and foundation to all relationships, especially the one you'll have with the Universe. And I'll help you figure out which benefits package you'd like to sign up for too."

Mia let out a deep breath. "Benefits package?" She appeared perplexed.

"You'll learn about everything in time," John said. "Take it one step at a time."

Mia nodded. "I guess there really is nothing left for me back home anyways… like you say."

She stared off into the distance as she thought about it.

A moment later, a big smile lit up her face.

"Okay, I'm ready to walk away from that life and join the 'Justice League.' I'm all in for inter-dimensional travel—and superpowers," Mia said with a grin.

"Superpowers? Dear Lord, slow down. We're dealing with new clear energy, remember? The only thing I want you thinking about is easy, gentle, and soft," John said, shaking his head.

"Well, if we're going to save the world, then clearly, the benefits package will need to include more superpowers," Mia laughed. "And how will I find you? Do I just come here? Will you know when I'm here? How do I get a hold of you? Can you hear my thoughts from far away too?" Mia's questions tumbled out of her, giving John no time to answer.

"Good grief," John laughed. "Yes, as loud as your thoughts are, I hear you wherever you are."

"Thank you," Mia said. "Thank you for finding me and helping me and believing in me and for all of it—really, there just aren't enough words to express how much gratitude I feel for this."

She leaned over and gave him a hug.

"You're welcome, Mia. Stay focused and hurry back." John hoped it wasn't a mistake to let her leave. "And remember to call on the elements if you get into trouble. Don't let your mind start talking you out of all this; you know how talkative the mind can be, especially in the stillness of the night when you can't sleep, so be wary of that and stay focused.

"In fact, as soon as you get up to your room, write about everything you've just experienced so that you can read it again when your mind tries to tell you that you're crazy."

"Don't worry, John, I'm all in. I won't change my mind."

With that, Mia hopped out of the truck.

5

Saying Goodbye

Mia made it back home in record time. Her mind had been lost in replaying the events of the past few days, so the drive passed quickly. She was excited for this new direction her life was taking and was eager to wrap things up and get back to Sedona.

For the first time in her life, she felt sure of what she was supposed to do with herself.

Although she didn't fully understand the specifics of what she would be doing, she knew with all her heart it was where she was meant to be. With all the information she had received so far, surely, she would be guided on how to proceed.

She went to work the next morning, gave her boss her letter of resignation, and cleared out her desk. She had been bored with work for a while, so she was happy to have a reason to finally leave the place. With a decent amount of money in savings, if she got into trouble, her family would help her out. Besides, John had been right about everything else so far, and working for Mother Earth sounded like a lot more fun than a forty-hour workweek.

She rented a storage unit and started packing up her belongings, though still unsure what she should tell people. Only someone who had experienced what she had would think her decision made any sense whatsoever. *I'll just tell people I'm going to take some time off and travel,* she thought. It was the easiest explanation since plenty of women her age did that kind of thing.

Most of the people close to her knew she had been unhappy since her breakup, and time off to travel was certainly something they would understand.

Plus, do I really care what they think?

The tightness in her stomach as she thought about her family's likely response was the answer to that question; she realized she was lying to herself.

She was disappointed in herself for still caring what they thought, but she didn't want to upset them or make them worry about her at the same time... This was all so hard to navigate.

But there was no way they would understand her decision.

They wanted her to find happiness, but this decision would definitely be too far "out of the box" for them. The more her mind thought about how her parents would react, the slower her packing became. She decided to take a break.

I'll do something else for a while to stop these thoughts spinning inside my head.

I'm going to get vertigo if I carry on like this!

There was only one person she could tell, just one who she knew would be supportive. Her friend Amy was into weird stuff, loved going to psychics and was always getting astrology readings. She had even done Ayahuasca. The stories Amy had told her about that experience made a lot more sense now. *Although I don't know why anyone would want to throw up for five hours when they can have the same experience with breathwork,* she mused.

She called Amy on the phone and told her just a fraction of what had transpired over the last few days. "... And so, I've decided to quit my job and move to Sedona for a year."

"Wow, Mia, go for it! Look, I know you haven't been happy here for a while now. It'll be great for you. A change of scenery and some fun new people. And *amazing* experiences!"

"It's going to be so hard to tell my family," Mia said, thinking of what was to come.

"Yes, but you can't let that stop you. This is going to be so good for you," Amy said. "You need to get away from all the bad memories and go have some fun. Plus, Sedona's so magical, and that vortex energy's insane. You should have sex on a vortex while you're living there!"

"What! Oh, my God! Amy, that's not at all why I'm going there," Mia responded, shrieking with laughter at her friend's one-track mind.

"You may laugh but I'm serious; it would be such a powerful experience. If you won't, then I'll have to come visit you and find some hottie to hook up with."

"I have no doubt that you will," Mia said, still laughing. "If anyone would, you would."

"We need to mark this momentous occasion with a celebration. An initiation into the new chapter of your life."

"Well, I'm planning on leaving as soon as I'm packed up, so maybe just a small dinner with some of the old group?"

"No, dinner's much too boring. We need to do something big. This change is epic, Mia. I'm so proud of you and really want to do something special. I know what we can do! My dad and his business partners are thinking of investing in a yacht down at the marina, and he wants me to go check it out with him. I'll tell him we want to take it out this Saturday night and cater a party on it to see if it's a good investment for him," Amy replied. "Sounds credible. What do you think?"

"Oh gosh! That sounds amazing but I don't want you to go to that much trouble. I wasn't really planning on telling that many people the reason I'm leaving. Let's just keep it simple."

But Amy couldn't be talked out of the idea once the inspiration had taken hold of her.

"It'll be perfect, Mia—one final third-dimension celebration before you go off into the fifth," Amy said, laughing. "We can even make it a costume party and tell everyone to come as their favorite ascended master or spirit guide."

"Amy! You know I love you, but it's just too much. I feel uncomfortable having a big party."

"Nonsense, you deserve some fun after everything you've been through these past few months," Amy insisted. There was just no way she'd ever back down on this.

Mia was hesitant, but she didn't want to hurt her friend's feelings. Plus, she already felt defeated on the matter as Amy had a way of making everything sound like fun and Mia didn't want to disappoint the only person she felt understood why she was doing this.

So she finally gave in.

Getting back to packing didn't seem too hard to do now. She threw herself into the task, hoping she could be ready to leave after the party. She even found an old Wonder Woman costume that would be the perfect party outfit since she was going to be saving the world.

I guess it's meant to be. Besides, it'll be good to say goodbye to my old friends before I go. I don't know how much contact I'll have with them after I leave, Mia thought.

She gave herself permission to relax and have fun instead of worrying so much about everything. Now feeling better, she gave her parents a quick call and let them know a rare opportunity had come up and she was going to be traveling for a while, helping people.

"I don't have all the details yet but I'll check in with you once I'm settled," she said.

"All right, honey," said her mother warmly. "You sound so happy, Mia. I can't tell you how much better that makes me feel. We really hope you'll find what you're looking for."

6

Getting Drunk

———

"You look amazing, Mia!" Amy exclaimed when she saw her.

Mia actually felt a little uncomfortable in her Wonder Woman costume. It was shorter and tighter than she had remembered but she hadn't had time to go out and get anything else.

She felt as if she was spilling out of the top.

Amy was dressed as the Egyptian goddess Sekhmet and looked gorgeous as always.

"You're going to die when you see the yacht! It's epic! I believe the Universe wants us to be abundant and enjoy the best life has to offer, so this will be the perfect send-off to your new life in Sedona. This way, the Universe will know that you're not giving up a life of comfort and luxury just because you're going to live in the woods, and you'll be blessed with a fifth-dimensional garden of paradise to live in. How amazing will that be?"

Mia wondered how Amy had come up with some of the

ridiculous things she believed, but hey, if she could get an up-grade from the Universe, she was willing to play along.

They arrived at the marina and boarded an immense yacht.

Amy had excellent taste and everything she did was always first class. There was live music, a dance floor, a free-flowing bar, and waiters serving appetizers. Mia saw friends she hadn't seen in years, feeling touched that everyone had shown up to say good-bye to her. But then she realized it probably had more to do with not wanting to miss one of Amy's spectacular parties. As she looked around, she saw there were several people there that she didn't actually know.

"Oh yeah...Um, a *slight* drawback, but understandable, is that I had to invite Dad and his investors tonight, but don't worry, they'll stay out of our way."

Amy waved to her dad, seated inside at a table with several older men.

As the yacht set sail, Mia decided to make the best of it and enjoy her evening to the fullest. Amy made a speech welcoming everyone aboard "the cruise ship to the fifth dimension."

"And let's all wish Mia a bon voyage on her new adventure," she added, raising a glass.

A few friends came up to ask Mia about where she was going, and she kept it simple. "Well, let's just say I'm heading off on an Elizabeth Gilbert *Eat, Pray, Love* adventure."

That answer satisfied them; they had all seen the movie or read the book.

The band played a bunch of eighties' cover songs, quickly get-ting everyone in the mood to dance. The sway of the ocean and the smell of the salt air combined with everyone's laughter and excite-ment created an illusion in which it was easy to get caught up.

I think it will be okay if I have just a couple of little cocktails, Mia thought.

Even though John had told her to stay away from alcohol, she told herself it would help her feel more connected to her old friends and more at ease in her costume.

She danced with her friends, allowing herself to let go of her inhibitions. She had been a wild party girl for well over a decade, so one last "hurrah" seemed like a great idea.

She also had to concede to being happy she'd let Amy have her way. As the band played AC/DC's "You Shook Me All Night Long," Mia let herself fully embrace the night's festivities, dancing until her feet were almost begging her for a break. Later, sitting at a dining booth, Mia had a chance to talk to more of her friends, all so curious about her adventure.

She had planned to keep the details all to herself, but of course, she was now buzzed on alcohol and less inhibited about sharing the details of her recent experience. Most of her friends were inebriated too, and in light of that, what Mia told them even seemed to make sense in some way. Feeling that her friends understood her gave her more confidence, helping her feel more connected to them. Now she was also feeling silly for having worried about what their reactions might be. They were all so supportive and so happy for her.

Eventually, her friends made their way back to the dance floor and Mia found herself sitting alone when an older man she didn't recognize came up to the table.

"I couldn't help but overhear you talking about your experience in Sedona. It sounds fascinating. May I sit down and ask you more about it? I'm Frank."

"Of course," Mia responded. Her heart was wide open, and she was feeling connected to everyone, even the men who had accompanied Amy's father to the yacht.

She hadn't felt this free since her time in Sedona and wasn't thinking at all that the drinks she'd had could be a part of what she was experiencing.

"Listening to you reminded me of an experience I had a few years ago, though mine was on a smaller scale. It was a dream actually, but when I woke from it in the middle of the night, I felt as if I was still in it. Have you ever experienced that, Mia?"

He did not even wait for a response, but her smile must have shown that yes, she knew that experience very well. He continued, "I felt connected to all of life, that we are all One, that there is no separation, and that we all must learn to love each other again. It impacted me so profoundly, I actually stayed up the rest of the night writing about it..."

He fell quiet, contemplative for a moment. Then he added, "I don't know, maybe I'm delusional, but it felt real."

"Oh, I definitely think it was real! That was the message I received over and over during my experience in Sedona. The solution to everything is returning to a state of love and feeling our connection with all of life. It's only our judgment and fear that make us feel separate from and threatened by one another," Mia responded enthusiastically.

"You glow with light the more you talk about this. Your energy is so beautiful and I feel really comfortable talking to you. I've never been able to talk to anyone about this. I'm really happy I came tonight. I think it's a sign."

"A sign for what?" Mia asked.

"Well, your friend Amy, her dad invited me here tonight to see if I wanted to invest in this project with the yacht. I wasn't interested, but decided to come and just enjoy myself because who doesn't enjoy a party at sea? But now I think it's because I was supposed to meet you."

He moved a little closer to her.

Mia laughed uncomfortably. *Is this man interested in me? He's old enough to be my own dad. Surely he doesn't think he has a chance with me...Does he?*

She continued smiling but it felt as if her facial expression had frozen.

So uncomfortable was she!

If this man, Frank, had picked up on that discomfort, he was not showing it or easing off his great enthusiasm. "I've never met anyone like you before," he went on. "It gives me hope for the world that there are people like you who want to help others. You are so inspiring."

Mia relaxed. *Oh, he's just being nice and feels connected to me because of my energy.*

Amy came by the table.

"Okay, enough talking, you two. Let's get back out on the dance floor!" she demanded.

Mia slid out of the booth with a sense of gratitude, following Amy, who decided to stop at the bar and do a quick shot of tequila on their way to dance. What Mia didn't notice was that Frank was following them; she was oblivious until he reached his hand out to spin her around on the dance floor. Having convinced herself that he was a harmless old man, she innocently continued to dance with him.

After a few more songs, the band took a break during the serving of their buffet dinner.

Mia made up a small plate for herself, stepping outside the cabin to get some fresh air. She was feeling pretty drunk and wanted to eat something to help her sober up. As she stared out over the ocean, she marveled at how peaceful and calm the water seemed compared to all the noise emanating from the party. She wandered farther away from the cabin to enjoy the quiet, standing on the boat's bow, marveling at the beauty of the city lights in the distance.

"It really is beautiful out here, isn't it?"

Frank's voice startled her; she hadn't heard him approach.

"Yes, the city looks so peaceful from out here," she replied.

"That's my building with the green lights," he said, pointing to the skyline's tallest building.

"It's beautiful," she responded. "What do you do in that big building?"

"Oh, I don't actually work there. I own a commercial real estate investment company and we have properties all over the world. I just recognize that one because of the green lights."

He laughed.

"It reminds me of the green light I saw in Sedona. The energy of Mother Earth is that color."

Mia blinked to focus her eyes, realizing the green halo she was seeing around the building was her vision blurring from all the alcohol she'd consumed.

She started to feel dizzy and wanted to put down her plate of food and drink so she could steady herself. As a wave rocked the boat, she lost her balance, toppling toward Frank.

"I've got you," Frank said, grabbing hold of her waist.

But she really wanted him to take her plate or drink out of her hands, not hold onto her.

"Thanks, I'm okay," she said, regaining her balance.

The wind picked up and the formerly calm ocean became choppier.

"You really are so beautiful," he said, not letting go of her waist.

Mia didn't like the way his hands felt on her.

"Could you hold my drink?" she asked, hoping that would get him to let go of her.

A high wave splashed against the bow and Frank had to grab the railing to keep from falling backwards. Mia's body fell forward into him, and she dropped her drink and plate.

"Here, let me help you," he said as he wrapped his arms around her.

Mia couldn't tell if he was trying to help her or cop a feel. She was agitated, uneasy.

"Let's go back inside," she said, trying to break free from his embrace.

"We're safe here," he said as he pinned her against the railing with his body. "Don't worry I won't let you fall in."

"I'm not worried about..."

Mia couldn't finish her sentence before Frank pressed his mouth against hers. She tried to pull her head back, but he had moved his hands and was now holding her head in place. She kept her mouth closed but could feel his tongue trying to part her lips.

What the fuck's happening? Mia's mind screamed.

She was finally able to push him off her as he laughed playfully. Still in shock, Mia just turned and got away from him as quickly as she could.

She found Amy, who told her some unexpected, good news.

"The captain's decided to take us all back to the marina because of this unexpected change of weather," she said.

Relieved that she would be getting off the boat soon, Mia decided not to ruin Amy's night by telling her what had just happened. Amy was going through the crowd now, inviting everybody back to her house for an after-party. Mia decided to take the opening to sneak away.

She planned to head back home, no longer feeling like celebrating.

An hour later, Mia was in a taxi on her way home, still feeling gross every time she thought about Frank touching her. *God, I am so naïve to have assumed he was just a nice old man.*

She realized that everything he had said to her about the spiritual stuff must have been absolute bullshit and that he'd just been saying it to try to connect with her.

Tears streamed down her face as she felt sorry for herself for always having such a hard time knowing how to deal with these types of situations.

Her phone chirped from inside her purse. She pulled it out and stared at the small screen. It was a text from Richard, bearing the words, "I miss you."

She had been ignoring his texts for months, but tonight, feeling sad and angry and still drunk, she decided to respond, though her mood was no more conciliatory than usual.

Mia: So are all your other girlfriends busy tonight?
Richard: There's never been anyone but you. Don't know
    why you keep saying that.
Mia: I don't believe you. You're a liar.
Richard: I love you, though. I'm not lying. Just wish you'd
    believe me.
Mia: You're full of shit, just like all men. You're all assholes.
Richard: Baby, what's wrong? Are you OK?
Mia: Don't act like you care about anyone but yourself.
Richard: You know how much I love you.

Mia put her phone back in her purse, seething. The cab pulled up to her house and she got out, not even looking at the other messages that Richard had sent.

One said, "Let me come over and show you."

Mia stumbled into her house and threw her purse on the floor. She was still dizzy and needed to eat something after her plate of food had ended up on the deck of the yacht. She found the box of pizza left over from lunch and dug in.

She had just finished eating her third slice when there came the sound of loud banging at her door. "Mia, are you in there?"

Richard's voice! What the hell? She went to the door.

Richard stared at Mia, still wearing her Wonder Woman costume, her hair disheveled from blowing in the wind, mascara streaming down her face from crying, and red pizza sauce on the corner of her mouth.

Without waiting for an invitation, he stepped inside and wrapped his arms around her.

"Oh my gosh, baby, what happened to you?"

She hated to admit it, but his arms wrapped around her felt amazing. He still smelled the same; his embrace still felt the same. All her feelings came rushing back.

"Did someone hurt you?" he asked again.

"You did," she responded coldly, forcing herself to push him away.

"I never meant to hurt you. I still love you. My life's been so empty without you," he said, pulling her back to him. "Nothing means anything to me without you."

"Well, I have news for you. You need to leave. Go back to your wife," she said, mustering all her strength to try and stop her body from melting into his.

"I don't think you're okay, Mia. I think you need me to stay."

"I'm fine, just get out," she said as she started to cry.

"Why are you doing this to us? Why are you pushing me away when all I want to do is love you?" he insisted.

"Me and every other girl you decide to seduce," she said, pushing him away again.

"There's never been anyone else, Mia! You are the only woman I have ever loved," Richard yelled. He gripped her shoulders tightly and then lifted her chin. "Look at me! Look me in the eyes and see how much I love you. See that I'm telling you the truth."

"No, you're a liar," she insisted, but the alcohol in her was starting to believe him.

"I have loved you from the moment we met, and I never stopped. Tell me you don't love me anymore," he said.

Mia cried harder and Richard pulled her back into his arms.

"I love you, baby," he whispered as he kissed the top of her head.

She knew she shouldn't do this, but it felt so good to be held. Her drunk mind justified that it wouldn't hurt this one last time. She'd had a terrible evening and at least she knew what kind of man Richard was. *Better the devil you know,* her mind reassured her.

Sensing the drop in her resistance, Richard picked her up in his arms and carried her toward the bedroom. He was so focused on getting her into bed he didn't even notice all her stuff was packed in boxes.

Mia woke up with a headache as the sun illuminated the darkness in her bedroom. She knew by the sound of his breathing that Richard was still asleep next to her. Her first response was to beat herself up for having given in so easily, but her brain hurt too much to think.

I can punish myself later, she decided as she slipped out of bed to get some aspirin and a glass of water. She looked around at the boxes in the kitchen and started to wonder what the heck she was going to do. *Is moving to Sedona still an option after what happened last night?*

That thought made her brain hurt even more. She'd just go back to bed, having already screwed things up. There was no reason to try to fix anything this early in the morning anyhow.

She tried to slide back into bed without waking Richard, but he smiled as he opened his eyes to find her lying next to him. He reached out and pulled her closer.

"Good morning, beautiful," he said as he spooned her. "This is the first morning I've woken up happy in months."

God, he's not going to make this easy, Mia thought to herself. *He's really laying it on thick.*

"It feels so good to have you in my arms again. I'm never going to let you go," he whispered as he held her even tighter.

It did feel good to be in his arms, dangerously good, her body responding to his touch the way it always had. The voice inside her was screaming, *What the fuck are you doing, Mia?*

But it was barely audible at this point. The voice that was saying, *He's already here, you might as well just enjoy it,* seemed to make the most sense.

The chemistry between them had always been off the charts, Mia always thinking it was as if he had been given the secret manual to her body. He knew exactly what to do, when to do it, where to do it and how, rendering her completely powerless and overwhelmed with ecstasy.

While she should have been too sore from the hours of sex they'd had last night, that never seemed to be a problem for them. Throughout all the years they had been together, there seemed to be no limit to what they could achieve sexually. As his hand caressed her skin, she could feel the familiar dampness returning between her thighs. He kissed her neck, and she felt a wave of desire wash over her that left her intoxicated. Within seconds, she responded like a hungry addict, spreading her legs for him, urging him to hurry up and get inside her.

"Tell me you need me," he whispered in her ear.

Oh my god, just fuck me already, she thought.

"I need you," she said, knowing he wouldn't give her what she wanted until she said it.

As he slid inside her, everything magnified: the desire; the intoxication; the ecstasy.

She felt as though she would die if she couldn't have him. She *did* need him, she really did.

She couldn't exist without this feeling, and he was the only one who had ever made her feel like this. This was why she had waited so long for him.

This was why she put up with all his bullshit. There was something amazing between them, something only the two of them could understand. Whatever this was, it had to be right.

"Oh god, yes!" she screamed as he continued to pound into her, flooding every ounce of her with pleasure.

"Tell me you still love me," he said as he slowed, holding very still inside her.

She opened her eyes and looked into his, as high as a kite on his energy. She would say anything in this moment to get him to keep going.

It's true, she thought. *I can't live without him...I need this...I need him.*

"I still love you," she lied, digging her nails into the small of his back.

"And not just because the sex between us is amazing?" he wanted to know. "Tell me that it's more than that. Tell me that you still love me, that you're still mine and that you'll never leave me again. Tell me that you need me and want me."

He was loving the power he had over her in this moment.
She knew she shouldn't say it, but couldn't help herself, caught in the spell he was weaving and intoxicated by her desire. She wanted to fall into his web, to be seduced by his words. She wanted him to keep going. She opened her mouth to speak, but no words came out.

He thrust deeper into her.

"Tell me," he whispered as he kissed her parted lips. "Tell me you're mine, that you'll always be mine."

"Mmmmm," was the only sound she could make.

"Say it, Mia. I can see it in your eyes but want you to tell me.

We belong together. We're perfect for each other and you know it. There's no reason for us to be miserable and alone."

"Yes," she whispered, wanting him to bring her to climax more than she had ever wanted anything.

"Yes, what?" he asked her, thrusting into her again.

"*Yes* to everything: yes, I want you; yes, I need you; yes, I won't leave you; yes, I am yours." Her spine arched from the waves of pleasure racing through her. She felt out of control, unable to stop herself; she didn't *want* to stop herself.

She surrendered fully to him, not caring about anything else in the world at that moment.

They stayed in bed all day, getting lost inside each other, taking naps in between orgasms, and only getting up a couple times to finish off the leftover pizza in the fridge.

Richard didn't leave until he had to go to work early Monday morning. By this time, Mia's addiction to him had returned so powerfully that she made him promise he'd come back at lunchtime. She wandered around the house trying to figure out what to do with herself.

She didn't know whether she should keep packing or start unpacking. A part of her still knew Richard was lying to her but she didn't care. She hadn't forgotten everything she'd realized about him; she just thought she could handle it now she knew the truth.

I don't need him to marry me, she told herself. *I can just enjoy this as long as it lasts this time. And maybe he has changed a little bit after losing me. Maybe he did realize what he gave up.*

She plugged her dead phone in, powering it up to see that Richard had already sent her three 'I love you' messages. She lay down on the couch, beginning a conversation with him that quickly escalated into sexting. He kept her drunk on sex talk all day, promising that even though he had to cancel their lunch plans, it would mean he could come over earlier at the end of the day.

He could also stay the night with her again.

He did come over at four and they had sex for two whole hours before he made a revelation.

"Well, I'd best get going," he said, checking his phone for the time.

"What? You're leaving?" Mia sat bolt upright, annoyed and perplexed.

"Yes, of course. I need to pick up the kids!"

"That makes no sense," she remonstrated. "You said you'd stay all night!"

Is he really pulling this crap on me again already? This is unbelievable!

"Baby, I'm sorry. Promise it won't happen again. But I couldn't get out of it. I mean, what can I do? They're my kids," he pleaded. "How was I to know I'd have to have them tonight?"

Oh, so all these plans have been made between our agreed arrangement and now? You could have told your ex you weren't available and let her figure something else out the way she does when you're traveling, was what Mia wanted to say. But she didn't want to fight with him.

She especially never wanted to fight with a man about his children because if there was one way to alienate someone, it was to argue about childcare and responsibilities toward the kids.

"I want to take you away this weekend," he managed in the next breath. "Go somewhere special to celebrate our new beginning." He reached over, taking her hand. "Don't be mad at me, baby. I'll not screw this up this time. I'm going to tell her I want a divorce this week and…"

"Wait! What do you mean you're going to tell her you want a divorce? I thought you *already* did that. You sent me all those messages when we were apart, telling me you finally ended it with her. Was that all bullshit too, then?" Mia said, pulling her hand away sharply.

"No, I did tell her. I did move out and get my own place and I started the divorce, but you wouldn't speak to me, and my kids were really upset, so I went back," he responded.

"Your kids were upset that their parents were getting divorced? Uh, yeah. What a surprise! What did you expect? That they'd be deliriously happy? You're so full of shit. You were only going to divorce her to get with me...and you never really wanted to. That's obvious. You just want whichever woman will have you at the time, so it happens."

She stood up to walk away from him.

He reached out and grabbed her hand.

"You wouldn't speak to me, Mia. I thought I'd lost you forever. I gave up on ever being happy, so went back because at least I could make my kids happy, and they could make me happier by me not having to be on my own. I'm not full of shit. Give me a chance to do this. I just got you back. I love you and I'm not going to fuck this up this time!" he said emphatically.

Mia said nothing.

Richard stood up, wrapping his arms around her.

"I can't lose you again, baby," he said with tears in his eyes. "Please. Please do not do this to me. It will destroy me. You're all that matters to me."

In all their years together, Mia had never seen him cry.

Maybe it's all true. Maybe he really will make it right this time, she thought.

"Please don't shut me out again, baby. I can't live without you," he pleaded.

Mia's anger melted as Richard held her tighter. His lips found hers again and it wasn't long before their clothes fell off their bodies and they found themselves intertwined.

"I want you to be my wife. I want you by my side always. I don't ever want to have to leave you," he whispered in her ear, bringing her to climax over and over.

Between his visits over the next several days and the nonstop sexting while he was away, Richard managed to keep Mia sedated all week. He had her convinced he had changed, that he was ready to get divorced, that he would take care of her, and that he'd take care of everything.

Anytime that he sensed her starting to pull away, he would rush right over or seduce her with some grand gesture. On the one day he just couldn't leave the office, he sent a car to pick her up, sneaking her into the building. Mia had always thought she hated all the sneaking around, but now that she was in the middle of it again, she realized something she had never known before.

It was that the risk only made things all the more exciting.

7

The Devil

Mia had moments of clarity in which she asked herself what the heck she was doing. John was expecting her back in Sedona. It seemed as if every time she started thinking about Sedona, Richard would show up, either in person or on the phone. Plus, she felt so embarrassed. She was sure John must have given up on her by now. *As intuitive as he is, he probably knew the second I relapsed. Relapsed? That's an interesting choice of words,* she thought.

She felt bad that he'd wasted so much time on her.

He really did try to help me, and it was a super-great experience, but I'm really not the type to live in the forest or be some sort of healer gypsy, Mia thought. *And there are way more qualified healers to help save the world. Seems so silly now that I even contemplated doing that.*

She thought she felt a tiny swirl of energy in her palms as she thought about being a healer but a knock on her door interrupted the thought. She was expecting Richard; he was taking her out of town for the weekend tonight and he'd made reservations at some fancy resort in the desert.

"Look, it doesn't even matter where we stay, does it?" she'd said to him. "We both know we'll never get out of the bedroom! Any old motel would have done."

They had giggled about it like a pair of teenagers, but still, he wanted to give her a treat and who was she to complain? She opened the door, her eyes going wide upon seeing a vase of red roses at her feet and a floral delivery van still backing out of her driveway.

Why would he send me flowers when we're leaving for the weekend? she wondered as she brought the roses inside. As she read the card, she understood why.

"Forgive me, baby. I can't leave tonight. Something came up. I'll be there tomorrow morning, I promise. Can't wait to see you. I love you, Richard."

Mia wasn't sure how to feel. Annoyed? Upset? Hurt? "Something came up" was hardly a respectful, detailed explanation for why he would stand her up for a whole goddamn evening.

Is this the same crap that he used to pull? Should I be understanding or pissed? The roses are a new touch, I suppose; he used to just cancel with no explanation.

But what's "come up"? Why couldn't he leave tonight?

Has something happened with work, or at home?

Her thoughts were racing. But it was more likely to be a home problem, otherwise he'd just have said that it was down to work. Or he would have called her. It sounded like a *wife* problem!

Her phone chirped and she expected to see a text from Richard, but it was not.

Amy: "How's the packing going? You still in town? When did you sneak off the other night?

Drinks tonight?"

Mia: "Yes! Let's get drinks right now and I'll fill you in on everything."

As they split a bottle of red wine, Mia did give Amy the whole picture.

"Oh my gosh, Mia! Why didn't you tell me what Frank did to you? I would have slapped him for you! I'm so glad Richard was there to comfort you! That was lucky, wasn't it?"

"Really?" Mia asked. "You don't think it's really awful that I'm with him again?"

"No, not at all. Why would I? You two have always had this unexplainable thing. And living without you this year was probably the wake-up call he needed," Amy responded. "Everyone can change. And everyone deserves a second chance."

"Yeah, but what about him canceling tonight? I don't know, this feels like the same old crap he used to pull—always getting cold feet and backing out when it came time for him to act."

"That's very true but the way I see it, you've got nothing to lose. If Richard leaves his wife, you two can finally be together. If he doesn't, you can take off on your adventure. Either way, you're guaranteed some excitement," Amy said.

Mia laughed. "This is why I love you, Amy. You always find a way to turn things into a happy outcome. And you're right, I've already proven to myself that I can walk away from him, so if I need to do it again, I will. And he better have a damn good reason for changing our plans."

"His postponing your romantic weekend allowed us time to get together, so I'm selfishly happy he did," Amy said. "Besides, there's a reason for everything."

"Well, I'm still punishing him for it. I've turned off my phone, so he won't be able to reach me if he tries," Mia said snidely.

Mia enjoyed her night with Amy, and as usual, one bottle of wine turned into two.

Mia turned on her phone the next morning to see what was happening with Richard. To her surprise, there were no messages from him. Her heart lurched. Now she was upset.

And now she was angry too...Until she remembered.

Shit! Why did I turn off my phone? Now I don't know if he called, do I? Maybe he did but just didn't leave a message. He could have been calling all night for all I know.

That shit's backfired on me. Trust me to make a bad decision to turn off—

Wait, no, that doesn't make sense; why wouldn't he leave a message? Unless he was pissed that I'd switched off my phone. Probably thinks I was being moody and petulant, which I was.

Or maybe he didn't call once! Probably because he finally told his wife, and they spent the evening talking about the divorce. But then why wouldn't he call to tell me that? He hasn't gone more than a few hours all week without communicating with me, and now, nothing?

Hell. Maybe he told her about the divorce and she got upset, and they've reconciled!

Mia's stomach started to hurt as she tried to figure out what was happening with him. Finally, she couldn't take it anymore and sent him a text.

Mia: Where are you? What's the plan? Are we still going?

She waited for a response, but none came. She even powered her phone off and on again to make sure it was working right. She waited all day, staring at the phone endlessly.

But she never heard back from him. He had not even read the message.

Has something happened at work? Has he been in an accident? Did his wife freak out? Did he change his mind? Mia was pissed. *Fuck him for not answering me,* she thought.

She threw the roses in the trash. *I don't need this bullshit!*

She grabbed a box and started packing again.

That's it, I'm done with him. I'm leaving, she thought, as she grabbed everything left in the living room and stuffed it into a massive box.

That's weird that he never even asked me about all the boxes in the house either.

How could he not have noticed? Is he so self-absorbed that it doesn't even occur to him to ask me about my life? She realized she hadn't told him anything about Sedona either. *He never asked what I've been up to, what my plans are. All he wanted to talk about was us getting back together. It's always all about him, him, him. That seems weird to me.*

She taped up another box. Before she knew it, she had finished packing everything.

Shit, now what do I do? Can I still go to Sedona? Is that still an option? Is John even going to want me around after what I've been doing all week? Why would he want me as a part of his community when the second I leave Sedona, I end up back in bed with the devil?

Thinking of Richard as the devil made her sick to her stomach. She lay down on the couch and started to cry, feeling so lost, confused, and hopeless. And she couldn't just stay. She had quit her job, given her landlord notice, and packed up everything. The fact that she hadn't heard from Richard by now confirmed her suspicions that he was up to his usual bullshit.

The question mark now was John.

Can I still go? Would they still want me, or have I ruined everything?

A knock at the door startled her.

Oh shit! she thought. *Is Richard finally here? And if he is, do I even want to answer the door?*

She walked quietly over to the door and peeked through the peephole.

What the heck? she thought as she saw Nick standing at the door.

"Open up Mia, I can see you looking at me."

"What are *you* doing here?" Mia asked as she pulled the door wide.

"John thought you might need some help getting back to Sedona, so I'm here to be of service."

Mia threw her arms around his neck. "You have no idea how happy I am to see you! And your timing is perfect!"

"Of course it is, although I have to give John the credit for that. He contacted me this morning and told me to be at your door by five this afternoon, so here I am," Nick said.

He surveyed the room full of boxes.

"Well, it looks like you're ready to go but you reek of entities. What's been going on here?" Nick asked.

"Ugh," Mia sighed. "I'm too embarrassed to tell you."

"I'm not here to judge you, sister, I'm here to help. So confess your sins and get over the shame. We've got work to do." He walked inside and took a seat. "Come on, let's hear it. It can't be all that bad and at least your stuff's all packed. I'm not in any hurry and have time to listen."

He placed his hands in his lap, cocking his head, waiting in an *I'm listening* pose.

Mia told him the story, starting with the going-away party and ending with Richard's disappearing act today.

Nick let her talk without interrupting except for the occasional "Yup...," "Sounds about right...," "Uh huh...," "Figures...," and eventually, "Dear Lord!"

"Well, I'm not going to lie to you Mia, it's pretty bad. You relapsed hardcore and ended up in a worse place than you were in before you came to Sedona. You were smoking the heroin right out of that man's penis," Nick said, shaking his head. He wasn't even laughing when he said it.

"I was what?" Mia asked, hoping she'd misheard.

"Oh, you heard me, sister, and you also know I'm right. But don't worry. This doesn't make you bad. It makes you normal. To be honest, I was pretty relieved to know that you fucked up and needed help. Brings you back down to our level, you know? You're not some miraculous superhero. You're like the rest of us, fallible and susceptible to the dark side's seduction."

Mia stared at Nick, not sure how to respond.

"Aww...I'm just giving you a hard time. John suspected this might happen because it happened to all of us once we started the work. The dark side actually starts to work harder to sabotage you once you answer the call of the light team. Clearly, John's been tuned in to you this whole time because he knew when there would be an opening to come help. So what do you say, Mia, are you ready to put down that penis crack pipe and get sober again?"

Nick was grinning.

"Oh my gosh, stop saying that! You're freaking me out, though your summary is disturbingly accurate. Yes, I'm ready. Let's get the heck out of here," she said emphatically.

"Great. Let's load up your car with the stuff you want to bring, and we'll have the movers put the boxes in storage for you on Monday. Is there a neighbor or someone to leave a key with?"

"Uh, yes...but um, this feels sort of fast. Are you wanting to leave tonight?"

"Girl, we've got to get you back in detox before that motherfucker shows up here with another bouquet of red roses." Nick nodded toward the trash can. "That energy isn't going to give up, and as soon as he senses you pulling away, which is going to be any second now, he's going to reach out or come over. And I certainly don't want to get my ass kicked trying to get you away from your entity. Besides, he'll probably think you're having revenge sex with me."

Mia stared, appalled at the suggestion despite the obvious twinkle in Nick's eye.

He was only teasing her, but he did have a point.

"So come on, let's go!" he added.

She knew Nick was probably right, and while it made her uncomfortable, she agreed.

"All right then. Tonight it is."

As they were loading up her car, she looked around, then looked again. There wasn't another car in her driveway.

"How did you get here? Didn't you drive?" she asked.

"Nope, I teleported; it's better for the environment."

Nick loaded Mia's suitcases into the back of her car.

"Wait, what? *Really?*"

"Ha, gotcha! No, not yet, but soon. I plan on having that superpower eventually. I caught a ride with a buddy who was heading this way. Figured it would be better if we drove back together in case you tried to run off and disappear," he said, laughing again at her expense.

Mia just shook her head and rolled her eyes in an exaggerated fashion. To be honest, his bad-taste humor was at least a welcome distraction from thoughts of Richard.

"Hey, I didn't know how willing you'd be to come along," Nick said. "You're exhausted for one thing. Look at the state of you; sure you don't want to catch up on your missed sleep on the back seat? From the look of you, you've been hitting that pipe pretty hard!"

He was cracking himself up again.

That reference again. Mia flinched at it.

Miraculously, Mia was able to coordinate everything with the movers and her neighbor, and within a few hours they were ready to hit the road and head back to Sedona. Nick insisted on driving, which was fine with her. She had finally turned her phone back on, and at last, there was a string of messages from Richard. It left her feeling shaky, hesitant to even read them.

The timing was bad, and anyway, she wouldn't be able to call him, not now, not on this trip with Mr. Comedian alongside. And when they got there, she would have a new life, new responsibilities. No more opportunities to deal with the devil and his crack pipe.

She did read the messages, of course, curiosity winning her over.

Richard was promising to explain everything, saying that he'd be over as soon as he could, and that he couldn't wait to spend his life with her and make her his wife. As she thought about him arriving at her empty house, frantic at not knowing where she'd gone, she felt a pang of guilt.

He'd look through the windows, seeing that everything had been removed, the whole space cleared out. It was a cruel, callous way to behave even if he'd let her down more than once.

"Nick, can I just send him a message explaining that I'm leaving? I feel bad taking off like this. I know I can't be with him, but I don't want to hurt him even so..."

"Oh Mia, you are so naïve! Look, where does he live? Let me show you why you don't need to worry about that motherfucker," Nick responded.

Mia hesitantly gave Nick directions to Richard's house.

What would happen when they arrived? She felt uneasy.

Is Nick going to knock on the door? No, that doesn't make sense. He won't want to get in a fight or create more drama; he's just not that kind of person. What in the world could he be thinking this is going to accomplish? Mia thought, too afraid to ask and hear Nick's response.

Nick parked across the street from Richard's house, turning off the car lights.

"Wait for it, Mia," he said, sensing she was finally about to ask what they were doing here.

Within a couple of minutes, Richard's car drove up and pulled into the driveway. He got out, walking around to the passenger side in a truly gallant manner.

He opened the door, holding out his hand to help his wife out of the car.

Mia gasped. Between the house lights and the streetlights, Mia could see as clear as day that his wife was pregnant—*very* pregnant. She was probably due any day now, judging by the difficulty she was having getting out of the vehicle.

Once Richard and his wife were inside the house, Nick started the car and drove off.

"Did that look like a man who was planning on spending the weekend away with you or a man who is telling his wife he wants a divorce? 'Cause from where I was sitting, it looked like that motherfucker's about to become a daddy again," Nick commented.

Mia was speechless. And *pissed* was nowhere near strong enough to describe how she felt.

I mean, I already knew he was a liar. But why make plans to go away with me for the weekend if he had no intention of going? None of it makes any sense.

Why didn't he just tell me instead of keeping me waiting in silence since yesterday?

Oh...Maybe his wife had a medical emergency. Perhaps they thought the baby was coming. So maybe he did plan to come away with me but then, 'something came up,' as in, she ended up in the hospital! Then the baby didn't come after all and—

Oh Mia, shut the fuck up. Stop overthinking.

You have no idea what's gone on, only that he's a rat. A scumbag.

"I don't get it," she finally said out loud. "So is everything with him always a lie? This doesn't make any sense. What was he thinking? Why did he bother starting things back up with me when, clearly, he's not going to take it anywhere?"

"You can't try to make sense of it, Mia. You just have to know how it operates."

"How *what* operates?" Mia asked.

"Richard," Nick said quietly.

Mia ranted on as if she didn't hear him. "And how the heck did you know they'd be arriving home at that time? How did this all happen so synchronically?"

"I wish I could take credit for it all, but John actually told me to take you by Richard's house on our way. So whoever's helping you on the other side is giving John some pretty clear windows of time, because that was pretty impressive, even for him. The angels are going out of their way to help you, Mia."

"Well, this definitely makes it easier to leave, although I feel completely sick to my stomach now after seeing that."

"Detox symptoms!" Nick laughed. "Your entities just realized you've cut off their connection to the head demon."

"Do you really think that's what he is?" she asked. "*That's* why you've been calling him *it!*"

"Yup! I mean, if you want to use layman's terms, we could also call him a sociopath and a narcissist. But demon seems fitting for that son-of-a-bitch. Don't try to figure it out, Mia. Don't give him any more of your energy. We'll have John do an exorcism on you and you'll be fine.

"Why don't you just relax and enjoy the drive? You're safe now, and your life is about to get a whole lot more interesting."

Nick settled back in his seat and turned on the radio.

Just then, a shooting star fell through the night sky.

8

Healed by Fire

"Are we here?" Mia asked. "What time is it?"

Mia stepped out into the cool night air, wondering, *how long have I been asleep?*

She was surprised to see a small house set back into the trees and the welcome of a porchlight to greet them. She had been expecting a tent and a sleeping bag or a cave set into the red rocks. She took a small turn to take in their surroundings, then gasped as she looked up.

How clear the sky was! The stars were sparkling like a sea of diamonds and seemed close enough to touch. "I can see the Milky Way!"

"Yep. That's it, all right. The night skies are pretty good out here," Nick said, stretching a bit after the drive. "It's about two in the morning. And yeah, this is John's place. He likes to be out a ways for the quiet, and the stars." Nick smiled, gazing up into the night. "He rents a house now and then and members of the team stay with him when they need to. Given all the detoxing you're going to be doing, he thought it would be best for you to stay here."

"Surely he doesn't think I'm going to relapse after what I just found out?"

"Well, I imagine you've been confident about not relapsing many times before," he said, laughing. "Don't worry about why you're staying here, just trust that you'll be grateful you are."

They made it inside, and Nick showed her to her room.

As she expected, it was nothing fancy, just the essentials—a bed, a night table, and a lamp. The only décor on the wall was a Native American dreamcatcher over the bed. Worn out from the day's drama and the long drive, Mia fell asleep as soon as her head hit the pillow.

Richard visited her dreams.

"Mia, you have to believe me. I'm getting a divorce," he insisted.

"You think I even care, Richard? After the lies you've been telling me, yet again? Like the old saying, *a leopard never changes its spots*. You're no better than you used to be. Probably worse, in fact, because now, you have a pregnant wife, and you've been messing around with me."

The whole thing was disgusting. It made her shiver to think of it.

"Can't you get the message, Richard? I don't want you anymore. I'm not that gullible."

She would never trust him either, she told him in the dream, but he didn't seem to care.

He moved his things into her house, advising her they were getting married regardless.

His wife showed up with the kids and they were happy Richard was there with Mia, welcoming her into the family with open arms.

They were about to sit down together to a breakfast of bacon and hot coffee when…

Mia woke up, slowly realizing that the bacon and fresh coffee were right here where she was, the aromas wafting into her nostrils. *Wait*, she wondered, *where am I?* She opened her eyes to bright morning sunlight, catching sight of the dreamcatcher above her head. *Sedona!*

After washing her face and brushing her teeth, she wandered out into the kitchen.

"Good morning! How'd you sleep?" John asked, looking up from the stove.

"I slept okay. *Very* weird dreams, but I guess that's to be expected."

"Yes, well, those will probably continue for a while. Are you hungry? You're welcome to make yourself some eggs. You do know how to cook eggs, don't you?" John teased.

"Yes, I know how to cook eggs!" Mia was relieved that he was being playful with her instead of punishing her for having relapsed. She poured herself a cup of coffee and helped herself to a slice of bacon, noticing John had cooked the whole pack. "Who else is joining us?"

"I never know with this bunch; I just know no matter how much bacon I cook, it all gets eaten." John reached into the fridge for a carton of eggs.

"I'm making myself soft-boiled eggs and if you want, I can cook yours for you too, so you don't catch the house on fire," he said, trying to hold back a chuckle.

"That would be great."

Mia found herself hoping that his teasing was his way of making her feel more at ease.

She had worried the whole way up here that he wouldn't want her around anymore, although that clearly didn't make sense since he was the one who had sent Nick to get her. Mia's mind was still spinning with confusion when John set a plate of bacon and eggs down in front of her.

"Maybe if you start expressing some of those thoughts, you won't be so confused anymore." John wanted to help Mia free herself from this endless circling.

Mia sighed.

"I fucked up, John. After all the work we did, I blew it. Nothing's changed. I didn't make better choices. I'm still a mess and don't know why you would want to have anything to do with me ever again." She set her mug of coffee on the table. "Clearly, I'm just wasting your time."

"And yet, you came back, so some part of you must believe there's still hope for you."

"To be honest, I'm not really sure how I got here. If Nick hadn't shown up, who knows what I'd be doing right now?" Mia looked down at her hands, fidgeting with her fingers, agitated.

"Yes, Mia, you did relapse, but I'm more interested in where you go from here. Do you need to keep beating up on yourself or are you ready to find the solution?"

John leaned back in his chair.

She answered, "With all the work we did last time, how could I still not be healed? How could I have experienced so much love and clarity and ended up back in the arms of my addiction?"

She lifted her eyes to meet his. She looked red-faced, slightly teary—and embarrassed.

"I debated whether or not you were ready to go back home; it was a big step for you to pack up your life and leave everything behind. Your spirit was asking a lot of you *and* there's a reason this happened. It says to me that there was something we missed." John took a sip of coffee. "I should have known an energy this big wouldn't release so quickly, so maybe I'm the one who failed you,

Mia. But this is a journey of healing, a journey of self-discovery for all of us. Reproaches serve no purpose, Mia, no function at all. We must learn as we go and move on.

"The good news is that you're here now and we know there's something more that has to be healed." John's gaze sharpened, though his posture remained relaxed.

Mia sighed, relieved that John wasn't blaming her for screwing up.

"If you trace back over your steps Mia, when did you first start to feel wobbly?"

"Well, I guess I started questioning myself when I thought about having to explain to people what I was doing. I was worrying about what they'd think, so decided not to tell people the truth," Mia began. "Then I started to get more uncomfortable when my friend Amy was planning a going-away party for me. She was just being nice, but I didn't want one. I didn't want to hurt her feelings, so just went along with it, even though it didn't feel right. I tried to just make the best of it but, every step of the way, was compromising myself."

Mia inhaled deeply. "And ugh! That man, Frank, at the party!" Mia scrunched her face in disgust. "I was just being polite and friendly and the next thing I knew, he was trying to shove his tongue in my mouth. I was so shocked, I didn't know what to say."

Mia looked at John with a half-hearted smile.

She continued, "I guess it was one step and then another, and add in alcohol and the experience with Frank, and it was a perfect setup for my letting that creep Richard back in."

"Fascinating." As Mia spoke about all that had happened, John could see a web of dark energy unfolding around her throat. John leaned forward in his chair. "Actually, all this makes perfect sense and I can't believe it didn't occur to me earlier."

Mia noticed the way John was looking at her, having seen this look on his face before. It made her feel as though he could see through her. "What didn't occur to you? What makes perfect sense?" Mia had no idea what John was talking about.

"Were you ever a smoker?"

"Um, yeah, years ago."

"Hmm...and how old were you when you started?"

John tilted his head a bit, still eyeing Mia's throat.

"I probably had my first cigarette when I was thirteen or fourteen. Why? What does that have to do with anything?"

"I can see traces of where the energy was." John was captivated by what he was observing.

"What do you mean?" she asked.

"I'm actually surprised you were able to quit. The wound it was numbing is still there; it's caught in your throat."

"Oh, wow, really? Well, it was the hardest thing I've had to do. I just couldn't stand the judgment and shame attached to being a smoker anymore, so I finally quit. You know, when it came down to it, quitting wasn't even that difficult because it had so much negativity attached."

Despite opening up, Mia wondered what the heck this had to do with anything.

She had successfully kicked that appalling, nasty habit, so why was he bringing this up now, when she had bigger problems that needed healing?

"How do you feel without the cigarettes?" John asked.

Mia thought about the question for a while.

"Well, I'd say I'm proud to be a nonsmoker now but there's still this feeling, you know, like something is missing. I suppose that's hardly hot news; every addict must have this feeling."

"Close your eyes and connect inside to that feeling that something is missing."

John watched Mia's throat begin to tighten.

"What is it that is missing, Mia?"

Mia had assumed the answer was a simple one: cigarettes were missing. She was wrong.

To her surprise, she suddenly felt sad. As she looked inside herself, she saw her energy like a column of light but there was a pocket of dark energy, too. As she sent her awareness inside of the dark energy, tears started streaming down her face.

"Love...*love* is missing. There's this small dark space. It's the belief that I'm not lovable, and therefore, I'm less valuable than people who *are* lovable."

Her breath caught in her throat.

She sucked in a deep breath and went on. "When I smoked, I didn't have to feel that. The cigarettes filled that emptiness for me." Mia's tears eased her heart.

It felt as though they were washing away the sadness. As strong as her emotions were, Mia couldn't believe how easily all this was revealing itself to her.

"Great! Now let out a really loud yell and release that darkness."

John gave a nod as he placed his hands over his ears.

Mia screamed, though her yell sounded more like the cry of an infant than that of a woman. She saw the dark energy dislodge and begin to release. As it was traveling up and out of her body, a piece of it got stuck in her throat. She felt as though she might choke, and started coughing nonstop, anxious as she looked to John for help, her hand on her neck.

John saw an obstruction in her throat preventing the energy from fully being released. He took a piece of sage from the abalone shell resting on the table and lit it, circling it.

The soft tendrils of smoke drifted around Mia's neck.

"Okay, great—you got most of it out, but this wound's bigger than just you, Mia. It's a belief handed down through your lineage," John explained. "It's all connected—the belief that you weren't lovable, that you couldn't ask for what you needed, and the feeling that you weren't important. This runs deep in you and is especially strong throughout the women in your family."

Mia tried to respond but no words came.

"Oh, it definitely knows we're onto it." John chuckled, reaching for another piece of sage.

Mia kept trying to speak but her voice was gone.

Finally, she just mouthed the words, "What is happening to me?"

"Your body's showing us how big of a block this has been, Mia. The dark energy is an entity energy, controlling people by taking their power away. And in you, it's operated by taking away your voice. That's where this energy is still stuck inside you—it's why your voice is gone right now." John lit the second leaf of sage, this time using a feather to send smoke toward the center of Mia's throat.

"Every time you didn't speak your truth, whether it was to protect someone's feelings or to be polite, you gave up your power. You deferred to other people to be liked and accepted by them, fearing that if your opinion was different than theirs, they would reject you. As you did these things, you told the Universe that others were more important than you, that you weren't as valuable, implying the Universe didn't have to acknowledge you either."

John looked at Mia, holding her gaze. "When you don't claim your power, you're telling the Universe you don't believe you have the right to be here, Mia."

Mia was quiet for a while as she contemplated what John was saying to her. Finally able to whisper, she said, "I hear you, and while what you're saying makes sense, there's this feeling in my body that it would be impossible to respond any differently. What was I supposed to do?"

"As long as that energy is still in your throat, it's not going to feel possible, but once we get it out of there, that feeling will change, Mia. Then the answer will come, and you will know."

"That would be amazing, to actually be able to say what I really think and feel and not worry about upsetting anyone. That would be the best superpower of all. I would be completely free to be myself," Mia whispered.

John smiled at her realization that being herself would be the best superpower of all.

She smiled as she tried to imagine her life with no limits. Feeling better now, she got up and started to clear the table.

"I didn't know you knew how to do dishes," John teased.

She elbowed him in the ribs as she walked by. It was fun how John and Nick teased her; somehow, she had always belittled *herself*, and now she knew there was no purpose to it. When these men teased her about her purported deficiencies, it was humorous because it was untrue.

"Ouch!" he responded loudly to the jab in his ribs.

"What's going on in here?" Nick asked as he walked into the kitchen.

"Mia's beating me up! You'll have to save me!"

"Ha!" she said. "I think I'm the one being messed with."

"Well, I must say, I'm relieved to see you two playing around this morning. I was worried you would still be in bed under the blanket, not wanting to face the world. So what's the plan for today? Are we going to slay any demons?" Nick asked.

"Mia's going to pick up sticks and chop some wood." John smiled, waiting for Mia's reaction.

"I'm going to what?"

Is he teasing me again? He must be!

"Nick, you can help. Take Mia out on the trail behind the house and show her the kind of wood we'll need for the fire. She'll need to gather some small branches to get it going and several larger pieces so we can keep it burning for a while. I have some aspen wood that we can use behind the shed in back, but the logs need to be split. Let's see if Mia here can handle an ax without hurting herself. I'll check in on you two in a few hours."

Mia still thought he was kidding until he left the room. She looked over at Nick, trying to read his expression, looking for any signs that this was a joke.

"Alrighty then, you'd better go change and put on some shoes and I'll go grab us some things from the shed. Meet me outside when you're ready." Nick noticed Mia's hesitation. "Just head out the kitchen door and you'll see the shed out back. The path we'll take picks up there."

Nick seemed to find nothing strange about John's instructions.

Mia went to change into jeans and a T-shirt. When she joined Nick at the shed, he handed her a water bottle and nodded for her to follow. He started down the path pushing a wheelbarrow.

What is this all about? She was still wondering at what point she would grasp her role.

"Why is he having me pick up wood? I don't get it, Nick." Mia stopped walking. "And what's the deal with me needing to use an ax and split logs?"

"Seems to me he's going to use fire to heal you."

"He's going to what? How's he going to do that?"

"Well, I don't want to ruin the surprise since this will be your first barbecue."

"Barbecue? I don't understand. Do you mean a real barbecue? Or is that code for something else? You're not going to cook me, I hope." Levity was one way to make herself feel better.

Nick laughed. "No, cooking you is definitely not on today's agenda. Maybe tomorrow." He winked. "And if John wanted you to know ahead of time, he would've told you. Instead of asking so much, why not start picking up sticks? Don't worry about splitting wood right now."

Nick nodded to a fallen branch just to the left of the path. "There's a good one, Mia. As you pick it up, you need to connect with it; tell it your story, tell it what happened to you, tell it what you need help with. Heck, tell it the story about all the women in your lineage."

"Okay, but I don't know how any of this is connected to Richard, or how it's going to prevent his energy from getting back in." Mia's voice grew quiet. "I dreamt about him last night and—"

"I'm going to stop you before you finish that sentence! Forget his name. Never speak it again—don't give him any of your life force energy. Don't waste any more time on that miserable excuse for a man." Nick's tone was sharp as he looked at Mia. "You understand?"

"I'm just *trying* to understand."

Nick paused and took a breath.

"I know, I'm sorry. I'm feeling really protective of you, and don't like that guy at all. I know how his type operates. He's not going to give up easily. And where awareness goes, energy flows. If you keep thinking about him and talking about him, he'll keep coming back around. You've got to cut those ties, Mia. Sever them. Imagine using the ax to cut them right off."

"Okay, that makes sense. I'm ready to do that. Still, can you tell me how gathering wood is connected to my relapse?"

"Well, what were you and John talking about when I walked into the kitchen?"

"We started off talking about when things first got wobbly, and we figured out it was when I stopped speaking my truth and let other people's preferences take precedence over mine. Then John did that thing where he tilts his head and it feels like he's looking through you."

"You mean when he's looking through the dimensions?"

"Oh, is that what that is? I never really knew what it was, but could tell it was something unusual. Anyway, then we talked about when I used to be a smoker and we released a belief that I wasn't lovable."

"So you identified another addiction besides Dick's crack pipe, connecting it to not feeling lovable and to using something outside of you, like cigarettes, to fill up the emptiness inside.

"And now he wants you to connect to the women in your lineage who didn't use their voice—who didn't feel deserving or good enough or valuable enough."

Nick shrugged. "Mia, you can't connect the dots to how this is tied into you dating a married man who compulsively lies? Really?"

"No, I mean, sort of, but it's foggy; can you offer more clarity?"

"Lord! Do you want me to pick up all the wood for you too?"

Mia looked down at the ground and let out a deep sigh.

"Oh, all right, but only because you're hungover and probably going through withdrawal."

Nick's manner eased. "Self-love is the only thing that can fill us up, Mia. The fact that you were dating that dick says you were seriously lacking in it. Today, you looked deeper into your history, but none of this started with just you. Now it's time to trace back through your lineage.

"You need to find beliefs like these: *I can't trust love; I don't deserve love; I'm not worthy of love; I'm not valuable; my voice doesn't matter*—do you get the idea?"

Mia gave a weak smile. She certainly recognized each of these, and many more. These were the many stories she had been telling herself for such a long time, longer than she could even remember. Some were tales she had heard from others in her past, her legacies.

Others were messages she had constructed for herself.

"As you find these patterns within you and throughout your lineage and become open to loving yourself in it all, you bring more light into the unconscious patterns that have been controlling you. And it goes further than you and your lineage. Historically, the feminine energy has suffered from not having a voice, from not being treated as equal in value to the masculine, and from being controlled or dominated by the masculine. He wants you to dig deep inside, bringing the full story into your conscious awareness."

Mia looked at the ground.

"Mia, does this all make more sense now?"

"I think I understand. Thank you, Nick." Mia gave a small smile, grateful for Nick's help, yet to her this was still confusing.

"I'm going to head back to the house for a bit," said Nick. "Are you good with picking up the wood? As John said, we'll need a mix of smaller pieces to use for kindling, and if you can find some larger branches, we can split them up to fuel the fire. You'll be helping the forest, too, by clearing up deadwood. Just remember to connect to the pieces you gather, okay?"

"Okay." She felt resigned to the confusion swirling around inside her. Couldn't Nick tell this was way over her head? *I guess I shouldn't be surprised, given that everything I've done with John has been strange,* Mia thought. *Tell the wood my story. What do the women in my lineage want to say? I don't know...that they're tired of being valued only for their beauty? That they have ideas and information to share that is of value? That they're afraid to speak up?* That thought caught Mia mid-stride. *Interesting—I wonder why they were afraid to speak up?*

She bent down to pick up the fallen branch Nick had pointed out to her.

"Ow!" It felt as though the branch was searing Mia's hand and she couldn't let it go. Images of women burning at the stake flashed in her mind, their voices rising through the flames.

This is why we are afraid to speak.

Mia saw lifetime after lifetime unfolding before her, countless women burning alive, taken by flames. She could hear their screams and then their silence. As it all unfolded before Mia's eyes, she knew these women had burned for speaking their truth. There had been no crime beyond being themselves. Nauseated by what she saw, she fell to her knees.

Tears ran down Mia's cheeks as her vision carried her further. She saw centuries of women—dying by the rope, by drowning, by guillotine, by stoning. She saw the silent ones standing, forced to watch their sisters or mothers or friends die. She saw in them an emptiness and realized they had hidden within their own bodies, choosing silence to survive. Finally, her hand opened, and the branch fell to the earth. Her arm went limp, falling to her side.

Nick was back at her side. He put his hand on her shoulder, "Mia, are you all right? I heard you scream. Did you hurt yourself?"

She looked up, tears in her eyes.

"So many women...so many times. Why? Nick, why?"

"I think that's what you're here to figure out, Mia."

Mia nodded, staring into the distance.

Her body trembled with the intensity of all she had seen.

"There were so many of them, Nick. I mean, I knew about the Salem witch trials, but that was just a small part of it all. This went on for centuries, a genocide of women whose only crime was being connected to Earth, to nature. They lived in relationship with Her, recognizing the bounty of Her providence and learning from Her. They could heal and find water and nourishment with an ease and a surety of knowing, something that frightened those who had long since chosen to live separate from this inherent connection to life."

"Wow, you got all that from the first branch you picked up? I wonder what will happen when you pick up the second?" Nick did his best to sound lighthearted.

Mia was brought back to the task at hand. "I'm going to need to know exactly what the heck it is that I'm picking up this firewood for! I know the phoenix rises from the ashes to be reborn and all that good stuff, but I'm not letting you guys burn me!"

"I promise you are not going to get burned. And on the contrary, you are going to have a very healing experience." Nick sat down beside Mia. "Do you remember what you were thinking when you picked up that branch?"

Mia thought for a moment. It seemed as if it had been so long ago.

"I was doing what you told me to do, telling the trees my story, and thinking about what the women in my lineage wanted to say. Oh! I know! I was wondering why they had been afraid to speak." A wave of understanding rushed through her. "Oh…Now I see. The branch was showing me the answer."

"Exactly. Just ask the trees to be a little gentler with you. And maybe ask to receive your answers in a way that will allow you to keep picking up wood, 'cause at this pace, it's going to take you all day! And maybe into tomorrow!"

"Ha!" Mia welcomed the laughter rising through her voice. "Okay, good advice. Thanks."

She reached down, quickly touching the branch to see if it was still hot.

It wasn't, so she picked it up.

Nick's laughter followed as he stood, helping Mia to her feet. "Gently, Mia."

Mia walked over to the tree from which the branch had fallen.

It was a juniper, a grandmother tree by the looks of her wide trunk and wizened branches.

She stood straighter than the whirled junipers Mia had seen in the canyon, Mia noticing her clusters of blue-gray berries nestled in green, branching needles. Mia inhaled their spicy, earthy scent as she stepped under the tree's canopy, placing a hand on the aged bark with the intention of connecting her heart to that of the tree. Still feeling the power of all that had just moved through her, Mia's gratitude flowed through her thoughts.

Thank you...Thank you for answering me. Thank you for showing me. If it's possible for your messages to be a little gentler, I would welcome that, but really, I trust you to show me things in a way that will help me understand. I love you.

Tears were streaming down Mia's face again.

She was filled with love for this tree, for her ancient presence, and as Mia's senses opened, she realized she felt this love, too, for all trees. She felt Earth's sadness over all the blood humanity had spilled, knowing the sadness the trees were feeling for the roles they had unwillingly played in the burnings, the hangings, the beheadings, and all of the tortures inflicted.

Nature wanted no part in the violence humans were inflicting on one another.

Mia felt a loving tenderness arising from the tree, then a fierceness that surprised her.

Her vision opened to a raging fire deep inside the earth, a fire promising a transmutation of humanity on Earth, a fire that would burn away hatred, fear, and suffering.

It was a fire that would consume everything in its path as it reclaimed the Earth. Mia understood, and was unafraid, somehow determining it made sense to her.

She's coming back and needs you to be ready, conveyed the tree.

Will you show me how? Will you help me be ready, please?

The tree answered through a gentle surge of energy. Mia felt it flowing into her hand as the tree spoke again. *Pick up my fallen branches and use them for your fire. This will help you.*

Only your branches? Mia asked her.

All branches are mine, dear Mia. We are all connected. Tell each piece what you need it to release for you. Connect to the gift of transformation our wood offers. And consider, Mia, how much of your story are you willing to let go of today? You won't be done until you let go of it all.

Mia pondered on the words.

What do you mean by letting go of my story? How can I let go of it? It's what I have lived through, all the things that have happened to me.

She heard, *It's only your perception of what has happened to you. You carry your life experience and all that you have inherited. You've not been burned at the stake, yet you're afraid to speak your truth if you think it will cause someone not to like you. Your story and that of all of your ancestors is carried in your DNA. The women in your lineage need you to set them free.*

As you step free of the fears within you, you free them each from remaining trapped in their fear. The Goddess needs a body that is willing to speak the truth.

This is what She asks of you.

It did not all make sense to Mia.

What do you mean the Goddess needs a body?

Mia listened again for an answer yet heard only the wind moving through the branches.

She had been given what she needed for now, realizing it, knowing it was time to get back to her task. She took a deep breath, rich with the spicy scent of the junipers around her.

She knew the trees around her now as friends offering their wisdom.

Thank you, Mia offered once more, this time to all of the trees in her vicinity.

As Mia brought her focus to gathering the many fallen branches, she began to feel a tsunami of sadness rising. From the depths of her being, an ocean of pain began to overwhelm her. As she struggled to remain afloat, she realized: these emotions were not just hers. It was the overwhelming, tumultuous sadness from which everyone in her family had been running.

Some had avoided it by staying too busy to feel, others by staying too drunk.

Some had escaped to their intellect to avoid the feelings in their bodies.

She could see now how with each passing generation, the repressed sadness was only growing stronger, each child inheriting the pain that their parents hadn't allowed themselves to feel.

And because no one was willing to feel it and live it, it had kept moving through the lineage, a force so overpowering it felt futile to try to change its path; surely, she would drown in this.

One piece at a time, Mia heard.

Mia picked up a stick and offered it a piece of her story. *Please hold the belief that my only value is my appearance.*

She found her next fallen branch. *I give you the belief that I have to earn love by being perfect and I release to you the belief that people will hate me if I show them who I am.*

Mia was on a roll and the wheelbarrow was filling with branches. Some of the things that came out of her mouth surprised her, but she could feel the truth of them in her body. She felt as if she was in a trance and that each of her ancestors was speaking up one by one, taking advantage of the opportunity to be set free.

Take the belief that I'm not good enough, that I'm not doing enough, that I'm a fraud, that I'm guilty and deserve to be punished.

I give up the belief that no one will ever really love me because of how messed up I am and that I'm an inconvenience and no one wants to be bothered by my needs.

I release the belief that I can only give to others, that I'm not allowed to receive.

I free the belief that no one wants to hear what I have to say and that what I have to say isn't worth saying.

I let go of the belief that I have to earn my right to be here and relinquish that I have to prove I'm of value.

She found a large, heavy branch and dragged it over to the wheelbarrow. *I give you everything that has to do with Richard and my addiction to his energy and his attention.*

Tears filled her eyes and fell into the barrow, coming to rest on the branches she was collecting. She cried from the depths of her being as she released the sadness and pain from all the stories she was carrying. While she could relate to most of these from her personal experiences, she could also see the faces of countless women who had felt each of these beliefs.

Mia recognized that her tears were those of her ancestors, the tears of the women who had never set themselves free. By the time the wheelbarrow was full, Mia felt as if she had cried a tear for every woman who had ever existed. Like the roots of trees connecting underground, she felt herself connected to everyone in all time and space.

Mia felt a heaviness in her body and was a bit dizzy again. She drank some water.

I'll have a quick rest before taking the wheelbarrow of branches back to Nick.

She lay in the shade of a nearby juniper, letting the earth cool her as she relaxed into the sandy ground, hearing a hummingbird trilling in flight. A gentle breeze stirred the air, and she could feel the edges of sleep finding her.

Just let go, Sophia whispered.

The spicy, rich fragrance of the junipers held her. Mia drifted, letting her senses carry her. She didn't resist when her dizziness grew in intensity; instead, she leaned into the sensation. Her surrender to it came naturally, no part of her feeling a need to fight.

Mia felt her body flowing into the earth, a vastness of love holding her.

All the sadness, the fear, the rejection, the struggle, the inferiority, the powerlessness melted away, a gentle wonder filling her. She realized herself as a part of Earth, so very alive and deeply known. She belonged here, able to see herself as a part of the whole of life.

The idea that she had to prove herself to someone was as ridiculous as a tree having to prove it was a tree. The fact that she existed meant that she had the right to be here and had value.

She could feel in every cell of her body how valuable she was to Earth, how loved she was, and how she had never been alone and never would be.

The afternoon sun peeked through the branches, warming her skin, bringing her attention back to her physical body. The contrast between feeling connected to all of life and the awareness of being in a body caused her to wonder, *What am I?* Her swirling thoughts deepened the hypnotic trance holding her between the etheric and physical planes of existence.

A breeze picked up, brushing strands of her blonde hair across her face.

It's time for you to start remembering who you are, Mia, and why you came here, Sophia said.

Yes, I'm ready. Mia knew this with a certainty she had never felt before. Her heart was full.

The sound of a hawk screeching in the sky above her echoed through her mind.

Who am I?

The love moving through her body was a current that could carry Sophia's words with ease.

I've been waiting for you to ask. You've already begun your journey through all the healing you've been doing. The first step is to realize what you are not. You will continue burning away everything that isn't you, all the thoughts that aren't yours, all the energy that you've carried for everyone else. Releasing all of that will help you get clear, and you will begin to remember.

Ask to be shown. Ask for clarification. You must participate in this transformation.

I want to know what my mission is, who I am, and why I'm here.

Mia reached for the words to express all she was feeling.

I'm ready to be done with my human life. Through all of my trying, I haven't been able to make it work out the way it was "supposed to," and I'm willing to do whatever I need to see this through. More than anything I've ever desired, I want to be filled with this love from the earth.

Mia heard another shrill cry of a red-tailed hawk as the breeze stirring the air grew into a brisk wind. She felt her breath becoming a swirling current of energy rising within her.

I am ready to give my body to the Goddess, to live at Her service in gratitude, honored and humbled to do so.

Mia listened for an answer, yet all was quiet.

The wind had stilled as quickly as it had risen. She remembered the directive to ask, to participate, and so gathered her courage.

Why am I here? Will you show me who I am?

Mia became aware of herself seeing through another's eyes.

She was sitting in a white circular room and could sense that she had been gathered there with many others. There was a brightness all around, diffuse yet almost tangible. The light moved in iridescent waves, making it hard for her to see clearly.

This is the Galactic Council, Mia.

They have been watching over Earth since the beginning of time. Listen...

A voice said quietly, *Sophia, we called you here because it is time.*

The words coming from a tall luminous being with large eyes were directed at her.

The being continued, *Our Earth is in dire straits. The volatility on the planet is so high, we don't know how many will be able to make the journey with Her.*

She felt the body through which she was looking nod in understanding.

I fear the density on the planet is too great, another voice replied. *If the Goddess returns to the surface at this time, the shift in energy will be so immense that all of life will be wiped out.*

Mia looked to see who was speaking, seeing a shimmering blue being at the end of the table.

The body through which she was seeing stood and spoke. *Our only hope is to send in a team to break up the layers of unconscious energy and raise the vibratory frequency on Earth.*

The person sitting beside her stood as well. *There will still be great disruption as these shifts occur, yet if the team can succeed, we will see much life preserved.*

Mia realized the person speaking was John.

They addressed him as Melchizedek in the Council.

She heard herself saying, *I am ready and will leave upon your command.*

Melchizedek—John—added, *Let me go first and prepare for your arrival.*

Mia listened as other voices joined in agreement, a team forming to open wide the way for the Goddess to return.

The red-tailed hawk circling above Mia screeched again.

Mia felt a wave of gratitude rise up from the earth and flow into her body, filling her with a burst of green mist that opened her heart in all directions. Her body softened as she allowed herself to receive this gift from the Goddess.

Thank you for agreeing to come here. And for helping them remember.

Mia answered, *I want to help in any way I can, but I'm not sure I know how.*

You have come to help humanity's people let go of their pain so they can reconnect to their hearts, reconnect to love, and feel Me again, in just the way you have.

I really do feel You, responded Mia with all of her heart. *I feel Your love coursing through my veins. I feel You in every fiber of my being.*

Mia's body was electrified as the green energy spiraled through her.

Help them remember, Mia. Help them remember that Love is who they are, that it is Love holding their very cells together. Help them know that Love is their birthright and not something they must earn or for which they have to search.

Mia asked, *But how do I help them remember? How do I help them let go of their pain?*

The answer came: *The same way you let go of yours. Teach them what they need to know.*

Mia inquired, *What do I teach them?*

Teach them about Me. They have forgotten because I was pushed underground into the shadows, but in truth, I have never left them. I have been here the whole time, underneath every footstep, waiting for them to remember. I cannot get through to them because of all the layers of pain they are carrying. I need you to set them free, Mia, so I can reach them.

I need you to do it before they destroy themselves.

Mia's heart felt heavy. How could she meet this task? The weight of the world seemed to rest on her shoulders, pushing her body into the cool, damp ground. Her mind was struggling to understand what practical steps she could take to save planet Earth.

The Goddess said, *While I love all my children unconditionally, most of them remain unconscious, living unaware of how they use the resources I give them, never saying thank you or expressing gratitude. They take and take, trying to fill up the emptiness they feel inside, not realizing that what is causing that emptiness is that they are disconnected from Me, from life, and from the very essence of themselves.*

Mia was finally beginning to understand how it was all connected.

The loss of the relationship with the Goddess was the cause of all the pain humanity was suffering. She wanted to ask again what practical steps to take, but before she could, she heard, *Tonight, you will remember more.* Then the voice was gone, leaving just the whispering wind.

Mia opened her eyes to see if she could find Her outside of herself. But all she saw was a spider spinning a web in the branch above.

She let the fragrant scent of juniper fill that place inside her that wanted all the answers.

Footsteps sounded on the path behind her, and she turned to see John approaching.

"You always seem to know exactly when to show up," Mia said.

John smiled. "Looks like you've done a good job of collecting branches for the fire. Nick saw you were in deep, so he's splitting the firewood, by the way. Guessing you might be ready for some lunch about now? Why don't you head on back to the house for a bit while I take the wheelbarrow over to the firepit? I don't want to engage you in too much conversation.

"You may not realize but you're in a trance-like connection to Mother Earth and it'll be better for you to stay in it. A lot of magic is in store for you in the night ahead, and the more you stay in your experience, the deeper you'll be able to go."

After having a bite to eat, Mia stood on the porch, watching the shifting light of the sun reflected on the trees around. She felt more grounded, her heart feeling full and open. She looked around for John, curious about what he was doing with all the wood she had collected.

She remembered him saying something about a firepit.

Ah, there he is, but what's he doing? she wondered as she saw him crouching, holding a log up in the air. His face was turned toward the afternoon sun, and it seemed he was offering the log in its direction. As Mia grew closer, she saw John place the log carefully into a stone-lined firepit before him. She stood nearby, watching him do this over and over, offering one log after another to the sun and then placing it in the firepit.

John did the same with all the branches she had gathered that morning.

The large branch to which she had offered her struggles and heartbreak around Richard flashed in her mind. She didn't see it in the now nearly empty wheelbarrow, yet she couldn't place it in the carefully layered wood in the firepit, either. It had been the largest branch she had found, heavy and wide at its base and tapering into a Y-shape at its top.

She remembered its weight too, having needed to drag it over to the wheelbarrow. Recent rains had layered coarse desert sand into its surface, and Mia's hands were tingling as she recalled the feel of the sand and roughened bark. Then her eyes caught its Y-shaped top near the center of the firewood. John must have broken it into smaller pieces to fit.

As she looked closer, recognizing more of the branches she

had gathered, Mia could see dried stems of grasses and flowers along with the thinner branches nested in.

Her curiosity grew. John was giving his full attention to the stack of split wood to his left. It felt to Mia as if he was deep in conversation with the wood. He leaned in and chose a piece, stepping back to the firepit and crouching to the ground before it as he lifted the wood toward the sun. This time, he started to place the piece and seemed to change his mind. He circled it around to the left, stopping just before the place in which he had begun to set it initially.

What is he doing? she wondered.

"I like to let each log know the stored sunlight inside is going to be released if it chooses to be a part of our fire. I ask each piece and listen for its agreement. I lift the pieces toward the sun to activate them before placing them in the firepit. Even the kindling has been set with intention."

Mia nodded as if that was the most reasonable thing she had ever heard.

"I also like to honor the four directions and the circle energy, so I start by placing the first log to the east since that is where the sun rises. Then I continue clockwise through the directions. See the four central pieces? They're anchoring in each direction, providing the structure that supports the rest of the wood. As I place these anchoring pieces, I ask each direction for assistance to support us in doing our healing work."

John chose another piece of wood, lifting it to the sun.

He paused before setting it into place. "When you saw me circle that last piece around, I was also honoring the energy of the circle. I moved the wood around sunwise to place it, rather than moving it backward to the place it wanted to be."

John gathered a handful of what looked to be kindling, yet finer in consistency. He offered it to the sun and the directions, then sprinkled it over the stacked wood. Mia caught scents of juniper and sage and a sweetness she couldn't quite place. Next, he held out a dried bunch of tall, silvery stems with feathery leaves and purple flowers.

"Mia, would you like to place these?"

"We've done this before, haven't we?" Mia stepped onto the weathered flagstone circling the firepit, moving sunwise toward John. As she took the fragrant stems from him, she felt tears gathering. "Watching you do this ceremony with the elements, the honoring and intention you bring to it...it all gives me a deep feeling of peace..."

Mia gently placed the sweet-smelling bundle against the layered wood.

"Yes, you are right. We've done this before, many times...So, you're starting to remember?" John smiled at her.

"Yes, I am. I see different faces but all have your eyes, and you're teaching me, or at other times, *reminding* me about the elements. There's something different about it this time, though. As if all the times before were merely in preparation for now."

Mia was staring at John yet looking beyond this current time and space. Her third eye was wide open, allowing her to see through the dimensions in the same way as John could.

"Yes, they were. No more dress rehearsal; this time is for real. Hand me the lighter. It's time to get this fire started."

John placed a bunch of honey-brown dried stems with curled leaves and tiny clusters of paper-thin spheres nestled in, laying them alongside the silvery bundle Mia had set in place.

Mia watched as the balled-up newspaper ignited at the center of the logs. She hadn't noticed it earlier, nested inside the kindling of dried grasses and twigs.

They caught as the paper flamed, and the larger branches

followed suit. Within a few minutes, the fire was raging, flames leaping several feet in the air.

Mia was transfixed by the dancing, flickering fire, its rhythm coaxing her deeper into her trance-like awareness. The fire seemed to be talking to her, beckoning her to open her heart. Its flames swirled uncontrollably as they worked to release the logs' energy. Oranges, yellows, blues, greens—even bright whites—the colors weaving throughout the flames mesmerized her.

Waves of heat rising from the burning wood met her skin with stinging sharpness. Mia could feel her heart gripped in fear. All she could think of was the destructive power of fire.

In how many lifetimes did I burn at the stake? she wondered.

Not very many, she heard the fire answer. *You haven't been here many times.*

What do you mean? she asked.

You only incarnate during times of great change. Your experiences here on Earth as a human have been few. In the times that you were at the stake, your suffering in the heat of my flames was brief. You burn very quickly.

She asked, *I do? Why do I burn quickly though?*

The fire answered, *There are those of you who carry a quality of gathering inward. You are able to pull me inside you with one breath and release your life at that moment.*

Mia said, *So you say I carry this "gathering in" quality?*

Yes, said the fire. *You are one who carries the gift of gathering in. You bring the "in-breath of God" into the world. There are also those who create expansion and forward movement in your world, bringing the "out-breath of God" to humanity. Each who comes here to Earth to assist in Her healing carries one of these two qualities.*

Mia considered the fire's words for a few seconds.

I bring the "in-breath of God." What does that mean?

The fire replied, *You and those like you are here to gather others* and bring them back to the truth of who they are. As you do so, they can once again recognize their sacredness. You, Mia, are here to gather everyone back into the heart of the Goddess. You have an important role.

As it spoke, the fire danced higher, showering its energetic sparks into the air.

I've been held in the heart of the Earth; She gathered me into Her, Mia responded. *I'm seeing connections, yet your voice differs from those I hear when talking with the Earth, the trees, and the waters. Are you also the Goddess?*

Yes, we all belong to Her and are a part of Her. The simplest way to understand it is that the earth is Her body, the waters are Her blood, the air is Her breath, and I, fire, am Her spirit. You will understand more as you continue your work with us. Your relationship with each of us will be a foundational support in your mission. We are all here to support life and the Goddess.

How do I create these relationships with each of you? Mia asked. *Is that how I will gather everyone back into the heart of the Goddess? And what does it all really mean? All this sounds so beautiful, but I still don't know what I'm actually supposed to do.*

The response came, *This isn't something your mind can understand, yet your heart already knows. Right now, just keep releasing all the sadness, pain, fear, and anger. As you free your body of these lower vibrational energies, you will find it easier to carry higher frequencies. All that you are doing now is preparing yourself for what is to come.*

A log cracked in half in the fire, sending a shower of sparks into the air. Mia jumped back, startled by the sharp burst of sound. She looked around and saw John and Nick watching her from across the fire. How long had they been there and why were they were keeping their distance?

The shadows of the trees falling over them caught her attention. She looked to the horizon and saw that the sun was starting to set.

Where did the day go? she wondered. *It seems I was just picking up branches and it wasn't even noon yet.*

Stay with the fire, she heard John say, although she couldn't tell if he had said it aloud or if she was hearing him in her thoughts. She looked back into the fire, searching for its voice.

Are you still here? she asked it.

I'm always here, but you can only hear me when your heart is open.

But I didn't do breathwork today. In fact, I haven't done any in a few weeks. What caused my heart to open?

The fire replied, *When you lay on the ground this morning, you surrendered all your burdens to Her. You allowed yourself to be loved by Her. That was when your heart opened, when you received the support and love that Earth was offering you. Breathwork is a powerful tool, and you will use it regularly to quiet your mind and release the wounds inside you, but nature also has the ability to open your heart.*

Mia nodded, thinking through all the words.

These wounds inside me, how long will it take to heal them? It feels as though they are never-ending, and even when I release them, it seems they just keep coming back.

When I tune in to the pain they bring, it feels like they're bigger than I am.

The fire said, *That is because they are bigger than you, Mia. They belong to everyone. As you heal each wound, you create an opening in the grid that allows others to do the same. And in this, you are helping Mother Earth to heal.*

Grid? I don't know what that is, Mia said.

There is a grid of energy within which this planet exists. All beings are a part of the energy of Earth and so also a part of the grid that holds Her. The energy of all life experience flows through Earth, and the grid is what holds it all in place. At this time, the weight of humanity's collective pain is so great that it is constricting the grid and deeply affecting Earth.

As you heal through the breathwork, you free your body to recover the natural state of connection to Earth and life that much of humanity has lost. All the wounds you've collected your whole life have been for this purpose so that as you healed them, you would create a pathway for others to follow if they too choose to heal.

Well, Mia was not so sure about all that!

That sounds terrible! Why in the heck would I do that? I mean, I'm happy to help others, but I'm not a martyr or a saint.

She sounded so introspective, momentarily immersed in her own words and in her self.

But the reply to come was understanding and empathic, not judgmental.

Through your deepening connection with Mother Earth, you are also assisting Her in releasing the weight She has carried for humanity.

Each person choosing to heal also helps Earth and all of humanity.

Well, I certainly haven't spent my life thinking about other people, Mia retorted. *I've been caught up in my own story my whole life. Like most people, I think.*

She gazed into the fire.

Exactly. And as you separate from "your story," others will also find it easier to do so. As you heal beliefs such as "I'm not good enough," or "I'm not lovable," or "There's something wrong with me," you open the way for others to follow.

At last, Mia nodded in acceptance and understanding.

Okay, so it's all a part of me doing the healing I'm learning to do?

And I'm still not quite sure I get the whole "grid" thing, yet what you say about opening a path for others to follow does make sense.

There's still more, Mia, answered the fire. *As you recognize and sever the ties to the entity energies that have intentionally misguided you in your life, you open the way to ending the control they have over humanity and Earth. As their hold weakens, Earth's grid will open to the healing energies the Goddess will bring as She returns.*

The fire snapped and popped, but this time Mia didn't jump. She could see the part of her brain that wanted to continue asking questions, never satisfied with any response it received.

She could also feel through her heart that for the first time in her life, everything made sense. This was her destiny and purpose, and even if she didn't know the specific steps to take, she knew she would be guided. She was incredibly valuable to the planet, to life, to the divine. She was loved and protected, and was powerful. The thought made her pause.

I am powerful, Mia thought. *I can help millions, no, billions of people.*

I am here to help bring back the Goddess.

Her mind went silent, feeling a stillness and expansion inside that she had never experienced before. It was as if the entire Universe existed inside her.

They want me to remember who I am because that is how I access my power. That is when the entire Universe can flow through me. It's not my personality or my humanness that has this power; it's my divinity. My job is to get out of the way.

"As you learn to stay in your heart, you will find that you can maintain this greater awareness of who you are more and more," John said as he came to stand beside her. "And the healing you are doing is getting your body ready for the higher frequencies the fire was speaking about."

Mia tried to respond, but her mouth wouldn't move. She tried to turn to look at him, but she couldn't move her head. Her body felt as though it was made of stone. Suddenly, it was hard to breathe, and her heart felt as though it couldn't continue to beat. She felt something cold on her cheeks and the top of her head, hearing John chuckling as he splashed water on her.

"You're okay," he said. John and Nick moved her away from the fire and wrapped her shoulders with a big towel.

John's voice reached her from what seemed to be far away.

Everything was blurry when she opened her eyes, yet soon Mia felt her vision begin to clear. She saw Nick's face in front of hers, smiling.

"We haven't even gotten to the fun part of the evening, and you're already cosmically inebriated?" Nick laughed, watching her trying to regain the use of her body.

Nick rubbed Mia's shoulders for a few minutes to help her get back in her body, and then firmly patted her down her arms and legs.

Mia took a deep breath. The sensation of air moving effortlessly into her lungs was incredible.

"She's back," Nick said, which made her smile.

"Wow, that was a trip. I was aware of everything, but couldn't get my body to respond the way I wanted it to." Mia dried her face and hair with the edges of the towel resting on her shoulders. It felt good to do such a simple thing.

She wasn't sure she'd ever appreciated the warmth of a towel like this before.

"You know, it was sort of like those stories I've heard of people who have a near-death experience and go into the light, except in my case, it was the light coming into me."

"That was a huge dose, but nowhere near all of it," John said. "Your body will get used to holding the light. Just like strength training, you're getting used to this new clear energy flowing through you. This whole time, you've already been opening to it, though in smaller increments than what happened just now. Your system is being strengthened—upgraded, you could say—to carry the energy of bringing your spirit fully into your body. This is the way of bringing heaven to Earth, Mia."

Mia nodded. The pieces were finally starting to come together.

Mia decided to sit for a while longer and watch the fire. She didn't feel ready to be up and moving. After making sure Mia was comfortable, John and Nick continued preparing for the firewalk, and Mia relaxed into the warmth and gentle sounds of the fire.

She must have drifted off, as the first thing she knew was when she heard Lori's soft and sweet voice bring her back to the present moment.

"Mia, are you feeling okay?"

She opened her eyes and saw Dominique standing with the fire, Lori by her side.

"I'm starting to feel better. The fire took me through a lot just now. I guess this whole day's already been a lot. Thanks for checking on me." Mia smiled. "What's in the bowl you're holding? Wait—you're not going to pour more water on me, are you?"

Mia laughed.

Lori chuckled. "No, no water here. It's the prayer mix for offerings to the fire. Did Nick or John talk to you about them?"

"No..."

Lori placed the large bowl in Mia's lap and began to point out the different offerings.

"This is dried tobacco. John grows this from seeds he has been saving through many generations of plantings, ever since he was a young boy. These are white sage leaves, and these silvery stem pieces and purple flowers are Russian sage. The base of the mix is mulched tree clippings gathered from tending the land around here."

"Is this like the offerings that John scattered when I hiked with him in Boynton Canyon?"

"Yes, exactly. Tonight, we'll make offerings to the fire as we ask for what we need healing or help with. We'll also thank it for its gift of working with us tonight and offer gratitude for all that fire provides to our lives every day."

"Do the different offerings have special meanings?" Mia asked. "And John grows tobacco? We just did a healing on my throat from all the years I was smoking cigarettes..."

"I can see how that might seem strange," Lori offered. "This tobacco has been grown to be used as a prayer offering. The intention connected to it has always been one of Love. John has a long connection to tobacco from growing it on his family farm, and he's also learned about ceremonial traditions through working with Native elders. Ceremonial tobacco has long been a sacred plant to many Native American peoples; their relationship with tobacco is one of reverence, and when burned ceremonially, the tobacco smoke carries their prayers to heaven."

Mia touched a delicate, curling leaf. "Is it okay if I pick up this stem?"

"It's perfectly fine, Mia!" Lori smiled.

Mia chose a stem that had round pods and several larger dried leaves. As she brought it to her nose, she heard a rattling sound.

"Those are seed pods," Lori offered.

Mia noticed a clear, sweet scent, nothing like the cigarette smell she was used to. Placing the stem back in the bowl, she picked up a dried silver-leafed stem with soft purple flowers.

"John offered me a bundle of this earlier, to place on the wood before we lit the fire," Mia mused. She brought the stem to her nose, inhaling its almost pungent fragrance.

"It's Russian sage. It grows well in dry climates, and bees love its flowers," Lori said. "John grows some around the garden and gathers their branches at the end of the growing season. The bundles smell nice and including them as prayer offerings just came about naturally.

"Whether he's tending to a tree that needs pruning or clearing the land to help it stay healthy, John saves all the plant material he gathers. Once it dries, he chips the trimmings into this base mix for offerings. He likes to make use of all that Mother Earth offers us."

Mia smiled.

"I think I'm starting to understand that about him. He does things with great care, doesn't he?"

"Yes," Lori answered. "It's one of the best things I've learned from him, I think."

Mia watched as Nick took a handful of prayer mix from Dominique's bowl and held his fist to his heart. He closed his eyes for a moment as he infused the offerings with his heartfelt desires.

"I ask for greater clarity and discernment. May I be able to recognize the energies that will try to sabotage me." Nick tossed the prayer mix into the fire.

He's always so sure of himself. I'm surprised he feels he needs help with that, Mia thought.

"Do you feel strong enough to come join us?" Lori asked, moving toward the fire.

"You go ahead. I'll be over there in a few minutes," Mia replied.

Dominique scooped up a large handful of offerings, handing the bowl to Nick. She stepped closer to the fire as she said, "May I no longer need to hide from those who seek to destroy me."

Sparks flew as the fire incinerated her offering.

Who's trying to destroy her? Mia wondered with alarm.

Lori set her bowl on the flagstones and gathered her offerings, stepping to the fire, holding her prayer mix to her heart. Her voice was steady as she spoke, saying, "May I always remember my value and recognize the gifts I bring to the world."

Again, Mia was surprised. *How could Lori ever doubt her value or her gifts? She's so easy to be around and so nurturing.*

John leaned down, grabbing a handful of prayer offerings. He playfully tossed it in the fire, "Let it be easy and a lot more fun!"

The others had been so serious, the change in energy inspired Mia to take her turn.

She walked over to the bowl sitting near Lori and picked up a handful of prayer mix. As she held it to her heart, she decided to follow John's lead.

"I'm willing for it to get a lot easier and to have even more fun than I'm already having!"

The fire sizzled and popped as her prayer was lifted to heaven.

"You're learning quickly!" John was happy to see that she was starting to understand this journey didn't have to be hard.

"I don't know about the rest of you, but I'm hungry!" John said with a grin.

"Dinner's almost ready," Lori said. "There's just the grilling to do while we dress the salad!"

"Ah, the beauty of teamwork. Thank you for getting dinner going," John said.

"Of course! We knew you'd want to eat before we do the fire-walk, so Dominique and I got a head start while you were all getting the fire ready. We weren't sure how many were coming, so we made plenty. Leftovers never seem to last long around here," Lori said.

"Yeah, I'm not sure how many are coming either," John replied. "Feels as if maybe there'll be a dozen of us. I'll start grilling the elk burgers if you've got them ready."

"We have some portobellos and zucchini for the grill too," Dominique added.

"Hey boss, you need a hand?" Nick asked, starting to get up from the table.

"Nah, I'm good. You keep an eye on Mia," John said.

He gave a wink as he headed out to the deck.

"I heard Lori say 'firewalk.' Are we going to be walking with torches somewhere?" Mia asked, joining Nick at the table.

"Didn't the fire tell you? We're going to be walking *on* the fire, not carrying it, although torches would be fun," Nick mused.

"What do you mean, *on* it?" Mia asked.

"Haven't you ever heard of anyone walking across hot coals?" Nick asked, laughing at Mia's panicked expression.

"No! Why would anyone do that? It sounds dangerous... and painful!" Mia was sure Nick was joking. "You *are* kidding, right?"

"Really, Mia? After the connection you just made with the fire?" Nick paused and decided to go a little easier on her. "Hey, don't you trust John and me by now? There's nothing to worry about. I promise it will be amazing and that the experience will transform you."

"So you've done this before?" she asked.

"A few times, but only with John; he's the only one I'd trust to do this with."

"So it is dangerous?"

"Well, it is fire. We have to always be respectful of the fire's ability to burn, but everything you did today was about building that relationship. We had you pick up the branches so you could connect to the spirit of fire." Nick paused, giving Mia a sidelong glance. "We were going to have you help with splitting logs, too, but after what happened when you picked up your first branch, I wasn't so sure about you and an ax."

Nick grinned.

Mia relaxed a bit, Nick's offbeat humor having a way of setting her at ease.

"John said you split the wood; it sounds like you did my part too, then. Thanks for that."

Mia smiled.

"Seriously, though, I've never seen anything like what you experienced today. As deep as you went with those branches and then with the fire just now, I'm not sure what will happen when you walk across the coals tonight. But I'm also not worried about you at all.

"You've got work to do here, Mia. Mother Earth isn't going to burn your feet and delay you getting started on your journey. That is what you must understand and really absorb."

Mia watched as Nick shoveled hot coals from the fire, spreading them along the path that John had marked off. Everyone had taken part in setting up for the firewalk.

The feeling of teamwork added to the magic.

Several others had joined the group, though Mia couldn't remember their names.

She experienced a myriad of emotions seeing the coals laid out on the path she would soon walk. She looked up at the stars, remembering John's words:

Pick a star—a fire in the sky to connect to before you walk across the coals. Your star will help you keep your attention focused upward, toward the heavens and not on your feet. We will all be chanting loudly, "My body will do whatever it must to let me walk on fire." This will get us into a trance state. When you walk, we will chant the word you choose for your walk.

Mia had asked John how to choose her word. Would it help her to be unafraid?

A good way to find your word is to consider your intention. Who do you want to be on the other side of the path? What are you asking the fire to help you with?

Where do I begin? Mia wondered. *I want to let go of so much—my fear, doubts, judgments, confusion. I want to erase every memory of Richard and so much from my past.*

Mia thought about all she had experienced since her first trip to Sedona.

I want to believe all the amazing things that have been happening. I love that I might have a purpose and one so pivotal to humanity's awakening. Yet it still doesn't seem real.

Who do I want to be on the other side of the path? I want to be someone who believes in herself, to feel confident and courageous to do what I need to do and express whatever I want to say. I want to forgive myself and be kind to myself, to always feel the love that I experience when connected to Earth. I want to feel that way about myself, too, to love myself and be the woman that spirit says I am. I want to let go of my smallness, my hiding places, and this feeling of doubt that I carry with me. How do I say all this in one word?

LOVE, she heard clearly.

It's true, Mia realized. *Love does encompass everything I've been thinking about. If I love myself fully, all of the wounds will dissolve, and my positive qualities can become stronger. If I trust the love I feel when I connect to Earth, it will guide me.*

"You ready?" John asked.

"Yes," she heard herself say before she even had a chance to get nervous again.

The group formed two lines on either side of the path of hot coals, beginning to chant, "My body will do whatever it must to let me walk on fire."

John had prepared them well, everyone moving quickly across the coals while staring up at the stars rather than down at their feet. Keeping focused upward on their star would keep them in a trance state while looking down might re-engage the mind.

If the mind and any fear got into the mix, there would be the potential to get a burn. There would be a person waiting at the end of the path to catch each person as they came off the coals.

John ran across the coals first to make sure it was safe for everyone else to go. He moved quickly, crossing in five long strides.

"Whoa! That's a hot fire!" he exclaimed as he came off the coals.

Mia felt a flash of worry. *Is he serious, or is he teasing?* She watched as he cooled his feet in the wading pool off to the side, returning to the path of coals. He seemed to be walking just fine.

"You ready, Mia?" he asked, smiling at her.

It was as if everything faded into the background until it was just her, John, and the coals before her. The sound of the group chanting, "My body will do whatever it must to let me walk on fire!" seemed somewhere in the distance, although they were right there alongside the path.

"What's your word, Mia?" John whispered.

"Love..." Mia felt her voice waver.

"Come on, Mia. Feel all the support here for you and give us your word again like you mean it!" John encouraged.

"Love!" Her voice came through stronger this time, and Mia could feel a shift in her heart as she offered her word to the path of coals ahead, her voice meeting the steady chant of the group cheering her on.

"Perfect, Mia." John held her by her waist. "Now look up and find your star."

Mia lifted her eyes to the clear night sky; there was her star.

"Now pick up your feet. Start marching in place and keep focusing on your star. It's time to start chanting your word," John spoke with a sureness in his being.

"Love, love, love..." Mia's voice grew stronger with each repetition.

Soon everyone was chanting the word "love" with her.

"LOVE, LOVE, LOVE, LOVE, LOVE, LOVE," echoed around her. Mia fixed her gaze on her star. Its glow brightened, and it seemed to be growing bigger.

"Let out a loud yell, Mia..."

"AAAAAAAAAAAAAHHHHHHHHHHH," she screamed.

"Go!" John said.

Mia tried to move her body quickly across the coals the way John had, but her legs wouldn't cooperate. Instead, she marched across, stomping firmly into the ground.

As Mia's feet moved across the bright-orange flaming coals, she felt as if walking on sand. There was no sensation of heat, just of support.

As her feet made contact with the coals, the fire codes that she had received when she had first arrived on Earth were activated within her. The fire now existed inside her. And though she wouldn't know it for a while, she now had the ability to work with fire—to ignite or extinguish it, or to request that it burn strongly or softly.

She held her gaze steady on her star as it glowed brighter and brighter.

She didn't know how many steps she had taken, her body moving on its own without her awareness. Suddenly, her guiding star flashed, blazing bright before disappearing into the night sky. Mia felt herself stepping through what felt like a field of plasma.

Everything seemed to slip into slow motion.

She felt layers coming off of her as if she were shedding her skin, as if the fear she had been carrying for decades was being melted away by the fire.

It felt as though she was stepping out of her old body, leaving the past behind in the ashes. And then suddenly, Mia was taking her last step on the glowing coals, meeting the outstretched arms of the "catcher" who lifted her off the coals in a great big hug.

"Get her over here!" Lori yelled. "We need to get her feet in the water. She was walking really slowly!"

As Lori helped her step into the cold water, Mia noticed discomfort on the bottom of her feet. *Oh shit, did I burn myself?* She looked at her soles, expecting to see charred flesh. All she saw were a couple of small, sharp pebbles she had stepped on while walking to the pool.

Laughter took Mia over. "I can walk across fire and not feel pain, but the tiniest little rock jolts me right back to reality!"

Lori laughed too as she helped Mia dry her feet. "Put your shoes back on so you can go stand along the firewalk path to support the others as they cross the coals."

Standing there chanting with everyone, Mia looked down at the glowing embers.

Every few minutes, Nick would spread a fresh layer of hot coals onto the firewalk path. She could feel their heat as she was standing nearby.

If I can walk on fire, I can do anything! she thought. She looked up at the sky, remembering. *I wonder why my star disappeared. Is that supposed to happen?* She felt different inside as if she had changed in a way that would be with her always. *I'll bet John will have some answers for me,* Mia thought, turning her attention back to the path of coals.

After everyone had walked, Nick sprayed down the path with water from the hose.

The coals sizzled, steam rising as the embers were extinguished.

Everyone helped clean up the fire area before going inside for dessert. Mia lagged behind, hoping to get a chance to talk to John alone.

"Looking for something?" John asked, startling her.

"As a matter of fact, I am—my star. First, it got bigger; I wondered if maybe it was a planet. It kept getting brighter and bigger, though, and then it was gone." Mia gathered her breath. "It disappeared while I was walking across the coals. As it did, I felt as though I was moving through a thick, jelly-like substance, and all the fear was melting off my body. I felt as though I was walking out of my body." She looked at John. "Does that happen to everybody? And how did my star disappear? Was it even a star? Or something else?"

"Yeah, I saw your star disappear too, Mia."

"So that part was real? That really happened?"

"Yes, the star thing happened in this physical reality. Someone up there is sending you a message, which usually happens before a big change. As for the rest, it sounds like you shed your lower-density body. That usually takes years, but I'm not at all surprised with the accelerated path they have you on that it happened like this."

"What's a lower-density body?"

"The negativity that's held in your aura, the energy field around your physical body."

Mia still looked unsure.

"Negative emotions such as fear, anger, or sadness get trapped in pockets of energy around the body. From what you described, the firewalk tonight burned away those pockets of trapped energy," John explained.

Mia smiled, saying, "Earlier today, I had a vision of some sort of council meeting, and the Goddess was saying that She needed me to help break up some of the density on the planet so that She could come back without taking everyone out."

"Do you remember seeing me at that meeting?" John asked, smiling.

"I do! You were right next to me."

"Yes, I was." John smiled.

"I think they addressed me as Sophia. Is that my real name?"

"It's the name of the aspect of you that's most connected to the Divine."

"Meaning?"

"Think of it as your higher self's name, your spirit's name."

"Who are the Council?"

"Representatives of all of the tribes of humanity, as well as of other galactic races that have been assisting Earth since human beings arrived on the scene."

"So that meeting was the day you and I decided to come to help?"

"Not just you and I; we were *all* there, too. We all agreed to be a part of this mission. I've been gathering us together for the past few years." John looked at Mia with a shake of his head. "Things seem to have shifted into quite a high gear now that you've arrived. Feels like it's time to put all the training into action and get out there and get to work."

"That's the part that I'm still confused about. What is it that we will actually be doing besides healing ourselves? And what about that green energy in Earth's center that I'm supposed to spread around the planet? What about the trees helping me? Is that all symbolic or real?"

Mia's voice took on an edge.

She did not wait long for a response before asking, "I mean, how do we even do that? I honestly don't know. When I'm in these visions, it all seems so simple, yet when I come back to reality, it seems either impossible or as if I'm missing a lot of the steps."

"Easy there! That's a lot of questions!" John answered. "Mia, it's okay. Everything will reveal itself as it needs to. And yes, as we heal ourselves, we are already helping other people heal. Remember what the fire said about you creating an opening in the grid for others to follow?

"Some will be open enough to receive healing spontaneously. And there will be those who are open and ready enough to find their way to us, just like you did. These will be the ones who'll go deeper with the work and help take it out into the world."

"Okay," Mia said. "I feel as if I'm getting a better idea of it all."

"At the heart of our mission is teaching those who will listen how to be more conscious in their relationship with Earth, and a big part of that is helping people see how they can be more mindful in their use of resources and the ways they interact with Earth in their day-to-day lives. I've also seen that we will be called to certain places on the planet to help heal the land or the water, and probably the air as well."

"Where do we begin? How do we get started?" Mia sighed. "How can it feel so simple and yet so overwhelming at the same time?"

John laughed, amused by her eagerness as well as her confusion.

"We'll let our intuition guide us, Mia. We'll follow the signs that show up in nature. Earth will guide us. That won't be the hard part; the hardest bit will be getting through to people," John said, looking at her.

"Don't you think people will want to heal themselves and help Earth once they find out it's possible?"

"I wish it were that easy, but in my experience not everyone even wants to heal. They don't consider it, being so attached to their own insular stories that they don't want to take responsibility or put in the work to change their lives. They hold onto their beliefs and the security of them, not realizing they're stuck in illusion and disconnect. And the worst are deeply addicted to the love of power, one of the greatest destructive forces on the planet today."

John looked to the stars as he inhaled the cool night air.

Then he continued, "I've found that until people want to see in a new way, they'll resist everything we have to say. I do mean they fight against absolutely *everything*. But Mia, we'll keep at it anyway. We must. Even if no one's ready or willing to listen, we will say what needs to be said. We will be Her voice and help awaken as many as we can."

Mia could hear a note of sadness in John's voice.

How long has he been carrying this burden?

"Can't we force them to change? Blast them with some sort of love ray? You know, like shoot them with unconditional love so that they wake up and realize what they're doing?"

John laughed, although his face soon regained its serious demeanor. This topic troubled him.

"Sometimes, I wish we could do something like that. But we have to respect people's free will and the agenda that their higher selves are holding for their evolution."

"But don't you think their higher selves want them to wake up as fast as possible? I think we would be doing them a favor."

"We would be, but it wouldn't work. Trust me, I've tried." John exhaled deeply. He sounded a touch exasperated, though Mia knew it was due to the situation and was not directed at her.

"You don't sound very hopeful," Mia said softly.

"Oh, I suppose I'm just a bit jaded. When I first came to learn the truth about healing, I was so excited to share it. I thought everyone would want to learn about the breathwork's healing power, that I'd have to rent out auditoriums because so many would want to come and heal."

"Yes, that's what I see—or at least in a dream I had the other night, you were on stage speaking to a huge crowd, and I was helping you."

"Well, maybe eventually, people will become more receptive… We can but hope, can't we?" John's voice trailed off as he shook his head slightly. "I wish it could be that way. It sure would be a nice surprise." John felt a glimmer of hope that Mia's dream might be prophetic.

"Yes, it's strange. While there's a part of me that has no idea *how* we are going to do this, another part of me sees it all happening easily and quickly," Mia said enthusiastically. "I know you're right, and there'll be a lot of resistance, but it feels as if the entire Universe is conspiring for our victory. I really feel it, John."

"Well, I'm willing for you to be right, Mia. And who knows, maybe now that you're here with us, things will be different." John smiled.

"And if wrong, I'm sure Mother Earth will get their attention soon enough as the environmental changes continue to happen. I'll bet people will come running for help at that point!" Mia laughed.

Gazing up at the night sky, they saw a shooting star, then looked at each other and smiled.

"And so it is, Mia." John put his arm around her shoulders as they turned toward the house. "Let's see if they left us any dessert."

9

Dreaming

Mia fell asleep as soon as her head hit the pillow, slipping effortlessly into the dreamworld that had beckoned her. Fueled by her connection to the fire, her consciousness traveled deep into the astral realms in which she found herself on the balcony of a crystal pyramid overlooking the ocean. She stared out into the horizon, hypnotized by the sound of crashing waves below.

She was startled by a dolphin leaping out of the water's edge toward her. It twisted in the air, touching its nose to her third eye. As she came to herself, she looked for the creature in the waters below. Instead, she saw its body broken on the rocks.

Mia hurried to the shore below, gathering it in her arms as tears streamed down her face. In a breath, she realized the creature had sacrificed itself for her awakening.

Mia's dream then carried her to a time in Egypt when she had been a priestess at the Temple of Isis. Dressed in white linen, she was lining her eyelids in gold and silver.

She had devoted this lifetime to studying the ancient ways of the Goddess, now preparing for an initiation that would awaken her healing powers. As represented in the adornment of her eyes and the embroidery of the ceremonial robes she would wear, she was to merge gold and silver, sun, and moon, bringing into union the masculine and feminine within.

She stood before an elaborate altar as Isis, Mother Mary, and Mary Magdalena appeared beside her. They anointed her body with oil of spikenard, singing ancient chants in blessing.

As Mia embodied her divinity, the temple filled with a golden light.

Mia could see this light reaching far beyond the temple, a beacon calling worshippers to its healing energy. As she watched time unfolding before her, she realized it was she who had transformed into this radiant golden light.

Mia's awareness shifted to a dream within a dream, set in the realms of the goddesses of India.

Durga, the Goddess of War, riding astride her tiger, slaughtering the demons that controlled the ego. Kali, the Goddess of Death, followed after her, destroying the darkness.

Mia learned that she could fight evil with force, but that the battle was never-ending. Mother Mary then appeared before Mia, holding the whole world with compassion.

She said to Mia, *The path to freedom is through the heart.*

Mia's dream now placed her in a large room filled with people lying on the floor. She found herself working alongside John as he was leading the group through breathwork.

Mia moved through the room, placing her hands on people's bodies. As she did, she saw the white light of their spirits amplify, transmuting all fear in their bodies into love. As Mia left the event to drive home, a tiger stood in her path. She realized it was there for her, to be her companion, her ally, her guide.

The big cat climbed into the passenger seat beside her and they traveled on together.

Mia told John about her dream the next morning over coffee on the front porch.

John nodded while sipping his drink, enjoying the breeze as if the strange things she was relating to him were completely normal.

"The Goddess will probably be speaking to you regularly now. She has taken many forms to help get humankind back on track. And yes, there have been those times when force was necessary. The Goddess will not hesitate to use it if She needs to, as we humans can be really hardheaded, but love and compassion are definitely Her preferred modus operandi."

He paused, watching a hummingbird that had just appeared, hovering between them.

"My sense is that the dreams were messages to you about the future, as well as some memories from the past."

"What do you mean, from the past?" Mia's voice rose. "I haven't done any of these things!" The hummingbird zipped toward Mia's forehead before darting upward and away.

"I mean past lives—to help you remember who you are," he said, watching for Mia's response as he took another sip of coffee.

"A literal past life? I mean, how is that even possible? Was Isis real? I thought she was just a mythological being. And how can Mother Mary and Mary Magdalena even be in the same dream as Isis? Ancient Egypt was thousands of years before the Marys were even born!"

John hadn't realized that Mia knew anything about ancient Egypt.

This could get interesting, he found himself thinking.

Hearing his thoughts, Mia responded, "I've always been fascinated by ancient Egypt. I've been reading books about Egyptian civilization for as long as I can remember. And I've watched lots of documentaries. Nick and I were even talking about the early Egyptians on the drive up here. He believes aliens helped the ancient Egyptians evolve as a civilization."

"What do *you* think about that?" John asked and looked over at Mia, surprised by this turn in the conversation.

"Honestly, it's the only thing that makes sense. There's no way ancient humans could have built those pyramids on their own, right?" Mia looked at John, her curiosity growing. "Do you really think I lived during those times?"

John wondered how much he could tell her. He knew for sure she had been there because he had too. She seemed to be connecting the dots pretty quickly, yet it would probably be best for her to remember as much as possible on her own.

"Keep asking these kinds of questions, but instead of asking me, ask your spirit and Mother Earth when you do the breathwork, or when you connect in other ways," John offered.

"So I have to get lost in a trance every time I want to know something?" Mia shook her head. "That's insane. Can't you just tell me?"

"I don't necessarily have all the answers," John laughed. "I've learned that it's my questions that bring the information to me. One way is to ask your questions at night before you go to sleep. Then your dreams can bring the answers you are looking for."

"But I don't always understand the messages I get in my dreams, and it's hard to tell what's symbolic and what's literal. I see so many things in my dreams, and they only make me feel even more mixed up than before." Mia didn't feel convinced. "Maybe if you help me understand last night's dreams, I'll be better able to interpret the next ones," she offered as a compromise.

"Well, wouldn't you rather I teach you how to get your own answers, instead of you being dependent on me for everything?"

"Well, yes, but can't you just tell me a little more?" Mia asked sweetly.

"Fine, but only because I can tell you're not going to give up."

John took another sip of coffee, thinking about how much he should say. "All of us here—I, you, Nick, Lori, and Dominique—were there in Egypt during that time. This isn't the first time we've come together as a team to help create shifts for humanity."

"Wow, we really are like the Justice League! A team of superheroes!" exclaimed Mia.

Her face lit up at the thought.

"Sure," he laughed. "You can look at it that way."

"So what about our superpowers? When do we get those? Will I really be able to heal people by placing my hands on them?" Mia was on the edge of her seat with excitement.

"Superpowers aren't always a blessing, Mia. They can come at a high price."

"Why do you say that? Don't we need them if we're going to save the planet?"

John looked up at the clouds, today moving quickly across the bright blue of the sky.

"Well, in truth, Mia, Love is the only superpower we need. It is the single key to unlock any gifts the Goddess has decided you will need in this lifetime."

"Why do you say superpowers aren't always a blessing?"

"Mostly, it's because of how different it makes you. You would never be able to fit in with the rest of society once these gifts are activated. Possessing such a gift can be pretty isolating. For one thing, not many people would understand you, and for another, you'd have to keep parts of yourself hidden. Are you ready to give up your life as you've known it just to have powers?"

Mia was quiet. She hadn't thought about it that way.

"My advice to you is just to stay focused on what's unfolding in front of you. Keep doing the work and learning how to help others and the planet, and trust that any gifts you need will reveal themselves when it's time."

"I can do that," Mia said, smiling. "It feels simpler when you put it that way."

As Mia settled back into her chair, she noticed one of the warblers adding to its nest in the honeysuckle. *One step at a time,* she thought.

"So," she began. "I should focus on the moment, keep practicing the breathwork, and learn how to guide others. Oh, and ask my dreams for answers. Do you have any advice on how I can learn to understand the messages in my dreams?"

"You can start by writing them down. You'll gain a lot of insight just by doing that. I'd also say take it a step further. Keep a journal about what's happening in your life. It will help make sense of things, making it easier when it comes time for you to share your story with the world."

"Share my story? I thought you just said choosing this life path would mean I won't be able to fully reveal myself to others." Mia shook her head, feeling uneasy again. "Who is it that I will be telling my story to?"

"One promise you made to the Goddess was to write your story for Her children, Mia."

"What? When did I make this promise? I don't even like writing. I'm no good at writing either! Well, I keep a journal, but never write for someone else. What all is going to be involved in this?" Mia's exasperated tone startled the warbler from its nest-building.

The tiny bird flitted away, taking flight across the yard.

John chuckled. "Lord, Mia. Just relax, it'll be fine."

"Just when I think I'm getting a sense of what's going on, you tell me a new piece. It seems like there are all these plans, yet I'm in the dark about so much," Mia continued, bringing her voice down a bit. She hadn't meant to startle the warbler.

"You're right, maybe I haven't been sharing enough of the basics," said John. "You jumped in so deep right away, I lost sight of the fact that you haven't been with us that long. Here's what's been coming to light as the group's been working together these past few years."

Mia let out a breath she hadn't even realized she'd been holding, pulling her knees up as she settled deeper into her chair to listen.

"We're going to be accomplishing our mission on several fronts," John went on. "By healing ourselves, we'll open our hearts, giving the Goddess a place to reside within us. That's what you've been experiencing. As you've released pain, fear, and sadness from your body, the energy of Mother Earth—the energy of the Goddess—has been able to flow into you. The more healing we do, the more of Her energy we can carry, which in turn is what will help us bring healing to the places we are called to, and to others who are ready. Our open hearts carrying Her energy will be like a beacon to those who need us."

"And writing my story fits in how?" Mia asked.

"By writing about your journey, you'll help others awaken and find their own way forward. Our team can do a lot, but any way that we can extend our reach will help more people begin to open their hearts. It's important to help humanity shift in a big enough way to keep things as gentle as can be. If humanity stays stuck, Mother Earth will have to bring more dramatic events to wake people up. Those whose hearts and minds remain closed will create a resistance, a polarizing pull in the opposite direction."

John's gaze sharpened. "Mia, we need to tip the scales in our direction in every way possible. That's what your dream last night with Isis and the Marys was telling you."

"That's where the darkness lives, isn't it?" Mia said. "Inside those whose hearts and minds remain closed." She felt a chill go up her spine.

John nodded.

"So, in my dream, when Mother Mary said, 'The path to freedom is through the heart,' she was referring to opening our hearts so we can carry the energy of the Goddess?"

"Yes...and..." John waited for Mia to connect the dots.

"The path of the heart is about love and compassion, for ourselves and others."

"Mm-hmm."

"But how do we have compassion for those people who are hurting others?" Mia asked. "I mean, is healing with compassion going to be enough? It seems we have to fight against the darkness with everything we've got, versus just loving it to death if we are going to have a chance at all." Mia could feel her desire to punish people who were causing harm.

"Well, I think that's what Kali and Durga were showing you."

"Right, they used force to battle the darkness. So why can't we do that?"

"Force creates more polarity, which is what we're trying to soften for Mother Earth. We don't want to get trapped in the duality of right and wrong or good and evil. Judging something entangles us with it. We end up matching the frequency of whatever we're pushing against. Judgment blocks our ability to love," John said, watching the warbler return to her nest.

"We have to rise above the duality into oneness," he continued, "and from there, we can take inspired action and follow the guidance of our heart, of the Goddess." The warbler chirped.

"And loving something to death," John went on, "is a lot more powerful than it sounds. We do engage with the darkness, as we did with your entities, but the light of our consciousness is what we use to transmute it into love. In the dream, you realized that battling the dark forces was exhausting, remember?" John pointed out.

"True," Mia agreed. "I had a strong feeling there had to be another way."

Mia thought back to her dream and to how it felt to experience the constant state of battle.

She asked, "So are you saying that if we used force, Mother Earth would need to have more cataclysmic natural disasters to balance that energy?"

"Well, put it this way...She's *really* tired of us fighting," John said, and looked away. Just thinking about it, he could feel the deep waves of Mother Earth's pain. "She feels every blow."

Mia inhaled quietly. She'd never thought of it like this before.

"Earth carries the lived experiences of all the lives lost in warfare." John exhaled. "And it's not just the death and destruction we bring that affect Her. Our fear, our anger, our grief, even our hopelessness—these toxic emotions flood Her senses."

Mia listened quietly, realizing how deeply this was affecting John. It reminded her of all the pain she had felt as she'd picked up branches for the firewalk yesterday.

"We agreed we would do it differently this time, that we would find a way that didn't create more separation," he said with conviction.

"And is that where Mother Mary comes in? Does she symbolize the compassion we will use instead?"

"Well, it's not symbolic, Mia. That is what she and Mary

Magdalena taught you in the temple along with all the other mysteries of the Goddess."

Mia's jaw dropped.

"Well, shit! I just told you a whole lot more than I meant to."

"Wait! What? You're saying that dream was a real past life? But I turned into a golden light! How is that even possible?" Mia's voice rose higher.

"Dammit, Mia, I've already said too much." John slapped his hand on his thigh.

"According to whom? Why do you have all these rules?" Mia's eyes flashed. "Why don't you just tell me and let it be easy for once? Isn't that what we asked the fire for?"

Mia set her mug on the table, sitting upright in her chair.

Looking at the gentle warbler as it busied itself cleaning its nest, Mia took in a deep breath, gathering her thoughts. "Look, if I'm going to have any hope of understanding this whole mission and my part in it, not to mention write my story about it, I have to know what these things mean. I'm going to know all of this at some point, right?"

"Oh, all right," John said, irritated by it all. "You did have the dreams for a reason. Maybe it is time to fill you in. Here are the dots I'm willing to connect for you today. You might want to settle back into your chair first, though."

Mia laughed, saying, "You're probably right."

"The crystal pyramid is from our time in Atlantis."

"Wait! Atlantis was real?" Mia said, nearly coming out of her chair again.

"Yes." John waited for her to relax before continuing.

"And you said, 'our time'—you were with me?" she said, her voice rising.

"I've been with you every time you've been on Earth."

"Every time? Wow, so we are like family." She smiled, finally leaning back into her chair.

John nodded.

"And what about the dolphin I saw? I think it sacrificed itself to help me open my third eye. Why would it need to do that?"

"The dolphins are galactic beings from the planet Sirius, here to help humanity evolve. You've had many lifetimes on Sirius, and you still have many allies there who continue to help you. Are you not aware of that? Have you not felt them around you?"

"Whoa! Really? That's crazy!" Mia shook her head as if that might help all of this begin to sink in. "This is all so cool. But why did the dolphin have to die? I can't begin to describe how broken I was to see it and to hold it. Such a beautiful creature had to surrender itself for me."

"It didn't, really, Mia. That being assumed that form merely to accomplish its mission, and once it had achieved it, it did not need that body anymore. You need not feel bad about it."

"Okay. But with all these beings helping Mother Earth along with us, how is it that we haven't succeeded already? Why is the darkness so powerful? Where did it come from?"

John sighed. "It's very complicated, but I'll do my best to simplify it so that it'll make sense."

"You're going to dumb it down for me?" Mia laughed. "You don't think I am capable of comprehending it in its entirety?"

"No, that's not what I meant. It's a conversation that could go on for days, so I'm trying to think of the easiest way to explain it, that's all."

John leaned back in his chair.

"When this planet was created, we existed in the fifth dimension, meaning that we were aware of our connection to Source in its wholeness."

"And by *Source in its wholeness,* you mean...?" Mia asked.

"The combined aspect of God and Goddess, our Cosmic Mother and Father."

Mia closed her eyes and tried to let the idea of Source as a unified Cosmic Mother and Father sink in. *Help me understand this,* she said to her heart, then began to sense a vast field of love.

As it moved through her awareness, it seemed to be a presence that was aware and alive. She asked her mind to help her understand, seeing the love appear like a deep, warm embrace. At the center of this bright ocean of light, Mia saw Earth.

"John! Their love created our Earth?" Mia exclaimed.

John chuckled. "I see you are starting to get the picture."

"So some believe the fall to the third dimension, the dimension of Separation, was created on purpose to see if humans could find their way back to the truth of Oneness. Others believe things got so out of hand in Atlantis, we accidentally cut ourselves off from the awareness of our divinity."

"So it was either because of an experiment or an accident that we believe we're separate from the pure love that Source is?" Mia asked.

"Yes, exactly." John straightened in his chair. "The story goes that after the fall, the Goddess refused to let Her children be alone on Earth. She left the Heavens and came to Earth to take care of us, yet doing so also meant separating from the Cosmic Father. Once on Earth, She did Her best to hold Earth in balance, yet found She couldn't create and sustain life the same way She could when She and the Cosmic Father were One as the whole of Source."

"It seems like a magical tale, even with all I've experienced these last few months. Yet if the Goddess is really here, why are most people only aware of the masculine aspect of Source?"

"The ancient civilizations were aware of the Goddess."

Mia nodded, remembering the world history classes she had taken in college.

"But why did that change?" she asked.

"I told you this wasn't an easy story to explain. I'll get to all of that. What I'm saying won't make sense to your mind, but listen instead with your heart, and it will help you understand."

John rested a hand on his chest. "The way the story is remembered and told glosses over a few key points. When Earth fell to the third dimension, it created a tear in the fabric of space, and this tear in the dimensions left the planet vulnerable."

What did he mean by a tear in the dimensions?

She wanted to ask but her heart could already feel the answer. In it, she could sense the ripping apart of the Cosmic Mother and Father that had happened in the fall.

Her chest tightened; the two great beings whose love had created all of existence had been torn apart. It was one thing just to talk about it, and another thing to feel it as Mia was doing, and she struggled to catch her breath. How had Earth ever survived a rift so deep?

"The Goddess struggled to regain balance once separated from Her Beloved. Though it was Her desire to journey with Earth and all life created here, She'd had no way to realize how deeply the rift would reach through Her, and how deeply it would reverberate through the planet. Many celestial beings were helping Her to support life through the great changes that occurred, but even so, it wasn't possible to keep the planet in balance."

Mia heard herself speaking before realizing her thoughts had taken form. "So, the love of Source in its wholeness is what created everything in existence. With the fall between dimensions and the Goddess being torn apart from Her Beloved, the very fabric of Earth's existence tore too?" She was trying to place what she was feeling into words. "Is this how the darkness came to exist? Was it created in the act of tearing apart?"

"Well, it's not so much that it was created as that it was given an opening to arrive."

Mia took a minute to think.

Was it due to the caffeine or all she was trying to take in, that she was feeling a little dizzy?

"Are you okay? We can stop if you need to, Mia, and pick this up later."

"No, I'm good. I think I just need a few deep breaths and maybe some water."

"I'll go get us both some water and maybe some fruit and toast." John stretched as he stood. "We aren't even at the really *out-there* stuff yet."

Mia rested against the back of her chair, enjoying the gentle breeze and shifting patterns of light. She was just drifting off to sleep when she caught the scent of pure heaven.

"Bacon?" she exclaimed, sitting bolt upright.

"We got lucky! Nick's been busy in the kitchen, and we have bacon and eggs to show for it. Fresh-squeezed juice too."

Mia looked appreciatively at the tray laden with their breakfast. She hadn't realized it, yet the rumbling in her stomach let her know it was definitely time for some nourishment.

As they settled in to eat, John picked up the story.

"The tear in dimensions and the instability that it brought to life on Earth acted like a beacon to opportunistic beings living between dimensions. Always on the lookout for their next hunting grounds, so to speak, the planet's vulnerability created the perfect conditions for them to thrive. The rift in Earth's energy field was their way in, and a humanity deep in the confusion of separation energy was their perfect energy source."

Mia coughed as a piece of toast caught in her throat.

John reached over and refilled her water glass. "Easy now."

Once she could get the words out, Mia's voice cut through the air. "Hunting grounds? Energy source?" Mia looked at John, wondering what she was doing there. "You sound like an outer space movie where invaders from another planet come and eat all of the sleeping humans."

"Well, Mia, you're not that far off, really."

John took a bite of bacon and chewed quietly, letting Mia settle a bit.

"As humans grew further from their knowledge of their connection to all life in Oneness," he continued, "they lost touch with the love in their hearts. Fear and negativity began to take over, clouding their minds and senses."

He looked up at the blue of the sky, taking in the scent of the nearby jasmine.

"This disconnect in which humanity became caught gave the beings the perfect opportunity to influence us through our thoughts, amplifying our fear and negativity and creating great discord and strife. All of this unrest generated a powerful energy of darkness."

Mia felt her mind clearing. "The darkness! The beings feed on it!" She sat up in her chair. "So, the more they can stir up fear and anger, the more energy they can...*siphon* from us?"

"Not just fear and anger—sadness, grief, and even confusion too."

John wondered what had brought about the sudden shift in Mia. Whoever—or whatever—had helped out, he was glad for the assistance.

"So the beings worked to stir up more discord?" Mia asked.

It felt to Mia as if there must be something she was missing.

"Eventually, fear and distrust infected the whole of humanity. It spread like wildfire, and over time, morphed into evil. Human beings became more deeply caught in the illusion of separateness, no longer remembering they were One with all of life and Creation.

"They forgot about the Goddess, beginning to believe that God was a jealous and punishing force. They forgot the truth of unity and Love."

John exhaled deeply, looking out into the yard.

"It wasn't supposed to be that way, Mia," he said. His voice caught, and he cleared his throat. "It never should have gotten this bad. It's why we've come back now to help."

Mia realized he had tears running down his cheeks. She had never seen him get emotional.

Sophia started sending images into Mia's mind of all that had happened.

As if a movie had commenced playing in her head, she watched as Atlantis sank into the ocean, also seeing the entire planet Earth nearly being destroyed. Few civilizations remained after the fall from grace. Yet under the care of the Goddess, life slowly regenerated. People still remembered their Oneness sufficient to keep love in their hearts, living in a way of goodness, and if their sense of balance and harmony—with Earth, the elements, each other, and life around them—ever wavered, they knew they could call on the Goddess to help them.

Then Mia saw the beginning of something else.

A darkness grew, the parasitic forces finding their way to Earth and beginning their work of destabilizing humanity. They found an opening to bend thoughts and hearts toward distrust.

To Mia, it looked as if they could even influence the way people saw or perceived each other, as if even their sense of sight became unclear. She watched as the sickness growing in humanity began to affect all life around them, and even Earth Herself.

As this state of instability grew, humans spiraled into more profound unrest, beginning to blame the Goddess for their pain and suffering, also longing for salvation from a distant god.

Images continued to flow into her third eye.

The chaos on the planet was also continuing to spiral out, humanity locked in fear.

People's hatred and blame toward the Goddess began to be enacted upon the priestesses of Her temples, forcing them to take Her teachings underground. Her priestesses embodied Love, and this had kept them from being infected by the fear now rampant in the world.

As the hold of evil deepened, the Goddess saw that many of Her children would perish in its grip. Yet there would be a day when the healing wisdom of Love could rise once more.

It was for that time that She must prepare. She would transmit the knowledge of how to release fear from the body to those who remained faithful to Her. They would be carriers of this knowledge that would one day help humanity return to Love.

Priestesses in the temples of Inanna in Mesopotamia, Ishtar in Babylonia, and Isis in Egypt were infused with the ability to heal the body of fear.

Hidden deep within their wombs was the gateway back to Love. In this way, the teachings would remain protected from the fear that was seeking to destroy all memory of the Goddess and Her love and the knowledge of the unity of Love as the Oneness.

Mia could see the path of these protected teachings moving throughout time, golden threads being carried heart to heart in the lineage of those early priestesses of the Goddess. And as she watched, Mia realized why she had been in the temple with Isis in her dream. Both Mother Mary and Mary Magdalena had been there as young women, training in the ancient ways. Mia's body started to vibrate as she recognized that she had been one of the early priestesses training alongside them both, a protector of this ancient lineage.

Mia's vision carried her to a garden.

There, she caught sight of a man and woman sitting, deep in conversation.

As her vision followed their time together, Mia came to realize who they were. It was Jesus and Mary Magdalena, and they were in love.

In the way he interacted with her and sought out her wisdom, Mia could see Jesus held Mary Magdalena in great regard. He knew who she really was, knew her contribution to be equal to his own. Mia realized Mary's love and strength were vital elements in Jesus's life.

As time moved forward in her vision, Mia knew that it was through their deep love and passion that Jesus was able to complete his mission on Earth and that this would remain a carefully held secret until the Goddess could return to the consciousness of humankind.

The vision carried Mia back to the same garden, yet this time she was sitting with Jesus and Mary Magdalena, enjoying food and conversation as longtime friends. As she felt the surprise of this, Jesus looked into Mia's eyes, speaking directly to her soul.

When you come back in two thousand years, you will help them remember.

Mia's body felt as though it was on fire, the energy spiraling inside her faster and faster. Waves of dizziness overtook her, causing her to fall out of her chair.

"Whoa! I didn't see that coming. Are you okay?" John asked.

He checked to see if she was still conscious.

"Uh-huh," she mumbled.

"Here, let's put this seat cushion under your head. Stay down there as long as you need to, and I promise the spinning will stop eventually. Guess that's as much as you get to know for now," John said and laughed. "I've never had anybody fall out of their chair before."

Mia came back to a full state of consciousness on the cool wooden porch boards, sunlight slanting across her face. Her mind was still spinning, however, trying to understand and to process all she had just seen, too dizzy to sit up.

I'll have to just rest a bit like John said I should. Take as long as I need.

"I'll have to remember this next time you're bombarding me with questions," quipped John. I only have to have Sophia overload you with visions, then I can enjoy my breakfast in peace."

"How's it going out there?" Nick asked.

"Thanks for breakfast. You could have come out and joined us," replied John.

"I thought you might be discussing something private," Nick shrugged.

"Private? In this house? Not possible!" John chuckled. "With Lori and Dominique here, too, every thought is like a live broadcast."

"You're probably right. I suppose we are an intuitive bunch." Nick laughed. "Speaking of, where's Mia?"

"Oh, she saw Jesus and fell out of her chair." John's expression didn't give much away.

"What do you mean she saw Jesus? Like in a vision?" Nick perked up. "Don't leave me hanging here..."

"It looks like the firewalk opened some things up for Mia. She had some pretty big dreams last night that walked her through several past lives. She was asking me so many questions it activated her third eye," John said.

"Ha! Well, that makes sense. A third-eye vision is worth a thousand words—or something like that." Nick laughed. "Wait—you mean Mia's actually lying on the porch right now, passed out? And you just left her?" Nick shook his head as John joined him at the table inside. "Seriously, though, is she okay?"

"Yeah, I waited until she came around. She *is* still on the porch floor, though. I thought it would be good for her to learn what happens when you want more than you're ready for."

"What does happen when you want more than you're ready for?" asked Dominique, walking into the kitchen.

"John told Mia some of her past life with Yeshua, and she fell on the floor," replied Nick.

"Umm...I thought that was a no-no, that we had to wait until we could see it for ourselves?"

"Yes, I did share a bit more than I intended to, but it all began in response to a series of dreams she had last night," John said.

"Ah, so you were just helping her clarify," Dominique replied.

"You really showed her the life in Egypt? The priestess one?" Nick chimed in, his curiosity revving.

"Yes, I even showed her a little bit of Atlantis. I didn't tell her about Lemuria, though, or who knows what would have happened to her!" John laughed again.

"Which part of our lifetime with Yeshua did you show her?" Nick asked.

"The talk in the garden when Jesus told her she'd help people remember the truth of the Goddess in two thousand years' time."

"Right. I remember." Nick's voice fell. "I thought that lifetime would have shifted things in a bigger way. Humanity really got Yeshua's teachings messed up, didn't they?"

"It was all part of the grand design," replied Dominique.

"Bah!" snorted Nick. "Grand design, my ass."

"Well, it was," Dominique snipped. "It all had to do with where

Earth was in Her cycle of Yugas. It was a time of moving away from the center of the galaxy, making humanity's journey into falling asleep and forgetting the truth inescapable."

"Okay, whatever." Nick rolled his eyes. "I know about all of that, and it doesn't change what happened. Humanity still distorted his teachings about love and just used them as a way to judge one another. Then Constantine got his hands on the sacred writings and took out all references to reincarnation, leaving a Bible empty of the greater picture. That one really got me."

Nick couldn't stop remembering. "I thought when the Dead Sea Scrolls resurfaced, humanity would take the hint." He gestured in emphasis. "But no—they dismissed those and chose to remain ignorant."

"Again," Dominique interjected, "I remind you that in the spiral of evolution, based on Earth's location in the galaxy, the consciousness of humankind couldn't fully receive Yeshua's teachings. He brought as much light to the planet as He could, but Earth is just now traveling through the photon belt that will allow humanity's consciousness to evolve."

Nick rolled his eyes and shook his head.

"What's your perspective on all this, John?" asked Dominique.

"Well, I think you're both right; in the cycle of Earth's spiritual evolution, the last few thousand years, we were moving away from the light. That timing definitely let the entity energies take a greater stronghold than anyone ever imagined," replied John.

"Guess that's who I should blame then, the damn entity energies instead of humanity," Nick scoffed.

"Actually, Nick, there's no point in blaming anyone, humanity, or those damn entity energies," John replied. "We have a job to do, and that's why we're all here now. Speaking of which, I'd probably better get back outside and see how Mia is doing."

Nick followed him out, helping Mia get back in her chair.

"Were you there, too, in the time with Jesus?" Mia asked Nick.

"Of course, didn't you see me?" Nick replied.

"I don't think so. I did see John. Actually, I don't know if I saw him. I think I just sensed him there. I did see Jesus and Mary, though. I was even sharing a meal with them in one part of my vision! Can you believe I knew Jesus?" Mia's expression still held a dazed glow.

"Of course. We all go way back with Yeshua," Nick said nonchalantly as if everyone could expect to sit and eat at the table with Jesus any day.

"Who's Yeshua?" Mia asked.

"Jesus. It's the Aramaic pronunciation," Nick replied.

"Oh, okay." Mia was feeling a little better now that she was sitting up again, feeling more or less all right. "John, were you in the garden when I was talking to Jesus and Mary—"

"Hey, you're out of questions for the day, missy. If I answer any more, you might pass out again. It's important for you to remember who you are, but if I just give you information, your mind will get in the way just like it did a few minutes ago. Learning information like this starts to unravel the identity that the mind has created, and there's only so much it can take before it shuts the body down," John explained. "I also need to check in with the powers that be to make sure I didn't already upset the apple cart by showing you too much."

"So what's the plan for today?" Nick asked.

"I want you guys to practice holding space for one another with the breathwork. Mia needs to begin learning how to hold space for others. It will help her begin building the confidence she needs to discover her unique gifts in assisting people in their healing journeys, so the more time she gets in, the better." John paused in thought. "I have a feeling that the time is coming for us to step up our work in the world, and we're going to need all of us fully on board."

Nick nodded in agreement. "I've been feeling the same thing, boss."

"You good with leading the group today?" John gave Nick a pat on the shoulder. "I've got some business to tend to."

"You've got to find someone, you mean?" Nick arched an eyebrow. "I saw you looking around into thin air again."

"Yep. You don't miss much, do ya?" John smiled. "Teach Mia everything you know about breathwork and get Lori and Dominique to help out as well. I'll come check on you guys in a little bit."

"You got it!" Nick replied.

He found himself excited to lead the group and share his knowledge with Mia.

10

Angelic Activation

"Meet us in the living room in a few minutes," Nick said as he left the kitchen.

"I'll be right there," replied Mia.

Nick had filled in Lori and Dominique on all the plans for the day, and they were getting everything set up for breathwork. It was time for Mia to learn how to facilitate a healing session.

Mia came into the room as Nick was clearing the space with a spray of sage and cedar. She saw two blankets laid out lengthwise, each with one to the side, already folded for sitting.

"All right! Let's get rolling," Nick said, clapping. "Lori, Dominique, go ahead and lie down on a blanket."

"Mia, you take the folded blanket beside Dominique. You'll be guiding her through a breathwork healing session today," Nick instructed.

Once everyone settled, he continued, "I'll be demonstrating on Lori as if it's her first time breathing so that you can learn each step." Looking at Mia, he decided to add, "All you'll need to do is follow my lead and repeat what I do as you guide Dominique."

Mia nodded. She hadn't realized she'd be learning to lead the breathwork sessions so soon.

"Don't worry," Nick offered. "You've done the breathwork, so most of this should be familiar."

Dominique had now taken a lying position on her blanket, Mia kneeling alongside.

"I'm the one who needs to be worried!" Dominique chimed in, elbowing Mia in the knee as she flashed a big smile.

Mia laughed, grateful for Dominique's teasing.

"Any questions before I start the music?" Nick asked.

"We're good," they all replied.

Mia watched Dominique's body, observing the breath moving through her. Following Nick's instructions, she did her best to *just hold space and stay neutral.*

The magic happens in our willingness to witness spirit do the work. All you have to do is stay present.

Mia tried to tune in to Dominque's mind, quickly halting on realizing there was too much happening in there for her to make any sense of it. She let out a deep exhale and pulled her energy back, now witnessing patterns of color moving through Dominique's body.

Her own body started to tingle as she felt Dominique's spirit moving through the room. Nick had told her there was nothing more she needed to do once spirit came into the space.

Huh, well that was a lot easier than I thought it was going to be. I didn't have to DO anything.

Mia stayed focused on Dominique until the playlist shifted.

"Just breathe naturally and allow your body to rest," Nick told Lori and Dominique, reaching the end of the breathwork's active portion.

Now, Nick explained to Mia that it was important not to disturb them during the resting phase. "This is the part where the breather gets to soak up the frequency of love that's moving through them. We'll let them rest here for a few minutes."

Mia watched as Dominique's body relaxed even more deeply, seeing vibrations of energy rising off of Dominique, reminding her of heat rising from the asphalt in the summertime.

"Thanks, Mia," Dominique said, smiling as she began to stretch gently. "I could feel your presence and support while I was breathing."

"Yes, that was great! I got a lot done!" Lori shared, sitting up enthusiastically. "Thanks for holding space for me, Nick."

"Okay, team, time to switch places!" Nick directed.

As Dominique helped Mia get ready to breathe, Mia realized that by holding space for Dominique, she was already in an expanded state. She began the active breath, discovering that her body was vibrating by her third inhalation. *Ah, this is going to be easy,* she thought.

Suddenly, her back began to arch, which took her by surprise as she had just begun to breathe.

She felt the green life force energy rising from the earth, traveling into the soles of her feet.

It shifted up her legs and along her spine, all the way to the crown of her head, rocking her entire body in a rhythmic, wavelike motion. As the energy flow heightened, her arms began to shake and flap wildly, the waves of energy starting to lift her torso off the floor.

So much for easy! Mia thought.

She could feel what her body was doing, yet it was as if the breath was *breathing her*, rather than her breathing it. The energy was taking over, and she was no longer in control. Her limbs were flailing, and her body couldn't breathe fast enough to meet the demand of the energy flow.

"Ahhhhh…ahhh… ahhh!" Mia moaned, her torso lifting with shocking intensity.

The energy was electrifying.

Hearing all the sounds, John had entered the room to be of assistance.

He spoke calmly, advising, "You need to sit up, Mia. Can you do that?"

Her kundalini energy bolted through her spine, whipping her upright. Her arms began moving faster than she thought possible, then the energy transferred into Mia's fingers.

Her hands started forming shapes so quickly that everything became a blur.

"Mudras!" Dominique exclaimed. "Her hands are shaping mudras!"

"What are your hands doing, Mia? Why are they moving like that?" John quietly asked.

Mia heard him clearly. Although her body was doing things beyond her understanding, her mind was strangely calm and present. She asked her hands what they were doing through her thoughts and heard Sophia answering instantly.

"I am…balancing the…masculine…and feminine…energies in my…body. They are…communicating…through…my hands," Mia stammered.

Centuries of conflict were being resolved through her hands.

The pain of the women in her lineage, their repressed anger, the fear with which they all had lived, it was all flowing out of Mia's left hand. The masculine side of her was angry too.

He had tried so hard to provide and to protect the feminine. Yet the feminine had never appreciated what he had done. All the responsibility had fallen on his shoulders. There was so much pain inside him, but he wasn't allowed to express any of it.

The more he felt, the more he tried to control.

As Mia's fingers expressed this battle, the mudras instantly transmuted the energy until the channels of her body had become clear, allowing the energy to flow unimpeded through her.

As the energies became freed, a blinding flash of light flooded Mia's senses, transporting her awareness into a future moment in which she saw the pure energy of the Goddess rising through her body. It shot like lightning through the soles of her feet, bursting through the crown of her head in its bid to reach to the heavens.

A sonic thunderclap pealed and she realized she was witnessing the force of the Goddess rising to meet the full light of God, and that it was all happening through her body.

Mia could hardly bear the force of the power released as the energies joined, these intertwined energies racing downward now, Mia's body their conduit as they traveled deep into the earth.

She watched as the pure energies of Earth and the heavens, now reconnected, flowed through her, a living current traveling between Earth and sky. A deep pulse, much like a cosmic heartbeat, filled the air. A merging was happening within her body. As the energies of Goddess and God reached full union in her heart, a blinding white light emanated from her chest.

"Mia, I need you to stand up now, okay? Keep breathing, though."

"Dominique and Lori, come over here and help me guide her closer to the wall."

"You can lean here if you need to." John gently moved one of her hands to the wall behind her to help her get her bearings.

Mia didn't think the energy could move through her any faster, but as soon as John let her go, her breathing kicked into overdrive, her legs shaking front to back and side to side.

Her arms flew above her head, fingers pressing back into the wall to steady her body.

How could she possibly hold that position? But there seemed to be an intelligence in the energy moving through her, taking care of her, no matter how out of control she looked.

Mia could feel her body moving in all directions, but she felt energetically supported, also able to feel John, Dominique, and Lori helping.

"Let's clear the furniture out of the way and Lori, if you could place some blankets and pillows around her in case she collapses..."

"I can see the energy codes traveling through the room. I recognize this pattern, iridescent white strands moving in a double helix; it's angelic!" said Dominique with surprise.

"You're right, she's receiving an angelic upgrade. Looks like she'll be getting those superpowers she keeps asking about," John replied.

"I didn't think humans could carry angelic DNA," Dominique said with concern.

They all felt the shift. If the energy before had been like an earthquake, this was like a parting of space and time. Angels arrived in an opening of light. It was time. Mia was to be the first human carrier of angelic DNA. Once it was integrated into her body and then activated, Mia would be an anchor on Earth for angelic wisdom. The three of them watched in amazement.

"Her spirit has been assisting humanity in the angelic realms for centuries, and that's why they're blessing her with these upgrades. But..." John got real quiet for a moment.

"But what?" asked Lori. "Why do you suddenly look so concerned?"

"I think Mia's about to find out why superpowers can be a blessing and a curse. This will likely place her in danger."

"Danger from whom?" Lori asked.

"Or rather, from what?" Dominique interrupted. "The dark force energies are going to come after her now, aren't they?"

Lori gulped.

"It's imperative that we keep her cloaked, well-hidden from the dark force energies. We can't let them find out who she is yet. This is why she had to wait to receive these gifts.

John said, "If she'd been born with activated angelic DNA, her light would have drawn them to her at a time when she had no protection against them. I had to work for years strengthening my abilities in order to remain undetectable to them. Now, I have to teach Mia to do this far more quickly than that." John's brow furrowed.

Mia could hear what they were saying but none of it was registering. A yell escaped her lips as her body was rapidly bending backward toward the floor. She wasn't flexible enough to move into a backbend unsupported, needing someone to help her. John rushed over to help her as much as he could. Once Mia's hands hit the ground, her feet lifted onto the tips of her toes. Her eyes rolled back in her head and her gaze fixed on her pineal gland in the center of her brain.

Lori and Dominique both gasped and then giggled, watching John try to figure out what to do next. Mia didn't know what was happening to her body, but her mind was too expanded to care.

She felt like a puppet on a string, a marionette being made to dance or perform speed yoga.

Her body held the backbend for several minutes and then collapsed.

She rolled over onto her hands and knees, once again carried by the energy moving through her. Her spine arched up and down as her body attempted to handle the force of energy releasing through her crown and root chakras. The flow continued, shaping Mia into a rapid succession of spontaneous yoga postures. The intensity built until the energy bursting through her crown chakra drew her head downward with a strength of desire that held Mia's full attention.

She needed her legs in the air more than she needed anything at that moment, yet her neck didn't feel strong enough to manage a headstand. The energy's pull was irresistible. It required a direct line into the earth, and she was its chosen conduit. Her breath too fast for words, she remembered her connection with John and thought *headstand* as loudly as she could.

"Ah, shit!" John said as he got the message loud and clear too. "You two better come help me. She needs to be completely upside down."

Lori and John each grabbed an ankle while Dominique steadied Mia's hips.

"You'd better not let her kick me!" Dominique yelled.

"Well then, you'd better hold her tightly in case her legs start flailing around like her arms were doing a moment ago," John replied.

"Oh shit!" Lori laughed. "Let's hope that doesn't happen."

As the energy poured out of Mia's head into the earth, her body stabilized.

The sun's energy was now streaming through her, flowing into the heart of Mother Earth, the very center of the planet. Mia's awareness traveled down with it, and she found herself in the green misty cave she had visited prior to incarnating into this body.

She saw misty swirls of purple light streaming out of her, the green and purple swirling together, embracing like two long-lost lovers. The cave filled with the deepest love Mia had ever experienced. There was a feeling of relief too, a sense of letting go, a surrender as if someone had been holding their breath for way too long and was finally able to breathe fully.

They all felt the earth rumble beneath them as the windows of the house shook.

"What was that?" exclaimed Lori.

"Little earthquake is all," John tried to say, as if he considered it no big deal.

"Since when are there earthquakes in Sedona?" Dominique asked. "The presence of angels in the room has disrupted my ability to tune in and get answers."

"As I sense into it, all I feel is deep love, and overwhelming relief," John replied.

Mia's awareness was wholly captivated by what she was witnessing. The Divine Masculine, the light of the sun, had traveled through her to find its way back to the heart of the Goddess deep inside Earth. Mia's body had been the conduit facilitating them to reunite for the first time since the fall from grace. Mia could only hold this awareness for a few seconds before her body became overwhelmed by the intensity of the vibration of love.

She felt herself melting into its encompassing presence.

Luckily, John and Lori still had a firm hold of her ankles, and Dominique was steadying her hips. As her body gave way, they were able to gently lay her back down on the floor.

She rested there peacefully and motionless, unable to move or speak.

11

A Ring of Crystals

———

"Wow! That was amazing!" Nick shouted, sitting up from his breathwork session.

Dominique laughed, then exclaimed, "Oh my! With all the commotion, I'd all but forgotten you were lying there breathing this whole time."

Nick looked at her oddly, not understanding whether she was teasing him or not.

"I just had the best breath session!" he said. "I traveled down into the darkness like I usually do and was able to get deeper into the den of demons; I was blasting them all with love, sending them back into light, when a legion of them was suddenly neutralized. It was crazy—I had maybe seven or eight I was targeting, and then 'whoosh!' Six thousand disappeared! I don't know how I did it, but it was awesome," Nick said excitedly.

"Well, I don't think you were the one who did it," Dominique said.

"That must have been what caused the earth to shake," Lori said.

Nick commented, "You guys felt that too? Wasn't it just an energetic experience?"

Nick wondered what the hell Dominique meant by that comment; he'd just told her what he was doing. How could it not have been him?

"Do you think holding Mia upside down and letting all that energy pour into the earth is what annihilated Nick's buddies?" Dominique asked John.

"Hey! They're not *my buddies!* And what do you mean by 'upside down'? What was going on in here?" He suddenly noticed the pillows and blankets were all the way across the room from where they had been when they'd set up to breathe.

"Well, the short explanation is that Mia received an angelic DNA upgrade that apparently allowed her body to become a conduit to connect Father Sun into the heart of Mother Earth for the first time since the fall from grace," John said.

"The heart of Mother Earth—or the WOMB?" Dominique smiled. Her intuitive powers were back online now that the angels had left. "That earthquake might have been orgasmic in nature."

Lori giggled.

"Nice! Mother Earth's orgasm wiped out a legion of demons!" Nick puffed out his chest a little. "I'm cool with that, and happy to have played my part in the battle."

John glanced down at Mia, concerned.

"What's wrong? Why are you looking at her like that?" Lori asked.

"A big part of the success of this mission is Mia remaining undetectable until it's time. A legion of entities being wiped out isn't going to go unnoticed by the dark forces and they'll likely come looking for whoever caused it," John said, his brow furrowing.

"Can't we cloak her? Or rather, can Mother Earth or the angels or someone on her team provide some sort of protection?" Lori asked.

"Yeah, or maybe there's some sort of talisman or spell we can cast?" Nick said.

"Do you know any, Nick?" John asked.

"Not off the top of my head, but I can certainly find out. I'll get to work on it," Nick replied.

"Great, but hurry; it's possible we may not have much time," John replied.

"What about you, Dominique, do you have any ideas?" John asked.

"I can cloak her for a few hours to give you time to find a solution. They won't be able to detect her," she replied.

"Really, you can do that?" Nick asked, his tone disbelieving.

Dominique looked at him, annoyed.

"Well, obviously, if I've avoided capture for the past three hundred years, surely you can see I've got one or two tricks up my sleeve! Plus, why would I say I could do it if I couldn't?"

Nick said quietly, "Dominique, it was just a turn of phrase. I wasn't doubting you."

"That can work, Dominique," John interrupted, obviously wanting her to put the cloaking into action as soon as possible and not let the time get lost in her and Nick's petty disagreement. "How much time can you buy us?"

Dominique tuned in to Mia's aura to see how brightly she was shining.

"Well, she's really lit up right now, so probably no more than four or five hours."

Nick went back to his bedroom to look through his books and see what he could find on cloaking. John went to his meditation mat to travel and ask the Galactic Council for help.

Dominique brought her chest of crystals from her bedroom

and joined Lori and Mia in the living room. Lori helped Dominique find all the black tourmaline crystals she would need to make a circle around Mia.

They created an outer ring of rose quartz to amplify the love from Mother Earth.

"This reminds me of my dream the other night," Mia said, eyeing the crystals surrounding her.

"What was it about?" Lori asked. "Can you remember much of it?"

"I was with someone—a woman—in a field, telling her that we were going to walk backward in a circle and that all the entities would be released from her body when we did. I had a hand on her shoulder and a fluorite wand in my other hand, pointed at the ground. There were also dust devils all around us and funnel clouds in the distance."

"Hmm…backward circles or more of a counterclockwise spiral?" Dominique asked.

"I'm not sure," Mia replied. "Why?"

"This could be the death spiral. That would make a lot of sense, actually," said Dominique pensively.

"Why? What's that?" asked Mia.

"A clockwise spiral brings spirit into matter, and a counterclockwise spiral releases matter back into the spirit realm. We could create an outer circle of fluorite to set up a vortex so that Mother Earth can just recycle any entities that get too close," Dominique suggested.

"How do we set up the vortex?" Lori asked.

"Hopefully, John got the answer to that question," said Dominique.

She looked at him hopefully as he walked back into the room.

John nodded. "I got some guidance from the Galactic Council. The fluorite is a good idea."

"How much do you think we'll need?" Dominique asked, exploring her chest of crystals.

"There's no telling; we'll have to experiment and see," he said, carrying over a large fluorite slab that had languished in the corner of the room. "This one can get us started, and I'm thinking three more big pieces along with this to anchor the four directions and go from there."

"Do you have any, Lori?" Dominique asked.

"I don't, but Nick might; he's still back in his room, looking through his books."

"I'll ask him and check in on his progress, too," John offered.

"How's it going back here?" John asked, standing in the hall by Nick's door.

"Good. I think I've found a couple spells we can cast that will keep her cloaked," Nick replied.

"You don't happen to have any big fluorite pieces, do you?"

"I don't. Wish I did, though, and now I'm curious—"

"Great work on the spells," John replied. "Come with me, and we'll fill you in on the rest."

"Lori and I are going to check the crystal shops in town," Dominique said. "I'm guessing we can't have too much protection in this situation, anyway."

"Hey, you two, the bigger, the better, and yes, get a few extra just in case," John said. "And give me a call and let me know what you find. Nick and I will work with Mia and Mother Earth to see if we can get an exact formula, so if we need anything else, I can let you know."

They found Mia sitting in the center of the black tourmaline and rose quartz crystals.

"Tell us about the dream you had," John said.

As Mia was recounting her dream, she remembered something new.

"There was just one funny thing...I was calling the crystal an ametrine," Mia shared. "I know ametrine is purple and gold, though, and the crystal I was holding in my dream was green and purple. Like fluorite." She paused, her eyes widening. "Just now in the breathwork, I traveled down into Mother Earth, and there were purple and green spirals everywhere—that has to mean something! Don't you think?"

"Do you think we need to call them and tell them to buy an ametrine as well?" Nick asked.

John let the images move in his mind's eye. "Purple and green...the Divine Masculine and Mother Earth coming together...Aah, that would be the complete vortex Mia would be making in the future. So what does the ametrine mean? Oh, of course! Purple and gold are the colors of her cosmic lineage. The Order of Melchizedek is the purple, and the gold is Sophia, her spirit. I think Mia is the ametrine. We just need to help her activate its colors within herself. Hmm. I wonder if the way to activate the vortex is for Mia to remember more of who she is?"

"What do you mean I'm the ametrine?" Mia asked.

"Nick, do you have a spell that can help her remember?"

"But you told me to stay away from that kind of magic—"

"Yes, and I know how well you listen. So do you have a spell?"

"Well, yes, but won't that affect the timeline? Isn't that why you told me not to mess with it?"

"I don't think that matters at this point." John looked sharply at Nick. "If we don't keep her safe, there won't be a timeline for much longer! And you nitpicking won't help right now."

"Oh shit! Okay. Yeah, I see where you're going with this. But how will helping her remember help with the vortex and the crystals and entities?"

"To be honest, I don't know exactly." John exhaled a long breath. "My sense is that if she knows who she is, she'll be able to carry more of her cosmic energy in her body," John explained. "And from what we saw today, the energies are working into her from both above and below. Maybe having more memories in her body will help get her mind out of the way and speed up the process."

"Is anyone going to explain this all to me?" Mia asked. "It sounds like a foreign language."

"We don't have time, Mia," John answered. "Not right now, anyway. You just lie down and start breathing gently. Nick, go get whatever you need for the memory spell."

John stepped to the edge of the outer circle, picking up a leaf of sage.

"Really?" chimed in Mia, catching John by surprise. "You're going to do a spell on me and not explain any of it? I'm just supposed to trust you and go along with things?"

"Oh, I'm sorry, Mia," John replied. He set down the sage leaf in the bowl on the altar. "I just assumed you were on board with what we're doing and knew we're only trying to help—"

"I'm just messing with you. Of course, I trust you—let's do this!" Mia laughed.

John chuckled and shook his head.

Nick came back carrying a leather satchel, then he placed several candles in a circle around Mia. He burned copal in the incense burner and smudged himself with sage. After this, he took up a kneeling position next to Mia and pulled out a Sacred Rose cross.

Using Hebrew letters, he created a sigil, a symbol containing magic, using the first letter of each word from the sentence, "I remember who I am."

Taking a deep breath, he began to trace the sigil onto Mia's forehead with frankincense oil.

"Close your eyes and start breathing. This might hurt a little… or a lot," he said to Mia, grimacing, not sure what might happen.

"What…do…you…mean?" Mia asked, between breaths.

"Well, we're sort of making something happen before its natural unfolding. You would eventually have remembered after you'd been doing the work long enough; the illusion would have faded away on its own, and the truth would gradually have come to reveal itself. Since we're forcing things to happen here, there may be some unpleasant side effects. I could be wrong—but I'm probably not."

Mia mumbled something, her words incoherent.

Her awareness of everything around her started to fade, and in its place, there came a horrendous stabbing pain in her forehead as the frankincense oil permeated the skin and her third eye began to open. It felt as though the sigil was being carved into her skin fraction by fraction.

She tried to speak but couldn't move her mouth.

Mia felt her face contorting, like a mask being removed, and then another and another. All of her masks were lifting off, all her false identities, all the layers of her ego peeling away one by one. Mia managed to let out a scream, startling John and Nick. She could feel the layers being stripped from her, each of the identities she had created to fit in with the world being eliminated.

Mia was struggling, her body squirming as all her ideas of who she had believed she was, became lifted away. She saw the endless stories of her mind, the trap of all its judgments. There was no way to win; no matter how much she did or didn't do, her mind could always find something else to judge. She saw how much of her life force energy was wasted on these scenarios created by her mind. They were all traps.

She could see no way out, no solution.

Despair and a sense of utter powerlessness flooded through her, completely overwhelming her. She felt as though there was a boulder on her heart, this pain so immobilizing.

She was drowning in its sadness, and there was nothing she could do to fix it and no story onto which she could grasp to explain the pain.

The feeling of powerlessness tried to tie itself into a sense of victimization, but that mask had been removed, leaving her no longer capable of viewing herself as a victim. Still, the sadness continued to weigh upon her heart, so dense and heavy that she felt her heart begin to crack.

The supposed "shields of protection" she had built around her heart began to crumble and Mia let out a cry from the depths of her being. It was as if all of humanity's pain was being expressed through her. Mia saw herself wanting to detach from the pain in her heart, trying to escape to her mind, but there was nowhere to hide, all of her "stories" now obliterated.

She couldn't blame anyone for what she was feeling, not even herself. She felt herself wanting to withdraw from life, but the fact was, life wouldn't let her go. So she fell momentarily into numbness, but all she found in there was the judgment of "not doing enough," of "not being lovable enough," and the loneliness of isolation.

But the story she needed to be able to stay in that isolation and numbness no longer existed. There was no place for her to remain, no place to hide as the masks continued to lift.

She tried to find a sense of Self in her accomplishments and in all that she had created in her life, but the judgments of her mind destroyed her ability to find any comfort there.

She felt as if she was moving from her mind to her heart and back again, searching for answers in a place where there were none to be found. Yet no matter how much she wanted to end the struggle, she couldn't set herself free. She felt as though she was covered in slime, a thick, filmy layer that she couldn't escape. No matter which way she went, she still found herself stuck.

Nick looked up at John and shrugged. "Do you think it's working?" he asked, hoping John could see some sign of progress under all the discomfort Mia was demonstrating.

John's face indicated that he was as uncertain as Nick about this.

"It's your spell, so don't you know if it's working?" John asked sharply.

He felt frustration in not knowing what to do to help.

"Well, I've never actually used it full strength. I've helped people remember things, but never to the intensity of what she needs to remember. I didn't think it would be this bad," Nick offered sheepishly.

"No, it's fine. I'm sorry. It's just hard to watch. I think this is good; I mean, I think it'll work. Of course, unraveling the ego can bring pain. We have to trust the breathwork, trust spirit that this will help her remember. It's all we can do."

John leaned down, picking up a leaf of sage.

He said, "The best thing we can do for Mia right now is to stay strong in our faith and hold some solid space for her. Let's both burn some more sage and get this fear and doubt out of the space."

Mia's body was exhausted from the struggle; there was no place to hide, no way to win, so she surrendered. As she let go of the fight, let go of trying to find the solution, a tunnel of light opened up in front of her. As her consciousness went into it, she was transported once again through the dimensions, feeling as though she was falling through space and time, although at times, it felt as though she was floating upward, as she possessed no sense of direction to know in which way she was moving. After what seemed like an eternity, her awareness exploded into a golden ball of light. She felt as though she was melting into honey, the viscosity of her surroundings thick, yet liquid. There was no ending or beginning in her awareness of herself.

She was pure, and she was light, every particle of her being made of infinite love.

I am the right hand of God, she heard Sophia say. *I come from the womb of the Cosmic Mother. I AM the mighty I AM. The Order of Melchizedek requested my presence on Earth during the return of the Goddess. I have assisted in the liberation of hundreds of planets, although this is the first time I've done so in a human body. I am you; you are me.*

I am the energy that sources you.

As you heal and release the density of the ego, I will be able to merge fully with your body, and our consciousness will become one. It is essential that you feel the truth of this in every cell of your body. The fear will never stop trying to destroy you, and as long as it has power over your body, I cannot reside within you. Yet once I am within you, it can never return, for we cannot occupy the same space.

Your task is to continue to choose love. No matter what happens, choose love. Love is always the answer, and fear nothing but an illusion. Love is the only thing that is real.

But I do not mean to imply that fear is powerless, for its illusion is in control of your planet. I am telling you that the solution, the answer to all your questions, is LOVE. Remember who you are, for that is where your power lies. You are Love vibrating in human form. Every cell of your body is made of Love. As you continue to love yourself, you will heal the world.

Then everything went black as Mia fell back into her body.

John and Nick watched as she lay motionless.

"I don't think she's breathing," Nick said.

"I don't either," John agreed. He placed his hand on her chest, sending a bolt of energy into her heart. Mia's body gasped for air as her spine arched violently upward.

"Fuck! Goddammit! Shit! Fuck!" Nick yelled.

"You already said 'Fuck,'" John said, laughing.

Mia opened her eyes, smiling at them both.

There was a golden light emanating from her, its vibrant glow filling the room. She couldn't speak yet, but the message of *Thank you, I love you*, was clearly heard and understood.

Dominique came through the door in a rush, crying out, "Why didn't you answer your phones? We've got the crystals in the car and need your help unloading them."

"All this energy in the room must have disrupted our cell service," John said. "Mia, you stay here and don't leave the stone circle. Come on, Nick. Let's get this protection vortex activated before her golden glow brings every entity in the state of Arizona our way!"

Nick and John followed Dominique outside, where Lori directed them to three large pieces of fluorite nested carefully in the seats of their cars, and several smaller pieces as well.

"Wow, these are beautiful!" John exclaimed. "You two did a great job."

"Yeah, and it's amazing that you were able to find such big pieces with traces of purple and green in them," Nick said, admiring the crystals, tracing his fingertips delicately across one.

"I'll grab the fluorite in my room and start in the east," John said. "Who wants to set a stone in the south?"

"I'll take the south," Lori answered. She chose the smaller of the four large fluorites, though it still weighed about ten pounds.

"Okay, then I'll take the west," Dominique said, touching the fifteen-pound crystal.

"Well then, I guess that leaves me in the north with this humongous mamma jamma," Nick said, pretending to struggle as he lifted the thirty-pound crystal.

"How wide should we make the circle?" Dominique asked. "These beautiful crystals are bound to draw attention if anyone passes by."

"I agree," John answered, coming from inside the house with his fluorite. "Let's keep it as close to the house as we can while still forming a perfect circle."

He looked for a layout where the stones could be protected from view. The trees and natural rise and fall of the ground would help.

"Okay, I'll go around to the east, set my stone, and begin pacing out the rest of the circle. You all meet me in the directions with your crystals," John told them.

John checked on Mia as he walked through the house toward the east boundary. She was still glowing, still smiling, and still speechless. He could see by the light that was now filling the house that Mia would have to stay well inside the circle until the threat was over.

John placed his large fluorite piece at exactly ninety degrees east, set about five feet away from the house. The compass app on phones these days sure did make things easier. He'd picked up two of the smaller fluorites that Dominique and Lori had brought from town, choosing the larger of the two, placing it about a foot away from the eastern boundary piece.

He set the smaller of the two new fluorites right alongside it. Now it was time to anchor in the energy of the east. He went to the large fluorite piece, placing the palm of his hand on its cool, smooth surface. He asked it to hold the energy of the east, telepathically sending it images of what he needed it to do, waiting to see if it agreed. Once he felt its agreement to this purpose, he moved to the larger of the two small pieces, placing his hand on it in the same way, asking if it would consent to being the gateway to the circle. He asked the smaller of these two to be the key that would activate the vortex once all the stones were joined. They agreed to his request, and John thanked each of them before standing to pace out the circle's path toward the south.

He found Lori waiting with her fluorite and showed her the point of 180 degrees in line with the circle. After she set the stone in place, John followed the steps to request that it hold the energy of the south. He walked the circle to meet Dominique in the west, then Nick in the north.

Once their stones were in place, he returned to the east to complete the circle. With all stones in place and the circle joined, John activated the vortex and set the gate and key.

Nick, Lori, and Dominique joined him at the east boundary.

John reminded them that they would need to exit and enter the circle only through the gateway set at the east for the duration of the period it remained activated.

"How long do you think we'll have to leave it up?" Lori asked.

"Honestly, I have no idea. I'm counting on us getting a clear message once it's safe to take it down," John replied. "Thank you again for going to town to find the crystals," he said.

"Of course, happy to help," Lori replied.

"How do we know if it's working?" Dominique asked.

"Wasn't this your idea? How can you not know if it'll work?" Nick rolled his eyes.

"Dominique, why don't you enter and find out? With your superpowers, I'm sure you'll be able to feel it," John said.

Dominique made a face at Nick before entering through the gate, then she turned in a clockwise direction to honor the energy of the Feminine. As soon as she completed the circle, she felt the buzz of Mother Earth moving through her nervous system.

"Oh, this is awesome. It's definitely working; it feels like one of those giant bug-zapping lights!" She giggled.

Nick, Lori, and John lined up to enter the doorway of the circle. It was going to take careful attention to remember to do this anytime they came into or left the house. Once they were all inside the boundary circle, they went back into the house, finding Mia sitting up.

"I'm starving!" Mia exclaimed.

"Me too!" John replied.

"Me three!" Nick chimed in.

"I'm way ahead of you guys!" Lori said, smiling. "I've got dinner in the crockpot. Just give me a few minutes to set everything up.

"Oh, I love you so much! Let me help you," Nick said, joining her on her way to the kitchen.

"So, Mia, now that you're able to talk, why don't you tell us about your experience while Nick and Lori get dinner ready?"

John took a seat in the chair across from her. Mia was still sitting on the floor inside the tourmaline and rose quartz circle Dominique had created for her earlier.

Mia smiled. "I don't know if there are any words to explain what happened. All of my breath sessions have been amazing, but there was something different about this one. I feel more connected to myself. My truth feels stronger inside my body; it feels like no matter what happens, that truth can't leave—that I can't un-know what I now know. At least I hope that's true, right? I can't un-know it, can I?" Mia asked.

John laughed. "No, you're right, you can't un-know it. You might forget it for a moment or two, but it feels to me like you've shifted into knowingness and that you'd easily come back to remembering if something did happen to cause you to forget."

"I feel like I'm done arguing about my worthiness for this

mission. It is what it is and it's what I was created for, and actually, I'm pretty excited about it." Mia paused for a moment, searching for the words to match what she was feeling. "Well, it's more than that. It's like knowing who I am and what my purpose is makes everything make sense.

"I can see how everything I've been living up to now has been about getting me here. Seeing it this way, I accept my past, and everything and everyone who played a role in getting me to this moment. I don't need to beat myself up about any of it anymore." Mia shrugged as she looked at John, needing to know he understood her.

"Sounds like you're all in!" he said, smiling.

"I am!" Mia grinned.

"Dinner's ready!" Nick called from the kitchen.

12

Alien Apocalypse

———

Mia went to bed, excited about the direction in which life was taking her. She drifted off to sleep, imagining a kind of future she had never thought possible before. Her consciousness traveled to the astral realms, and she found herself sitting in the back seat of a four-door sedan.

Nick was driving, Dominique was in the front passenger seat, and Lori was sitting in the back seat beside Mia. They were headed to meet John.

"Holy fuck!" Nick yelled, slamming on the brakes as a building just ahead began collapsing.

"Aaaaaahhhhh!" Dominique screamed.

Mia froze with fear and Lori started crying.

The earth was shaking violently, and everything on Her surface was being diminished to rubble. Nick's quick reflexes kicked in as he saw a streetlamp giving way, arcing toward them.

He floored the gas, maneuvering them safely out of its path.

In a matter of minutes, the city lay in ruin around them.

"Holy shit! Holy shit! Holy shit!" Nick kept screaming as they sped along, falling debris crashing around them. After what felt like an endless scene in a terrifying movie, he saw a clear space ahead, using it to pull over and stop the car.

They would be safe here; everything around had already fallen.

"Oh, my God! What do we do?" cried Dominique.

Mia was in shock, unable to speak.

As the last of the tremors stilled, the silence was deafening. There were dark clouds in the sky and the wind began to pick up. Mia felt as if Earth's tremors were still shaking her body.

She sought to connect into Mother Earth to calm herself, but the energy of the planet was far too intense. She looked up, seeing a funnel cloud in the distance, headed toward them.

Lori got down on her knees and started to pray while Nick paced back and forth, muttering curse words.

"Well, I guess John was right," Mia said.

"What? He told you this was going to happen?" asked Dominique.

"Not this, specifically, I just mean he was right about big Earth changes he said would be happening," Mia answered.

"Did he also happen to mention what we should do when the apocalypse began?" Nick asked.

"He said something about help from above…"

Mia's dream shifted, and the next thing she knew, she was on a spaceship high above Earth with tall, luminescent beings watching her intently. Mia realized she had seen some of them in the meeting of the Galactic Council. "Where are we?" she asked.

"You are on the Solar Wind. We've brought you here so that you can see—"

Mia turned toward the voice.

She found an extraterrestrial being, seated in a commander's chair. The being gestured toward a viewing gallery, holographic images of Earth flashing in rapid succession.

Mia saw Earth in turmoil, volcanoes erupting, hurricanes ravishing the coastlines, fires burning, rivers flooding. Like a dog shaking off an infestation of fleas, Earth was ridding Herself of the parasites; the purification of the planet had begun.

A part of Mia wanted Earth to destroy it all. It was humanity's own damn fault for abusing Her and one another. How could humans not know how harmful their actions had been for so long? They lived as if what they did could just continue without consequence, as if they were the owners and ultimate rulers of the planet, freely able to decimate it with their grievous habits.

Well, here were the repercussions of endlessly violating the Feminine. Yet would most of humanity even realize their part in it all?

"Please make it stop," Mia finally said.

"We told you this would happen if your humanity didn't change the way you treated Her," the extraterrestrial responded.

"I know, and we're really sorry," Mia said. "Please make it stop."

"Are you willing to take responsibility for them?"

"For whom?"

"For the humans who keep fighting with each other, perpetuating the fear and pain that is destroying your planet."

"Yes, I'll do anything to save Her. Tell me what I can do to fix things."

The ET contemplated Mia's request before finally answering, "Fine, I will make it stop..."

Mia's body softened in relief.

"... but you'll have to nurse my baby while I do."

"What?" Mia was sure she hadn't heard clearly or that this was some sort of symbolic request she didn't understand.

"You need to nourish, nurture, and care for the little ones in exchange for us helping you," the commander responded, elucidating but not looking away from the console.

Mia still didn't understand.

She was nervous to ask again, yet soon had her answer. A door behind them opened, and what Mia supposed was a nursemaid approached her, carrying a baby ET.

The ET placed the baby in Mia's arms. "Don't worry, he ate a little earlier, so you'll only need to nurse him for a short while."

Mia looked down at the baby. He smiled up at her, revealing two teeth, one on top and one on the bottom. *Oh God, I hope this doesn't hurt,* she thought.

Dear Lord! What the heck does that mean? Mia woke with a start, the dream clear in her mind. *I definitely didn't sign up for that!* She reached down and touched her breast, still feeling the dread of having to nurse a baby alien. *Everything just keeps getting weirder and weirder!*

Hoping John would have some answers for her, she dressed and headed into the kitchen.

John seemed to take it all in stride as she told him about her dream. He almost choked on his coffee, though, when she told him about nursing the baby.

"Sounds like you got your first mission!" John laughed, eyes still wide.

"What do you mean? Breastfeeding an ET?" Was he teasing her?

"Well, I don't know about that." John chuckled. "What we do know is that you're here to save the planet, and clearly, you need to contact your galactic friends to ask for assistance."

"What galactic friends? Are you messing with me?"

"Maybe. What did the beings on the ship look like?" he asked.

"They were tall, luminous beings with large heads and big eyes," she replied.

"Sound Sirian to me. You didn't recognize any of them?" he asked.

"I guess I did, sort of. They looked like some of the beings I saw at the Galactic Council meeting. But..."

"What?"

"Well, I mean, I know aliens exist, and that's fine, but I thought I was working more with angels and Mother Earth and Goddess divine energy stuff."

"So what's your question?"

"Well, how do they fit together? The one seems more like a sci-fi mission and the other a spiritual one. How are aliens supposed to help save Earth? I thought the Goddess and Mother Earth were saving themselves."

John was quiet for a while as he contemplated her question.

"What is it about the two subjects that feels like they don't mix for you?"

"Well, one sounds like a *Star Wars* movie and the other a Bible story."

John laughed. "I see what you mean." He took a sip of coffee. "So what if both are true? Can't there be angels and Mother Earth and divine God and Goddess energy, *and* extraterrestrials? You know now about your lifetimes on other planets, don't you? Think about what you heard when Nick did the remembering spell on you."

"Okay...but then, are you saying that angels are aliens?" she asked.

"No, angels are beings in their own separate category. What you're referring to as aliens are merely inhabitants of other planets. To them, we are aliens, which we are. *Alien* means literally that: a being hailing from elsewhere. Many of these beings have been assisting humanity for a very long time. So your dream makes perfect sense—well, except for the baby alien part." John laughed again, slapping his knee as if he just couldn't get over how funny the imagery was in his mind. His eyes were filled with tears.

"You know, I'm not even sure I want to know what that means!" he said.

Mia tried to overlook his mirth; she still had questions to which she needed answers.

"The name of the ship was the Solar Wind. Does that mean anything to you?"

John was quiet for a moment.

"Yes, actually, it does. Your dream makes a lot more sense to me now."

"How so?"

"We both know that spaceship quite well. Interesting that the Council decided to send you this dream now."

"Why? And you still haven't said what you think nursing the baby ET was about."

"Oh, it's probably more symbolic, like feminine nurturing is what saves the world—you know, the whole thing you got in your vision yesterday about knowing that you are Love and Love being the answer. And breasts are connected to the heart chakra. That whole thing."

John felt a little awkward talking to her about her breasts. Or *any* breasts, come to that.

"Breasts? What about breasts?" Nick asked, walking into the kitchen. "What did I miss?"

He saw that John was blushing.

"She'll tell you—I need to go check on the vortex boundary circle outside." John stood abruptly and headed out.

Mia told Nick about her dream as he poured himself a cup of coffee.

"Holy amazeballs, that's an awesome dream! Of course, my driving skills saved the day! But what the heck about the apocalypse? What did John say about that part?"

"Basically, that it's about the overall mission of us saving the planet versus there having to be an actual apocalypse, although it's what will probably happen if we don't succeed. I mean, I've seen lots of other visions of catastrophic natural disasters. Maybe Mother Earth doesn't know how much force She'll have to use to heal Herself."

"Interesting though, about the aliens being able to stop it. So that means there's some sort of alien technology that could heal Mother Earth? And all you had to do was ask and apologize?"

"No, that's not all I had to do! I had to nurse a baby alien—and it had teeth!"

Mia laughed, clutching her breasts as if protecting them.

"Yeah, for real! What's that about? What did John say?"

"He didn't really. He said it was probably symbolic, then got uncomfortable and left." Mia shrugged.

Nick chuckled. "Poor guy, I think he's been single for too long."

"What's his story? Has he ever been married? Does he have any kids?"

"I know there's at least one ex-wife and a few ex-girlfriends, but none that I've ever met. He doesn't say much about his personal life."

"What about you, Nick? Have you ever been married?"

"Hell no!" He laughed. "Just kidding. I mean, I haven't been married, but do plan on finding the right woman someday. Like you, I was confused about love and found myself in an unhealthy pattern. I decided to take a break until I could get clear about self-love."

"That seems smart. I think I'm going to be on a forever break after the chaos of my last relationship. Mother Earth will probably require me to take vows of celibacy so I don't jeopardize the mission!" Mia chuckled.

"I hate to disappoint you, sister, but I don't think any of us are going to get off that easy, including John. I think there are too many valuable lessons to learn from being in a relationship. And not only that, but I also believe you're going to have to find your man to complete this mission." Nick was watching for Mia's reaction.

"Why do I need a man when I've already got you and John around, and all the love of the Universe flowing through me?"

"Because all that kundalini energy you've got flowing through you is sexual energy, and I think you're going to need a man to help you ground it!" Nick laughed.

Mia furrowed her brow.

"I just can't imagine trusting someone again after what I went through," she said softly.

"You're going to attract a different kind of man now that you're learning about boundaries and self-love." Nick got up to hug Mia. "I'm sure Mother Earth has someone special in mind for you, someone who'll be grounded and connected to the earth, someone who has superpowers like yours and will be your equal. In other words, someone deserving of your trust and love."

"What are you two talking about now?" John interrupted, returning from checking the boundary circle.

"Oh, we're still talking about her nursing baby aliens," Nick proclaimed, laughing loudly as Mia swatted him playfully.

"She was saying that she's done with men, but I was telling her I still think there's one out there for her." Nick swatted her back.

"Ha! There sure is. I'd say he's about six-two with dark hair..."

John tilted his head as if seeing through the dimensions again.

"I'm definitely not ready for a relationship. Honestly, you two—I've got way more than I can handle going on in my life right now," Mia said.

"Normally, I'd agree with you," John replied. "Especially after your last relapse, I'd want you to be 'sober' for a while before re-engaging with the opposite sex, but the Goddess may not be able to wait that long."

"How does my love life affect the return of the Goddess? Isn't that a lot to ask?"

John replied, "I don't know that we need to get into all this right now."

He was regretting having rejoined the conversation, still worried about all they had done last night without the Council's approval.

He was also feeling unsure of how much he should be telling Mia about her mission.

"Well, if we're on an accelerated timeline, I would think it would be beneficial to bring me up to speed," Mia replied.

John shook his head.

"Can you at least tell me if he's human or alien?" she asked, trying to be funny.

John smiled. "Does it matter?"

"I guess not. I mean, a few days ago, it would have mattered, but knowing what I know now, I guess it doesn't," Mia answered. "Will he at least look human, though? You said six-foot-two and dark hair; that sounds human to me. Don't you agree?"

"Yeah, but he could be purple or green," Nick chimed in. "Maybe that's what the baby alien dream's all about."

They all laughed.

"Just stay open to the idea and trust that the Goddess will send you the right man at the right time," John said.

"How will I know, though?" Mia asked. "You're relying on me to recognize him?"

"I can tell you with absolute certainty that you won't miss meeting him. I mean, it won't just go by you that it's him. You're going to know it. So, until he shows up, don't worry about it, Mia. All you have to do right now is stay focused on the mission."

"What about my partner?" Nick asked. "Can I get some details too?"

"Oh Lord, now look what I did," John said, shaking his head as he walked out of the room.

As they gathered for dinner that evening, John informed them he had received further guidance from the Galactic Council during his meditation.

"Apparently, Mia's sped up the timeline again," John said.

"Huh? How did I do that and what does it even mean?" she asked.

"Remember the story I told you the other day, outside on the porch?"

Mia nodded.

"Well, since Earth fell from the fifth dimension to the third, the Divine Masculine hasn't been able to be on the planet. In order for humanity to experience itself as separate from the Divine, the Divine Masculine had to leave. Given the state of the collective, we weren't expecting Him to be able to return for quite a while, but due to the work we've been doing with Mia, He saw an opening and went for it. When He and the Goddess reconnected through Mia's body, the pure love vibration this created filled the room, giving Nick the turbo boost he needed to defeat all the demons he was battling, along with most of their affiliates."

Nick smiled and puffed out his chest.

"The Council said because of this, we should expect things to move into overdrive from here on out."

"Overdrive? Really? Is it even possible for things to speed up any faster?" asked Mia. "I don't know how much more my body can take."

"Yes, apparently the reunion of the Divine Masculine and Feminine, even for that one moment, created a whole new opportunity, an opening that we need to take advantage of so that we can accelerate their full reunion."

"Okay, so what's that going to look like? How long do I need to stay in the cloaking vortex? When can I move freely again?" she asked.

"A few weeks should be long enough for the entities to give up trying to figure out what happened. We all need to keep doing the breathwork daily, to keep our vibration high and our energy clear. Mia, you need to keep upgrading your nervous system to hold the new clear energy that will be flowing through you."

Mia nodded.

"The good news is, after that, we're all going to Hawaii!" John exclaimed.

"Really? That's cool. What for, though?" asked Nick.

"We're all due for some energetic upgrades. Then we'll be doing some deep healing separately. The women will participate in a priestess training and you and I will be working on healing the masculine wound."

"Tell us more about this priestess training," said Lori.

"I don't know any of the specifics, other than I'm not qualified to help you with it," John said.

"Thank God for that," replied Dominique. "And as far as I remember, men weren't even allowed in the temple of Isis. It's a very sacred teaching that can only be handed down through her priestesses."

"Priestesses of Isis? Are there really any left?" Lori asked.

"No, the information was lost thousands of years ago and has only been regained by channeling the goddesses," Dominique answered.

"I don't know that I trust channeled information; I mean, how do we know for certain who they are channeling?" Lori asked.

"Oh, I hear you," Dominique said. "I don't trust most of the information out there, which is why I always verify everything with the Council first. But since the Council is sending us directly to this woman, I'm actually really excited that we'll be going."

Mia's curiosity was piqued.

"I dreamed about the Temple of Isis the night after our firewalk. I was a priestess being prepared for a ceremony with Mother Mary and Mary Magdalena!" Mia's excitement grew. "Can you tell me more about all of this, Dominique?"

"Of course! In ancient Egypt, the priestesses devoted their lives to serving the Goddess Isis. They were trained in a form of sacred sexual alchemy that was incredibly healing."

"What is sacred sexual alchemy?" Mia asked.

"These priestesses carried a sacred healing energy in their yonis. They were powerful women who were highly respected and revered in their time and they knew their bodies were holy and weren't confused about sex the way humanity has been since the patriarchy took over.

"Men who were afraid of the power these priestesses carried began saying they were practicing prostitution, which was looked upon as a sin in their patriarchal view of the world. So, of course, the priestesses were persecuted, and their temples destroyed. The ones who survived carried the teachings underground, yet all was eventually lost."

"Well, except for tantra," Lori added.

"Tantra? Isn't that all about orgies and endless orgasms?" Mia asked.

"No. In its pure form, tantra is a spiritual practice using sexual energy to connect with the Divine. It is a form of sacred sexuality based on a heart connection. Over time, many of the teachings became distorted, so many practices have lost the true meaning of the ritual and are taught as being all about sex," Dominique shared.

"So do you think that's what we're going to learn in Hawaii? How to use sexual energy to connect with the Divine?" Mia's expression revealed her uncertainty around it all.

"I hope so!" Lori grinned.

Dominique laughed. "Mia, you do know that the energy that moves so strongly through you when you practice breathwork is sexual in nature, don't you? It's your kundalini."

"Uh, well, it is orgasmic sometimes, but I thought it was just life force energy, the energy of the Goddess."

"It is—and it's also sexual energy."

"I guess I'm just confused. What I feel when I breathe isn't what I think of as sexual energy. Sex between Richard and me was intense, and I became so addicted to it, it took over my ability to think rationally. I'd rather stay away from anything that can make me that powerless again."

Lori rested her hand on Mia's shoulder.

"I understand why you feel that way, Mia, but this will be something totally different. This will be a sacred teaching, an experience that I believe will give you back all your power."

"I've always gotten too much sexual attention from men. I don't want to do anything that's going to give me more sexual energy," Mia responded.

"Girl, that's because you've never owned your power!" Dominique said adamantly. "This experience will give that back to you.

You will be in charge of your sexual energy, and no one will be able to take it from you or abuse you with it."

They spent the next few weeks practicing breathwork sessions with one another while waiting to hear from the Galactic Council that it was safe for them to leave.

Mia's breathwork experiences evened out, meaning she was able to carry the energy flowing through her without too much difficulty. Initially, she had wondered if she was doing something wrong when she only felt tingly during the breath. But this was a good thing, John had explained, and a lot more was happening than she was aware of.

"Your body's being prepared to carry that new clear energy, so just enjoy the ease of your sessions right now," he reassured. "And if you're missing the intensity, I'm sure it'll change once we get to Hawaii."

"Okay. I do keep seeing this hurricane when I breathe though. I've also had a few dreams about a big storm coming. Do you think that means anything?"

"Hmm...I'm not sure but I'd definitely pay attention to anything that keeps showing up. Is there a feeling that goes along with the visions or in the dreams?"

"It's kind of confusing because there's a sense of danger and something really bad's about to happen, but at the same time, I also feel really peaceful and centered."

"Is the hurricane in the distance or are you in it? Is anyone with you?" John asked.

"It's always just me. Sometimes I see it approaching, and at other times, it's overhead. Sometimes it feels like I'm the hurricane, and at other times, I'm in the eye and it's all around."

"Okay, well, definitely keep asking for more information," John replied. "Remember what happened in the cave that day with the rain clouds. This is probably something you're going to have to help Mother Earth with. You've been getting messages about natural disasters for a while."

The night before they were scheduled to leave, Mia dreamt that she was on the plane headed to Maui. She was going to a mystical part of the island that only she could access.

She didn't have a place to stay, so she started to look for hotels online.

In the dream, a handsome young man sitting next to her told her that she could stay with him.

"I have a friend who owns a house with twenty bedrooms, and it's located at the entrance to the mystical part of the island."

"Wow, really? That's incredible," said Mia.

She felt so relieved at this fortunate turn of events. They landed and soon arrived at the grand estate.

"Are you hungry?" he asked next. "I'm going to order a pizza."

"Yes! Pizza sounds amazing," Mia replied.

Dialing the number, he was suddenly overcome with fear, unable to speak. He fell to the ground and curled up into a fetal position. When she went to help him, a golden light began to emanate from her vagina, and she instinctively knew that if she had sex with this man, all the fear would be released from his body. Then she woke up.

She told Dominique and Lori about the dream over breakfast.

"I told you, Mia!" Dominique said.

"You told me what?"

"That your kundalini was sexual energy."

"I love this dream for you!" Lori smiled.

"Why? What the heck does it mean? I don't want my super-power to be sexual alchemy!"

"Why not? That sounds fabulous to me!" Dominique teased.

"Seriously? You think it would be great to be obligated to have sex with everyone to heal them? To have a golden light coming out of your vagina?" Mia was incredulous.

Dominique laughed. "Yes! Absolutely!"

"Well, that part is probably symbolic," Lori assured.

"So it's not enough that I have to nurse baby aliens. Now I have to have sex with everyone?" Mia laughed.

"What's going on in here?" Nick walked into the kitchen, eyebrows raised. "What are you three laughing so hard about?"

"Oh, not much. Mia was just telling us how she's going to heal the planet with her golden yoni." Dominique tried her best to keep a straight face.

"What? You three...I don't know..." Nick shrugged.

Mia shook her head and Dominique started laughing again.

"I still think it's a beautiful dream," Lori said.

"I'm going to go finish packing," Mia said as she got up from the table.

"You're not going to fill me in?" Nick leaned against the counter.

"Lori can do that," Mia said, heading for the door. "I gotta go pack for our trip."

13

Aloha

———

Mia felt as though she was in heaven. Enjoying sliced pineapple, she stared out at the turquoise ocean as the waves washed up on the shore. They had arrived last week, but Mia was already feeling as if she'd been here forever. This place felt more like home than any place she had visited on the planet. It wasn't her first time on Maui, but those earlier trips had been about partying and having "fun." Her values and priorities had changed drastically over the past few months. She didn't need alcohol to have a good time; she could feel so much more with her breath. Her heart was full of gratitude and awe for the beauty before her.

She felt a deep peace anchored within her, lacking for nothing in this moment.

They'd managed to avert any trouble with the entity energies their last few weeks in Sedona.

"Ahh, it feels good to be here. I didn't realize how stressed I was until I got here and was able to relax," he said.

"It does feel great. Do you think the danger with the dark forces is over now?" Mia asked.

"I feel confident that Mother Earth will keep us safe on top of her volcanoes. Did you eat all the pineapple?" John teased. He sat down next to her, appreciating the shade of the lanai.

"There is so much pineapple!" she said, her mouth full as she smiled up. "Here—have a slice."

As he bit into the cool, fresh fruit, its juice ran down his hand.

"Wow, this may be the best pineapple I've ever tasted!"

"I know, me too," Mia said, picking up another slice.

"Hey, I want some!" Nick exclaimed.

"Don't worry, we have plenty," Lori said, walking out with another tray.

"None for me; it makes me break out, as does all this sunshine," said Dominique.

She applied another thick layer of sunscreen.

"I don't think there's any chance of the sun hitting your skin with that giant hat you're wearing, but maybe you should just go back inside," Nick replied.

"Oh, you're just still upset that you didn't get upgraded to first class with the rest of us," Dominique dismissed.

"Well, that was total bullshit," Nick said.

Mia was still so blissed out, their bickering didn't even register in her awareness.

"When do we get to start exploring?" Mia asked.

"We're going out today," John replied. "Our guide Bree will be here soon."

"Guide? What kind of guide? Who's this Bree person?" Nick asked, wrinkling his nose.

"Why do we need a guide?" Dominique added. "Can't we guide ourselves?"

"While it's nice to hear you two finally agreeing on something," John answered, "just relax. Bree's great, and you're going to love her. She's part of the team. Think of her as being from another division, yet still on the same mission. She's been living on the island a while and she's been developing relationships with the locations of the strongest activation points."

"Welcome to the island!" a cheerful voice called out.

Mia turned to see who the voice belonged to, finding herself surprised by a bright, genuine smile that radiated *Aloha*. A sparkle in the woman's eyes highlighted the pink plumeria behind her ear, and she looked every bit an islander in her yellow bikini top, multicolored sarong tied around her waist, and with several white *leis* adorning her arm.

"Aloha, everyone! I made leis for you all this morning. Maui's happy to have you here. Aloha." Bree walked to Mia and placed a lei over her head, then over Lori and Dominique's as well.

"Oh, wow! Thank you," Lori beamed. "They're beautiful!"

"They are made of *pikake* flower, reserved for honored guests," Bree shared. "I chose the traditional *kukui* nut for the guys. I was feeling you might be a little more conservative. Aloha!" Bree smiled as she placed a lei on Nick. "Now that I see your mohawk, I don't think conservative is the right word!"

"You must be Bree," John said.

"I am indeed! Are you John, fearless leader of this pack?"

"He is indeed. I, however, am Nicholas and I am charmed to make your acquaintance." Nick took Bree's hand, dipping into an elaborate bow.

"Oh Lord! Here we go again!" Dominique rolled her eyes.

"I am pleased to make your acquaintance, kind sir." Bree played along, holding out the edge of her sarong as she dipped into a curtsy.

"Thank you, Bree, for these magical leis," Mia said. "Their heavenly scent opens my heart."

"That's exactly what they are here to do. We're going to want everyone's heart chakras as open as possible, given the day the Goddess has planned for you."

"How do you mean?"

Given her experiences with the Goddess, Mia had developed a healthy attitude of caution.

"It's like stretching your muscles before going on a run: the wider your heart is open, the easier it'll be for the island energy to flow through you."

Mia took another big whiff of the pikake, feeling her heart expand.

"Bree, why don't you tell them about yourself and the work you've been doing here on the Islands?" John suggested.

"I'd be happy to, but we do need to get on the road soon to miss the traffic. How about I fill everyone in on the way?"

"Really? Traffic in Maui?" Nick asked.

"The road to Hana can get pretty backed up this time of year with all the tourists," Bree explained.

"Damn tourists," Nick grumbled.

"I think you'd better give Nick a pikake lei, Bree...His heart needs all the help it can get staying open." Dominique tried to place her lei around Nick's neck. "Here, you can have mine, grumpy..."

Nick ducked away. "Stay away from me, woman! I like my heart just the way it is."

They all laughed.

The road to Hana was a single-lane, winding road through the rainforest side of Maui. The scenery was spectacular, making the drive itself the destination. Dense, green forest opening into black

sand beaches and clear ocean waters, hillsides of rainbow euca-
lyptus or bamboo giving way to beaches of red sand, each turn
presented something new to admire.

Bree entertained them with stories of her adventures on the
island, pausing to comment on unique land aspects as they drove.
Nearly an hour flew by as they learned more about Hawaii, realizing how much they all had in common. Pulling off the curvy
road, Bree managed to squeeze the van into a tiny opening on the
roadside near a tourist-filled path.

"Well, this is disappointing. Did we get too late of a start? How
are we going to get any spiritual work done here with all these
people?" Nick wrinkled his nose.

"Stop being so negative, Nick," Dominique chided.

Bree giggled. "Fear not! This isn't our final destination. Just be
careful of the mud. This trail to the waterfall can get slippery."

They hiked back into the rainforest, climbing over large boul-
ders, under vines, and weaving through stands of bamboo.

"Ta-da!" Bree opened her arms toward a pristine waterfall;
there was no one else in sight.

"Oh, wow!" Mia turned in a circle to take it all in. "This place
is amazing."

"Hola, everyone! I'm Marco," came a rich, deep voice.

"Hopefully, he's the one from your dream who needs the healing," Dominique whispered to Mia as they looked in the voice's
direction.

"Oh shush!" Mia said, elbowing Dominique in the ribs.

"Oh good, you made it!" Bree waved Marco over. "Come meet
everyone. Marco only arrived in Maui a few weeks ago and hasn't
had a chance to visit all the activation sites yet. I thought it would
work well to have him come along."

"It's a great idea!" Dominique winked at Mia.

Marco was incredibly handsome, so much so that Mia could

barely look at him. And Dominique's teasing was making her uncomfortable.

Marco made his way around, greeting everyone. John and Nick each gave him a hug, saying they didn't do handshakes anymore, especially not with team members.

"In my country, we greet women with a kiss on the cheek. I know it is not the custom here, so I've learned to ask first," Marco said as he made his way toward the women.

"That sounds like a wonderful custom to me." Dominique laughed, looking at Mia as she accepted a kiss on her cheek from Marco.

"Me too," Lori agreed, enjoying the greeting.

When it was her turn, Mia smiled, willing herself to look at Marco. *What's wrong with me? Why am I acting like a silly schoolgirl? I'm here to embody the Goddess; surely I can act normal around a hot guy.* Mia inhaled. *What if he can hear my thoughts?*

Marco kissed her on the cheek before making his way over to Bree.

"*Hola, bellissima!*" he said as he gathered her in a giant hug, twirling her playfully.

She laughed.

The group settled down and stood in quiet awe, taking in the beauty of the waterfall.

The sky had been cloudy and misty on their drive, parting now to the bright sun. As sunlight shone through the falling water, tiny rainbows arched all around.

The wet rocks looked almost black, and the foliage around them was lush and wild. Vines and tropical flowers added sprinkles of vibrant color.

"Don't be shy, you can all go on in; the Goddess has been waiting for you," Bree encouraged.

Unable to wait a second longer, Mia set down her stuff,

stripped down to her bikini, and jumped in the water. It was cool against her skin, feeling so good after hiking through the humid forest. She giggled as she floated around, feeling very much like a mermaid.

The others began to ease their way in. John was moving the slowest.

As a triple Earth sign, he was far more comfortable on land than in water.

As the negative ions from the waterfall infused everyone, all stress and tension melted away. The waterfall cast Her spell, filling them with love and happiness.

Bree was delighted seeing the island work Her magic. No matter how many times she had seen it happen, it never got old. She was honored to serve as a guide to these islands, bringing to Her sacred healing spots those who had great work to do for Mother Earth.

Mia couldn't stop giggling. She felt as though there were bubbles of joy all around her and that everything was filled with magic.

"Damn, this place is fucking amazing!" Nick floated by Mia, grinning. "I didn't think any place could impress me the way Sedona does, but man, this is legit."

"I've never felt this happy in my life," Mia replied, still giggling.

Dominique and Lori swam over, both smiling ear to ear.

"I have no words to describe this feeling," Dominique said.

"I want to stay here forever," added Lori.

"*Que rico la agua!*" Marco exclaimed.

"You've done a great job with your team," Bree remarked to John.

She had joined him at the spot where he was leaning against smooth black stone rocks, comfortable in a pool of waist-high water.

They had a perfect view of the team splashing and playing, taking turns climbing up onto rocks on the bank and diving into the deep pool near the waterfall's cascade.

"Aww...I didn't do much. They just needed a bit of polishing," John replied humbly.

But Bree's clairvoyance had already shown her the transformation they had undergone in John's care. "You've done more than polish, John," Bree said. "They wouldn't be able to take in all this love from the waterfall if they hadn't released so many of the blocks around their hearts—and they may well be the most 'love-drunk' group I've ever seen."

John laughed. "Yeah, it looks like even Nick can't keep up his cynic act here. He's all heart, that guy, but doesn't like to admit it."

John closed his eyes as sunlight danced upon his face. Bree could see light codes streaming into him and knew he'd be receiving messages for a while.

"I can't believe you didn't tell me about this place sooner, Bree," Marco said.

She swam over to him.

"When was there time? We've been working nonstop since you got here!"

"I know, but still, *este lugar es increíble*! I haven't laughed and played like this since I was a young boy."

"I think we all feel that way!" Mia yelled, giggles taking her over again.

They all gathered closer so they could hear one another over the roar of the waterfall.

"Aside from the opportunity to swim in paradise, is there anything else we should be focusing on while we're here?" asked Dominique.

"Look behind the waterfall," Bree said, pointing as she swam in place. The five of them looked but couldn't see anything through the cascade.

"Is there a cave?" Nick's face lit up.

"Yes! It's a pretty special one, too," Bree answered.

"How do we get to it?" asked Nick.

"You can climb to the rocks behind the waterfall when the flow's lighter, but you won't be able to get there that way today. The other way in is by swimming under the waterfall, but you'll have to trust your intuition to guide you."

"So there's no easy secret way in?" asked Dominique.

"There might be, but I won't deny you the opportunity to figure it out on your own," Bree teased.

"Oh, I see how it is now." Nick pretended to feel rejected.

Bree swam over to the rock where she could relax and observe them.

They began searching for a way in.

Every time they'd get near the cascade, its force would push them under and soon they would pop up again, laughing. It was as though they were being blasted with a firehose full of love.

"Let's try going at it from an angle." Nick waved his arms in an exaggerated gesture to communicate above the roar of the water.

"Let's make an offering!" Mia yelled. Shielding her eyes against the sun, she looked up to the top of the falls. The rock ledge high above reminded her of the path she had walked in Sedona and the spirit guardian who had granted her passageway. "That's it! The waterfall will have a guardian! We just have to ask to be allowed behind the waters."

"*Buena idea!* Who has something to offer?" Marco asked.

Mia swam back to shore, grabbing an apple from her bag and gathering up the leis that Bree had made. She looked around for John to see if he wanted to join them.

She saw him looking settled on the smooth rocks nearby, deep in meditation.

Lori waved everyone over to a grouping of rocks off to the side of the waterfall, having discovered a flat stone perfect for their offerings.

Mia gave everyone an item to place as they said a prayer to Maui, asking for Her blessing to enter the secret cave. In an instant, Dominique received an image showing the way in. They would climb onto the rocks alongside the fall, hold hands, and jump in together to reach the still waters deep beneath the cascade. They could swim easily from there to the cave's opening.

"We've got it!" Nick yelled out to Bree. "Dominique saw the way in!"

"Way to go!" Bree called out, giving a big thumbs-up. She was pleased. This group was something else, and that had been a fast response from the Goddess.

They climbed up to the rock Dominique had seen in her vision.

Laughing, they joined hands, took a deep breath, and jumped. As they plunged into the water, it was as if someone was grabbing them by their feet, pulling them rapidly down.

They tightened their grip on each other's hands as a flash of fear passed through them, and then, just as quickly, they relaxed, finding an overwhelming feeling of love taking its place.

You are safe and protected, they heard loudly inside their minds. They broke the surface behind the waterfall into slanting sunlight that revealed the cave ahead. They looked at each other, excitement shining in their eyes as they took in the moment.

"We made it!" Dominique laughed.

"Wow, that was amazing," Lori exclaimed, giggling.

"Woohoo! Let's do this!" Nick enthused.

Mia and Marco looked at each other, laughing.

"What are we waiting for?" Marco grinned. "Vamos!"

As they swam into it, they realized the cave opened into another and another.

Once they were far enough from the sound of the rushing waterfall, they gathered long enough to decide to swim as far as the caves kept going. Swimming further in, they weren't sure where the light was coming from but could still see clearly, and it felt as though they were being directed to keep going, as if something were pulling them forward.

Reaching sections too narrow for swimming, they found holds in the rocks to climb through the damp, cool passageways into the next cavern, and the next.

Mia wasn't sure when it had begun, yet she realized that the light around them was now a misty green that she knew well. "Ah!" she sighed, feeling the sweetness of Mother Earth's energy all around. "Thank you, sweet Mother."

She turned in a circle in the water, her soft words moving into the mist.

As she breathed in the green light, she heard, *You'll now be able to breathe underwater.*

Perfect timing, Mia thought.

Their path ahead was a narrow tunnel below the water, offering no way through but to swim. The others hesitated, but Mia assured them it would be fine.

They swam down into the tunnel, the green light illuminating the way.

And as the voice had told them, they were able to breathe as they swam. The tunnel led them to a large underwater cave, the water here unlike anything Mia had ever experienced.

She felt as if being purified in its vibrant energy. It was also so crystal clear that Mia could see every detail of the cave around them. Looking down, she realized the green light was coming from below. As they swam toward it, they discovered that the cave was itself a cavernous tunnel leading downward. Magnetized by its presence, the group followed the green luminescence.

They traveled deeper and deeper through the waters.

As they swam into what seemed to be the depths of the earth, they unlocked the doors to their unconscious minds, soon seeing a hall of doorways with a human figure standing in each one.

Some of the figures were light, and others dark.

The light figures were the parts of themselves they had already accepted back into wholeness, and the dark figures were parts remaining wounded, lost, or rejected.

At the end of the tunnel was a lush green forest inside the Earth.

"Whoa, this place is amazing," said Nick. He turned around, taking it all in.

"My body's vibrating really intensely," Dominique said.

"Mine too," said Lori.

"Where are we?" asked Marco.

"In the heart of Mother Earth," replied Mia.

"Really?" asked Marco.

"Yes, I recognize it by the green mist. I've been here a few times."

"But I thought this was your first time at the waterfall," said Marco.

"It is—I've accessed Her heart through different locations before. The green light has always appeared to guide me."

Marco got down on his hands and knees, kissing the earth.

Mia smiled, loving the way he was acknowledging the sacredness of this place. Mia placed her palms to the ground to connect more deeply with the earth, the green mist surrounding their bodies like a blanket of love, filling Mia with awe and wonder.

Suddenly, Mia started coughing. Soon she was choking and felt as if she couldn't breathe.

"Are you okay?" Marco placed his hand on her back.

Mia was coughing too much to respond, black smoke pouring out of her lungs.

She doubled over as black shards of crystallized energy were violently expelled from her body, tears cascading down her cheeks as she painfully released these streams of darkness.

Marco patted her firmly on the back to help release the energy. As the last of the shards flew from her, her body relaxed, but the black smoke continued to bubble up from her throat. She tried to speak, yet the smoke filled her mouth, obscuring her voice.

You are releasing the control the patriarchy has had over you. All the beliefs you breathed into your body. Giving up your power in order to survive, the pain of being dominated, oppressed, and exploited. This social system crystallizes in the lungs to prevent women from ever finding their power, she heard the green mist say.

The lower vibrational energies fled Mia's body through any opening they could find, only to be instantly transmuted by the green light of unconditional love surrounding her.

Mia collapsed.

Sitting beside her, Marco caught her and gathered her into his lap. "Are you okay?" he asked.

"I am now. That was intense. Thank you for helping me."

She still seemed overwhelmed, breathless.

Mia looked up at the others, seeing Dominique twisting in pain, the green light wrapping around her body like tendrils or a knot of vipers.

She could see and hear what everyone was experiencing.

Now Dominique found herself at an Egyptian archeological site.

Someone needs to know what I went through; this trauma needs documenting.

She saw an image of scribes etching hieroglyphs into the stone, recording the suffering of humankind. Fear wanted the story to be told over and over; that was how fear could remain in control, its voice having long been embedded in the cells of her body.

I know what you went through; you don't have to hold onto the story, the mist assured her.

No, someone needs to know how much I suffered, she remonstrated. *They need to know what I went through, and I need others to know so that I won't feel so alone.*

Her many wounds were insistent, her body continuing to contort and writhe in pain.

I know what you went through because I was with you, and you were never alone. I never left you, even though you thought I did. You were never alone, and never will be.

The green mist flowed around Dominique's body, holding her in its light.

Dominique's spine arched, lifting her chest to the heavens.

She gasped, inhaling deeply as the green light flowed into her. The wound of separation that she was carrying deep within her cells was now bathed in the love of the Goddess. Every nook and cranny, every tiny spot where darkness had been hiding was saturated with light.

Mia was about to get up and go to her, but she noticed Lori had also collapsed, and she could feel her pain and hear her thoughts. Lori lay on the ground, the green energy swirling around her.

Your body is my temple; it is perfect as it is, she heard the light say. *My temples come in all shapes and sizes, and it is I who decide how big or small they will be.*

All the memories of the years she had been struggling with her eating disorder flashed before Lori's eyes like a movie reel replaying, but at the same time, her body was racked with pain.

Her body's agony was created by the demands of perfection society had forced upon women.

"I'm so sorry," Lori cried to herself, devastated to feel how deeply she had been rejecting herself over such a protracted period. "I am so, so sorry, please forgive me."

Tears streamed down her face as she realized how she had bought into society's distorted beliefs of physical perfection to try to get attention, approval, and love from others.

The green mist lifted off the wounds of the objectification of the female body. As Lori forgave herself, the deepest feelings of love and gratitude filled her. She was now recognizing and accepting the sacredness of her physical form, vowing to treat it as such.

The green mist swirled around Nick so rapidly that it lifted him off the ground, holding him floating, his body twisting and contorting as toxic energy was released from his cells.

He had spent years self-medicating with drugs and alcohol, and though he had managed to stay sober for a long time, there were still traces of those substances in his cells.

He felt as though he was being wrung out like a well-used washcloth as the blackness was expelled from his body, being replaced with the vivid green light.

It is safe for you to be vulnerable, the green light said to him. *You do not need to hide your tender heart from the world anymore; your vulnerability is what makes you beautiful and powerful, true strength coming from an open heart.*

When you fear nothing, then fear cannot affect you.

Nick's body arched 180 degrees as the green energy shot through the back of his heart, removing all his shields.

You'll have access to all your power with an undefended heart, said the green light.

Marco and Mia got up, walking in Nick's direction.

But Marco was only able to take a couple of steps when he was brought to his knees.

The Masculine needs to atone for the wounds done to the Feminine. The patriarchy has done so much damage, inflicted so much pain. It is not enough for the Feminine to rise up and claim Her power; the Masculine must rise up alongside Her, supporting Her.

Marco was devastated, feeling the immensity of the pain that women had suffered at the hands of men. His body slumped in shame as images of the atrocities flashed before his eyes. He let out a sob, tears rolling down his cheeks. *How could we have done this?*

How could we have failed to protect those who bring life to this planet?

The green mist engulfed Marco, purifying his body. It lifted his devastating heartache, but the burden of atonement still weighed heavy on his shoulders.

The green mist then enveloped all of them, and although they had each received a specific individual healing from the green light, they had also each been given the benefit of all that had been healed in all of them. The green light then filled their bodies, going to the spaces and places that the entity energy had once occupied, replacing it with the love of the Goddess.

Their bodies felt healed and light; every cell was filled with love.

They felt loved, nurtured, and supported. They started giggling and laughing, overcome with bliss, hugging one another and crying tears of joy.

Eventually, they perceived the impulse that it was time to get back, being guided to the portal of water that led them back to the base of the waterfall.

As they surfaced from it, they found Bree waiting for them.

"You all look different," she said to them, smiling.

"I feel different, not just emotionally, but physically and mentally as well," Mia said, her complexion as if glowing and radiant. "It's like there's more space inside me, yet I'm all filled up. My mind feels quieter too, as if there's a lot less to defend against."

"YES!" Nick interrupted. "Less to defend against; that's it! There's less fear inside me; I feel like I'm more present in my body."

"Yes, as if I've landed, as if more of me is here," Lori added.

"As if the past is over," added Dominique.

"What about you, Marco?" Bree asked as they all looked over at him.

"I've got a lot of work to do; we've caused a lot of damage." He knit his brow, his face pale.

"What do you mean, Marco?" Bree asked, looking a little deflated at how he had brought down the mood for them all.

"I'll tell you all later; I'm still trying to process it all."

The clouds rolled back in, covering up the sun.

Soon they were all feeling a little too cold to be in the water and they made their way back to the pool's edge, where John was just returning from his journey.

"Where have you been?" Nick asked. He noticed John still looked a little out of it.

"Solar Wind," John said, before splashing his face with the cool water in an attempt to get grounded. "I wasn't expecting the transmission, but as soon as the sun hit my eyes, I was gone."

"Anything new to report?" Nick asked.

"Yes, but we can talk about it later over lunch. Who else is hungry?"

"I am!" said everyone in unison.

"I've got the perfect place to take you," Bree said, leading the way back to the van. Marco had gotten a ride there from a friend, so he also had to squeeze into the van with them.

Sitting next to him, Mia asked, "Marco, are you okay? How do you feel?"

"*Si*. I'm okay," he responded quietly. "It was just a lot to take in, that's all. I felt the devastation the Masculine has inflicted on the Feminine and was told I have to atone for it," he said, looking down at his hands. "I feel as if I'm carrying this heavy burden. There was so much pain, it's unspeakable really..."

His voice trailed off as he turned away, staring out the window.

Mia looked so unsure. How could she tell him that she had seen and felt his pain? It felt as if he would be more uncomfortable if he knew how much she was aware of.

She sought the right words inside her mind, finally saying, "I had an experience once, one in which I felt the pain of all humanity," Mia said, hoping it didn't sound boastful as this was far from her intention. "It was brutal, but the breathwork was what shifted it for me. Did you not get filled with the bliss at the end when we were in the cave?"

"I did," he answered. "You're right, and I don't feel anywhere near the depth of pain I was feeling inside the waterfall, but I do feel the responsibility of this task, and have no idea how to do it. I've never actually experienced the breathwork; maybe you could teach me. Could you?"

"Yes. Well, you should get John to teach you because he's the master at it, not me."

Marco nodded.

Bree drove the group to a "locals only" spot that offered fresh organic juices, salads, spring rolls, and acai bowls. They filled their bellies with food that felt alive and nourishing as John told them all about the message from the Solar Wind.

"We need to fill up with as much life force energy from Mother

Earth as we can. Our capacity to hold light will increase while we're here, requiring us all to deal with whatever remaining shadow aspects we have. Things are going to be happening fast once we get back home. This is our time to train, expand, and nourish ourselves," John said.

"What things are going to be happening fast?" Mia asked.

"Earth changes. Getting the people and planet ready for the next dimension. Things are going to be speeding up. Originally, the Council thought those not vibrating at a high enough frequency could be left behind," John answered.

"Left where?" she asked.

"In the third dimension. But the Council voted against it. Now they believe if we can get just forty percent of the population reconnected to life's meaning, connecting to their hearts instead of the fear in their minds, it will be enough to shift the whole planet into the fifth dimension."

"What percentage is already reconnected?" asked Dominique.

"Twenty-seven percent," he replied.

"And how long do we have to accomplish this?"

"Twelve to twenty-four months."

"How are we supposed to get thirteen percent of the population to let go of fear that quickly?" Nick asked.

"That's around nine hundred million people!" said Marco.

"Mia knows how to release fear from the body," Dominique said, chuckling, unable to resist.

Mia gasped, elbowing Dominique in the ribs. "Shush!"

She glared at her, pretending to be offended.

Nick laughed, catching onto the reference of the golden vagina dream.

John, Marco, and Bree all looked confused as Dominique, Lori, and Nick kept laughing, and Mia was blushing top to toe, her face so flushed it felt as though she was burning up.

"Let's just say I think the priestess from the Temple of Isis is going to have the answers we need," Dominique offered.

"When do we meet the priestess?" Lori asked.

"The plan is that we'll go together to the sacred sites on Maui first, then split up for our separate initiations," John answered.

"And how long will that take?" Dominique asked.

"Until we get you all up to speed," Bree responded. "However long it takes us to get to all the sites. And however long it takes for your bodies to adapt. Judging from how quickly things happened today, I don't think it'll be too long."

"Exactly," John said. "It'll take as long as it needs to take."

"Have you done the priestess training, Bree?" Mia asked, hoping Bree could tell her what to expect.

"I haven't yet, but I'm super-excited to do it with you all," she replied.

"And what training will you men be doing while we go get our goddess on?" Dominique asked playfully.

"We're going to find the answer to Marco's mission," John replied.

Marco looked at him quizzically. "How do you already know? Oh, did you hear Mia and me talking in the van about breathwork?"

"Oh, he hears everything!" Mia replied.

They all laughed.

14

Haleakala

A few days later, the team was up before dawn, waiting for Bree and Marco to arrive.

Bree had sent a message the day before, saying she'd be picking them up to watch the sunrise at the top of Haleakala. She had warned them that the temperature at the top of the volcano would be below freezing, so they should come prepared.

Bree had been checking the weather forecast, waiting for a day with less cloud cover so that they could witness the sunrise ten thousand feet above sea level.

"Haleakala is the volcano forming most of Maui," Bree said. "The native Hawaiians consider it a sacred site. *Haleakala* means *House of the Sun.* Legend has it that the demigod Maui lassoed the sun to lengthen the island's daylight. Maui is the one who gave humans the secret of fire."

Bundled in blankets, in addition to the heavy jackets they were wearing, everyone followed Bree from the parking lot. Instead of having them watch the sunrise with all the other visitors waiting at the lookout point, Bree led them on a ten-minute hike to a more remote viewing area. There, they all sat close together on the crunchy black cinder cone ground.

"I suggest we all meditate and connect with the spirit of the land as we prepare to welcome the sun," said John.

As Mia sent her consciousness into the volcano, she felt the intensity of the energy, so expansive and fiery, unlike her experience grounding in other locations. There was raw power here. This aspect of Mother Earth felt fiercer; there wasn't the nurturing that Mia was used to.

The only words she could think of to describe it were, "Don't fuck with me."

She always approached Mother Earth with humility and reverence, but this time, she did so with a little bit of trepidation. She could feel the magma beneath Earth's crust to which this volcano had access, finding herself hesitating to connect completely.

Are you really going to keep me waiting? said the spirit of the volcano.

Uh, no, of course not; I just wasn't sure you wanted me here, Mia replied.

If I didn't want you here, you wouldn't be here. I know who you are, my child; I feel your reverence and humility. I know the pureness of your heart and the work you agreed to do for me.

With those words, Mia allowed herself, on an energetic level, to fall completely through the volcano, throwing herself into the fire, allowing herself to be consumed by it.

The volcano laughed with delight as Mia surrendered to the flames.

What am I here to learn? How may I be of service? Mia asked.

You're going to need me, replied the fire. *You are very comfortable with water, expanding and feeling everything around you. You like the safety and grounding of the earth, but you will need more fire if you are going to succeed.*

Okay, so what do I do?

Become one with the destructive power of fire.

Feel its ability to transform and consume everything with which it comes into contact. Find the fire within yourself, and don't be afraid to use it to transform the energies that would get in your way. Allow the fire to connect to your masculine side.

Mia felt the fire anchor into the right side of her body.

"Mia, the sun is rising," she heard Lori whisper as she nudged her.

Mia opened her eyes and saw the fire rising in the sky, the darkness all around her disappearing as the light spread over the horizon. The sea of clouds glistened as the sun's rays created iridescent rainbows on their soft, pillowy curves. Mia leaned into the sun, allowing the fire within her to ignite, feeling it coursing through her veins, suddenly growing extremely hot. She let the blanket she had wrapped around her drop to the ground. The sun beamed into her forehead, activating her third eye; swirls of color appeared, and her vision became blurry.

"Look through the dimensions." She heard John's voice behind her.

She didn't know what he meant, but said yes anyway. As she gave herself permission to see, her vision blurred and then came into a soft focus. Suddenly, she found herself in another reality, standing on the sand at the edge of a tropical jungle. Everything felt familiar, and she knew she was at home here. There was a feeling of great love, and a sense of someone there, a masculine presence; she looked around but couldn't see him, but she knew he was there regardless.

She felt him come up behind her and wrap his arms around her.

I'm here, he whispered in her ear.

His breath on her neck made her heart beat faster. She leaned back into him, feeling the electricity moving through her body. She turned to see his face, but all she could see were his eyes—big brown eyes that looked right into her soul.

"Aren't you cold?" Lori's voice brought her back as she felt her putting the blanket back up around her shoulders.

Mia couldn't speak. She turned to ask John who that was, and he just smiled back at her.

"Soon," was all he said.

"But why the sun?" she asked.

"Divine Masculine energy finding you, Momma Earth," he said, chuckling.

"Me, Momma Earth?" she asked.

"Yes, you've embodied quite a bit more of Her energy since we've been here. He'll be able to find you once you're done," John replied.

"Who is he?" Mia was hoping he'd keep answering her questions.

"You saw him. Who does your heart say he is? What was your relationship to him?" John answered.

"He was my husband, my lover, my friend, my strength, my home, my heart, my..." Her words trailed off as she felt their connection once again. Tears filled her eyes. "We've been apart for a long time."

"Yes, but that was your decision," John said more sharply than he had intended.

"It was? Why did I do that?" she asked.

"Well, I could say why I think you did it, but you can find your own answers inside of you."

Mia closed her eyes and connected to Sophia.

Because I wanted to be in my full power when he arrived this time, so that we wouldn't have to deal with the complexities of human relationships, she heard inside her head.

Mia looked at John. "I think that's a good reason. I mean, look at my track record so far; clearly, a love as sacred and pure as his is worth waiting for."

"I agree; I just didn't want you feeling sorry for yourself that he wasn't here yet, and to realize you wanted it this way. Knowing that will also make it easier for you to stay focused; embodying the Goddess is what brings him to you. I just wanted you to know he was coming, which as why I told you to look." John smiled, turning and walking over to Bree, preventing Mia from asking any more questions for now.

Bree led them farther down the trail through the black lava cinder cones to the crater floor. Mia felt as though she was on the surface of Mars; the topography was so unlike anything she had seen before.

Bree told them the crater was three thousand feet deep, seven and a half miles long, and two and a half miles wide. "It's big enough to hold the city of Manhattan," she added, giving them a broader perspective. "It rises ten thousand feet above sea level, but there are another 19,600 feet hidden under the ocean, making it taller than Mount Everest."

Bree winked at Marco, knowing he had climbed Mount Everest several years ago.

Marco laughed. "And yet so much easier to get to. Good to know I finally made it to the highest peak."

"Well, technically, you haven't. Mauna Kea on the Big Island is four thousand feet higher, measuring thirty-three thousand feet from the ocean floor. How high is Mount Everest? Twenty-nine thousand?"

"Yes, twenty-nine. I guess I'll have to visit Mauna Kea next then!" he said, and laughed.

Bree smiled and put her arm around him. It was the first time she'd heard him laugh since his experience in the waterfall.

Mia's body was buzzing with all the energy flowing through it as she walked across the top of the volcano. She thought about those big brown eyes, wondering when she would see them again.

Nick interrupted her thoughts as he caught up with her on the trail.

"Any messages you want to share from the volcano?" he asked.

"I'm supposed to become fierier and incinerate people who annoy me," she said, extending her arms in front of her, pretending that fire was emanating from her palms.

"Ha!" he laughed. "So you're turning into a dragon?"

"Maybe!" she said.

"I got the opposite message; I'm supposed to let the fire melt my heart all the way open and use it to ignite my passion for writing. Apparently, I'm supposed to write a book."

"Ugh, John told me a while ago that I should write one too," Mia sighed.

"Why the resistance?" he asked.

"I'm not a writer; I don't have the patience for it. It just feels hard and tedious," she answered.

Nick chuckled. "Well, did he say why you have to write it?"

"He said I promised Mother Earth I would write a story for Her children to help them understand Her or to raise their consciousness or something—which I know is a great honor, and of course, I'll do anything to serve Her; it just feels really freaking impossible," Mia answered.

Nick chuckled again, not used to hearing Mia swear.

"That reminds me," Mia continued, "I need to ask John what fire letters are. I did get that message today, or maybe I saw them. Yes, I saw letters with flames on them," Mia said.

"Fire letters? That's awesome!" Nick said excitedly. "I hope I get to use fire letters too!"

"Oh, so you know what they are?" she asked.

"Yes, they're letters that carry the vibration of spirit to the reader. This makes so much sense. Mia, do you get what this means? No wonder he told you that you have to write."

"Maybe...I don't know. So are you saying that when I write, the energy transmission will happen to whoever reads it?" she asked.

"Yes! This is how you're going to help raise the consciousness on the planet and get people up to speed. Girl, I mean Goddess, you better get your ass writing; the world needs to hear your story—Mother Earth's story!"

"But what if it's too weird and no one wants to read it?" Mia continued resisting.

"Fire letters, Mia. It doesn't matter what you write—the fire letters will do the work for you. Have you started writing it yet?

"Yes, I started keeping a journal when I met John, so I've been writing every day about my experiences."

"That's fantastic! Keep doing it. We can hold one another accountable and make sure that we're both writing our stories!"

Realizing they were all running low on water, the group decided to head back to the car. The thin air was making them all thirstier than they expected.

"I'm glad we're done up here. The altitude's really starting to affect me. The thin air made it difficult for me to hold back my ability to see through the dimensions, so half the time I don't know which reality I'm walking through. I have to be careful to stay under the radar in the other dimensions because my cloaking only works in this one," Dominique said.

"I'll keep you cloaked," Nick said, trying to throw his jacket over her head.

"I'm going to toss you into another dimension if you come any closer," Dominique warned him. She moved her arms like a ninja, making everyone laugh.

When they got back to the house, John extended an invitation to Bree and Marco.

"You've got to stay for my famous Southern breakfast. It'll help ground everyone after being on top of the world," John said, his southern accent becoming more pronounced.

"Do you need any help?" Nick asked.

"Nope, I got this. Why don't you all go jump in the ocean? It'll help you ground and wash off some of that fire energy."

Nick, Marco, Dominique, Mia, and Lori changed into their swimsuits and headed down to the beach. Bree stayed behind and watched John as he pulled out the bacon, eggs, potatoes, and butter and got to work.

"How are you able to still eat like this?" she asked.

John just smiled.

"I'm serious, I had to switch to a mainly organic vegan diet to be able to maintain a high enough frequency to hear the transmissions from the Council. How are you still able to hear the messages when you're eating like this?" she asked.

"Love. I focus on love and gratitude while I'm cooking. I remember all the love my mom used to put into my meals as a kid when she'd cook for us. I stay in a place of gratitude as I prepare the meal. The whole process becomes a sacred ritual for me, a prayer, a meditation.

"I stay conscious and focused throughout the whole experience, so when my body digests the food, I'm filled with love and gratitude. I believe those are the keys to living in a state of harmony." He placed the bacon in the frying pan.

"Wow, thank you for sharing that, that's beautiful. I'm going to be grateful for this new information and see if I can talk my body into trying a piece of bacon," she said with a big smile.

"Thank you for taking us to Haleakala this morning. How often do you go up there?" he asked.

"At least once a month during the full moon. I usually get a big download of information while I'm there."

The others made it down to the shore. As Mia dove into an ocean wave, she felt the energy in her body soften. She thought she heard a sizzling sound, similar to the way fire would sound when being put out by water. She sighed with relief as she came up for air.

She looked around, seeing Dominique and Lori still negotiating with the water temperature by slowly walking in. Nick, on the other hand, had swum way out and looked as if he'd be gone for a while based on his current speed.

"How was your meditation this morning on the volcano?" Marco asked.

"Really hot!" She laughed. "How was yours?"

"It was humbling. I felt the fire inside Earth burning away my ego, showing me the places I still try to exert my will. I was grateful when John suggested we get in the ocean. He seems like a great guy. How long have you known him?"

"He is a great guy! He's changed my life completely; I'm so lucky to have found him. We met just a few months ago, but I was 'all in' right off the bat. It's strange how quickly things can change; I can hardly remember whom I was before meeting him. As you said, so much has been burned away, healed, washed away, purified, and cleansed that it's like I'm a totally new person. Have you talked to him yet about doing the breathwork?"

"Not yet. I'll ask him today once I check with Bree about our schedule."

"I like Bree a lot. She has fun energy, a bright spirit."

"Yes, Bree's amazing, the most positive person I've ever met. And wise beyond her years. We always end up talking for hours."

"How did you meet? Did you know her before you came to Maui?"

"I feel as if I've always known her; definitely a past-life connection with that one. I've spent the last few years traveling around, going wherever I felt guided to go. I had a spiritual awakening a while back on Mount Everest and I've been on this quest ever since."

They were interrupted by Nick swimming back to shore just as Dominique and Lori had made it waist-deep into the ocean.

"The water's so warm; what's wrong with you two?" Nick said to them.

"It's just such a sharp contrast to the energy of Haleakala, my nervous system needed a minute to adjust," Dominique replied.

Just then, they heard Bree holler from the porch that breakfast was ready. Everyone came out of the water, dried off, and quickly headed up to the house.

"I can't do it," Bree was saying as they arrived. She was looking at a slice of bacon sitting on a plate on the table. "As good as it looks, I'm just not ready."

"Let me save you from it," Marco said, helping himself to the piece that was on her plate.

"Thank you for saving me." Bree adopted the "damsel in distress" pose, putting the back of her hand to her forehead and leaning dramatically, making everyone laugh.

"I'm at your service, my lady."

As everyone ate, Bree updated them on the messages she had received up on Haleakala.

"Our priestess training will start in a couple of weeks. It will be held on the Big Island."

"What about us? Did they tell you what the men need to be focusing on?" Nick asked.

"Yes, you'll be going out into the wilderness, disconnecting from civilization to reconnect with your truth. Sort of like a vision quest, but you'll have one another since your mission is the same. John will get more instructions for you."

John nodded. "Yes, I've already started getting visions of where we'll be going and what we'll be doing. I'll fill you guys in as I get more specific information. As for now, what I know is that we'll be backpacking deep into Mauna Kahalawai, the West Maui Mountains.

"Sounds awesome," Nick commented.

"Yes, it does," agreed Marco.

"Um...I'm just gonna say I'm glad our training doesn't involve going without indoor plumbing," said Dominique.

"Agreed!" chimed in Lori.

"Totally!" said Mia.

They all laughed.

"Hey John, I was wondering if you could teach me how to do the breathwork?" asked Marco.

"That's a great idea, but why don't we have Mia teach you since she's been training in how to facilitate sessions for people," replied John.

Mia looked surprised. "Do you really think I'm ready to hold space for someone who's never done the breathwork before?"

"Definitely, and I'll be nearby in case any questions come up," said John.

"Is that okay with you, Marco?" John asked.

"Of course, I'd initially asked Mia, but she suggested I do it with you first." Marco smiled at Mia. "I'm sure I'm in excellent hands."

"We can go for a walk and have a chat about what you want to focus on, giving our bodies some time to digest this amazing breakfast John made us," she said, smiling at John.

"Sounds good to me," John said. "Come find me after you get back from your walk and I'll supervise the session. I'm going to take a little nap in that hammock outside."

He got up from the table and headed toward the door.

Dominique and Bree decided to take a nap as well, and Nick and Lori volunteered to clean up the kitchen.

15

His Story

———

Marco and Mia headed back down to the beach and walked along the shore.

"Thank you for doing this," Marco said. "I hope I'm not keeping you from resting along with the others."

"I'm excited to do it; my only hesitation earlier was that I thought your experience with me as leader wouldn't be as good as if John were doing it. He's a powerful healer, but as he'll be in the room, I'll get him to help out if I need to. Also, since you're going into the wilderness with him, you'll get plenty of time to experience his magic."

"I'm happy it'll be you; I've been feeling a connection to you since we were in the waterfall together," he said, smiling.

The waves washed ashore, wetting their feet as they walked.

"So what's going on with you? How are you feeling?" she asked.

"I've been pretty stressed out for a while now."

"You don't seem stressed at all. Every time I've been around, you seem happy and relaxed."

"Well, usually, you see me after my run," he said, chuckling.

"So what are you stressed about? The mission?"

"Yes. I'm trying to figure out how to fix everything, and it seems impossible."

"Are you trying to figure it out with your head instead of your heart?"

Marco laughed, saying, "Yes, I'm definitely guilty of over-thinking it all."

"So it sounds like all we need to do is get you more in your heart than in your mind—which is perfect because that's what will automatically happen during the breathwork. So I'm already guaranteed to impress you as a healer," she said, laughing.

"I'm already impressed after that experience in the waterfall and then this morning on Haleakala. If anything, I'm intimidated by how powerful you are."

She smiled. "Can you tell me more about your life? Like how you ended up on Maui?"

"It's a very long story; how much time do we have?" he replied.

"We have all the time in the world!" she exclaimed. "Or wait, maybe we only have twelve to twenty-four months!"

Marco laughed. "My story begins when I was on top of the world."

"Oh, when you were on Mount Everest? I definitely want to hear this story! I can't even imagine how physically challenging that was to climb. What made you decide to do it?" Mia paused, realizing she needed to stop asking questions if she wanted to hear his answers.

"It was the hardest thing I've ever done both physically and mentally. I didn't know why I was going, I just felt called. No matter how I tried to talk myself out of doing it, something inside of me kept pushing me to go." He looked at Mia to see if she understood.

She nodded quietly, intent on not interrupting him.

"Halfway through the trip, I didn't think I could keep going. I was exhausted, my entire body hurt, and the low oxygen levels were making it hard to think clearly. I was questioning why I was there and wanted to give up. It was an overwhelming feeling of everything being too hard.

"I was thinking too much about other things, not fully concentrating and letting my mind drift off. Well, you can't do that when you're halfway up a mountain and maybe that's why so many people choose to take time out *by* climbing mountains...because you have to leave the everyday stuff behind. All your worries, everything...you have to let them go and just focus intensely.

"So I say all that now, but at the time I wasn't doing any of that. I wasn't watching where I was walking, and stepped on a chunk of ice that gave way, Before I knew it, I'd started to fall down the mountain, tumbling over and over, picking up pace. Suddenly, I heard a voice from nowhere say, 'turn your body and throw your rope back toward the trail; She will catch you.'

"The voice was so commanding that my body responded to the instructions without even thinking about it. I didn't even know which way was up, only able to see flashes of swirling white; everything was blurry and then my body stopped. One of the Sherpas pulled me back up onto the trail, brushed me off, scolded me sharply, and told me to keep going."

Mia looked at Marco with eyes wide, urging him to keep going.

"That night at base camp, I was lying in my cot and remembered the voice that had told me to throw the rope. It sounded like a woman's voice, but there weren't any women on the expedition. I didn't know if the voice had actually been spoken aloud, or was it in my head?

"Did I imagine it? Was I delirious from lack of oxygen?

"That night, I dreamt I fell off the cliff and was caught mid-air by an angel.

"She took me to a crystal pyramid structure inside of Mount Everest, setting me down on a bench carved from ice, telling me to await my orders."

Marco looked at Mia to see if she thought his story was getting too weird.

"I have strange dreams all the time," Mia assured him. "It's not unusual, is it?"

"Not unusual, no," he agreed, though his face showed there was more to this tale than just the kind of thing a regular dream might deliver. "But there were countless other beings there, all glowing and moving about without touching the ground. No one seemed to notice me.

"So I decided to get up and explore, realizing that everyone was communicating telepathically and if I focused, I could somehow hear their thoughts. Everyone seemed to be managing complex tasks with great care, each with different assignments, but the overall mission was the same: it was all about love and preserving life on Earth. There was a feeling of certain victory, yet their focus indicated that they couldn't slack off in any way.

"They said something about the return of the Goddess. Some of them entered from below the structure as if they had been deeper inside Earth, others entering from places that were above me, inside higher parts of the mountain, yet I could also see the sun behind them.

"Then the angel came back, saying, 'You were told to await orders. Your life has a significant purpose, and you agreed to do something in this lifetime to change the course of history, well, *herstory*, to be precise. And while you have the free will to do as you please, to experience and enjoy all aspects of life on Earth, we can't have you falling off a mountain, getting yourself killed. She is going to need you, and you promised you wouldn't fail Her this time.'

"I didn't understand what the angel was talking about, but my heart ached, especially when she said, 'Fail Her this time.'"

Marco put his hand on his chest, still feeling the heaviness inside him.

"I didn't even know whom 'She' was, but I was overwhelmed with a feeling of responsibility for Her. And then the angel said it was time for me to wake up! And I did, proceeding to lie in the cot replaying the dream, trying to understand what it meant and whom this woman was, to whom I'd promised not to fail? Why did the thought of failing her feel like a fate worse than death?"

Marco looked out toward the horizon, letting a long sigh escape.

His sadness was palpable to Mia; she realized he still didn't have the answer.

"That morning as we were getting ready, the Sherpa who had saved my life walked by and patted me on the back. 'No fall today. She will catch you,' he said.

"I asked him how he knew about Her catching me and whom She was. He told me She was the Mother of the World and was protecting me and had sent him to help me.

"He then touched the center of my chest and I felt this spinning sensation. Everything became blurry and I saw a swirling, green light coming up from the center of Earth, burning through my feet, legs, up my torso, and out the top of my head. It felt like a firehose blasting through me, cleansing and purifying me. The light reached the sun and then came back down as a golden violet ray, the light pouring through me like honey down to the center of Earth.

"I felt simultaneously anchored to Earth and connected to the heavens, seeing how all of life was connected by love, and love was life's fabric and all there is. I felt expanded in all directions, able to feel every heartbeat on the planet. I saw this love healing everything on the planet too, and my experience was so intense that I was sure everyone around had experienced what had just happened. I expected to open my eyes and be living in heaven on Earth."

Mia smiled, remembering how exquisite that feeling of love and connection to all of life felt.

"Then I realized I was really cold and was lying in the snow.

"I opened my eyes to see several people standing over me, asking if I was okay. They were worried I'd had a seizure or some neurological event, and I looked around for the Sherpa, but he was gone. No one there had seen us talking. They said the Sherpas had all left over an hour ago to get a head start to the next camp. I never saw him again.

"For most mountaineers, the peak experience of hiking Mount Everest was reaching the summit and surviving the physical challenge of the journey. But for me, it had to be the experience of awakening, comprising so many things: my conversation with the Sherpa; speaking with the Mother; being caught by an angel; being inside the mountain; having my chakras opened...

"I realized I couldn't share these stories with the people in my life; they would think I was crazy. But this experience ignited a fire inside me that would become the guiding light of my life. I became obsessed with research, trying to find as much information as I could, even traveling to meet with spiritual teachers around the world to see if anyone could explain to me what had happened. I realized my experience had been bigger than that of most of the people I met, so there was little they could offer me."

"Is that the only time She's spoken to you?" Mia asked.

"After spending years seeking gurus, I gave up, deciding to go visit my old college friend Juan Carlos, who'd invited me to go sailing around the Caribbean. After a few days of staring out at the turquoise water, feeling the warmth of the sun and the smell of the ocean, I felt at peace again. We went diving that morning and managed to catch a couple of lobsters we planned on having for dinner. We were anchored just offshore from a small unin-habited island.

"I decided to swim ashore and take a look around, hiking until I found a cool spot in the shade of a large tree. I was more tired from the morning dive than I realized, deciding to rest for a while. The island smelled so sweet, like jasmine blowing in the wind.

"I fell asleep, soon dreaming that I was searching for her on the island. Then the tree under which I was lying absorbed me into Her, making me become a part of it, traveling down into her roots. This feminine being appeared, and all I could see was her silhouette and a bright, golden light around her. She said, 'Why do you seek Her outside yourself? Why do you think others will have your answers? You already have everything you need; look within your heart.

"'Your heart is the only guide you need; it will show you your next step. Learn to love yourself as much as you want to love Her, expanding your capacity to love. Live your life in service to Her; your service to the Mother is what will bring you two together.

"'And only your heart knows what that looks like, not your mind.' Then she reached out and touched my head with her golden light. As she did, black, snake-like strands of energy re-leased from my mind. She announced, 'You see, that is the by-product of having such a strong intellect.

"'You are used to finding your answers with your mind, accli-matized to figuring things out. That will only ever slow you down. Like I said, only your heart knows the way.'

"I asked her what the snakes were, and She said, 'They have

many names, many shapes and forms. They are anti-life, anti-love; they are parasitic, feeding off of your life force energy.

"'They are also spies, which is why I got rid of them for you. They cannot know when the Goddess is returning; She must take them by surprise so that they can't interfere with Her return.

"'Since you will receive information regarding the Return, you must remain clear of them.

"'They will, however, be targeting you, so remain vigilant, letting your mind forever stay in service to your heart, trusting your heart and letting it lead the way.

"'The mind can carry out the instructions, but it cannot be the one to lead. Your mind is quick; learn to slow your thoughts. Use your breath as it will help you. Find yourself in it.'

"And then I woke up. As I swam back to the boat, I replayed the dream a few times, wanting to make sure I remembered every detail, wishing I could talk to Her all the time, and then I heard, 'I am always available.'

"I said, 'What? How? No, you're not always available, not at all. In fact, I've been trying to talk to you since Mount Everest, and this is the first time I've seen you since then.'

"She replied, 'You were trying to find me with your mind, and that's not where I exist. You hear me only in the moments when your heart is open and being in nature makes it easier. You have a good relationship with water, which is why you can hear me now.'

"I wanted to cry, feeling so relieved. I finally knew how to talk to her. Though I was longing to stay in the water and continue the conversation, there was a storm coming in and we needed to get on our way. I asked Her what I should do next. And 'Maui' was all I heard."

Mia was listening intently, awestruck and enraptured.

"Wow! what a beautiful, crazy story, and now you're here on

Maui, about to do the breathwork...about to find yourself in the breath!" Mia exclaimed. "Finding yourself, just like She said!"

"Whoa! I didn't even make that connection about finding myself in the breath!" Marco stated.

Mia asked, "Do you still feeling the heaviness from the message you got at the waterfall?"

"I'm not physically feeling it as much as I was then, but I still have this ache in my chest." He lifted his hand to his heart as he gazed down at the sand.

"If your heart could speak, what would it say?"

She was attempting to get him to tune in deeper to his body.

"There's a feeling of devastation, like my heart is broken at the awareness of what the Masculine has done to the Feminine. It's not personal; I mean, I know it's not mine. Yes, I had to unlearn a lot of incorrect beliefs I picked up growing up in a *machista* country. I know I'm not the one who inflicted the damage, yet there's an overwhelming feeling of responsibility that I've been chosen to make amends for it. On the one hand, it's an honor, and on the other, it seems impossible that anything I could do could ever make up for it."

Marco looked out toward the ocean again.

Mia stayed quiet, able to see the tears that had welled up in his eyes. She had already known he was a good man, but listening to his story and seeing how he was still struggling with this made her like him even more.

"When I think about my culture, my ancestors, my lineage," Marco said, "I feel responsible."

"Maybe that's the key," Mia offered softly.

"The key to what?"

"John taught me that as we heal the energy, beliefs, and trauma that we inherited from our ancestors, the healing expands through time, forward and backward—so that our ancestors don't have to reincarnate and learn the same lessons, and our children don't have to inherit the same beliefs or wounds."

"Hmm...but how?"

"I don't believe you have to figure anything out; I think you just have to allow the healing to happen through you. I believe your willingness is all that is required," Mia offered.

"My willingness to allow it?"

"Your willingness to feel it, witness it, acknowledge it, take responsibility for being the solution."

Marco looked away again as he reflected on what she was saying.

"Of course, I am willing; it just feels insurmountable, like the pain is too big." His eyes filled with tears again.

Mia placed her hand between his shoulder blades. She was surprised by the energy she felt coming out of her palm and flowing into him.

Marco's body relaxed as he allowed himself to receive the support she was offering.

"Thank you," he said. "You're good at this."

"Thank you for being willing to heal this for the collective."

He was quiet for a moment. "Do you really believe that we can heal things for everyone through our bodies? You truly accept it's possible?"

"I'd never heard of the concept before meeting John, but after his explanation, I do believe it."

"How did he say it works?" Marco asked.

"Well, first he told me about the 'hundredth monkey effect.' You know, the theory Japanese scientists came up with that after one hundred monkeys learned how to do something, then the rest of the monkeys just automatically knew how to do it because it existed now in their collective consciousness. He said that the souls that came here to help the planet evolve had the ability to create an opening in the grid of the conscious collective, so once we healed something, it would then be available for anyone else to heal it as well. So the way I see it is that as you allow this to heal through you, men all over the world will be able to choose to do the same."

"So it doesn't automatically happen; they have to choose it?"

"Hopefully, only a hundred monkeys—I mean men—have to choose it before it becomes automatic," she said, grinning widely.

He laughed. "Okay, so let's do this! This monkey is ready!"

Mia laughed. "Great, let's head back to the house."

16

Healing

Mia set up a yoga mat and blanket for Marco to lie on. She showed him how to do the two-part breathing.

"It's two breaths in, the first breath in your lower belly and the second in your upper chest, and then exhale. The breathing is all done through the mouth because you can get more air in that way. Plus, it'll help bypass your mind and connect you more to your body."

He lay down on the mat and did the breathing as Mia instructed. She placed a lavender-scented eye pillow over his eyes to help his mind relax.

John, who was sitting in the back of the room, had given Mia a set of the essential oil blends he had created to help the energy move during the breathwork. She placed a drop of each oil on Marco's body at the location of each chakra, turning on some Native American flute music to help fill the space as Marco breathed. She watched him initially struggle with the breath as he worked to quiet his mind, and after a few minutes, he seemed to find his rhythm with it.

When she felt as if it was the right time, she told him she was going to cover his mouth with a towel and that she wanted him to let out a loud yell from the depths of his soul.

"Release the frustration, the tension, the pain, and stress you're carrying in your body with the sound," she instructed. That allowed him to access the sadness around his heart.

Unable to hold back his emotions, he started to sob.

Mia leaned in, wanting to help him.

"Stay back, Mia, let him have his experience. Trust the breath to do all the work," John said softly.

Mia sat up straight and moved back a foot, staying focused on Marco, watching the breath move the energy in his body.

Her third eye opened up and she could see what was happening inside Marco's mind.

He fell into the darkness and felt the pain his ancestors had inflicted on the feminine, witnessing the masculine energy trying to control and dominate.

Reaching the core of the wound, he saw that there was fear, and that the masculine was terrified of being abandoned by the feminine. Without her, he couldn't survive; she was what gave him purpose, bringing to his world beauty and softness; without her, it would be meaningless, cold and gray and hard. During the fall from grace, when the Goddess had been forced underground, man thought She had left him.

The pain was so unbearable that he withdrew into his mind so he wouldn't have to feel it.

It was at this point that the entities gained access, encouraging men to close their hearts, to protect themselves, making women less valuable.

Being vulnerable made men weak; it was safer to be stronger

and more powerful. Women were dangerous because men needed them in order to feel as if life was worth living; they needed to take this power away from them to be safe.

Marco's mind was caught in this trap, his body filled with the fear that his ancestors had carried. His teeth started chattering as his body temperature dropped.

"Put another blanket on him, Mia," John instructed. "He's releasing the fear from his lineage, which is making his body really cold."

As Mia stood over Marco, preparing to lay another blanket over him, the memory of the golden vagina light dream flashed into her mind. Since he had tuned in to her, John saw the memory of the dream the moment it flashed into her mind.

He now understood what Dominique had been teasing her about for the last few weeks.

"Should I give you two some privacy?" he asked, chuckling.

Mia glared at him, realizing he had just read her mind.

Trying to ignore John, she sat back down to hold space for Marco.

But her mind wouldn't let go of the dream. It felt as though it was real, as though she could release all the fear from Marco's body and that it was bigger than the two of them.

She knew the fear he was experiencing was greater than him, that he was feeling the fear held in the masculine collective. Yet she couldn't quite put all the pieces together. The key was the golden light, but she didn't know how to access it.

"Allow the mystery to unravel," John whispered behind her. "All you need to do right now is hold space for him; the golden light's dreams and messages will be revealed as necessary."

Mia relaxed and asked Marco, "How's your body feeling?"

"I'm really cold," he replied.

"You're releasing old fear from your lineage; you're doing really well. Surrender everything to your breath," she encouraged, placing her hand upon his chest to help his heart chakra open.

As she did, a white light energy flowed from the palm of her hand into him the same way it had earlier on the beach. Marco's chest filled up with light, his body beginning to heat up.

The fear melted away and his heart chakra opened wider.

He was filled with love, compassion, and forgiveness as if he was being held in the arms of the Goddess and all that was broken was made whole. Mia removed her hand, knowing that Marco didn't need her help anymore since he was connected to his Source.

She told him he could breathe naturally now and allowed him to rest and bask in the love he was receiving from spirit. As she saw the light of his higher self beginning to merge with his body, Mia felt something really familiar. She knew this energy, this spirit; it felt like home somehow. She looked back at John to see if he would help her figure it out, but he had left the room. She hadn't experienced this when she'd held space for Lori, Dominique, or Nick. With them, she just saw the light come in, but there were no feelings involved.

She decided it must be because of what had happened inside of the waterfall. Maybe she would feel this way now when she held space for the others. *It must be the oneness of the fifth dimension. Wow, we're really doing this.* She wondered how much fear Marco had released for the collective. *I wonder what percentage is left now that remains to be healed?*

After resting for ten minutes, Marco started to stir.

"Wow, that was the most amazing experience of my life," he said.

Mia smiled, remembering her own first breathwork experience. "How's your body feeling now?"

"I'm vibrating and tingling all over, yet I also feel deeply relaxed.

I feel incredible! Thank you, Mia, you are such a powerful healer. When you touched my chest, my whole body filled with light."

"You did all the work, I just held space for you. You healed yourself with your breath."

"How did you know to touch my heart in that exact moment? Your timing was perfect; I had just gotten to the point where it was so dark I felt I couldn't go on for one more second, and then I felt your hand and, bam! Suddenly, I was filled with light."

Mia laughed at how dramatically he described the experience. "I guess I just got lucky." She had learned from John that remaining humble was the key to allowing spirit to flow through her.

Feeling a little more grounded, Marco sat up and looked into her eyes. "I could even feel her energy, as if I'm closer to finding her now."

"Who?"

"The woman I'm here to help."

"Oh, I thought you meant you were here to help the Goddess return. I didn't realize you needed to find an actual woman."

Marco sighed, tears filling his eyes.

"I've been searching for her for years. And during the breathwork, I could feel that she was so close. I don't care what you say. I only know that you, your energy, your gifts, made that experience more incredible than it would have been without you and I am very grateful."

Mia blushed.

"May I give you a hug?" he asked.

"Of course."

As he wrapped his arms around her, she was filled with that warm, familiar feeling again.

"Your energy feels like home to me, Mia. We definitely must have known each other in many other lifetimes."

"I feel it too. Maybe if we ask, we'll be shown those incarnations in the next breathwork."

Bree poked her head around the corner. "Are you ready to head home, Marco?"

"Yes," Marco said. "Thank you again, Mia; that session was incredible. I'm so happy we did this today." He helped Mia fold up the blankets and gave her another hug.

Then he headed out the door with Bree.

Mia grabbed her laptop and went outside on the lanai.

Just start typing, she heard Sophia say before she could ask herself what she should write about. Words appeared in her mind faster than she could type the letters, her day pouring out on the screen effortlessly. She recounted her experience in the waterfall and this morning on top of Haleakala. She wrote about her healing session with Marco, doing her best to describe how his energy felt to her. She lost track of time until Lori came out and set a plate of food next to her.

"John told us not to interrupt you, but I thought you might be getting hungry since the rest of us have already eaten dinner."

"John's back? Have I really been out here all day? That's amazing! It feels like it's just been a few hours." Mia smiled, feeling good about how much she had accomplished. "Thank you for bringing me dinner!" She ate a few bites and then went back to typing.

The energy moving through her body made her feel energized.

She wasn't sore or tired, so just kept going. It was two a.m. when she finally decided that was enough for one day, falling asleep as soon as her head hit the pillow, waking the next morning to the sound of the birds singing. She got something to eat and then went back outside to write. The others were going snorkeling, but she had decided to stay and keep working on her story.

A storm blew in the next day, preventing them from going on any of the other outings Bree had planned, so Mia was able to keep going. Nick joined her and started working on his story as well. Lori and Dominique went to the spa, the movies, and read books to occupy the time.

By the time the weather cleared, Mia was ready for a break.

"I'm hungry and ready to go somewhere," she announced at breakfast.

"Good! 'Cause we have plans today. Bree and Marco should be here soon, so get something to eat and grab your swimsuit. Bring a towel too," John replied.

Bree and Marco arrived shortly and they all headed off to Iao Valley.

"This is my favorite place on the island," Bree said.

"Really? What makes it so special?" asked Dominique.

"The energy here feels really different to me than on the other places of the island. *Iao* means *cloud supreme*. It gets the most rain on the island, so the water in the stream is really fresh and pure. I feel as though I can access the different dimensions really easily when I'm here."

Dominique turned to John and said, "I'm going to need some help staying here or staying cloaked if this place is anything like the top of Haleakala. That was *no bueno* for me up there."

"My sense is that you'll be able to control it easier down here; it won't be as disorienting as it was in the high elevation. But just in case, grab a couple of rocks from the stream and hold onto them while we're here. Ask them to keep you grounded and safe. Remember, you don't have to do this all alone anymore, we're all here for you," John said, touching her shoulder.

"You're going to make me cry." Dominique wiped a tear from her cheek.

Bree looked confused, unsure what was happening in the row of seats behind her. Nick, sitting up front with her, explained that Dominique had been in hiding, that she was the queen of a Universe, but that there were inter-dimensional beings looking for her.

She had been hiding on Earth but had felt alone and isolated for most of her life.

"I thought you didn't believe I was a queen." Dominique was surprised by how Nick had explained her story to Bree.

"I'm a big softie now that I got my heart shields removed in the waterfall, so I don't have to be an asshole to you anymore. There's just no need to behave that way."

"That's going to make me cry even more." She looked for a tissue in her purse.

He reached back to pat Dominique on the leg. "Don't worry, sister; I've got your back."

Dominique let out a sob as Nick's words reached through the shields around her heart.

Bree parked the van and they all headed straight to the stream.

"I can't believe our luck!" Bree exclaimed. "It averages an inch of rain a day here, it's always cloudy, and yet today, the sun is shining! We are so blessed. This stream is fresh rainwater, so as you get in, allow it to connect you to the Cloud Beings and the Sky People."

They all climbed down the large rocks and into the stream. Marco helped Dominique and Mia navigate the slippery stones. As they settled at the edge of the stream, they instantly felt why this was Bree's favorite place on the island. The water here was soft and gentle, soothing and cleansing in a different way than the waterfalls had been.

"Splash your third eye one hundred times with the cold water to activate it," Bree suggested.

John laughed, saying, "I better not or I may never get it to close down again."

"I think I'll pass on that one, too," Dominique said.

"I'm in," said Nick.

"Me too," said Lori and Mia.

Bree asked Marco, Dominique, and John to help "float" the others once they were done splashing themselves.

"Once they're done, you'll support them in the water and let them expand into their experience."

The water felt ice cold at first as Mia splashed her face as quickly as she could. She laughed, then realized she'd better keep her mouth closed or she'd end up drinking the water.

Eventually, her face felt numb, and she continued to splash the cold water.

When she reached one hundred, she closed her eyes and lay back in the water as John floated her in the stream. He wondered what else she was ready to receive today, and being this close to her, he'd be able to see whatever she saw.

Mia felt her body dissolve into the water, becoming one with the stream as it traveled along the earth. She connected to all the life that depended upon this stream, eventually traveling up the stream and meeting the Cloud Beings, different from the Water Beings she had met earlier but very much connected to them. The best way she could describe it was that they were the elders, the ancestors of the Water Beings, the ones who held the power of where to put the water.

They got to decide the consistency of the water, be it light mist, heavy rain, hail, or snow. They could get close to Mother Earth when they wanted to or go up as high as sixty thousand feet. They welcomed Mia as they felt her approach.

Nice to see you again, Mia, came the message.

Again? asked Mia. *Have I been here before?*

Technically, no, but we were referring to our interaction in the cave in Sedona.

Wait, that was you? Mia wanted to know. *You are all the same clouds?* She said it while thinking that was probably a dumb question.

We are omnipotent Beings, so we know all things, and we definitely remember someone when they figure out how to summon us.

That was one of the coolest moments of my life. Thank you for making it rain when I asked you to. She recognized that it was a gift that they agreed to give and not anything special about her.

You're right that we agreed to make it rain, but we did so because you are special—not in a "more valuable than other people" kind of way, but in a "you are going to need to know how to access us to complete your mission" sort of way, they replied.

Seems like everyone knows about the mission these days, Mia said, and laughed.

We are grateful you are finally here. We see so much from our perspective up here. We try and nourish all of life the best we can, but the energy has gotten so polarized on the planet, there are areas we can't reach as regularly as we want to, and areas we can't leave that don't need us.

Sometimes, the Goddess needs us to wash out a large area to help her remain in balance. This has been happening more and more frequently; we need someone to help the humans wake up so that they can realize what they are doing to Mother Earth. It's not just the pollution; yes, that's bad and needs to improve—but mainly, it's their toxic emotions, their anger and judgments, the way they hurt one another, the unconscious behavior that disrupts the balance on the planet.

Someone needs to teach them how to feel their feelings, how to release them instead of numbing them; they need to realize that they are not victims.

The clouds went on explaining what humankind was doing to keep the planet out of harmony.

Mia knew that the "someone" they kept referring to was her—

and her other team members, as well as the others out there doing the same work. Everywhere she went, the Goddess was speaking to her, asking for her help. And Mia wasn't shying away anymore.

She was all in and ready to do whatever she could, feeling good that she had gotten a lot of writing done this week and excited to share it with the world.

We have a surprise for you! Mother Earth wants to thank you for all the progress you've made, for how dedicated you are to Her, and for writing Her story.

She's very pleased with all the writing you did this week.

Mia exclaimed, *Really? I mean, I believe you, but was just doing what I promised to do, and up until this week all I was doing was complaining about it, so I would think Mother Earth would be like "Finally! I can't believe she actually got it done!"*

The clouds laughed, making the sky rumble.

Writing is a spiritual practice, and spending time doing something that will end up helping others will bring a lot of blessings into your life.

Thank you, I am humbled and grateful for the blessings of Mother Earth, Mia replied, bowing her head. Suddenly, she was filled with rainbow light.

A rainbow had arched across the sky, passing right through her.

We bring the blessings from heaven to Earth, she heard the light say as it caught her consciousness.

I'm inside a rainbow! she exclaimed with delight.

In all the journeys in which she had participated, she had never become the light, or at least all the colors at once. She wasn't certain, but all she knew was that in this moment, this was absolutely amazing, experiencing the colors individually and collectively at the same time.

There was a sound inside each color, a harmonic symphony

that she felt vibrate through her being. The colors moved inside her, balancing her energy and she felt herself entering a great state of peace. The colors went where they were needed to heal her.

Once that was complete, the rainbow was able to communicate with her, although it was a strange form of communication, devoid of words, being simply a knowing and a feeling.

She felt loved and protected and that she was being reassured this would turn out okay. She felt as though she was being blessed by the rainbow, calibrated to be able to hold its energy. She saw prisms and angles, light being bent inside the density of the water.

John watched with interest as Mia's body started glowing.

At first, he thought something was causing her chakras to shine brighter, but then he recognized the vibrant hues of the rainbow. Looking up, he saw the rainbow in the sky.

He heard Mia say, *John, I am inside it*, followed by seven clicks as the colors connected to her chakras. She was locking in the seven rays, or rather they were locking into her.

To his knowledge, no one had ever fully embodied the rainbow.

Many beings had embodied certain colors, but he hadn't heard of anyone possessing all seven. He tried to tune in to see if he could access more information about what was happening, but he wasn't getting much. He tried to speculate. What would the end result be?

He asked, *Mia, what will you be able to do with this upgrade?*

Mia said, *The Rainbow Beings are saying that the Goddess wanted this done. What happened inside the waterfall and the deeper connection with the fire made this possible. I'm not only embodying the elements, but I apparently also have the ability to refract and reflect the light.*

John replied, *This could be really handy! I wonder if you'll be able to emit a rainbow ray and blast people with it? What do you think?*

That would be awesome! I don't fully understand everything, voiced Mia. *I'm embodying the water/ice in my feminine left side and the fire in my masculine right side, and will have the ability to refract the light through the water and reflect it back, something about being able to influence what people see or change the energy that's sent toward me, returning it as a blessing.*

I bet that's it! exclaimed John. *I bet you're going to be able to convert any energy that comes at you that isn't love, into love. That would wipe out the entities completely, rendering them useless. Not only would they be neutralized, but they would also be converted into forces of good.*

Yes! This will make victory possible, John said excitedly.

Mia responded, *They're saying something about a hurricane...*

Mia's body started to convulse in the water and John almost lost hold of her.

Marco looked over to see what was happening. "Do you need help?" he asked John.

"I'm not sure; it's hard because the water's so shallow; she'll collide with the rocks any second now. I'm trying to keep her face above the water so she doesn't swallow any and choke."

"There's a pool a few feet deeper just on the other side of this boulder. Can you float or carry her over there?" Bree suggested. "Is that possible?"

"I don't think I can carry her by myself because she'll probably knock me out or flop right out of my arms. Let me see if I can lead her by holding her head and keep her from breaking anything by smashing it into a rock." He looked at how deep and wide the stream was, from where he stood to where the deeper water lay. "Honestly, I just don't think I can do it alone."

"Bree, you take over supporting Nick and I'll help John," said Marco.

Bree traded places with Marco as he quickly made his way over to help John with Mia. Her arms were hitting the water by now, her legs kicking into the rocks of the shallow water.

John instructed, "Marco, if you can grab both of her legs, I'll keep one hand under her head and grab her left arm; then we can maneuver her to the deeper water. Let's just grab her and go and do it as quickly as we can; she's already going to have several bruises, so I'd just like to avoid anything worse." He caught Mia's arm as it was about to hit him in the face. "And avoid any injuries to us as well!" He guided her contorting body down the stream.

The two of them were successful in moving her to the deeper water with only a few scrapes.

Mia felt as though she was going to explode, the rainbow's intensity too much for her to handle. The angle to the light bending through her was something her body couldn't tolerate.

Eventually, the pain got to be too much, and she lost consciousness, allowing her body to fully surrender to the process. Her connection to Sophia was interrupted.

The Rainbow Beings had to work quickly, or things could go very wrong.

Normally, detaching a human from their higher self would result in the death of the physical body, but hers was being kept alive by the influx of life force energy the rainbow had initially given her on entering her body. The risk was too high that her body wouldn't make it, but the Goddess was keeping death at bay.

The fire inside her from the volcano was creating a shield around her, keeping her essence cloaked while the crystal aperture emanating her light into her body was recalibrated.

Mia thrashed around for another twenty minutes until the Cloud Beings covered the sun, ending the rainbow. John and Marco carried her out of the water, gently laying her on a boulder still warm from the sun. John put a towel over her, sitting at the edge of the stream.

Marco stayed next to Mia, waiting for her to regain consciousness. But why didn't John seem more worried about her? It was something Marco couldn't comprehend at all.

Nick and Lori had come back from their float by this time, and, given Mia's track record, they weren't surprised to find that she had been "taken out" by the experience.

"She's probably going to be out for a while, so do you guys want to go explore while we sit here with her, or should I carry her to the car and head home?" John asked the group.

"There's something I need to go look at by the Iao needle," Lori replied.

"Me too," said Nick.

"All right, well then, go do that and swing by again when you're done. We'll wait here as long as it doesn't start raining too hard."

He was looking up at the dark clouds moving in above the mountain.

Marco was surprised that no one seemed concerned about Mia or thought she might need medical attention. He folded his towel and put it under her head, to make her more comfortable.

"What was your message?" Lori asked Nick as they walked up the path toward the needle.

"To accompany you."

"Aww, that's sweet," she said. "What was your message?"

"I was told that there was something here for me to see."

They stood and took in the twelve-hundred-foot volcanic formation covered in green foliage. The clouds were coming down the mountain, filling the valley with mist.

Lori stared into the clouds, awaiting her message. Nick stared for a while too, but then got distracted by the tourists behind them.

"I just realized why I'm here. I need to shield you from the tourists until you get your message."

"How are you going to do that? This is a public place. Maybe we should just go."

"Just because your gifts aren't as pronounced as those of the rest of us doesn't mean you don't have the right to be here and take up space. You don't have to prove your value to any of us. We all see it very clearly. And it's not because you always keep us fed; your gift is way more than being of service to us," Nick said emphatically.

"Thank you, Nick, but they have a right to be here too. I don't want them to get upset."

"Let me do my job and put my prickly personality to work. I've mastered the art of being an asshole as you well know. And this vanilla group of Minnesota tourists is no match for me."

Lori giggled.

"Are you fucking kidding me?" Nick yelled. He pretended to be looking at a message on his phone. "No fucking way!" he said even louder. "Goddamn motherfucker!"

Now he was waving his arms in the air.

And sure enough, the group turned and left, leaving Nick and Lori all alone.

"I love you," Lori giggled.

"I know, I fucking love you, too," Nick replied. "I'm going to stand in the walkway and cuss some more to keep any other looky-loos away."

Lori stared into the clouds again and fell into a trance, words softly beginning to flow out of her. "I see patterns starting to form. The clouds have no real substance, yet they can cover everything from view. They don't have to be solid or dense like

Earth; they can float and roll wherever they want to be. Even though they are 'soft,' they are very effective.

"They are like me, in fact. My gifts are not as obvious as the others, yet I am able to accomplish just as much. Because I am so light, my energy touches everyone, allowing me to help the group in so many ways. Dominique and Nick's energies could clash with one another, but my energy provides a buffer. The nurturing I provide to everyone creates a field of love that holds the group together. Physically, they wouldn't survive without me, too caught up in the other dimensions to remember to take care of their bodies. My role is vital. My heart opens wider as I acknowledge myself and my contribution. I am enough, and I claim my right to be here!"

Thunder echoed in the sky.

"*Aho!*" exclaimed Nick.

"*Aho Mitakuye Oyasin!*" Lori cried out. "To all my relations, I give thanks for all of creation!"

The clouds opened up, sending rain pouring from the sky.

Lori and Nick laughed as they hurried back down the path, running into Bree and John on their way back to the car. Marco was carrying Mia, who was still unconscious.

"Looks like you two were successful," Bree said, noticing their big smiles.

"Just a little claiming and cussing was all that was needed," replied Nick.

"What?" asked Bree, confused by his response.

Lori laughed. "Just ignore him. He created some privacy for me so I could understand my deeper purpose as a part of our community."

"Mmm. Sounds lovely," Bree smiled.

"Is she going to be okay?" Marco asked John. He put Mia in the back row of the van.

"I hope so! She's our secret weapon; it'd be bad if she was out of commission before we even got started!" he joked.

Marco looked confused.

"This happens to her a lot," John explained.

"She does lose consciousness a lot. Glad I'm not the secret weapon! Seems like a tough job," Dominique commented.

"What do you mean by 'secret weapon?'" asked Marco.

"Hasn't Mia told you who she is?" Nick asked.

Marco looked confused. Evidently, Mia had not told him at all!

"What do you mean? Who is she?"

"She's here to save the—"

John cut Nick off before he could finish his sentence. "She's a valuable member of our team is all, and we don't need to be talking about this out in public," John said in a hushed voice.

He was glaring at Nick.

"Oh, uh, right, yeah, let's load up and get out of the rain," Nick said.

Lori filled everyone in on her experience and the revelations she had received. She added, "Nick, you did an excellent job scaring off the tourists!"

When they got to the house, Marco dashed forward to assist Mia, but both John and Nick piped up in unison, "It's all right. We can get her inside on our own."

"No, I'll carry her," insisted Marco.

While they waited for Marco to return to the van, Bree told John to reach out to her when Mia was back online.

"Hopefully, she'll be feeling better in time for our priestess training," said Bree.

"I'm sure Mother Earth will make sure she's feeling better by then," said John.

"My understanding is that you guys will join us after your vision quest so we can swim with the dolphins in Kona," Bree stated.

"Yes, I got the message about swimming with the dolphins. Thanks for all your help with everything," he replied.

"Of course! This past month with you guys has been amazing. I can feel all the upgrades and blessings my body has been absorbing just holding space for you all."

"Keep us updated on how she's doing. I'm really worried about her," Marco said to John as he came back outside.

John placed his hand on Marco's shoulder. "I promise you she's going to be just fine. If she were in any sort of danger, you know I'd be the first one to take her to the hospital."

Marco relaxed a little, hearing the sincerity in John's voice.

Mia was unconscious for three days, and by that time, a distressed Lori was now starting to wonder if they should take her to the hospital, but every time John checked in, he was told she would be fine and to just let her body keep processing the upgrades.

He placed his trust in that advice.

Mia did come around, of course, but she was confused when she finally woke up because for her, time had stood still. She was shocked to find that three whole days had gone by. She felt okay, just a little weak. Lori cut up a fresh pineapple, setting it in front of her at the kitchen table.

"What do you remember?" John asked.

"I remember being in the water, talking to the Cloud Beings. They said I would receive a blessing for my role in helping Mother Earth. Then I found myself inside a rainbow. Weren't you there with me, John? I seem to recall that you were."

"Not actually with you, no, but I was communicating with you while you were in there."

"Ah, okay, that makes sense. At first, it was magical, then they warned me that it was going to hurt but that I would be safe. And that was it; then I woke up here. I feel different though, as though this isn't my body, even though it looks the same. I don't know; it's hard to describe, like I'm occupying my body differently. Do I look different?" she asked.

"Yes!" They all answered in unison, making her laugh.

"How so?" she asked.

"You look taller, like you're occupying more space although you do look really thin from not eating for three days," Lori said.

"Your energy feels different, but different in a way that's more completely you. Does that make sense? Like you're not watered down anymore, just full-strength Mia," Dominique said.

"Yes," Nick said. "You're SOOO MIA!"

"Look me in the eye. Let me see if Sophia's all the way in there," John said.

Mia looked at him.

"You're not fully merged yet," John replied.

"Merged with what, or with whom?" she asked.

"That must be why we have to go see the dolphins," John said, more to himself than the others.

"I'm merging with a dolphin?" Mia asked, looking concerned.

"Like a mermaid, you mean?" asked Lori.

John laughed. "No, Mia's merging with her higher self, with Sophia," he answered Lori. Then he turned to look at Mia, smiling at her. "But right now, Mia, it still feels like there are two of you in there. The dolphins will be able to use their sonar to help you integrate with one another. Don't worry, it's a good thing, a really good thing."

Mia smiled, asking, "So when do we leave for Kona?"

John laughed. "I'll let Bree know you're back and eager to go."

17

The Priestess of Isis

_____

Mia was surprised at how different the Big Island looked compared to Maui.

Miles and miles of black lava made her feel as though she was on a different planet again. The energy feeling so unique and unusual here. While Maui had felt soft and juicy to her, the Big Island felt primal and fierce. It still felt magical and amazing too, but there was a rawness to the island that she'd never experienced anywhere before. The land around the airport had been so barren, she was delighted to observe that it became lusher the farther they traveled south.

They drove past Kona to the temple where they'd be meeting the priestess.

Bree, Dominique, and Lori were chatting away, seemingly excited and eager to get there. Mia still had mixed feelings; she knew it was divinely orchestrated and guaranteed to have a beneficial outcome, but she just couldn't completely wrap her mind around it. She'd spent decades being confused by sexual attention and as far as she could tell, her sexuality had only ever gotten her into trouble. She had experienced the energy of the Goddess running though her and knew how powerful it was; she just didn't experience it as sexual energy.

"Don't you agree, Mia?" she heard Dominique say.

"Huh? Sorry, I wasn't listening. What did you ask me?" Mia responded.

"Where are you?" Dominique asked.

"I'm still wondering about where we're heading and what will be involved with this initiation," she admitted.

"Are you worried there will be group self-pleasuring sessions?" Dominique said, continuing to tease her.

"Ugh," Mia groaned, wrinkling her nose. "No, not that! I just need the initiation to feel sacred and not creepy."

"It will be, Mia, I promise," Lori reassured her. "The Council wouldn't have sent us here if it wasn't in complete alignment with our mission. You know that's true, don't you?"

Bree, too, was nodding in agreement.

"I think it's a good thing that your resistance is coming up," Bree added. "This is the final piece of the embodiment process, and any parts of you that are still not up to speed are making themselves known. By holding them with compassion, you'll be able to transmute them."

"And I was just teasing you earlier," Dominique added. "Trust me, if I felt this wasn't going to be a sacred experience, I'd be the first one to back out."

Mia relaxed. "You're right, thank you. I feel more at ease about it. I think I just needed to be heard and witnessed."

Bree turned off the highway onto a winding road. After a few miles, they pulled onto a private driveway surrounded by dense foliage. As soon as they got out of the car, Mia could feel it.

She sighed and took in a deep breath.

All the nervousness she had felt about coming melted instantaneously, as if dissipating into the fresh air of nature. The beauty of this place was breathtaking. The temple was a large white Mediterranean-style building with fuchsia and purple bougainvillea cascading all around, and beautiful stone statues of the goddesses had been placed throughout the garden.

The sound of running water from the fountains and birds chirping filled her ears, while the view of the turquoise ocean to the west was magnificent too.

To add to this sense of perfection, the soft breeze felt as if it was caressing her skin, and the sweet and heady scent of plumeria seemed to be welcoming her home.

This place was magical and sacred, and Mia could feel it with every ounce of her being.

As they unloaded their suitcases from the car, a woman dressed in white carrying four leis came out to greet them.

"Aloha. Welcome to the Temple of the Cosmic Mother," she said.

"Aloha," they responded, smiling back at the beautiful Hawaiian woman in front of them.

"My name is Ke'alohilani. I am the caretaker of this property and assistant to the High Priestess."

The women introduced themselves to her as she placed a lei around each of their necks.

"If you are ready, I will show you to your rooms and then take you on a tour of the property." She indicated that they should follow her down the walkway leading around the main building.

The path led to a series of small white cottages, each containing two queen-sized beds.

Dominique and Mia set their bags inside one of the cottages, and Bree and Lori placed theirs in the one next door. The grounds immediately surrounding the property were manicured, but the rest of the landscape was made up of natural Hawaiian foliage.

Ke'alohilani showed them the saltwater infinity pool overlooking the ocean and the hot tub as she led them to the meditation garden. Beyond that was a trail leading down to the ocean.

"It's just a ten-minute walk and there are many dolphins in the bay early in the morning," she reported.

"Thank you, Ke'alohilani. Your name is so beautiful. Does it mean something in Hawaiian?" asked Mia.

"It means *the brightness of heaven*," she said with a bright smile, indicating they should keep following her.

They made their way back up to the main building and she led them inside.

The main room was white and filled with light as there were many windows, and the west wall comprised a series of sliding glass doors opening up all the way to the lanai.

Images of the Goddess in all Her different forms adorned the walls.

A large altar was set on the room's eastern wall, filled with flowers, candles, crystals, feathers, two bowls of water, and a golden statue of Isis at the center.

Pillows and soft blankets adorned the edges of the room, but the center was empty.

She showed them the kitchen, introducing them to Healani and Kiele, the cooks who would be preparing all their meals. Mia could feel the love with which these two women were working in the kitchen. They smiled warmly, greeting them while preparing their colorful feast.

Before Mia could ask, Ke'alohilani added, "Healani means heavenly mist and Kiele means fragrant blossom." Mia nodded; then Ke'alohilani said, "We will meet for lunch at noon on the upper lanai, and then begin with the training after that. You are free to get settled, unpack, or wander around the property until then."

She left them to go and greet the other women arriving. She had told them there would be thirteen women going through the initiation. Two of them, Michelle and Ana, were part of Bree's team back on Maui. The others had all flown in from different parts of the world.

Dominique, Mia, Bree, and Lori returned to their cottages to unpack. The rooms were exquisitely decorated, simple yet elegant, every detail of comfort taken into account. The white linens on the bed were soft and inviting, topped with an abundance of large fluffy pillows.

"I've gotten so used to the simple ways in which John does things. Don't you think this feels so rich and luxurious?" Mia asked.

"Yes, it's a feast for the senses," Dominique enthused. "My body feels so loved and supported in this space."

"Yes, I can't wait to sleep in this bed tonight," Mia said, throwing herself on top of it.

Dominique squealed with delight when she saw the large sunken tub in the bathroom. "You need to come check out this bathroom! I'm going to soak in that tub every night!"

Mia quipped, "Well, don't forget about the saltwater pool and hot tub! If you spend all night in the water, you might dissolve!" She set off laughing.

They met back up with Bree and Lori and walked around the temple grounds.

"The attention to detail's really impressive with this place," Lori noted.

"I agree; you can feel how much thought and intention were put into creating this temple," said Bree.

"Feels like a sanctuary for my mind, body, and spirit," said Mia. She opened her arms, spinning around.

"The love is tangible, with even the trees and plants feeling so happy. I've been to many beautiful places, but there's something really special happening here," Dominique said, gazing around.

There was a fullness to their experience; sight, smell, sound, and touch senses were satiated already, and the final sense—taste—would soon be too as they headed up to the lanai for lunch. There, they ran into Bree's two friends.

"Hi Michelle and Ana. I'm so happy you made it," said Bree.

"It's so nice to meet you all," said Michelle with a smile that lit up the room. She was a voluptuous black woman who exuded warmth and kindness.

"Yes, it's a pleasure to finally meet you all," added Ana, a petite Latina with large brown eyes.

They all sat together at one of the two big circular tables over-looking the ocean. Before noon, the rest of the women made their way up to join them.

Ke'alohilani had them all stand and hold hands as they blessed the food.

"Great Mother, we thank you for this food and for the hands that prepared it. May it nourish the temples of our bodies, hearts, and minds, so that we may be of greater service to you. Amama ua noa. Which means, this prayer is lifted, it is free."

The buffet was a feast of colorful salads and exotic Hawaiian fruits, carefully selected to provide a satisfying yet light meal.

To drink, they were served a tropical herbal iced tea with hints of pineapple, orange, and guava. They chatted and exchanged stories, getting to know one another over lunch.

Mia felt relaxed and connected to the group of women.

Looking around, she guessed they ranged in age from early twenties to late sixties, but it was hard to tell as each woman had a radiant glow about her. She wondered if it was the specialness of each woman creating this effect or the result of this sacred land they were on.

Probably a combination of both, Mia thought.

Once the meal was complete, all the women thanked Healani and Kiele again, heading into the main room of the temple.

Gabriella was standing in front of the altar waiting for them when they arrived. Mia could feel her energy as soon as she entered the room, just like the green mist energy Mia had experienced so many times inside Earth. She paused to allow the experience of Gabriella to wash over her. She appeared taller than she actually was because her energy took up so much space.

Her hair was long and dark, her bright smile and sparkling brown eyes were mesmerizing, and her face was rich with experience and wisdom.

There was a welcoming softness about her, a loving and nurturing gentleness to her presence making everyone feel at ease. Yet Mia also felt as though she was in the presence of royalty.

Never had she witnessed this combination of qualities before.

She wondered, *How can someone feel soft and powerful at the same time?*

"Thank you all for coming. It's an honor to have you all here," Gabriella said once everyone had entered the room.

"We are going to ease into our time together with some movement. Before we get to know one another with our words, with our minds, let's get connected to our bodies." She turned on the sound system behind her and Israel Kamakawiwo'ole's "Over the Rainbow" started playing.

"Close your eyes and just allow your hips to start moving to the music."

Mia smiled. She was lost in thought, feeling the warmth passing through every vein and sinew, remembering her time inside the rainbow. She let her body start swaying to the music, in fact quite powerless to prevent it even if she had wanted to, for it was a magical song. She felt joyful as she allowed herself to let go of all her thoughts, moving to the rhythm of the music.

"Now open your eyes and smile at the other women in the room," Gabriella instructed.

Mia looked around at the group of women with whom she would be spending the next few weeks, smiling at each one of them.

"Start to move around the room interacting with one another, admiring the uniqueness of each woman, seeing one another as beautiful flowers, all of us different and yet equally radiant." Gabriella weaved her way through all the women in the space.

"Bow to each woman, acknowledging the gift her presence brings to the group," she added.

Mia smiled, bowing to each woman, her hands in prayer position in front of her heart.

The energy in the room got stronger as they laughed and danced with one another for several more songs. When the music ended, Gabriella asked them to come into a circle, hold hands and close their eyes.

"Blessed Mother, we gather here to celebrate You, to celebrate one another. We ask that You bless each woman here, that You assist her on her journey of embodiment. May we all remember who we are, may we remember the truth of who You are, may we live our lives in service to the divinity that resides within each of us. *Amama ua noa.*"

"*Amama ua noa,*" they all repeated as one.

Bringing out the pillows and blankets, they created a comfy circle on the floor.

"One of the biggest lessons for women to learn," Gabriella began after everyone had settled, "is to change their relationship to their needs. Most of us have been socialized to put ourselves last, taking care of everyone else's needs first. The first lesson of being a priestess is to take precious care of our bodies. So while you're here, practice getting into the habit of really listening to your bodies and nurturing yourselves."

"Oh, I'm going to like this," Mia whispered to Dominique.

"Me too." Dominique smiled, her eyes bright.

"We're going to go around the circle and introduce ourselves. Tell us briefly who you are and why you are here. I'll start us off," said Gabriella.

"My family's originally from India, and I was raised in the Hindu faith. At twenty, I went to live in France and when I was there, I had a vision of Mary Magdalena. She told me that She needed me to help the world know who She really was. It was such a powerful experience for me that I immediately began a quest to uncover the truth.

"Eventually, my seeking led me to Her cave in southern France.

"There, I had another vision of Magdalena in which She anointed me, initiating me as one of Her priestesses, instructing me to create a temple for Her, a sacred place for women to gather and learn about the feminine mysteries. She said this lineage had begun in the Temple of Isis, but that the teachings had been lost over time—and that it was now time for them to be remembered.

"Teams of spiritual warriors would be awakening across the globe to assist in the spiritual evolution of humanity, She said, and that they would be filled with light, but they would not be able to hold this light steady in their bodies. The key, She said, was to bring women back into their bodies, helping them to remember the sacredness of their temples—to remember that a woman fully in her body is a force capable of bringing great change to the world.

"I was divinely guided each step of the way, being brought here to this sacred land, to be shown by Isis how to heal, restore, and reawaken the power of the Goddess in each and every one of you." She looked around the circle, making eye contact with each woman present.

She paused for a moment when she looked at Mia, as if she recognized her. Mia felt seen in a way she had never experienced before, as if Gabriella's gaze pierced right through to the very essence of her soul. Gabriella smiled and nodded, then continued around the circle.

One by one, the women introduced themselves, most of them sharing painful stories of heartache, abuse, trauma, and addiction that had brought them to their knees, followed by journeys back to wholeness and series of serendipitous coincidences that had led them here.

They felt a greater calling to be of service to the world.

Mia felt supported, knowing that she was amongst like-minded souls.

We are All saving the world, she thought. *What an honor that I get to spend this time with these brave women.* Her heart swelled with love and pride.

Finally, it was Mia's turn to introduce herself.

"Hi, my name is Mia and I'm really happy to be here. I was feeling a bit hesitant on the drive over, but I can tell now that I'm exactly where I'm supposed to be.

"I've been on an accelerated healing journey the past few months because the Goddess has asked me to step up and be of service. So I'm here because I need help getting my body up to speed to be able to handle the energy desiring to move through me. I had a dream that I was able to heal someone from all the fear they were carrying with the golden light emanating from my, um...well, first chakra. I believe the golden light activation is what I'm here to receive."

"You are, indeed, Mia. Welcome," Gabriella responded. "Pleasure is the language of the Goddess, and it's how She heals the world. To reconnect ourselves to sacred desire, we have to be in our bodies. Trauma, fear, shame, and pain have kept us out of our bodies.

"We have to heal those wounds in order to be allowed back in. You are all at different levels or stages of this healing journey; some of you have already done most of the heavy lifting and there's just fine tuning to do, a softening that will allow you to fully embody the rest of the way."

She glanced at Mia as she said this, then returned her gaze to the rest of the women.

Did she say pleasure's the Goddess's language? Whoa, what does that mean? Mia pondered.

"And some of you are here to further release belief systems that have long since been holding you back. You see, many of us were heavily programmed with the belief that women needed to be perfect and look and act a certain way, and even though you may 'know' it's not true, your body is still holding onto it and won't allow the wild and juicy part of you to take the lead.

"A part of you may still be afraid of the power of your sexuality, especially if you haven't had a strong voice to set clear boundaries," she said, catching Mia's bright gaze again.

Damn, she really does see right through me! She's as powerful as John, or maybe more so, she thought. *Shit, I wonder if she can hear my thoughts as well?*

Would Gabriella look at her again when she heard these deliberately strong thoughts?

Indeed, Gabriella looked at her and smiled, causing Mia to laugh.

"Throughout the training, we will be weaving in the ability to receive pleasure, awakening our sensuality, opening up, releasing old wounding, balancing our masculine and feminine energies inside of us so that we can fully reside in our bodies. So our focus will shift as needed, but we will begin with increasing our ability to receive pleasure."

Oh, here we go, thought Mia.

"I want you to spend some time walking barefoot in the meditation garden. Feel the ground underneath your feet, knowing how each sensation feels from the harsh gravel to the deep carpet of the lush green grass and the warm soil. Touch each one of the plants in turn, brushing your fingertips along each part, feeling their textures, experiencing how each part of the plant feels different from the stamen to the petal, to their prickly or their smooth, silken-soft leaves…

"Really move in close, becoming intimate with and smelling the flowers, discerning each tiny scent that goes toward creating the whole fragrance, learning to be fully present with everything and every element you encounter. Take in the beauty before you in all its fullness and glory. If you feel called to lie on the earth, do so. Soak up all the magic in the garden, letting yourself be satiated by nature. Invite nature into you."

Gabriella gestured, indicating that they should get up and get started.

Phew! Mia's body relaxed as she realized she was just going to connect with nature.

"I will come find you in the garden when it's time to shift our focus," Gabriella called after them as they headed out the door.

Mia stepped onto the dense, soft grass, her naked toes relishing the sumptuous carpet of lush, plump greenery underneath her feet. The earth felt warm as she slowly walked toward the small plumeria tree that had been calling to her since her arrival.

Hello beauty, she said tenderly in her mind, gently running her delicate fingers along the new green tree bark, taking her time before reaching for its fragrant soft pink-and-yellow flower.

Leaning in, she inhaled the sweet, perfumed scent that was filling her nostrils with delight and the profoundest joy imaginable. *Thank you, thank you for your beauty, for your magical fragrance. Thank you for letting me close enough to experience you.*

A flower dropped from the tree at Mia's feet.

She picked it up, gently fastening it in her hair behind her ear, feeling the love emanating from it as she did. And so, just as Mia loved the tree, she felt it loving her back wholly, completely.

The delicate and entrancing sound of wind chimes dancing in the breeze caught her attention, as did the birds chirping all around her, her ears and mind tuned into the minutest noise.

She allowed herself to be filled with the song of the garden, feeling held in the embrace of the warm, moisture-rich air all around. She noticed the small yellow butterflies visiting the six-foot kahili ginger plant with its deep blue-green leaves, its golden fragrant flowers containing a bright red stamen at the center. The scent of the plant was so powerful, Mia found herself slightly intoxicated. She focused her awareness back on her feet, touching the earth to help herself feel grounded. Now she noticed three gold dust day geckos scurrying across the grass.

She had never seen one before and even though she wasn't a huge reptile fan, she was absolutely enamored with the beauty of the little creatures' iridescent bright green bodies and light blue around their eyes and tiny feet. Ke'alohilani had told her earlier in the kitchen that they weren't native to Hawaii and had been brought over from Madagascar.

She wandered over to the shade drawn by the cup of gold vine with its dark green leaves and huge, vivid yellow coconut-scented flowers. Mia touched one, noticing its thick, leathery skin.

She complimented the flower on its beauty, scent, and texture, and in the process felt her heart opening wider. She noticed the sound of the buzzing bees working on the nearby magnolia tree.

There's so much activity in this tranquil garden, so much life happening that I would have missed if I hadn't been focusing on what's right in front of me.

Mia lost track of time, absorbing all the love from the garden.

Gabriella appeared outside with Ke'alohilani, Healani, Kiele, and several other Hawaiian women, and addressed all the women on retreat.

"Now that the garden has helped you awaken your senses and opened your hearts, these talented women are going to help you get deeper into your bodies. They are all trained in the art of *lomi lomi* massage. Half of you will go with them now for your treatment and the rest of you will go soak in the pool until it's your turn."

Several other women elected to have their massage first, so by default, Dominique, Mia, and Lori ended up relaxing by the pool. There, the expanse of clear water had been warmed by the sun, so it was easy to slip into. They shared their individual experiences in the garden, amazed at how such a simple exercise had helped them feel more connected to their bodies.

"I felt loved and nurtured by that experience, and I'm noticing that now I feel more open and receptive," Dominique said.

"Yes, I feel softer, more feminine," added Mia.

Gabriella walked over, carrying a tray bearing a pitcher and glasses.

"Excellent, you experienced exactly what I intended," she said. "Our feminine energy possesses all those qualities, those of receptivity, softness, love, nurturing, openness; it's inclusive, saying 'yes' to life." She offered them a glass of tropical iced tea, continuing, "The feminine is also timeless, so when we give ourselves permission to slow down and be with ourselves, we can access the magic all around us."

"But the goal is to balance the masculine and feminine energy within us, right?" asked Michelle.

"Absolutely, but because most of us have grown up in cultures in which the masculine traits were more revered, we've forgotten about the power of our feminine side. This is the balance we need to bring to the world," Gabriella said, smiling at Mia.

"Women tried to find their power in the world by becoming more masculine, becoming more focused, action-oriented, direct, more competitive, driven—and they did an excellent job of it, but they forgot about the gifts their feminine qualities brought to the world," she added.

"But what choice did they have when being female was seen as weak?" interrupted Ana.

"Oh, I agree. It couldn't have happened any other way. But the planet has really paid the price as humanity shifted even more into their heads and away from their hearts. The solution, the way we heal the world, is by reconnecting to our feminine side, allowing our bodies to come back into balance."

"But feminine energy can also be dramatic and exhausting, never accomplishing anything," Dominique added.

"Yes, I should clarify I'm referring to grounded feminine energy, healthy and balanced. A woman connected to the energy of the Goddess through her root chakra, her hips, her womb, up into her heart is a force to be reckoned with. That woman can heal the world!" she said, glancing at Mia again. "And once we do that, we can help the men reconnect to their own feminine energy. You see, the mind was never designed to be in charge; it's brilliant at solving the problems it creates, but it was never intended to be the captain of the ship.

"The heart was always meant to lead us through life, being connected to our divinity, to the force that guides us. It is our feminine energy that allows us to connect to life, to Source, to the divine. Men don't know this, but they need us in our feminine energy, because this is how we heal them. The masculine needs to rest in the arms of the feminine in order to be restored.

Gabriella commented, "Everyone out there is running around feeling empty and addicted; they are missing their connection to their Source, and the doorway back to the Divine is through the feminine. There are so many layers to this, and we'll be going more in-depth with all of it while you're here, but can't you already begin to feel the difference in your being just from the nurturing you've received since you arrived?"

"Yes!" they responded all at once.

After their massages, they showered and dressed for dinner. Mia noticed how much more present she was now feeling in her body, how much more alive and connected she felt. The peace and stillness she could usually only achieve with breathwork or a trip inside Earth now felt anchored within her. She felt more patient, more compassionate, more loving.

She took a deep breath, feeling as though she could send this feeling all around the world.

She thought about the guys, wondering how they were doing up in the West Maui Mountain.

The island must be loving them, but they're having to work a lot harder to get comfortable.

Their bodies are probably exhausted from hiking and carrying all their equipment. They're already amazing men, but how much more could they be if they were loved by a woman who embodied the energy of the Goddess?

She thought about John, too; she had always assumed he had it all figured out.

But now she could sense a little sadness running through him.

He's had his heart broken, and even he needs the love of an embodied woman. I wonder if Gabriella's single? What would happen if she got a hold of him?

That thought made her giggle as she imagined the two most powerful people she knew entangled in a passionate embrace. *Why can't they be the ones to heal the world?*

She looked at her hips in the mirror.

What will it be like when you're fully activated? she said to her body, moving her hips slowly and deliberately from side to side. *How much healing power will I be carrying?*

She slid her hands along the curves of her body. *Who will I heal with this body?*

Marco's handsome face flashed into her mind.

Just then, Bree and Lori walked in to accompany them up to dinner.

"Are you two ready?" Bree asked.

Mia blushed as if she had just been caught in the act.

"What are you up to?" Lori asked, noticing the startled look on Mia's face.

"Just finishing up," Dominique answered from the vanity in the bathroom.

"You look so beautiful, Mia," Bree offered, noticing how nice

Mia's tanned skin looked against the light pink halter dress she was wearing.

"We all look gorgeous," Dominique said, coming into the room, admiring everyone's outfits.

"True! Dominique, that fuchsia dress is fabulous on you," commented Lori.

"Thank you, and you look so pretty in yellow," Dominique replied. "Like summer, all wrapped up! It's nice to get dressed up for a change, isn't it? With John, we've all gotten into the habit of dressing in such casual and practical clothes. The same thing more or less every day."

"I have as well, living on Maui for so long," Bree added. "I'm always in something practical, but this feels really good. We look like all the colorful flowers we saw in the garden today."

They headed up to the main room, filled with all the other women who were also looking radiant and beautiful. Gabriella was especially stunning in her long green strapless dress that accentuated her abundance of curves. She turned on the music and soon had everyone slowly moving around the circle, dancing, flowing, swaying.

"Acknowledge the beauty in each woman by bowing and saying *'namaste'* as you cross paths," she instructed. "Allow yourself to be seen and appreciated. Receive the love from your sisters, feeling what a gift your feminine presence is to the world."

Mia noticed how connected she already felt to all these women, even though there were several to whom she still hadn't spoken. They were already a community, a sisterhood, bonded through their femininity, through their hearts.

Ke'alohilani appeared and announced that dinner was ready.

Mia wondered, *how can she look so radiant after working so hard all day? She must be connected to her heart, to all the love in this magical place.*

Yes, that must be it, she thought, noticing Healani and Kiele looking refreshed and relaxed too.

Gabriella blessed the food and the cooks, then encouraged the women to experience their dinner mindfully. "Really focus on the flavors as they make contact with your tongue. Notice the texture and temperature of the food in your mouth, savoring every bite slowly, appreciating the nourishment it is bringing to your body. Let yourself experience the love, the *aloha* Healani and Kiele have put into this meal, as well as the love from the food itself."

Mia admired the ahi *poke* salad placed in front of her.

The firm chunks of raw tuna had been arranged on a bed of mixed greens and seaweed salad surrounded by sliced avocado and pieces of mango. The seasoned salty taste of the ahi combined with the sweetness of the mango was a delight for her palate.

The main entree was Hawaiian shrimp kabobs with pineapple and bell peppers atop a bed of white rice. Mia savored the shrimp, which had been seasoned with garlic.

The grilled bell peppers were slightly sweet, but the grilled pineapple was her favorite.

For dessert, they had homemade coconut sorbet with a white chocolate macadamia nut cookie on the side. It was not difficult to appreciate the temperature and textures, and to feel the love.

They began each morning with deep hip-opening yoga to prepare their bodies to be able to hold the energy of the Goddess. During pigeon pose, Mia felt her eyes welling, her breaths almost choking in her throat as she wanted to burst out sobbing despite not knowing why.

Gabriella looked across, as she must have picked up on it,

softly explaining that it was a natural reaction, the pain and trauma of the feminine wound being held in the hips.

As Mia looked around, she also saw she was not alone in her tears.

After yoga, the group would sit in silent meditation, then gather for breakfast and spend a few hours afterward listening to Gabriella teach them about the sacredness of their bodies.

Then they would dance and move to anchor the teachings deep inside them.

Daily massages and body treatments were always available, and Mia indulged in a different treatment each day. The sugar cane body scrub with lavender-infused coconut oil left her skin feeling softer than it had ever been, and after that she tried the thermal bath soak infused with minerals and essential oils. The hot stone massage was one of her favorites.

She adored the sensation of the healing power of Mother Earth releasing the deep tension and soreness in her muscles. The reflexology treatments, on the other hand, were slightly painful but left her feeling completely reset. The sessions of myofascial release were a surprise, the tension in her muscles and tissues unwinding and her body shaking as the silent trauma she had been holding were released. The craniosacral massage tapped into memories she hadn't thought of in years and left her feeling balanced and centered in a way she'd never experienced.

Every meal was an exquisitely prepared feast for all the senses, yet healthy and light so they could move easily in their bodies. They meditated in the garden and swam in the pool and the ocean, also leaving the temple a few times to go on hikes around the island, connecting intimately with nature. Toward the end of the week, they took a day trip to Green Sand Beach, Papakole, at the island's southern end.

They brought a picnic lunch with them that day so they could really enjoy their time there. It was a two-and-a-half-mile hike to get there from the parking lot, but well worth the effort.

Mia had noticed since her arrival on the island that colors were impacting her differently.

At first, she became aware of how vivid all the colors were around her, no matter where she went. Then she started to experience the ways these colors made her feel.

When she saw her first rainbow since her experience at Iao Valley, she began to understand that the activation she had received had forever changed her relationship to color. Through color, a powerful gift was now available to her, one that she was only beginning to understand.

When she first laid eyes on the green sand beach, she was so overwhelmed with joy that she began to cry. The olivine crystals, from a forty-nine-thousand-year-old volcanic eruption that had made the sand green, were calling to her. She made her way as fast as she could and lay on the warm sand, her body so open and relaxed from all the nurturing and love it had received in the past week that she was able to instantly merge her consciousness with the green crystals.

She didn't think it was possible to feel any more loved than she already did, but that's exactly what she experienced, an infusion of love into her cells from green energy that originated from deep inside Earth, a love that allowed her body to soften even further.

Surrender all your barriers to love and release the remaining defenses around your heart, she heard the Crystals Beings saying to her.

Mia was surprised, as she thought she had already done this.

Where am I still defended? How am I still blocking love? she asked.

In her mind, she saw the judgments that still made her feel separate.

Give up the need to be right about what's wrong, she heard. *Judgment will always block the experience of love.*

Mia had been so happy all week that she hadn't heard the running commentary forever playing in the back of her mind. It had been there since she was a child, and because this week had been filled with so much nurturing and relaxation, her ego hadn't been on guard, creating the perfect opportunity for her to surrender that programming.

This mental programming was the foundation of what the entity energies used to keep humans constantly at odds with one another.

The need to be right about what was wrong created a chronic state of judgment, preventing humans from feeling the love that was all around them. And it was sneaky by design because judging something clearly wrong seemed, at least on the surface, beneficial.

Mia could feel that a big part of the reason this week had felt so amazing was because this mental chatter had been quieter. Her body sighed in relief as she recognized this. The green Crystal Beings showed her the amount of life force energy this programming consumed. No wonder most people were so exhausted; their judgments were draining them dry. The programming caused a drop in the frequency of their vibration, making it impossible for them to experience love. Earth was covered in this mental energy, and it was suffocating Her.

Love was Her natural state, and it was how She supported all of life.

If everyone on the planet focused on love and peace at the same time, said the green Crystal Beings, *Earth could regain her balance and heal Herself. But the incessant negative mental chatter keeps Her in a weakened state. As you already know, she regains her balance through what you call "natural disasters." The intensity of these has had to* increase, given that the Information Age has allowed individuals to ex-press their judgments on a global level.

Mia pleaded, *I never want to hurt Earth in any way. Get this thing out of me!*

That's the tricky part, the Crystal Being said. *The energy cords related to the programming are thick and sticky with barbed edges; be-cause of this design, we must remove them slowly and softly, letting them melt out of you into the earth.*

Any energy of force and the barbs will get tangled, keeping this mental energy inside you. Pay attention to any time you hear your mind complaining, blaming, or judging, and softly ease into gratitude. Let the neural pathways of gratitude become stronger in your mind. Only once you've released all of it can your siddhis be activated.

Mia asked, *Have the entities been blocking me from activating my powers?*

No, as a precaution, the siddhis remain dormant until the body is free of entity energies so that the entities can never access them. Can you imagine what would have happened if the entity energies could control humans with supernatural abilities?

Yes, she could imagine it; it would be a total disaster, Mia thought!

Keep softening and surrendering, loving and laughing, and opening your heart.

Mia came back to the present moment, feeling the water from the small ocean wave that broke on the shore reach her toes. It felt cool and refreshing after lying in the sun on the warm sand.

She noticed most of the others were swimming in the bay, so she decided to join them.

Loving and laughing, she repeated to herself as she swam over to the group of giggling priestesses. They splashed and played with one another until their sides ached from laughing.

They ate the picnic lunch Healani and Kiele had packed for

them, then explored the rest of the area. Once complete with their adventure, they hiked back to the van to make their way home.

Mia shared the messages she had received with the others in the van.

"I get so tired of listening to that negative voice in my head," said Ana.

"Or even worse, when that negative voice comes out of my mouth," said Michelle.

"It would be so freeing to never have to listen to it again," said Lori. I like the practical tool they gave you of softening into gratitude any time you hear yourself complaining, blaming, or judging. I'm going to set an intention and make that my new practice."

"Me too," said Bree.

"I will too, except when someone's wrong, then I'll have to let them know," Dominique said jokingly.

They all laughed.

18

Dragons

———

The next day in the main room of the temple, Gabriella announced that they would be changing their focus.

"I'm going to tell you a story. There are many versions of it. For some of you, this will feel like the truth; for others, it will sound more like mythology. And for the rest of you, it may just be a helpful way to conceptualize the information. Take what works for you and leave what doesn't. Does that make sense to everyone?" Gabriella smiled as she looked around the room.

Everyone nodded in agreement.

"This is a subject that can be tricky and activating, so I want us to hold a strong circle of support energy. And this is going to be a conversation, so please feel free to ask questions at any point if you need further clarification. If you have some information to offer, please do so. If you get triggered at any point while I'm talking, please speak up. Now, let's all take a deep breath."

Everyone in the room inhaled deeply, letting out an audible

sigh. The energy in the room was noticeably different than it had been since the women arrived.

"We've spent the last week getting all of you feeling relaxed, soft, and open so that it would be easier for your bodies to let go. Now we're going to energetically clean out your bodies, your sacred temples, your womb space."

Mia felt her root chakra start to spin as Gabriella spoke. *Here we go,* she thought.

"Just like Jesus in Jerusalem, we are going to cast the thieves from the temple. These thieves are part of the dark force energy trying to control humankind."

Gabriella let the words sink in before continuing.

At the mention of Jerusalem, Mia grew dizzy, and her vision became fuzzy. She could see and hear Jesus speaking about the den of thieves in the temple.

Her body became hot and she felt slightly nauseous as she tapped into past- life memories. Sophia recalibrated so that Mia could remain present.

"Some of you may know them as entity energies." Gabriella paused again for effect. "Their survival is dependent upon living off of our life force energy. And they have been manipulating humans since the beginning of time."

The tension in the room was palpable, several women squirming in their seats.

"Let's all take a few more deep breaths." Gabriella continued. "The imbalance of power between the masculine and the feminine on this planet didn't happen just because women are physically weaker than men. This was a calculated strike to keep humans from ever realizing their true potential, their true power."

"Don't you mean keeping *women* from realizing their true potential?" asked Ana. "Because men seem to have had no problem finding all the power."

"No, I mean humans. The power that men have found isn't true power; it's the limited power of brute force and the mind. Or what I like to call the Love of Power, which is nothing in comparison to the Power of Love, the power of the Divine."

"So you're saying these entity energies were the ones that caused gender inequality?" Ana asked.

"Yes."

"But why did this affect our ability to find our power?"

"To access the Power of Love, our true power, both the masculine and feminine must be valued and sacred. The subjugation of the feminine caused her to lose her value and sacredness." Gabriella was speaking slowly, methodically revealing each layer.

"And I'm purposely using the words masculine and feminine instead of men and women, or male and female; does anyone know why?"

"Because all humans are a combination of masculine and feminine energies," Mia responded. And these energies must be balanced within us before we can experience our divinity."

"Exactly, and I'll explain more on that later, but I mention it now because I want you to experience how this happened both in the external world and our inner reality."

"Sorry to be asking so many questions, but I'm still not sure I understand why this worked?" said Ana.

"No need to apologize; your questions are helping everyone understand. When the feminine was seen as less valuable, we lost access to the powers of the Goddess. Humanity has forgotten Her altogether. They have no idea who She is, and therefore have no idea of the real power of our sexual energy, our shakti, our kundalini, or how it was intended to be used."

Mia's body got hot at the mention of the word kundalini.

"Think of Shiva as the penetrating power of focused energy

and Shakti as the receiver of life, the creative force of matter and all that exists in the Universe.

"We all know what happens when an egg and sperm are joined: life is created. But the combination of this energy was meant for more than just procreation. Imagine what is possible when we merge the energy of the Goddess in our hearts with the energy of the Enlightened Masculine. The energy that creates life can also be used to heal our bodies, to connect to our divinity, and to co-create our lives on Earth like gods and goddesses."

Mia's body started vibrating and tingling all over.

"The dark force knew that if we ever figured this out, it would lose all the control it had over us. So the first thing the dark force did was to split humanity. By taking away our balance of power, the dark force ensured that the two components necessary to access the power of the Divine within us became lost."

"But I thought this happened because of the Kali Yuga, the cycle of darkness we have been in for the past several thousand years," said Michelle.

Gabriella replied, "Think of it this way: humanity couldn't access the solution because of the cycle of darkness in which we found ourselves, but now that we are moving back to the Satya Yuga, the Golden Age of Truth, the solution is available to us again."

Michelle nodded.

"The dark force achieved this split in the mind of the masculine by causing him to fear the power of Shakti. The entities went to work, convincing the masculine that the power of the feminine to create life was dangerous and that the masculine must act first and suppress the power of the feminine, or they would be dominated by it. They convinced the masculine to use the feminine energy for his own benefit without regard for her value and needs. By making the feminine subordinate to the masculine, by turning her into a sexual object, the female body suddenly became something that could be violated, abused, controlled, or possessed. The feminine was no longer in equal step with the masculine on the planet."

Gabriella paused to see if everyone was still following her explanations. She noticed some of the women were leaning back, almost lying down, falling out of the circle.

"Let's take a few more deep breaths together and make sure you are staying present in your body. Sit up straight, shaking off any heaviness that you're feeling right now."

Gabriella shook her shoulders, encouraging the others to do the same.

"What the masculine didn't realize is that by doing this, it lost its ability to access its divinity as well. In subjugating the feminine, it had discarded the other half of the equation that was necessary to experience its true power, the Power of Love. Because the feminine was considered less valuable because our power had been taken away, the kundalini life force, the energy of the Goddess, couldn't flow through the body. This life force had been designed to rise in the body and connect with spirit, and then bring heaven back to Earth through the physical body.

"But the Goddess's power, the sacred energy of desire, was perverted and twisted until it cracked, giving the dark force complete control of humanity.

"Pornography, prostitution, sex trafficking, rape, sexual molestation, deviant forms of sexual behavior, all these are the result of the loss of sacred sexuality. This loss of connection to the Goddess created an emptiness that humanity has never stopped trying to fill. Desire energy with no connection to the Goddess creates only addiction."

Mia thought about her breathwork experience in Sedona when she had felt the insatiable energy of desire overtaking her.

She remembered she had been told to *become that which holds all desire* and had then experienced herself becoming the Grand Canyon.

"As women, our bodies are carrying the scars of this violation, yet also the power to heal this. Restoring the temple so that the Goddess may return is how we heal ourselves and how we heal the masculine, and heal the world."

She looked directly at Mia, holding her gaze to make sure her words were sinking in.

"Our womb holds the memory of every sexual experience we have ever had. Most of us have had unwanted sexual experiences, whether we consented for the wrong reasons, were too young, unconscious, or inebriated to know what we were doing, or we never agreed to it, and it happened by force. The pain, the guilt, the shame, and the trauma are all energetically stored in the womb until they are healed. Even if you were fortunate enough never to have a traumatic sexual experience, just being in a female body on this planet has exposed you to this wounding.

"This is going to be a raw and difficult week for us; we need to hold very sacred space for one another as we go through this together. Let's hold hands again and call in extra support."

They closed their eyes as they held hands, focusing within.

"Beloved Mother Goddess, we humbly ask for your help. Please hold us as we seek to release the sexual trauma from our bodies. Give us the strength to share our stories with one another, and the courage to look at all the wounding we carry inside. Allow us to be the sacred witnesses for one another as we heal as sisters. Guide us to the depth of healing that we need so that we may restore the sacredness of our wombs and embody the golden light of the Goddess within us. And as we heal this for ourselves, may all women everywhere be set free. *Amama ua noa.*"

"*Amama ua noa,*" they repeated.

Mia's root chakra began to spin softly as Gabriella spoke those words, heat traveling up the base of her spine, causing her back to arch. *Here we go,* she thought, as she committed to healing herself completely. She could feel the heaviness in her body, the sadness and pain in her heart.

By now, she knew that a lot of what she was feeling belonged to her ancestors and to the women all around the world, understanding that the healing work she was doing was for the collective. And yet, she also knew she had several personal wounds to heal.

Given how messy my relationship was with Richard, I wouldn't be surprised if there was more to heal there. This thought caused her uterus to contract in pain. *Ugh,* she groaned silently. *And not to give him all the credit, there were many others before him.*

There had been several drunken one-night stands that she had regretted the next morning. And there'd been the times when she was younger and thought sex meant the promise of a relationship, only to find her suitor had disappeared the next morning.

And there were also the times when she had said no, but had been coerced into having sex. *Yes, there's a lot left for me to heal,* she thought, as she felt the heaviness in her body.

Gabriella had them split into groups of three, instructing them to take turns sharing their sexual stories with one another. "Imagine that as you share the story of what happened, you are taking it out of your body and laying it on the altar to be healed by the Goddess."

The energy in the room was somber for the next few hours as they told their stories. There were lots of tears and intermittent moments of silence as they struggled to find the strength to keep going. The women holding space offered energetic support yet remained quiet to allow the others to tell their stories uninterrupted.

After everyone had spoken, Gabriella had the group take a short break.

"Go outside, stretch your legs. If you've been crying a lot, splash water on your face. We're going to circle back up in twenty minutes."

The women came back into the room, still feeling vulnerable, tender, and even more connected to one another.

"The sisterhood of the Goddess is a bond that will support you for the rest of your life," Gabriella said, and smiled, feeling the compassion the women in the room had for one another.

Mia felt connected to every woman in the room in a way she had never experienced before. She already loved Dominique, Lori, and Bree, but she could feel how much deeper that love went now. *I feel seen and heard and so safe, even though I've been talking about some of the worst things that have ever happened to me.*

"Now I'm going to show you how to heal yourself with your breath," Gabriella said.

Oh, goody, breathwork! Mia thought.

"You will be taking two breaths into your body through your mouth. The first one you will breathe into your womb and the second into your heart. You will be breathing all the trauma from the second chakra into the heart so that it can be healed with love," Gabriella said, demonstrating the breathwork.

She turned on some music and had them lie down and begin the breathing.

"Let the breath flow gently into your body; let it be tender and easy."

This was different from how Mia had been used to doing it.

She wanted to push through the resistance and tightness she felt in her body with her breath.

How am I ever going to get there with a soft, gentle breath?

The feeling of heaviness in the room was thick.

This is too hard; I can't do it this way. It felt as though she was trying to climb an insurmountable mountain.

"Everything is given in the breath; allow yourself to receive it all. Breathe deeply into your womb, your hips, your ovaries, letting the breath all the way in," Gabriella encouraged.

Mia could hear some of the other women in the room crying, connecting her even more deeply to her sadness.

"Ask the Goddess to help you," Gabriella said.

Please help me, Mia pleaded in her mind.

And, as always, the request was answered immediately.

Mia surrendered to the support being offered to her. Her energy shifted as the breath found a gentle, rhythmic motion. All of the sadness inside her rose in front of her.

The wave of emotion parted like the Red Sea, taking her even deeper into her body. She kept welcoming the breath deep into her womb, her hips, all the way down to her root chakra. As the faces of her past sexual partners flashed in her mind, she released them to the breath. *I forgive myself. I release this shame and guilt from my body. I claim my innocence and my sovereignty.*

Because of all the work she had done with John, Mia knew she also had to forgive the men, setting them free being the way to liberate herself fully. She thought about the breathwork in the cave in Sedona and all the confusion she'd been carrying, all based around sexual attention.

We're all confused about it, all humans, she realized, allowing the blame to start to lift. *Everyone is wounded and seeking relief from the pain any way they can find. Even the predators are just trying to fill the emptiness inside them. The entities have been controlling everyone.*

She started breathing faster as she was filled with rage against the entities for all the suffering they had caused. Her ovaries contracted, sending pain shooting through her body.

She realized her hatred and blame toward the entities only made them stronger.

This is like the "need to be right about what's wrong," she thought. *I can't force it out or attack it directly. It has to be soft. I need my heart to guide me; I need the power of my feminine energy.*

She slowed her breath. *Maybe I can love it to death.*

She chuckled, amused that she still wanted to kill the entities.

Mother Earth, please help me! How do I transmute this poison from my body? That's it!

She realized the answer had been immediately given: she needed to transmute the poison into medicine. This realization strengthened the breath even further, sending it pumping through her body as if on autopilot. She thought about the green energy inside the heart of the Goddess.

She sent her awareness through her root chakra into Earth.

Knowing that accessing this energy was her birthright, she plunged right into it.

Please help me heal this, help me transmute the poison with your love, she humbly asked. Instantly, the green mist flowed up into her womb, wrapping around her ovaries.

The Goddess's energy transmuted the entities, transforming their poison into medicine. *You now walk with dragons,* she heard Her say.

Mia saw two green-and-gold dragons shoot out of her ovaries, bold and majestic. The entities had been converted into dragons designed to protect her.

The fierceness of the Goddess had now become the energy that would keep her safe. Mia laughed aloud, realizing that love had turned her perpetrators into her guardians.

The evil that had wounded her was now a magical force field of elemental love. "Protection" was the wrong word; the dragons had made her impervious to evil.

Mia realized that her body was now a vessel the Goddess could fully occupy. A surge of golden kundalini energy shot up her spine, causing her body to bolt upright. She sat there for a moment with her eyes closed, taking a couple of long, slow, deep breaths.

When she opened her eyes, Gabriella was smiling at her.

"Well done, Mia," she whispered.

Gabriella instructed the others to switch to their natural breath and let their bodies rest.

Mia decided to join them and lay back down, her body feeling strong and energized. She felt as if she was a fortress of strength, as though indestructible.

She realized the mental programming that all women had around physical safety was gone, leaving her feeling safe and secure in a way that she had never experienced before.

She closed her eyes to see if she could see the dragons again. Although she could feel their energy around her, she couldn't see them. *Maybe I'll be able to see them when they're needed,* she concluded. She thanked the Goddess, Mother Earth, and her body for doing all the work, and she thanked her dragons. She thought about what it meant that she had successfully transmuted the poison into medicine with the power of love.

I'm an alchemist. I did it, I really, really did it! What will happen now that my body is ready?

Gabriella interrupted her thoughts, having the women sit up and share their experiences.

"The shame I was carrying is gone," said Ana.

"Yes, and the guilt as well, I feel pure—holy even," said Michelle.

"I feel so much lighter," said Ana.

"Yes, and freer," added Lori.

"I feel clearer," said Bree.

"What we did today was a lot. I want you to take the afternoon to nurture yourselves. Let's end for today by coming into a circle and holding hands. Focusing inside, let yourselves feel all the changes, all the healing that happened today. We offer gratitude to the Goddess, to Mother Earth, and to all the beings that watch over us. I am grateful for this community, for this sisterhood of loving, caring, supportive women. Thank you all for answering the call of the Goddess, for your willingness to transform your lives and be of service. *Amama ua noa.*"

"*Amama ua noa,*" they repeated.

After a delicious lunch, they spent the rest of the day lounging in the pool. Mia told them about her dragons.

"I want dragons!" said Dominique.

"Imagine how different the world would be if women felt safe," Bree offered.

"If I had dragons, I wouldn't have to be in hiding anymore," Dominique continued.

"What would you do differently if you didn't have to be in hiding?" Lori asked.

Dominique paused for a moment, taking a breath as she allowed herself to imagine the unimaginable. "I'd go back home."

"And reclaim your kingdom—or rather, your queendom?" Lori asked.

Dominique looked away. "I'd probably go back as a civilian. As on Earth, my people need to learn to empower themselves and not wait for a messiah to do it for them. They gave me too much of their power and came to see me as their savior. Like what happened with Jesus, my teachings were eventually twisted by those who wanted to control others. When the dark force took over, my life was in danger, and not just the physical incarnation I had at the time; they wanted to capture my essence, my soul."

"What does that mean exactly?" asked Mia.

"If they had captured my essence, all traces of me would have ceased to exist. I wouldn't have been able to reincarnate, but even worse, it would have magnified their powers considerably."

"How so?" asked Bree.

"Imagine if you could harness the energy of the sun or a star, the amount of power that would give you. Yet by doing so, the star would cease to exist. It would have been something like that."

"Were you in a physical body, or actually a star?" Mia asked.

Dominique was shining so brightly Mia could hardly look at her.

"Well, a star is physical," Dominique replied coyly.

"Holy shit! You were a freakin' star!" said Mia.

"This explains everything," said Lori, laughing.

"How so? What do you mean by that?" Dominique replied.

"Well, your energy field's always felt so vast, you have a terrible time being human. You've got crazy clearance levels and connections, and Nick's always been so intimidated by your light. Oh, I wish he could be here for this conversation," said Lori.

"Nick found his light through his journey into the darkness. I have only known myself as light," Dominique replied.

"I didn't even know stars could incarnate into human bodies," Bree said.

"It's not typical, which is why it makes the perfect hiding place," Dominique said.

"My mind would be having a lot harder time grasping this if I hadn't already been having conversations with earth, air, water, and fire—and, of course, rainbows, clouds, and crystals," Mia said.

They all laughed.

"Consciousness can take whatever form it needs to evolve and experience life," Dominique said.

"How long have you been away?" Lori wanted to know.

"Long enough to have had multiple lifetimes on this planet," she said, sighing. "And it still isn't getting any easier. The complexities of being human and having such a limited physical vessel are things I think I'll never fully get used to, although this priestess thing might change all that, especially if they give me one of those golden lights like the one Mia has."

She winked at Mia, gyrating her hips under the water.

"Ha! Well, I'll have you know that I had a dream in which the golden light was also radiating out of my heart, and I was able to heal people by hugging them," Mia replied.

"Well, that's not nearly as exciting. Were you like Amma, the hugging saint from India?" Dominique asked.

"Well, no, it was still sort of sexual since there was kissing involved," Mia answered.

"Oooh, and you said 'people,' implying there was more than one?"

"There were two men, and by hugging the first, I dissolved the conflict that was about to occur, and we ended up kissing. Then the second guy was upset that I'd done that, so I did it to him so he'd understand. There was a golden light in my root chakra, but it traveled up to my heart chakra as well. The feeling of love in the dream was so visceral, to feel it emanate out of me into someone else just by touching them was incredible."

"I still like the way you did it in the first dream," Dominique teased.

"You must be getting closer to achieving this as you're having more dreams about it," Lori offered.

"Especially after the breathwork today," Bree said.

"I know. I'm super-curious to see what Gabriella has in store for us next," replied Mia.

The women spent the next few days continuing to heal the sexual trauma wounds they carried in their bodies. By the end of the week, they all felt lighter and clearer but also exhausted from the deep work they were doing.

"I'm very impressed with the way all of you dove into the core of your wounding these past few days," Gabriella said. "I know how challenging it's been, and you have my deepest respect. Get a good night's sleep, as we'll head to the Hilo side of the island tomorrow. And, if possible, please wear something red for our excursion."

They left before dawn, driving to the eastern side of the island, arriving just as the sun was rising. Gabriella had explained that they were headed to a sacred site known as Pele's Vagina Cave, an inactive lava tube that had been created thousands of years ago. The morning was cool and damp, and their shoes sank into the moist ground as they stepped out of the car. Silently, except for the sound of their squishing feet, they made their way to the cave's entrance. It was hard to find because of the overgrown vines, moss, and ferns covering its opening.

Gabriella had brought sage so that they could smudge themselves before going inside, and the smell of the herb always made Mia feel more alert.

The women had also brought offerings of fresh fruit, nuts, and seeds to leave at the cave entrance. Gabriella instructed them, "Gather around in a circle and hold hands."

Everyone silently gathered, reaching for one another's hands and gently clasping them.

"Mother Earth, Madam Pele, we humbly and respectfully ask permission to enter Your cave. We enter with pure hearts and ask that You help us reconnect to the sacredness of our temples.

"We have purified ourselves of the stories, beliefs, and judgments we once carried about our bodies and our wounds, offering our sacred wounds to Your fire so that they may no longer keep us from embodying the energy of the Goddess. *Amama ua noa.*"

"*Amama ua noa,*" they responded.

Mia's body started buzzing with energy. Feeling a little dizzy, she steadied herself as she walked into the cave. Inside, it was damp and dark, each of them carrying flashlights to illuminate the way forward. The cave was eerily quiet, seeming to absorb every slight sound they made as they walked, continuing ahead for about fifteen minutes through a narrow passageway until the cave opened up wider. Gabriella stopped and instructed everyone again.

"Here, everyone. Set all your stuff down."

She opened the canvas bag she had been carrying and handed everyone two red candles.

"This is where we'll do our ceremony. Set the candles in a circle and take off your clothes."

"I'm sorry, did you say take off our clothes?" Michelle asked, wide-eyed.

"Yes, we will bare ourselves completely before the Goddess," Gabriella answered.

"But aren't there bugs, possibly bats in here?" said Michelle. "Won't we get bitten to pieces?"

"You'll be fine, I promise," Gabriella replied.

They undressed, placing their clothes off to the side. After this, they placed lit candles in a circle in front of them at their feet, creating a beautiful golden glow in the cave.

"Now hold hands again," said Gabriella softly, beginning to sing in Hawaiian.

And though they couldn't understand the words, they all felt the power of the lyrics.

Tears streamed down their faces as they felt the wounding of the feminine, calling upon the fires of Pele to rise within them and transmute the pain into love, igniting their fierceness so they would never see themselves as victims again.

Gabriella had them speak the names of those who had wounded them, to be left forever in the cave. There was no echo in the cave as it absorbed every word they said.

"There is no looking back once we complete our time in the cave. We leave our abusers, our stories, our pain, our victimhood, here inside the fiery womb of Pele. As we exit the cave, we are moving forward, creating a powerful life for ourselves, no longer hiding or playing small. We claim our sovereignty and divinity so that we may help heal those who follow behind us."

Gabriella's brown eyes were glowing as she looked around the circle at each woman.

Mia's body was vibrating so intensely that she was surprised to still be standing, and though it was cold inside the cave, she was burning up, feeling as if she was going to pass out. She looked over at Lori for support, but could see through the darkness that Lori wasn't in any better shape.

The fire was cooking all of them.

Mia felt as though her body was melting, as if she was made of liquid gold. She closed her eyes, seeing her dragons before her. In the dream space, they guided her deeper into the lava tube where she looked down to realize she was walking on lava flowing from the earth.

Unbelievably, she walked on its red-hot stream until she arrived at the molten core.

There were no words, but she understood that the lava contained the love of Mother Earth, that it was pouring out of Her to heal the planet, continuing to flow in the four directions, north, south, east, and west, until it had surrounded Earth around the equator and from pole to pole.

How is this different from the green mist that will surround and heal Earth? she asked.

The green energy is from the heart of Mother Earth, and the lava from Her womb.

This is Her fire, the energy that creates and destroys. The dark force controlling your planet can't be removed with love alone, some aspects having become so twisted that they must be returned to Source to begin anew. The assault on sexuality can only be healed by fire.

The fire must purify it so that it can become sacred once again. You have done your part in allowing the fire to purify you, but now you must do it for all of the feminine. And once that is complete, you will use it to heal the masculine. First within yourself and then the world.

Her dragons encircled her, breathing the fire of the Goddess into her.

All of the energy that had been trapped inside the wound of the feminine was set free, and the story turned to ash. Mia let out a scream as the fire engulfed her.

Earth absorbed her cry as the sacred fire ignited within her.

Her awareness came back to the cave as she heard Gabriella singing, knowing intuitively that it was a prayer of gratitude, even though she didn't understand the words. Eventually, they all caught onto the chorus and started singing with her: *Mahalo nui no pomaika'i nei au,* meaning, "I am so grateful for all the blessings surrounding me."

They found their clothes in the darkness, making their way back to the opening. There, they emerged from the cave with their sacredness restored.

"I feel like a new woman," said Lori, moving her hips from side to side.

"I think we all are new women," Dominique said as she gyrated her own hips. "Although Mia, you don't look so good. Do you feel okay?"

"Yes, well, no, but I'm sure I'll be fine. I'm still really hot. Are any of you still feeling like you're on fire? Maybe I just need cool air and some water," she replied.

Lori touched Mia's forehead. "You're burning up; is it still considered a fever when it's induced by Mother Earth?"

Mia chuckled.

Dominique alerted Gabriella. "Is there a body of water we can get Mia into ASAP?"

Gabriella took one look at Mia. "Everyone get in the van," she said without hesitation. "There's a stream nearby where she can cool down; let's load up and we'll drive over to it."

Dominique nodded her agreement. "Mother Earth takes her out almost every time, but we can usually help her balance out with the help of the elements."

"At least I'm still conscious this time! And don't have to be carried," Mia said, laughing. "That's progress, at least!" Everyone seemed relieved that Mia at least felt well enough to make jokes about herself and the state she was in. It could have been so much worse.

They arrived at the creek and Mia took off her red dress as fast as she could and got in. The cool water soon began to ease the burning fire within her.

She could have sworn she saw steam coming off the water where she was lying. After several minutes, her flushed skin had returned to its normal shade.

"Okay, phew! You look a lot better now," said Lori. "You might be used to this, but I certainly am not. Especially when John's not around to take care of it."

Gabriella brought out the picnic breakfast hamper Healani and Kiele had packed for them the night before. It was filled with fruit, rolls, cheese, and hard-boiled eggs.

"Lori, I'd love some pineapple if you don't mind bringing me some," Mia said.

Lori smiled. "Thank you for knowing that I wanted a way to nurture you."

"Lori, you can always nurture me with pineapple, and any other way you want to. I always feel so loved and taken care of when you're around."

"And thank you for being willing to receive the gifts I love to offer you."

They ate their breakfast, sharing stories of their experiences inside the cave. They were all feeling different, as if the slate had been wiped clean.

They headed into Hilo, stopping at a large farmer's market. The booths spanned several city blocks and were filled with all types of vendors. There were also tables filled with brightly colored exotic fruits and vegetables that Mia had never seen.

Local artisans were selling their wares. There was intricate handmade jewelry, carvings, and paintings, while stunning sarongs of every color and hue were swaying in the gentle breeze.

In the center courtyard was a band playing traditional Hawaiian music while several Polynesian women performed the hula, dressed in bright green Ti leaf skirts and orange-and-red tops. They wore plumeria flower crowns on their heads and leis around their necks.

The rhythm of the music, the sound of the singers' voices, the graceful yet powerful way the dancers moved their bodies, were all hypnotizing. The dancers honored Earth, expressing gratitude, moving in unison. Mia felt her heart opening as she witnessed their prayer in motion.

After several songs, the dancers invited the onlookers to join in. Gabriella encouraged them all to dance too. "It will be so powerful after the morning we've all had in the lava tunnel."

"This is going to be amazing," exclaimed Lori, rushing over to join in.

"Yes!" agreed Mia, Dominique, and Bree, and they followed right behind her.

The dancers demonstrated the steps of the hula, breaking it down by movement and explaining what each one meant. They would honor the four elements as they moved.

They bent their knees, lifting their hips, swaying side to side as they rolled their arms like ocean waves. Bree was a natural, having studied many different dance styles.

Dominique and Lori picked it up easily too, rhythmically following along.

But Mia felt as though she was dancing in a brand-new body, still unsure of how to operate all its moving parts. As she continued swaying her hips, she felt her root chakra beginning to blossom. The energy flowing up her spine took control of her body, allowing her to move with the beat of the drums.

The women giggled as the joy effervesced from them.

Their open-hearted laughter was contagious, and soon the entire group was laughing like children, dancing and dancing until their bodies were too exhausted to move anymore.

They found a booth serving Kalua pork and decided their bodies could benefit from the grounding effects of the animal protein, even Bree agreeing her body was in need of some.

It came with a side of *poi*—a thick, slightly sweet paste made from the taro root—as well as chicken long rice, which were seasoned vermicelli noodles served in a broth with boiled chicken, and sautéed cabbage. The meat was tender, smoky, and juicy.

Mia felt more in her body than she had in weeks.

"Wow, my body really needed that. I feel so clear-headed and present," she said.

They ate until their bellies were full and then headed back to the temple.

19

Merkaba

Mia woke up early, quietly slipping out of the cabana so she wouldn't wake Dominique. The dawn hadn't started to illuminate the sky yet, so she figured it must be close to 5:00 a.m.

The air was thick and moist as she followed the path to the garden, relying on the solar lights that were still glowing. The garden was quiet except for the sound of the water flowing from the fountain. She took a seat on the stone bench, letting her feet sink into the damp grass, feeling herself easily connect into Mother Earth as her consciousness traveled down to the green crystal cave. She sighed, feeling the love surrounding her in this now familiar place.

You've done great work, my child, said the Goddess.

I couldn't have done it without everyone's help, Mia replied.

It's good that you recognize that. You are all connected and need one another. Humankind will accomplish so much more as you learn to co-operate and work together.

It is important that you teach them that.

Mia nodded in acknowledgment of the Goddess's words.

It seems there's so much to do to help heal Mother Earth and awaken humanity that it feels overwhelming at times.

The Goddess said, *And yet, all you need to do is keep your heart open. Allow me to do the rest.*

True. Mia smiled at that thought. *I am truly so grateful and humbled to have been chosen to be of service to you.*

I know. And your humility is why you were chosen, allowing you to access your vulnerability, beneath which lies your true essence. It is only through an open heart that I can merge with your essence and guide you to do my work.

As she heard these words, Mia could feel Sophia inside her heart, experiencing her as a bright golden light shining inside her chest. She felt powerful and invincible, and as though she was made of pure love. She took a deep breath, wanting to expand that feeling throughout her body.

Sophia allowed herself to do that, filling Mia up with her essence, sending swirls of energy emanating off her body. Mother Earth decided to join in the fun, sending a burst of green life force energy up Mia's spine to amplify the swirling energy, making her body tingle and vibrate.

The sun, now above the horizon, sent the morning's first light to her forehead, illuminating her third eye. *Soon you will be able to get Earth back on the proper timeline,* Sun said.

What do you mean? asked Mia.

You can see the world the way it's supposed to be and change it; it's one of your gifts.

But who are you? I have never heard your voice before, asked Mia.

I am Sun, pure divine consciousness.

How do I do this? she wanted to know, hoping He would explain it more to her.

He seemed to be a masculine force after all.

You already know how to do it; the dolphins will help you remember.

Mia's mind flashed to the dream she'd had a few months ago of the dolphin leaping from the water, touching her third eye.

What is the proper timeline? How will I know?

The timeline that allows everyone to remember the truth of who they are, the timeline that leads to the return of the Garden of Eden, to the Golden Age.

Mia felt a shimmering purple-and-gold light coming in through the crown of her head, making her dizzy. She squeezed her toes into the damp grass beneath her feet to help her ground.

Mother Earth responded by sending more of the green life force energy up her legs.

It's easier for you to hold my energy now, said the Goddess, *since we've been working together for so long. It'll take a while for you to get used to His energy.*

The rest of your team will help you with this.

Mia's mind flashed to John, Nick, and Marco. She had been so busy since she'd arrived on the Big Island, she hadn't thought about them much, but now saw them seeking shelter from the rain inside a cave. They were covered in mud and looked exhausted. All four elements were being ruthless with them. She understood that they were being tested, forced to surrender what was left of their egos to Pele. Their lack of sustenance and sleep was causing frequent hallucinations.

Marco looked as if he was losing his mind, haunted by the wrongdoings of his ancestors, centuries of controlling and disregarding women. He spent most of the day asking for forgiveness. Nick had spent years as an addict numbing his feminine side, dumbing down his tender heart and creativity. Pele was having him atone for silencing the voice of the feminine within him, flooding him with all the emotions he had been avoiding.

John was experiencing the repercussions of closing his heart to romantic love.

He had become too independent and was avoiding the possibility of getting his heart broken again, having never really trusted the love of a woman. Pele was igniting a fire within him, forcing him to confront the pain and beliefs that kept him isolated.

A part of Mia wanted to feel sorry for them, especially because she was being pampered in this temple, but she knew it was for their own good and they wouldn't have it any other way.

It seemed like the harder they struggled with their environment, the more they surrendered internally.

I wonder how long it'll be until I see them again.

As soon as you are all ready, replied the Goddess.

Mia took a deep breath before returning to the present moment, opening her eyes and taking in the beauty of the garden, now lit up by the morning sun.

The birds were starting to sing and she could smell the sweet scent of jasmine all around.

"Thank you." She smiled and looked about, loving and appreciating everything she saw. "I am so blessed." She allowed her heart to fill up with even more love.

Mia headed toward the kitchen to make herself a cup of tea. She found Kiele already in there, cutting up pineapple and mango for breakfast.

"Aloha," she said, smiling.

"Aloha! You're up early this morning," Kiele replied.

"I was so exhausted when we got back last night, I just showered and went straight to bed."

Kiele nodded. "I've noticed Madam Pele seems to be demanding more of you than the others. Your bowl of light is being purified."

"My bowl of light?" Mia appeared perplexed.

Kiele smiled, explaining, "Each of us is born with a bowl of light, connected to our true essence, our spirit. If we are taught to love and respect our light, we will know and understand all things. We will also be able to accomplish many magical things; we can swim with sharks and fly with the birds. But if we begin to judge ourselves and become fearful and ashamed, we begin to put stones into our bowl, and it blocks our light. Madam Pele is emptying your bowl of its stones." She put the plate of pineapple in front of Mia, having noticed how much she loved it.

"Yes, I'm definitely being purified!" Mia said, reaching for the prepared fruit. "I thought I'd already been cleaned out, but Gabriella's helping me find even more rocks in my bowl of light."

"Ah, she is a master at purifying the personality. By the time she's done with you, there will be only light in your bowl," Kiele replied.

"How long have you known Gabriella?"

"Since she opened the temple many years ago. I have been here since the beginning."

Kiele continued working as she spoke, putting the eggs in the pot to boil and turning on the kettle. "We've had many visitors over the years, but even more lately. People are starting to remember that life doesn't have to be so hard. They are starting to remember the path of Aloha."

Mia took another bite of pineapple, savoring the sweet and tangy flavor. Listening to Kiele made her even more hopeful about the future.

She turned to Kiele, saying, "Thank you for everything."

Then she went to dress for the morning session.

Gabriella explained that it was important for the women to integrate all of the healing they had experienced yesterday. She gave each of them a canvas bearing the image of a Merkaba, two intersecting tetrahedrons, representing the union of the divine masculine and feminine contained within a mandala. It consisted of three concentric circles, each adorned with lotus petals all the way around. They were to spend the day painting color into the image, creating a piece of art to represent the union of the masculine and feminine energies within them. Applying the colors of paint to the canvas had a hypnotic effect that took them all on a deep inward journey.

Mia decided to paint the top pyramid of her Merkaba bright purple to represent the Divine Masculine energy coming down from the heavens. As her thoughts drifted to the masculine, the memory of last night's dream came into her awareness. She had dreamt of Marco and herself.

They were together in many bodies, so many lifetimes, yet she could always recognize his eyes and the way his energy felt, his presence, his heart. He had always been by her side.

Sometimes they worked as a team, both leading the way. At other times, one led while the other would quietly assist from behind the scenes. She wondered why it had taken her so long to figure out who he was this time. *I did feel comfortable around him from the moment we met,* she thought. She laughed out loud, remembering how hard it was for her to look at him because she found him so attractive. *Okay, well maybe "comfortable" isn't the right word.*

I definitely felt a connection to him, and I liked him right away.

She realized as she kept painting that it was her fear of her own power that kept her from recognizing him. Her dreams had shown her the energy field that the two of them could create when they were together. It had something to do with the new clear energy, but she wasn't quite sure what. She only knew she had to be fully embodied in order to be able to hold it.

There was something about having that much power that scared her.

I was healing him.

She saw herself laying her hands on him, healing him from a bullet wound to the chest. Several other visions poured in, ones that hadn't been in her dreams. *I healed him in Egypt with my body and in Atlantis. He's always relied on me.*

The vision expanded, and she saw it was more than that. She wasn't just healing Marco; she was healing many people, all through his body. And she would have to do it again.

The dream in Sedona of the man who'd collapsed from fear flashed through her mind. She saw now that it had been Marco, only much younger than he was now. She was going to have to release the fear from his body with her own, the fear within the masculine that caused it to mistreat and try to control the feminine. Marco would need to fully surrender, letting in Mia's love. They would need to join their hearts, minds, and bodies for her to heal him.

Mia couldn't imagine this happening for a while.

How would she know when she was ready?

Gabriella walked up behind Mia's chair, placing her hands on her shoulders. "Trust me, there will be no doubt once the Goddess fully activates Herself in your body. And judging by the progress you've made on your Merkaba, I don't think it'll be much longer."

Mia felt chills and tingles all over her body as Gabriella spoke.

"Really? This is what activates it?" Mia asked.

"Well, it's helping to integrate all your experiences so your body can prepare for the next step."

"Hmm...Does it transmute fear as well? In the dream, I was hesitating because I was afraid of being too powerful," said Mia.

"Because what would happen if you were that powerful?" asked Gabriella.

"I don't know; I just feel this pit in my stomach."

"Close your eyes and go inside that feeling in your stomach and let it get bigger."

Mia put her hands on her stomach, allowing her conscious-ness to flow into her solar plexus.

"There's this fear that if I'm that powerful, I will be killed, re-jected. It's because I'm a woman; if I were a man, it would be okay for me to be that powerful," Mia realized.

"Mmm-hmm, what else?" said Gabriella.

"It goes beyond my lineage; it exists in all women. There's this terrible, devastating emptiness inside me, like a cavern, and I feel safe hiding in the shadows. I'm powerful, but no one knows it, and I have to remain hidden. Now I see a woman; it's Mary Mag-dalena. She is supporting Jesus, also doing so much more than anyone realizes. Only the two of them know. He is the external expression of the power of love; the world could only receive it from a man back then. They would have killed her if they had known how powerful she was. They were a team."

"Keep going," Gabriella encouraged.

"It still feels safe to be in the shadows, but the Goddess must return. And so it must be women leading the way. But I still feel this inverted energy inside me, and I want to stay in there. It feels like that's how I was designed, and I don't know how to change it."

"That has been true throughout history, but that's what you're here to change. Once the Goddess returns, it will be-come safe for women to be outwardly powerful again—not with the unbalanced love of power that controlled this planet, but rather with the power of love. The power that unites, heals, and harmonizes."

"So how do I convince my body to let the Goddess all the way in?"

"Look at your Merkaba. This image represents the merging and balancing of the masculine and feminine within you. It's al-ready happening. You must just release the layer of fear that's blocking the way."

"Do I need to do more breathwork?"

"I want you to keep working on your painting, but as you do, focus on all the ways that fear has kept you safe."

"But I thought I was supposed to get rid of the fear?"

"You are going to transform it, and the first step is to find all the ways it has benefited you."

"But I hate this fear; it's preventing me from being who I want to be. Why should I thank it?"

"You'll connect the dots as you focus on it. Trust the process."

"Okay." She sighed as if weary at the suggestion.

Mia stared at her painting, asking herself, *How has this fear served me?*

To her surprise, the answers appeared almost immediately.

It allowed me to remain invisible, so no one could see me. It allowed me to remain small so that I wasn't a threat to anyone. It gave me a place to hide. It saved me from conflict when I didn't have a voice to defend myself. It protected me.

Mia could see the paradox: the fear made her feel protected and safe, and yet, if she had access to her power, she wouldn't have felt so weak and defenseless.

She reached for the bright green paint that reminded her of Mother Earth. As she applied it to the bottom pyramid of the Merkaba, she saw herself as a little girl.

I really didn't have a choice; I was born into this lineage, born into a female body on Earth at this time, AND I know this all happened for a reason. Calling in fear for protection was the best I could do at the time, and it did save me from conflict and from being perceived as a threat to anyone. The more Mia thought about it, the less she hated the fear.

Thank you for protecting me when I didn't know where else to turn.

Thank you for being the perfect hiding place. Mia was genuinely grateful for this fear that had kept her small. She now allowed herself to feel love for the fear.

"Do you still need the fear, Mia?" Gabriella asked.

"No, I don't need it anymore. I'm ready to embrace my power now," she replied.

"So end your relationship with it and send it back to where it came from."

"How?"

"Use the power of your words. Command it away," Gabriella responded.

"Fear, I am ending my relationship with you. Thank you for protecting me when I thought I needed you. Thank you for making me invisible, but I don't want you anymore. And so I release you and send you back to your source." She saw the dark energy in her stomach spiral out of her body like smoke and instantly felt lighter.

"Is that it?" she asked Gabriella.

"Not quite. Now you need to activate something in its place. With which qualities would you like to replace the fear?"

Mia thought about it for a moment as she looked around the room to see what the other women were painting. Bree's mandala and Merkaba had a beautiful pair of horses, one on each side.

Lori's Merkaba was a beautiful rose-pink triangle merging with another that was midnight blue. Kuan Yin and a stunning pink dragon rose up from the swirling waters surrounding the lotus mandala. Dominique's mandala and Merkaba appeared crystalline, with a colorful ocean sunrise with leaping dolphins visible behind it.

She could see that, in each painting sadness or fear was replaced by something greater, whether it was the courage of Bree's horses, the unconditional love of Lori's Kuan Yin and the strength of her dragon, or the joy of Dominique's dolphins and the clarity of her sunrise.

"Love, truth, clarity, courage, and...balance. Yes, I want to feel balanced inside. To have that flow of strength and softness. Oh, and authenticity too," she said excitedly.

"Perfect. So claim those with 'I am' statements. I am love, I am truth, and so on. And repeat those mantras as you finish your painting."

Mia repeated the mantras, allowing the power of the "I am" statements to fill her up. She smiled at the green-and-purple Merkaba she had created, feeling the balance of the masculine and feminine within her. She painted the black around the Merkaba so it would appear to be floating in the Universe. She used gold to represent the light of her soul on the circles of lotus petals.

Now that these energies are united within me, they can be united outside me. Her mind flashed to Marco again; she was feeling nervous and excited to see him again.

What else do we need to do to be ready?

A vision appeared in her mind.

She was on top of the highest pyramid with Marco, they were working to bring the energy down to Earth. She was doing most of the work as Marco seemed to be struggling. At first, she worried it was too much for her to do on her own, but as she repeated the mantra, she felt empowered and unstoppable. She realized all the help that she had been given by John and the whole team, by Mother Earth, the fire, water, air, and the Crystal and Rainbow Beings—and now it was her turn, *their* turn, to help Marco. *I can do this; we can do this; this is who I AM; this is who WE ARE.*

Dominique gasped in delight as she walked by and saw Mia's painting.

Lori and Bree looked over, eyes wide. "Mia!" Bree said, "Your painting is creating a vortex!"

"Can you feel it too? When I looked around, I was so inspired by all of your mandalas, I feel as though all of our energy created the vortex," replied Mia.

Gabrielle smiled knowingly from across the room.

20

Sacred Sexuality

The next morning after yoga, Gabriella announced there would be no activity that day.

She said, "Everything we've done since your arrival has been in preparation for tomorrow. We've talked about ancient priestesses who knew the art of sacred sexuality and practiced it to connect to the Divine. The power they were able to generate could be used for healing, transformation, creating, and manifesting. Imagine a sacred practice that brings the energy of the Divine into form. These women understood that the gateway to access the Goddess was within a womb of light, an awakened womb. But because of the threat they posed to the religions that only worshipped a masculine God, they were persecuted, and their temples destroyed."

"You said this was orchestrated by a dark force that didn't want humans to know about their ability to create like the Divine. Right?" Ana asked.

"Yes, exactly. Because of all the damage and desecration done to the female body for millennia, it's taken a long time to restore the sacredness to our bodies. To this day, the vast majority of the population is confused about sexuality and continues to objectify and harm women. But deep within you, there's a seed of remembering the truth that has been dormant within your DNA. And you wouldn't have come here if it wasn't ready to activate within you."

Gabriella looked around the room at each woman.

"I suggest you spend the day in silence, contemplating and preparing for our final ceremony tomorrow. Is there anything remaining in the way of you embodying the Goddess? Are you prepared to stand before Her and fully accept Her into your body? Are you willing to live your life in service to the Divinity within you?" She paused, allowing the women to take in her words.

"We will meet at sunrise, and please, wear all white."

The next morning, Mia slipped on her white cotton sundress, placing the white shawl Gabriella had given her over her head.

The women gathered in the main room, then quietly made their way up the path to the top of the property, to a secret garden that had lain hidden from them by the vines of trumpet flowers.

As the sun peeked over the horizon, the light illuminated the immense beauty of this place. There was a small koi pond filled with white lotus flowers, while standing majestic in the center of the garden was a semicircle of concrete benches facing a small white building that appeared to be a miniature church. The structure had been intricately built with a steep tented roof and a Gothic-arched doorway. A round stained-glass rose window—tinted red—sat above the doorway, and the building was also surrounded by red rose bushes.

The Flower of Life was etched into the wall on one side of the door, an alcove with a golden statue of Isis set into the stonework on the other.

"Let us hold hands and ask for a blessing as we begin this ceremony," Gabriella said softly.

The women gathered in a circle, bowing their heads. Mia had not been able to sleep the night before and had a headache; she was struggling to pay attention.

"Blessed Goddess, we come to you with open hearts, purified minds, and bodies made whole. We come to be of service, to do your work, to be the vessels for you to embody. We humbly ask for the gifts that will allow us to help heal humanity and the planet."

Mia felt the air becoming thick like honey, the presence of the Goddess palpable.

The breeze picked up, swirling the scent of the roses among them. Mia inhaled deeply and felt her heart open. For a moment, the awareness of her pain dissipated.

Gabriella instructed, "This is the moment you have been preparing for since you arrived. Allow your consciousness to drop inside your heart as you review the journey we have undergone throughout the past few weeks. Honor the transformation that has occurred within you, feeling how much lighter you are now, how much more space has opened up inside you. Experience the openness of your heart, the expansion of your light."

Mia's heart was full of love and gratitude as she allowed it to open wider.

She thought of all the wounds she had healed since her arrival, feeling so blessed and ready for this next step. She wanted to fall even deeper into this state of love, but the pain in her head continued to distract her. *Please make it stop. I want to fully participate in this experience; please, please make the pain stop,* she begged.

Suddenly, Mia became aware of a sensation in her root chakra. It started to spin and swirl, and as it spiraled inside her, it became orgasmic. She could only equate it to the feeling of foreplay.

Oh yes! This is much better. She sent all of her awareness into the sensation of pleasure filling her lower body, her lips smiling as she floated in the ecstasy of the present moment.

"As you sit in meditation, I will be coming around and anointing you with spikenard, frankincense, and rose oil. I will let you know when it's your turn. Before entering the chamber, you will sit for a moment in this chair where Ke'alohilani will be washing your hands and feet.

"This is our temple of initiation. You will enter one at a time and spend a few minutes conversing with the Goddess. You can offer gratitude, you can ask for anything that you need, or if you are in need of further healing, you can also ask for that. She will have a message for you, so listen closely. You will enter with your heads bowed and kneel before the altar.

"When it is time for you to exit, I will ring this bell. You will then have a minute to leave. Please back out of the chamber with your head bowed as a sign of reverence, as we never turn our backs to the Goddess. You will then go and lie down while you integrate the experience.

"For now, while awaiting your turn, stay focused within in prayer with the Goddess."

The soft touch of Gabriella anointing her with the oils transported Mia back in time.

Her mind flashed to images of Mary Magdalena teaching her about the *hieros gamos,* the sacred marriage between God and Goddess. Spikenard was used to anoint the crown chakra by applying it to the hair and also the root chakra by applying it to the feet.

Mia saw Mary anointing Yeshua's feet and applying the oil to her hair.

The sacred marriage takes place first within you as you allow God and Goddess to be joined within your heart. But this can only take place within an undefended heart.

This will break open the power of love within you, and only then will you be ready to reunite with your beloved and the sacred sexual act between you can usher in the Golden Age.

Mia felt as though she was remembering the future in the past.

Had Mary given her the information for this lifetime over two thousand years ago?

That thought made her dizzy, so she grounded her awareness back into her vibrating root chakra. A bolt of energy shot up her spine, arching her back, causing her heart to open even more. Her body felt as if it was ready to go; she just hoped it would be her turn soon.

Sensing Mia's readiness, Gabriella touched her on the shoulder.

"Go sit in the chair so Ke'alohilani can prepare you for the bridal chamber, the room in which the sacred marriage of the Divine Masculine and Divine Feminine takes place, where two become one."

Mia attempted to stand, but found her legs too wobbly.

Gabriella supported her around the waist, escorting her over to the chair.

Ke'alohilani helped her settle, then placed Mia's feet inside a basin filled with warm water and rose petals.

Mia's mind traveled back in time again, seeing herself washing the feet of other women before their own initiations, the feet being sacred as the first point of contact with the earth.

Ke'alohilani washed and dried Mia's feet with such tenderness, this moment feeling so sacred as the love flowed between the two women. Next, she rubbed the essential oils on Mia's feet, causing her awareness to anchor deep inside the earth.

Mia sighed as her body relaxed.

Next, Ke'alohilani had Mia cup her hands over the basin while she poured rose water from a pitcher, then she dried Mia's hands with a soft cotton towel.

Gabriella reappeared, helping Mia to the door of the chamber and opening it for her.

Mia bowed her head as she entered, kneeling before the altar.

The table was laden with picture frames of images of the Goddess, Mother Mary, Mary Magdalena, Isis, Venus, Durga, Kwan Yin, Tara, Vesta, Athena, and several more, and there were candles and rose petals distributed throughout the room. Mia's impulse was to prostrate herself in front of the altar. But as she went to lie down, she heard a voice say, 'Stand up!'

As she stood in front of the altar, her kundalini thrust her hips forward and backward, the heat rising up her spine, arching her body in a rhythmic motion. She had to widen her stance so that she wouldn't lose her balance as the energy moved faster and faster.

A golden light appeared between her legs.

Mia couldn't tell whether it was emanating out of her or coming into her.

She heard the words: *"Equal in divinity to all beings on the table."*

That caused her body to thrust even faster, her arms flailing out at her sides, orgasmic waves of bliss moving through her one after the other. The golden light continued growing brighter, filling her entire body. From above, a violet light descended, too, pouring through her.

As Mia fully surrendered to the experience, love exploded in her heart and claimed all of her. She fell to her knees as love radiated out of every cell of her body.

Mia heard Gabriella ring the bell.

How can I make it to the door a few feet away?

But as the word "door" appeared in her mind, something transported her body in that direction with no effort on her part. She bowed her head in gratitude, backing from the chamber.

Gabriella led her to the blankets and mats under the canopy of white wisteria.

"You must rest, Mia," she said.

Mia felt as though she was lying on a cloud made to fit her body, and every fiber of her being basked in the feeling of a peace beyond understanding.

She closed her eyes, seeing the Universe spinning inside her heart, being as one with all of life, with all of creation. *I hope this feeling never ends. I feel so complete, every need and desire satiated. I could die in this moment completely fulfilled.*

Mia sighed, then welcomed a slow, long inhale into her body, each breath more exquisite than the last. *I am so in love with... everything!*

She allowed herself to drop even deeper into the feeling until all awareness of herself disappeared. She was now no longer the one experiencing the bliss; she had become the bliss and the love, and she was life itself. She followed the spiral as she expanded into life, then contracted into death...but the spiral continued birthing new creations infinitely.

She came back to her body when she felt Ke'alohilani gently massaging her feet.

Mmm...this is heaven. Mmm...no, I am heaven!

She opened her eyes, gazing with love at the white wisteria flowers hanging high above her head. She inhaled their sweet scent, receiving the love they were exchanging with her.

Mia stretched to help herself come back even more to this present moment, turning her head to see the garden filled with resting priestesses. She could see the energy grid now too; the priestesses were all connected into Mother Earth, anchored into their bodies and into the planet like never before. *A woman who is fully in her body can change the world.*

Mia could feel the truth of those words with every cell in her body, feeling the force of the elements inside her, the colors of the rainbow flowing through her.

She felt more alive and powerful than she thought possible.

Sitting up, she placed her hands on the earth, offering gratitude.

Holding all this power inside her filled her with humility, and she bowed her head to the ground, able to feel Earth's vibration against her forehead.

Spirals of green energy emanated out of the earth and into her body.

The more Mia loved the earth, the more love she received back, even feeling the plants all around her absorbing the love. All the creatures that were walking, hopping, creeping, crawling, or flying through the garden soaked it up as well.

This love sustains all of life and its source is infinite, for it is all there is.

This is my purpose, to be a conduit for love to flow through and radiate out of me, for this is how love heals the world. Using her powerful intention, she magnified this feeling as far out as she could, feeling everything for a mile in all directions…the fish, dolphins, eels, crabs, and starfish in the cove below, the birds flying through the sky, the dogs, cats, pigs, donkeys, mongooses, even the geckos walking on the earth.

Life was abundant and glorious. Yet the only thing she couldn't feel was the other people.

Not yet, she heard the Goddess say.

Oh, is that coming? She asked.

Yes, once you have help to amplify your field.

Marco's face flashed in her mind.

Once you initiate him, you'll be able to generate a bigger field of energy together.

Mia asked, *Marco? Am I the woman he's here to help?*

Her memories of her lifetimes with Marco slowly flowed into

her awareness. His appearance was always different, but his eyes remained the same—his big brown eyes.

Mia smiled as she thought about him.

So Marco is who I was feeling on top of Haleakala that morning. There is so much love between us. But why didn't I recognize him sooner, or why didn't he recognize me?

The Goddess responded, *You had to wait until you had embodied more of your spirit and were prepared for the mission or it would have distracted you both.*

Mia thought, *I wonder how he's doing. Surely, with all our past life connections, I can feel him, even though he's on a different island.*

She focused her attention on Marco, imagining her awareness traveling over to Maui. To her surprise, her awareness circled back to the Four Seasons Resort in Laulalai, just north of Kona.

What the heck? Why am I here?

She looked around. Then she saw the men sitting at the Beach Tree Bar and Lounge enjoying cheeseburgers and beer—except for Nick, who was drinking a Diet Coke. They were laughing and joking with each other, recalling their month camping in the West Maui Mountains.

They must have arrived yesterday, Mia thought.

Marco had insisted on treating everyone to a stay at the Four Seasons to recover from roughing it for so long. They looked good but also tired, all three of them thinner, and their muscles more defined. They all had beards and deep tans.

Mia allowed herself to know more about Marco, desiring to really feel who he was, allowing her awareness to experience his essence.

His heart is kind and generous; he's passionate and playful, but he's focused and committed to his mission. He's a good man, a really good man. Even though she already felt love for everyone and everything, she was sure that loving Marco as a man was going to be easy.

John said, *I wonder what Mia's up to?*

That's funny you said that. I was just thinking about her, too, said Marco.

Hmm, me three. Wonder if she's spying on us? said Nick.

Mia pulled back her energy, feeling as if she'd just been busted.

Ha! I told you guys we wouldn't have to worry about them knowing we were here on the Big Island, John said loudly. *Mia, we want to swim with the dolphins with you tomorrow. Meet us at the beach in the morning.*

Marco and Nick laughed.

Is that the extent of the communication we're going to rely on? You're not going to call or text them? asked Marco.

What if they have other plans?

How do we know they're even done with the priestess training? Nick asked.

Okay, well then, John replied, *how about, "Mia, I love you and would be honored if you would join us at beach in the morning if you are free." There, is that better?*

Well, we still don't know whether they got the message or not, said Nick.

Can you hear me, Mia? Give me a sign if you can, John said and then chuckled.

Mia laughed, imagining sending her affirmative in the wind.

Not yet knowing her own power, however, what she had intended to be a gentle breeze turned out to be a strong gust of wind, causing John to spill his beer on himself.

Oh, shit! Haha, see, she got the message! said John.

Mia infused them all with her love and returned to the garden.

Back in her body, she realized how hungry she was and got up slowly, not sure how well her legs would work. To her surprise, she felt strong and grounded. She was therefore able to meet up with Dominique, Lori, and Bree on the lanai and share their experiences in the temple over lunch. Mia also told them where John and the men were and what the plan was for tomorrow.

After dinner, Gabriella had everyone gather in the main temple where, as usual, they opened with a prayer and dance, but the energy in the room tonight was different.

Each woman seemed more present, more embodied, more fully herself, filling the room with far more light. There was so much love and gratitude for all they had experienced together, and for all that they had received. They knew they had forever been changed.

There was also sadness in the air because this was their last night together. They had become like sisters bonded through their love; they had been doulas for one another in birthing their true selves, and priestesses when they had witnessed the alchemy of transmutation. They would carry one another in their hearts, returning to the world to do their work for the Goddess.

"It has been my absolute pleasure to hold space for you, witnessing your courage, your open hearts; your transformation has been such a blessing. I know the world is in better hands because of the healing you have all done. I have great hope for our future."

As spokesperson for the group, Mia stood up and addressed Gabriella.

"We would like to thank you for following your vision and creating this sacred place, for your dedication and commitment to the Goddess, and for sharing your wisdom with us. I know that we all leave here better women because of you. We have some offerings for you, brought as a token of our appreciation. First, a lei that we made from flowers we collected in the garden."

Bree walked over to Gabriella and placed a lei of purple orchids around her neck.

"We also decided that as our queen priestess, you also needed a flower crown," said Mia.

Lori placed a crown of lilac orchids on Gabriella's head.

"Oh, thank you, these are so beautiful," replied Gabriella.

"And we ordered you something a while ago that luckily arrived just in time," said Mia.

Dominique placed a wrapped gift in Gabriella's lap.

Gabriella untied the red ribbon and opened the package, pulling out a white alabaster ovoid jar with a domed lid.

"This is magnificent!" gushed Gabriella.

"It's from Egypt, and it's filled with spikenard," said Mia.

"Oh, it's absolutely perfect!" Gabriella exclaimed as she opened the lid and smelled the semi-sweet, musky odor of the oil. "Mary Magdalena would be pleased. Thank you, ladies, so much; I am deeply touched by your generosity and thoughtfulness."

The women shared stories of their most memorable experiences on the island, laughing and crying until it was time to say goodbye.

21

Dolphins

———

Bree, Lori, Dominique, and Mia were the first to arrive at the beach and had the cove to themselves. They carried their towels, snorkels, masks, and fins and went to sit for a moment on the sand. They had planned on meditating for a while, but could already see the dolphins swimming in the cove. It was far too tempting to wait any longer.

"Bree, is there anything we need to know before we get into the water with the dolphins?" asked Lori. "As excited as I am, I'm also a bit nervous about swimming with wild dolphins."

"You're afraid of the dolphins?" asked Dominique.

"No, it's not that, I just don't want to do anything wrong," explained Lori.

"I appreciate you asking," said Bree. "And it's a really good and considerate question, in fact." She eyed Dominique as if to ensure she also was listening after her flippant comment to Lori.

Bree continued, "Most people get so excited to swim with

them that they forget they're entering the dolphins' rest area, and the dolphins will be slightly apprehensive too, despite being accustomed to people—because, of course, every person, every swimmer, reacts to them differently. So ask permission as you enter the water; take time over this, asking them to feel your intention. I know they're already going to feel how loving and gentle you all are, so I'm not that worried about it. Swim out there and hold still, float, and let them come to you. Please don't swim after them or touch them because the oils from our skin aren't good for them."

"Are we going in now, or should we wait for the guys to get here?" asked Lori.

"It might take them a while to get here since their hotel's so far north," said Mia.

"Plus, it's better if we go in individually instead of as a big group," Bree replied. "And there's no telling how long the dolphins will stay, so I suggest we get in the water with them, and the guys can join us when they get here."

Mia was grateful for Bree's response, not only because she was excited to swim with the dolphins, but also because now that the time was here, she was feeling slightly nervous about seeing Marco again. How would she explain everything to him?

In fact, should she even tell him what she knew?

The water was the same temperature as the air, so it was easy to get in and, one at a time, the group began swimming out toward the dolphins.

Mia's body was feeling so strong as she glided through the water; she knew the dolphins were close, but she couldn't see them yet. She pushed her body to swim faster, eager with anticipation for the first encounter. She could hear the sounds they were making, but still couldn't see them. *Oh, that's right*, she thought, *Bree said to hold still and let them come to me.*

She stopped swimming, allowing herself to float motionless in the ocean, focusing on her heart and offering gratitude for this moment. She allowed her body to relax and her mind to soften. As she did, her kundalini kicked in, causing her body to pulsate in the water.

She became aware of the feeling that someone was behind her.

She turned, expecting to see Dominique or Bree, but instead saw at least thirty dolphins swimming right toward her. She was momentarily overwhelmed.

Wow! How many there are! It's like a wall of dolphins! she thought, trying to regain her composure. There were so many of them that there was no place she could go to get out of the way. But there was no need for her to move; the dolphins swam past her but then circled her so that she was completely surrounded. There was a feeling of calmness and safety, a sense of certain protection, as if they were shielding her from the outside world.

She didn't understand at first, but then the message appeared in her mind's eye.

There will be many changes happening on the planet; many people will be in fear. We want you to know that you are protected.

Mia was surprised by the message.

She had already assumed that she was safe and protected; that's what her dragons were for. *What could possibly be about to happen that would require the need for extra protection?* She didn't ponder the question for long, however, as she was suddenly distracted by baby dolphins spinning playfully out of the water. Filled with delight and wonder, her heart opened even wider.

She felt as if she was home, that she knew these creatures on some intimate level. As the dolphins continued to swim around her, she now became aware that they wanted her to swim with them, that they were excited at her being there, so close.

She started swimming, and they swam alongside her, escorting her out into the deeper water. Bree had said not to touch the dolphins, but they kept swimming so close to her that it was hard to avoid contact. Two larger dolphins appeared along either side of her.

She wanted to follow Bree's instructions, but it felt as though these huge, loving mammals wanted her to reach out and hold on.

She extended her arms slowly, gently placing them on their dorsal fins.

The contact sent an electrical current through her body, images of tall, luminous beings flashing in her mind. She knew their faces; she remembered who they were. Her heart was overflowing with joy as she felt the love from her soul family.

I remember. I know who you are. I've missed you so much, she told them.

They all responded simultaneously, *I know. We've been waiting so long for you to return. When you left Egypt, we didn't realize you wouldn't be back until now.*

You've been incarnating here on Earth this whole time? she asked.

We committed to being here when the humans remembered. We had to help the planet as much as we could until then. But now that the Goddess is back, it won't be long now.

What won't be long now? asked Mia.

The time of the prophecy is now and we will be free to move on if we choose to.

Mia said, *Humanity owes you a great debt. Human beings have no idea how much you've helped them.*

We need you to come with us.

Where are we headed? Mia needed to know.

All the pieces are almost in place; it won't be long before your mission is fully activated. The amount of fire energy that will be running through you will incinerate you unless it's balanced by a proper cooling system. Water will be essential to the success of the project and, well, to your physical survival.

Mia was a little confused. *But I thought I'd already received a water activation.*

You did, but it will be a lot of fire energy, so you're going to need to embody the ocean.

Mia frowned momentarily.

The ocean? How the heck am I going to do that?

The voices came back, saying, *You don't need to know how; just allow it to happen.*

Right. Is this going to make me retain water? She giggled, amusing herself. *Will I end up bloated?*

As they swam deeper, Mia had a strange feeling that she had been here before. She had never gone scuba diving in Hawaii, so she knew it couldn't be from this lifetime. The dolphins slowed as they approached what appeared to be a swirling circle of energy.

Is that a vortex? Have I been here before?

It's the gateway to Lemuria, and, yes, you have been here before.

Before Mia could ask any more questions, she and the dolphins were swimming through the portal, through time and space, into the dimension in which Lemuria existed.

Once on the other side, they swam several yards toward a shore.

Is this really Lemuria? This place is real?

Of course it is. You called this place home for many years.

It feels familiar, but I don't remember any details.

You will remember what you need to help you complete the mission. Someone will be there to assist you. We'll wait here for you and escort you back once you're done.

Okay, Mia agreed.

Mia swam the rest of the way until she could stand; then she walked onto the shore and looked around, taking it all in. Her senses were overwhelmed by the beauty around her. She noticed that the soft sand beneath her feet was light pink, and the beach was overgrown with tropical foliage. The sweet scent of flowers hung in the air and the birds were singing loudly in the trees.

The sky was pale lavender. While a part of her mind felt as though she was seeing a strange new world for the first time, she also felt oddly at home.

I know this beach; I know these plants.

Mia paused to feel what she was experiencing, feeling the essence of every living thing around her, including the sand, the air, the trees. Mia knew them; they were a part of her.

Sophia allowed more of her memories to be revealed to Mia.

Mia saw images in her mind of the time she had lived here. She and all the people of Lemuria were tangibly aware of their oneness, their connection to all of life, living with love and reverence for all beings, in harmony. Harming another being would have meant they were harming themselves, so it would never occur to them to do so.

Sophia had been a priestess in this lifetime, a beloved and respected leader and a teacher in her community, and she was living her life in service to the whole. Having become one with all of the elements, she therefore had the ability to influence them.

This is why even the air feels familiar; I had merged with all of life. Lemuria and I were one.

She looked back at the sea, immediately able to understand what the dolphins had meant by embodying the ocean. She knew what it meant to feel that connection so strongly that there would cease to be any feeling of separation.

If I had been born into a world that remembered the Goddess, this is how it would feel. And I feel Her everywhere. Mia's heart expanded in her chest, feeling the love existing all around.

Wow, how do I keep this awareness with me? I want this to be permanent; how do I take this back to my world?

That was when she saw him. He came sauntering slowly out of

the jungle and Mia could feel his immense power from fifty yards away.

I know him. I recognize him from my dream.

He continued to walk toward her, his huge amber eyes fixed on hers.

Mia was filled with awe at his strength, the ground seeming to shake with every step he took. When he was in front of her, she kneeled so she could look him in the eye.

Then she reached out and touched his fur. Sweetly, he leaned his face into her gentle caress.

You are the tiger from my dreams. We were a team when I lived here. You helped me with everything. Her eyes filled with tears, remembering her love for this magnificent being.

It's good to see you in a body again, Sophia, he replied.

Mia touched her forehead to his, allowing herself to experience the depth of their connection. He was a companion spirit who had traveled with her throughout most of her incarnations, her current lifetime on Earth being one of the first in which he hadn't been with her in physical form.

They had battled evil together in other pockets of the galaxy, helping countless planets through their awakening processes.

For the record, I wanted to be with you in your dimension, but you asked me to wait here for you. You said you would come find me when it was time, said the tiger.

Thank you, my friend. I finally made it to you. She pulled her head back and smiled.

Where's Marco? Didn't he come with you? the tiger wanted to know.

No, he doesn't know who I am yet, answered Mia bluntly, as if it would make sense.

What do you mean he doesn't know who you are yet? Who's protecting you then?

I'm fine, asserted Mia. *My team has been helping me, and the islands have kept me cloaked.*

That's not enough. He needs to be protecting you. When they find out who you are, they will come after you. He needs to be there, the tiger insisted.

Well, I'm going to see him later today, so I'm sure he'll know by then, Mia said, indignant.

I would never have agreed to let you go alone if I had known how reckless your plan was.

Well, I couldn't very well walk around Earth in this day and age with a tiger by my side, Mia answered. *Somehow, I reckon that would have blown my cover right away! Don't you think?*

Mia set off laughing at her own humor, trying to diffuse the tension between them.

Yes, but I could have gotten you away from that entity you dated for so long, the big cat said.

Mia retorted, *But how else could I have learned to recognize them in human form? I needed that experience with Richard. It was useful for me, even if it wasn't exactly fun for me...*

The tiger huffed loudly. *Look, he almost killed you, Mia! He could have drained you of all your light if you hadn't gotten away from him when you did.*

Mia still wasn't ready to stop arguing. *Well, John and Nick got me away from him, so it all worked out. And they've done a really good job of keeping me safe.*

So they are with you now?

No, but they'll be arriving soon.

I see, said the tiger. *So who's protected you since you've been apart from John, Nick, and Marco? And what do you mean by Marco doesn't know who you are? How could he not know?*

It's a long story. Mia was starting to get frustrated. *Listen, thank you for being concerned for my safety but I promise I've been fine. In fact, just the other day, I got my dragons in place and was told I'm impervious to evil.*

Yes, but that's only on a personal level; once you get ready to activate the vortex to heal the collective, they will come at you with everything they have.

She snorted as if in derision. *And Marco will be able to protect me better than dragons can?*

She chuckled at the conversation she was having with a tiger in Lemuria, thinking how strangely magical her life had become.

Yes, he is the key. And I only agreed to stay behind because you two promised me you'd protect each other.

Okay, I'll make sure he knows who I am as soon as possible, conceded Mia at last, exhausted from this disagreement. *Now let's talk about why I'm here. I can feel the oneness and my connection to all of life in a way that I have only glimpsed in my dimension. It feels amazing and—powerful. I feel impervious to danger here.*

That's because there is no danger in this dimension, the tiger answered. *There is only love.*

But I also feel powerful; I feel the force of the wind, fire, water, and earth, all at my fingertips. Can't I take this feeling back with me? she asked.

What you're feeling is the power of love. Source exists in union with all of life here, not like the separation you experience in your dimension. But yes, this is what you came here to remember. You knew it wouldn't be possible for your human self to understand how to have the elements assist you in your mission unless you felt how it was to merge with all of them simultaneously. What you feel at your fingertips is the power of the perfect storm.

Mia asked, *Okay, but how do all the puzzle pieces fit together?*

You need the help of all the elements to bring the two aspects of Source into your body in your dimension. And you need Marco to help with the external aspect of the coming together of male and female.

Oh, I thought he was just my security detail, Mia teased.

The tiger ignored her comment. *Once all the pieces are in place, Source will be able to return to your dimension.*

Mia nodded and smiled, realizing her Sophia had kept the plan hidden from her so that the entities wouldn't be able to access it from her memories.

This is all I need, isn't it? What you just told me, and the experience of oneness, that's what I came here for.

Yes, the tiger confirmed.

Thank you, my friend. It's been really good to see you.

Mia wrapped her arms around his neck and hugged him tightly. She didn't want to leave him so soon, but a strong feeling that it was time to get back was pulling at her.

Now that you know how to get here, you can come back and visit me again.

I will, I promise. And I hope you'll keep showing up in my dreams. She kissed him on the forehead, then stood and took one last look at everything. She sighed and breathed in the love she could feel all around her. *This place is hard to leave.*

She swam out into the ocean and found the dolphins waiting for her.

That was amazing, thank you for bringing me here.

You're welcome, they said. *Now let's get you back to your reality.*

They swam through the portal, back to the third dimension. There was a layer of sadness inside Mia that she hadn't been aware of before. She realized that it had always been there, that as blessed and magical as her life was here, the absence of constant connection with Source was heartbreaking. *Have I lost the feeling already? I thought I was supposed to bring it back with me.*

The answer came.

You can never lose it; Lemuria is a part of you, your first home on Earth, and it is a vibrational match to the frequency of your soul. Lemuria is in your essence.

But I don't feel it the way I did when we were there. I feel this layer of sadness inside me. Do we really need to go back? Did I do something wrong?

It's still there; think of your experience of Lemuria as your destination, your North Star guiding you home. The sadness is an indication of the distance you need to travel. When your mission is complete, life on Earth will feel the same as Lemuria does to you.

Mia did as they instructed, visualizing Lemuria showing her the way forward. As she relaxed into it, she was able to focus more on the love and less on the sadness. She remembered John's words, *Where awareness goes, energy flows.* The thought that she would be assisting in bringing this feeling to everyone on Earth filled her with tremendous joy.

As they swam her back to shore, they sent more sonar waves rippling through her body.

All the pieces are now in place. You now know who you are.

Mia thought about it. *They are right.*

Oh, my gosh, it's true, I remember ancient Egypt as if it was yesterday—and wow, all of it! My awareness of myself is beyond this lifetime, this personality; it includes this version of myself, but there's also an infinite vastness, she said.

All the barriers in her mind crumbled; she now had access to all parts of herself. The sonar wave from the dolphins had dissolved the remaining limitations of her ego so that she could experience all of herself.

How can I ever thank you?

Just save the world and set everyone free, replied the dolphins.

Haha, okay. Only that?

She hugged them goodbye and promised not to wait so long for the next visit.

As she walked out of the water, she recognized John sitting by her stuff. Looking around for the others, she caught a glimpse of Nick's mohawk just as he went underwater.

John had been sitting on the shore, watching her verbal exchange with the dolphins.

He knew she'd soon be coming out of the ocean a new woman.

As she walked up toward him, he saw how differently she moved in her body, with a confidence that hadn't been there before, a strength, a sense of security; it was a softness of no longer having anything to prove because she knew who she was.

"You look like Venus emerging from the ocean," he said once she got closer.

"I certainly have been reborn today," she said, smiling.

"You look like you're ten feet tall—if we include your halo." He smiled.

She laughed. "Yes, please include my halo, especially now that I have my body."

"So should I call you Sophia or are you going to stick with Mia?"

"I'll stick with Mia, so I don't confuse anyone...although it feels like the two of us have merged into a whole new being. Maybe I need a whole new name!"

She sat down next to him on the towel.

"It's good to see you so fully in this body," he added.

"Feels really good to be here. These past few weeks have been transformative."

"I can see that. If I hadn't always known who you were, I wouldn't recognize you."

"Well, with that beard, I hardly recognize you either!" She laughed.

"Haha, yeah, Nick and Marco shaved theirs off this morning, but I decided to keep mine a few more days."

"I saw Nick getting in the water. Is Marco already swimming as well?"

"No, he should be back any second. He forgot his towel in the car."

Marco grabbed his towel and locked up the rental car. As he headed back, he saw Mia standing in front of John. She looked up and saw him, their eyes connecting.

To her surprise, Marco fell to his knees.

"Marco, are you okay?" she asked, quickly walking toward him.

John got up and headed toward the water to give them privacy.

"It's you. I couldn't see it before, but I do now. You're her, the woman I'm here to..." Marco couldn't finish the sentence. He stared at her, unable to say anything else.

Mia nodded. "Are you okay?" She could feel his heart pounding.

His eyes were brimming over.

Mia reached out and touched his cheek.

He placed his hand over hers. "*Lo siento.*"

"What's wrong?" she asked.

Marco closed his eyes and savored the touch of her hand on his skin. He took hold of both of her hands and took a deep breath, looking into her eyes once again.

"I am sorry for all the pain men have caused women. For all the wrongdoings, for the ways we have mistreated you. For the abuse and violation, and for all the unspeakable things men have been doing to women for thousands of years, I beg for your forgiveness. We should have been protecting you, celebrating you, worshipping you, and instead, we nearly destroyed you."

As Marco spoke, silence fell all around them.

The birds in the trees stopped chirping, the wind ceased blowing, and the waves were no longer crashing against the shore. Mia could see a purple stream of energy pouring down through the top of his head. She tilted her head sideways, seeing between the dimensions.

Marco is atoning for all of mankind, asking the Goddess for forgiveness through me.

Though everything was silent all around them, she heard glass breaking, immediately feeling the world come crashing down. The grid of the patriarchy was disintegrating with every word that he spoke as he took responsibility for the actions of all men at the foot of the Goddess.

The purple light of the Divine Masculine continued flowing into him, filling him up completely. The green light of the Goddess flowed out of Mia's hands and merged with the purple light in Marco's. Mia's mind wanted to say, *Marco, you haven't hurt anyone!*

But she knew he was healing this for the collective.

She felt so moved to hear the sincerity in his voice.

"I forgive you," she said, breaking the silence.

The birds recommenced singing as if they had been holding their breath, waiting for her answer. The ocean waves resumed their dance on the sandy beach.

She pulled Marco up and he stood in front of her.

"Thank you," he whispered.

She pulled him into her arms and pressed her body against his.

He wrapped his arms around her, closing his eyes, saying not a word as he was captivated by the moment. They held one another for what seemed like an eternity, neither one of them wanting to end the embrace.

Their hearts connected, remembering all the lifetimes through which they had traveled together. Though their appearances had been different each time, the light in their eyes was always the same. Mia smiled, remembering how much she loved this man.

She pulled her head back from his chest and looked up into his eyes.

Rising onto her tiptoes, she placed a kiss on his lips.

Marco wrapped his arms around her, picking her up and spinning her around.

Mia squealed with laughter.

"You have just made me the happiest man on Earth!"

He stopped and kissed her softly at first, savoring every sensation of the moment. He had searched for her for over a decade, and at last, he had found her. He felt her body quiver in response to his touch and deepened his kiss. The air around them felt warm and thick like honey. It wasn't really the air; it was the energy field they were creating, their energy particles swirling around one another, creating a spinning vortex between them.

She had known the moment they kissed would be significant, but this was more than she had ever imagined, everything around her feeling amplified.

"You two are glowing!" announced Dominique, walking back up from the water.

They broke their embrace and smiled sheepishly like two teenagers caught in the act.

"Maybe you should go cool off in the water," she teased.

"Oh, Dominique, be nice. They just found each other!" exclaimed Lori.

"I'm only teasing. I'm super happy for you guys."

"Who are you happy for?" Nick asked. He placed a handful of seaweed on Dominique's head, causing her to squeal.

"Nick!" she yelled.

"Did you miss me?" he asked, trying to hug her.

"No, now get away," she laughed.

John walked back from the water.

"Well, it didn't take long for you two to start teasing each other again," he said.

Nick hugged Lori instead. "It's good to see you beautiful women again. I got tired of only having these two hairy guys to look at the last few weeks. And you smell a lot better than they do, too! Wow, Mia, did you get taller? You're glowing."

"That's probably from kissing Marco," Dominique teased.

"Well, it's about darn time," said Nick.

"Yes," said Mia.

"Where's Bree?" asked Lori.

"She must still be swimming with the dolphins," said John.

"Do you want to go swim with them, Marco?" Mia asked.

"I do. Will you come with me?" he asked, not wanting to leave her side.

"Absolutely!"

Marco grabbed Mia's hand as they walked down to the water.

"Does it feel to you as if everything is oddly familiar and yet completely new at the same time?" Mia asked.

He smiled. "Yes, I feel like I'm experiencing the world for the first time with you by my side, and yet also that we've done this hundreds of times before."

"Like when you were holding my hand just now."

"Yes, and when I kissed you a moment ago." He pulled her close, softly kissing her lips.

Mia sighed. "Dominique may be right; I think we need to get in the cold water."

Marco laughed. "Yes, the dolphins may give up on me and leave."

They swam out and found the pod of dolphins. Just as the dolphins had done before with Mia, they swam in a circle around Mia and Marco, too.

It was hypnotizing to watch them move through the water. They started swimming faster and faster, creating a whirlpool around them.

What are you doing? Mia asked but didn't hear an answer. She looked at Marco, who signaled that they should raise their heads above water.

"I keep getting the image that our bodies need to be vertical and connected," said Marco. "I think the image is coming from the dolphins. I think they are trying to do something to our combined energy field."

"Okay."

Marco pulled her close and held her as they felt the water spin around them, its momentum pulling them beneath the surface. They could hear the whistles and clicks of the dolphins all around. Mia's kundalini turned on, her body tremoring as Marco held her tighter.

Together, they descended until they touched the ocean floor, both experiencing Mother Earth and anchoring their energy into Her. Then they heard the song of a humpback whale in the distance. As the sound traveled through the water, it was amplified by the spinning vortex around them, making them feel as if they were experiencing it in surround sound. As it got louder, the sound waves moved inside their bodies and Marco's body began vibrating in unison with Mia's. Though they were right side up, they both experienced themselves being upside down.

Marco thought he was going to lose consciousness, but willed himself to stay present, afraid of what could happen to Mia if he didn't.

Finally, the dolphins dispersed, and the vortex stopped spinning. Mia and Marco felt the earth releasing them, and they floated to the surface in a slow spiral.

"What the hell was that?" Mia laughed.

"I was hoping you would know," replied Marco.

"I only know that I need to get back on land. That made me dizzy," said Mia.

"Me too, let's go."

As they began to swim back, two larger dolphins swam along-side Marco and sent sonar waves through his brain.

Sorry, one last adjustment, they both heard the dolphins say as they swam off.

They made it back to shore and lay down on their towels.

"That was intense," said Marco.

"Yes," agreed Mia.

"They're getting your bodies ready," said John.

"Ready for what?" Marco asked.

"Let's just say I think you two should take things very slowly. The merging of your energy fields is going to change this planet. And you'll want to make sure all the upgrades are in place before you…Well, before you…get too intimate," John replied.

Mia blushed, burying her face in her towel.

Nick, Dominique, Lori, and Bree reemerged from the water.

"I'm hungry," said Nick.

"What about the rest of you? Is everyone feeling complete with the dolphins?"

"Definitely," said Marco.

Mia giggled.

"Yes, I'm feeling pretty waterlogged," said Bree, who had swum with them all morning.

"Where are we staying tonight? Did you guys check out of the Four Seasons?" asked Dominique.

"No, we haven't checked out yet. How did you know we were staying there?" asked Nick.

"I have my sources," replied Dominique.

"I got a suite for you ladies as well. Figured we could work out our plan from there," said Marco.

"Wow, thank you, Marco," said Lori. "That is so generous of

you. Should we drive back and have lunch there? Nick, can you wait that long to eat? I have a protein bar for you."

"That works for me!" Nick replied.

After showering in their rooms, everyone met in the lobby and headed to the Residents' Beach House restaurant for lunch. Sitting under the lanai at a table set for seven, they recapped the last few weeks.

"I heard you got some special kisses from the fire ants, Nick," said Dominique.

"Oh, man, that was terrible," Nick replied.

"Yeah, I thought we were going to have to cut the trip short after that. Nick was so miserable," said John.

Marco said. "I've done a lot of camping over the years, but this trip was definitely a humbling experience."

"We definitely got our asses handed to us," Nick quipped.

"Mother Earth reminded us of how vulnerable we really are without Her mercy," said John.

"What about you, ladies? How was the temple?" Nick inquired.

"It was a thorough cleansing," said Lori.

"Yes, I need a break from all this spiritual work...at least for a few days," said Dominique.

John nodded in agreement. "I think we've all earned a few days off."

"Marco, do you still want to go to Mauna Kea?" asked Bree.

"I do, but I probably need to wait at least twenty-four hours after being at the bottom of the ocean. You know, to adjust to the elevation change."

"We could wait and go later in the day tomorrow and stay for some stargazing," said Bree. "People say it's the most spectacular place to do that."

"I think I'll just relax here tomorrow," said Dominique. "Haleakala was too much for me, and feeling into Mauna Kea, it's even more powerful."

"Yes, it's considered the most sacred spot on the island," said Bree.

"Do you want to go?" Marco asked Mia.

"I do." She smiled.

He smiled back, gingerly placing his hand on her thigh. His touch sent a bolt of energy through her, causing her spine to straighten.

"Well, I better go to make sure these two don't set off the volcano while they're up there," commented John, chuckling.

"The crater on top's frozen solid, so we should be safe," Bree observed.

"I think John's right; with the way these two glow every time they touch each other, we'd better not take any chances," said Nick.

Mia blushed, and Marco laughed.

After lunch, Mia and Marco went for a walk on the beach.

"I want to know everything about you," said Marco.

"Don't you feel like you already do?" asked Mia.

"Yes—well, kind of," Marco answered. "But I still want to hear about your life, like where you grew up, and about your family. How did you meet John and end up in Hawaii? Oh, and at Iao Valley, Nick referred to you as the 'secret weapon'; what did he mean? We haven't even talked about the mission either; we should compare notes, see what each of us knows about it."

"Haha, oh my gosh, that's like a million questions. It's going to take hours to tell you all these stories."

"Good, because I want to spend the rest of the day with you."

He reached for her hand as they kept walking down the beach.

"All right, but I'm going to want to hear your life story as well."

"Then we may have to stay up all night, talking," Marco replied.

They walked for a while, then found a cabana by the pool where they could relax on the lounge chairs. Mia told him everything she could remember, but so much of her past seemed distant and unimportant. Neither one of them knew much more than the other about the mission.

"I know I'm supposed to bring heaven to Earth to help people open their hearts and remember our oneness, our connection to Source," said Mia.

"Hmm, that's interesting," said Marco. "For me, the message I kept getting over and over was that I need to protect you and help you complete the mission. But they didn't give me any specifics. Do you know any more details?" he asked.

"I think it has something to do with this," she said. Mia leaned over and kissed him.

"Mmm, really? This is the mission, is it? This is a good mission," he said, kissing her back.

Mia pulled back.

"Yes, but apparently as we…Well, when we…um…are eventually intimate with one another, something bigger will happen. And I kept getting the message about you protecting me too, so, apparently, there is risk involved. That may be what John was referring to earlier."

"Speaking of John, do you want to find the others for dinner, or should we eat on our own? It looks like the sun is about to set."

"Let's have dinner alone, just the two of us so we can continue our conversation."

They walked out to the beach to watch the sunset.

Marco stood behind her and wrapped his arms around her. She rested the back of her head on his chest as the horizon glowed deeper shades of pink, yellow, and orange.

Thank you, she said and sighed as her heart overflowed with gratitude.

"This may be the best day of my life," he said as he kissed the top of her head.

"Mine, too."

They stayed until the sun disappeared into the ocean and then walked over to the 'ULU Sushi Bar, where Marco entertained her over dinner and sake with stories of his adventures around the world. The stars gradually appeared in the night sky, and they talked until the restaurant closed and then walked back to her room.

"To be continued over breakfast?" he asked.

Mia nodded, stopping in front of the door to her suite.

Marco placed his hands on her waist and pulled her in as he leaned down and kissed her deeply. She pressed her body into him, wrapping her arms around his neck.

Suddenly, they both felt the hallway begin to spin around them.

"Whoa, is this getting stronger, or was that because of the sake we had at dinner?" Mia asked.

"Maybe both! It felt the same as it did in the water today with the dolphins."

"Okay, no more kissing tonight!" She playfully pulled away.

"I want to protest, but I think you're right. *Buenas noches, bellissima,*" he said, reaching for her hand and kissing it.

22

Mauna Kea

———

"Why are you driving so slow?" asked Nick.

"I don't know. I've got the accelerator pressed to the floor," replied Marco, puzzled.

"It's because of the decreased oxygen levels at this elevation; the motor can't perform as well," said John.

"I thought all the switchbacks and gravel roads were making Marco nervous," said Nick.

"Haha, no, that's not the problem. All the tingling on the top of my head is distracting, though. Anyone else feeling that?" asked Marco.

"No," replied Nick and Bree in unison.

"Only always," laughed John.

"I'm feeling it too. Maybe we didn't acclimate to the elevation change long enough at the Visitor's Center," said Mia.

"We were there an hour, and they said thirty minutes would be enough," said Bree.

"Yes, but Marco and I were at the bottom of the ocean floor a couple of days ago. Are you feeling nauseous or dizzy?" asked Mia.

"No," replied Marco, "but my vision seems to be playing tricks on me. I'm seeing energy waves rise off the gravel road like it's common to see in the desert, but it's too cold outside for that to be the cause of it."

"Dude, are you safe to drive?" asked Nick.

"Probably not, but if we stop and change drivers this car may not make it up the rest of the way," answered Marco, chuckling.

"Just make sure he doesn't drive off the road, Mia," John said from the back seat.

"They said it was only five miles from the Visitors' Center, so we should be pretty close to the summit," said Mia.

"My sense is that the tingling has more to do with your crown chakra opening up than the elevation," said John. "Marco's climbed Mount Everest; I'm sure he can drive us up the mountain!"

"Since we're entering the most sacred part of the island, we should all say a prayer and ask for permission to be here," said Bree.

"Yes, you're right. Thank you for reminding us," said Nick.

"I also made a few donations today to exchange with the mountain," said John.

Mia asked, "Which ones?"

"I donated to the Mauna Kea Forest Restoration Project," said John. "Among other things, they're working to protect the high elevation dry forest, the only place the palila bird inhabits. When they built the new highway up here, they damaged their habitat, and these beautiful little birds have been on the endangered list ever since. I like to support organizations that take care of the land. It's my way of exchanging with Mother Earth—and I have a feeling we're going to get our money's worth up there today."

They reached the summit and Marco parked on a gravel stretch at the end of the road.

"Ahh, finally," said Nick, stretching as he got out of the car.

"It's freezing up here!" exclaimed Mia, swiftly zipping up the parka she had last worn on top of Haleakala.

"Yes, but the crisp air feels so refreshing," said Bree.

"How long before the sun sets?" asked Nick.

"We've got about an hour," replied John.

Marco walked over to Mia and put his arms around her. "Are you warm enough now?"

"Yes," she replied, leaning into his hug. "Are you still feeling okay?"

"I am now." He smiled and kissed the top of her head.

Taking her hand in his, they walked from the parking lot to the lookout point. A thick sea of clouds had congregated below them, making it hard to see the land below. In the distance, they could see Haleakala rising out of the blue ocean.

"It's so beautiful up here," said Mia.

"Yes, and quiet," Marco replied.

"How're your vision and the crown of your head?"

"The sensation of energy pouring into me is increasing, and my vision's still playing tricks on me. Think I'll let someone else drive us back tonight. How are you feeling?" asked Marco.

"Really buzzy! Like my body might lift off the ground," she said.

"I better hold onto you extra tight then," he said.

"Hopefully it won't increase your symptoms; our touching one another seems to amplify everything."

Mia could sense that he was trying to be strong, but his energy felt wobbly to her.

"Do you need to sit down?" she asked. "You're looking a bit pale."

"Yeah, that's probably a good idea. I'm feeling pretty dizzy."

Mia helped him get settled on the ground and then signaled John for help.

"Do you see it?" John asked.

"See what?" Mia responded.

"The energy pouring into the top of his head," said John.

Mia took a couple of steps back and saw the stream of purple light flooding into Marco's crown chakra. "Whoa, no wonder he's dizzy. That's a lot!"

"Mia, put your hands on his feet and help ground him." John handed Marco his water bottle.

Mia pressed on Marco's shoes and massaged his calves and ankles.

Marco took a drink and closed his eyes, but the kaleidoscope of colors he could see from the sun's rays made him feel as though he was on an acid trip.

"Is he okay? Do you think we should head back down to a lower elevation?" asked Bree.

"No, this is happening for a reason," said John, "and I think his spirit's been preparing him for this with all the mountain climbing he's been doing over the years. It's easier for the Divine Masculine energy to flow into us at the highest elevations. My sense is he needs to fill up with as much of it as possible to complete the mission."

"Do you think my touch is helping or magnifying it? Things got pretty intense for us last night," said Mia.

John raised his eyebrows.

"When we kissed goodnight," she said, making a face at him. "That's all I mean."

"Well, let's trade places and see if it feels any different for him if I ground him," said John.

Mia stood up to let John take over.

He placed both hands on Marco's feet and imagined him sending roots into Mother Earth.

"Marco, keep imagining that you're sending the purple energy all the way through into the earth. Imagine that you are a part of the mountain," said John.

Mother Earth, ground me, Marco said as he imagined becoming a part of Her. Mia received the awareness that she could help him connect to the earth, so she seated herself behind Marco and wrapped her arms around him, imagining sending all of her energy deep into the green crystal caves and taking Marco with her.

I've been waiting a long time for you two to come here together, said Mother Earth.

Where are we? How did we get here? Marco asked.

We're inside Earth. I brought us here, said Mia. *We're safe. The voice you hear is Mother Earth Herself.*

Was John right? Mia asked Mother Earth. *Is Marco being filled up with the Divine Masculine energy so we can complete the mission?*

Yes, Mother Earth replied. *He has to be able to hold as much of the energy as possible for the sacred marriage. The deep love between you that has existed since your first incarnations make you the perfect souls to carry out the plan. As you can tell by the way the energy field responds when you touch one another, there is no time to waste. The fuse has been lit and you have to get this explosion of love to the right location, or its effect will be wasted.*

What do you mean? Where is the right location? asked Mia.

There will be two primary effects from the new clear vortex. First, it will transmute all of the darkness within the blast range, allowing humans to open their hearts.

Second, added Mother Nature, *it will balance my energy in that geographic region, saving me from having to do it with a natural disaster. If the sacred marriage happened on the island, it would benefit a few, but these islands are already filled with so much love it wouldn't do the most good. If, on the other hand, it happened somewhere densely populated, where people had little access to nature, and were in their minds more than in their hearts—in an area where life is stressful and busy—then it would create an enormous shift, sending the ripple effects reverberating around the globe. And if it happened in a city that was about to experience a hurricane, earthquake, volcano, or tsunami, it would save thousands of lives.*

So where should we go? asked Mia.

Mother Earth knew immediately, answering, *New York City. The northeastern seaboard is a few days away from getting hit with a category six hurricane.*

Six? I thought the scale only went up to five.

So far...

Ay, carajo, so we need to leave right away, said Marco.

Yes, replied Mother Earth.

Mia asked, *And we need to go to New York City? I didn't know hurricanes hit that far north.*

Anything can happen anywhere, Mother Earth clarified. *I am committed to moving to the fifth dimension and will make all the adjustments necessary to get there. There is no turning back.*

I understand, said Mia.

And Marco, remember that once you leave the islands, Mia will no longer be cloaked. She will be vulnerable and you will need to protect her.

Marco nodded, a look of the utmost earnestness on his face.

Their consciousness returned to the top of Mauna Kea so quickly that it was disorienting for both of them. Mia gasped for air as she felt herself arriving back in her body. She opened her eyes and, at that very second, felt Marco's body slump into her arms.

"Did he just pass out?" asked Mia.

"Yes, it looks like he's out," replied John.

"Oh no," said Mia.

"Well, he hasn't had all the initiations you've had, so he can't hold the energy as well as you can now. Remember how many times you passed out and had to be carried. He still has more wounds to heal. You'll have to help him with that so he can hold the Divine Masculine energy."

"You mean he's not ready yet to help me activate the vortex? Mother Earth said we had to hurry; thousands of lives depend upon it," said Mia.

"Clearly, he's not quite ready or he wouldn't be unconscious. What did Mother Earth say?" asked John.

"She told us that we need to activate the vortex in the place that will do the most good, where it can affect the greatest number of people and have the biggest ripple effect as well as averting a natural disaster. She said a hurricane is scheduled to hit the northeastern seaboard in a few days."

"Well, maybe you can talk to the elements and get them to give you enough time to get there. I don't think it'll take long to get Marco ready, but you definitely need to do it before you two...uh, ignite the vortex, or it might not work."

"Really? Do you think that's possible?"

"We're dealing with something that has never been done on Earth before, so I don't know for sure. But if Marco can't hold the energy, it either won't work, or it could destroy his body."

Mia took a deep breath. The thought of doing something that could hurt Marco was inconceivable to her. Yet the thought of letting thousands of other people die when she could prevent it would be something she would never get over.

Mia reflected on what she had learned during her time with Gabriella.

"We have to get him ready before the hurricane hits. I know I can do some hands-on healing that will magnify the light of spirit within the body. But I thought the biggest healing would happen during the sacred sexual act, and we can't be intimate until it's time to open the new clear vortex, so it feels like a Catch-22."

"You'll just have to get creative and figure out a way to make it work."

"What do we do with him now? Is the purple light still flowing into him? I can't see from my angle," said Mia.

"Yes, it's still flowing. I think we should stay out here until it's done."

"I'm getting pretty cold sitting on the ground, though," said Mia.

"You do remember you have access to the fire within Earth, don't you? Why don't you just heat yourself up?"

"Oh yeah. Can't believe I didn't think of that!" Mia closed her eyes and focused inside. She felt her body become strong and solid, connecting down to the fire. *I humbly and respectfully ask to be warmed up. I ask that it be gentle and comfortable for me. Thank you.*

She watched a thin stream of fire rise up from the earth, and within moments of her request, her body was feeling so warm and cozy.

That's perfect, thank you. I love you.

Mia adjusted her body, Marco's limp body getting too heavy for her.

"Want me to sit behind and give you some back support?" asked John.

"Oh my gosh, yes, that would feel much better. I'll share some of my fire with you, so you'll be warm and toasty."

John sat down behind her, facing the opposite direction, and leaned his back into hers. Mia sighed at the welcome relief from the tension.

John's body heated up the second he made contact with hers.

"I'm going to have to unzip my jacket, you're so hot," said John.

"Thanks." Mia laughed.

"Those were some serious grounding skills, by the way. And really helpful that you could take him with you," said John.

"I didn't even think about that. That's the first time I've been able to take someone with me. I wonder if I can do it with anyone or just with Marco."

"Maybe I'll let you try with me later. After you save New York."

John noticed Bree and Nick returning from the exploration and signaled them to come over. As the sun set, the stream of purple energy stopped pouring into Marco.

"Nick, help me get him in the car," said John.

"Too many upgrades from spirit?" asked Nick.

"Yup," said John.

"Reminds me of my drinking days," said Nick, chuckling.

"We'll have to skip the stargazing. Apparently, the mission clock's ticking," said John.

John and Nick each grabbed hold under Marco's arms and got him to the car, Marco regaining consciousness as soon as they reached a lower elevation.

"I'm sorry I passed out on you guys and that you had to carry me," said Marco. "How embarrassing."

"No worries, man, we're totally used to it with Mia!" Nick set off laughing again.

"How are you feeling?" Mia asked.

"I feel fine. But my head feels really strange, as though it's full of empty space."

Nick laughed. "Honestly, how can anything be 'full of' nothing? You mean, like an airhead?"

"Haha, well, sort of. More like there's a greater distance for my thoughts to travel before I can articulate them. As if I'm thinking in slow motion. My body feels really sluggish, too."

"Mia said you two need to get to New York as soon as possible. Do you feel up to traveling?" asked John.

"I should be able to manage. I'm just concerned because Mother Earth said I need to protect Mia once we leave the island because she won't be cloaked anymore. I don't feel like I can keep her safe while I'm in this condition."

"Well, let's not worry about that now. You may feel better by tomorrow," said Mia.

"*Lo siento, mi amor.* I know we need to get there quickly," said Marco.

"It'll be fine," Mia said as she squeezed his hand tight.

Once they had returned to the hotel, Mia decided she should stay with Marco so she could work on him. She ordered hamburgers from room service, figuring they could both use the extra grounding the protein would provide. Mia had Marco lie on the bed while they waited for the food to arrive. She placed her hands on his body to see if she could figure out what he needed. She felt the golden light within her turn on and emanate from her hands.

Skin to skin, she heard inside her head.

"Do you mind if I unbutton your shirt?" she asked.

"Not at all," he responded, smiling.

She lightly placed her hands on his bare chest, trying not to get distracted by his well-defined muscles. *Focus,* she told herself, feeling his body responding to her touch. She realized she could move the energy inside him. He was off-balance; the purple light hadn't made it all the way down to his feet. As she slowly moved her hands down his body, the energy followed.

"Does this feel okay? Tell me if it's too much," she said.

"It feels amazing," he said. "I'm enjoying the sensation of your hands on my skin. It's like nothing I've ever felt before."

Mia realized a lot of the energy was still in his head, so she stroked his hair, his cheek, and then his neck, moving the energy down into his shoulders.

She realized she needed to move the energy on both sides of his body simultaneously as it kept bubbling up the side she wasn't touching.

"I need to move the energy down both sides of your body at the same time. I'm going to have to get up onto the bed with you."

"I don't mind," he smiled.

Mia straddled him on the bed and again began moving the energy down his head into his chest.

She slid her hands down his abs toward his hips.

Suddenly, Marco grabbed her wrists and stopped her.

"We're about to have another problem," he said.

"Oh! What's wrong? Am I hurting you?"

"No! You're turning me on." Marco burst out laughing.

Mia laughed. "Well, think about something else. Trust me, I'm exerting a lot of willpower here, too."

"I just wanted to warn you, so you're not offended."

"I'm flattered. Now let me finish. I've just got to get it all the way down your legs."

"You're torturing me, woman," Marco groaned.

"Well, it's about to get worse 'cause I just realized I need to take your jeans off." She laughed, sliding off of him and letting him remove his jeans.

Mia bit her bottom lip as she looked at him in his black boxer briefs.

"Maybe we should finish this standing up," she said, placing her hands on his ribcage and slowly running them down the sides of his body, his hips, thighs, calves, and then holding her hands on his feet as she intended for the energy to anchor.

"How do you feel now?" she asked.

"Better."

"All the way better or just a little better?"

"Well, I don't think I'm going to feel completely healed until we're in New York!"

He was amused, pulling her up and hugging her.

Mia hugged him back and felt the golden light within her heart get brighter.

"Don't hate me for this, but I think we need to be skin to skin. I'll have to take my shirt off."

"If you must," Marco smiled. "Maybe the bra too?"

She took off her T-shirt and bra and pressed her body against his. The golden light from her heart poured out of her to fill up his chest.

"Oh God!" Marco said. The light caused his spine to rapidly arch backward.

Mia held on tighter, trying to keep him from falling over, but his weight and momentum were too great for her to counterbalance. He fell back onto the bed, taking her with him. Mia giggled.

"Whoa! What was that? What did you do to me?"

"I blasted you with my superpowers," she replied.

"I've never felt anything like that before. It was like getting hit by lightning and..."

"And having a full-body orgasm?" she asked.

"Yes! Wow, that was incredible."

"You're welcome." She started to get off of him, but he wrapped his arms around her.

"Where do you think you're going?"

"I think you're probably healed, and I also think that room service will be here soon."

"No, I'm not healed yet. I need more skin-to-skin contact," he playfully insisted.

Mia kissed him on the lips, making the energy in the room

start to swirl around them. Their kiss was interrupted by a knock at the door.

"Room service."

Mia jumped up and put her bra and shirt back on as Marco grabbed his jeans.

They devoured their burgers, trying to distract themselves from what they were really hungry for.

"I'm assuming you felt the room start to spin as soon as we kissed?" asked Mia.

"Yes." He looked disappointed. "This means you won't be kissing me again until New York, doesn't it?

"Probably safer that way. How do you feel now?"

"I actually feel great. Better than normal."

"Do you think you're strong enough to travel?" she asked.

"Yes. In fact, I was thinking we could leave tomorrow."

"Well, if we can find a flight that soon, I guess we could do that," she agreed.

"I'll arrange for a private jet to take us. It'll be safer and faster that way too."

"A private jet? Really?"

"Yes. I'll call and arrange for one," he replied.

"Isn't that really expensive?"

"I think it's worth it to keep you safe."

"Wow, I'm so excited; I've never been on a private jet before."

He placed his hand on top of hers. "Caring for you is my only priority."

Mia smiled, allowing herself to receive everything he wanted to provide for her.

Marco called the concierge, asking them to arrange the flight and a suite at The Plaza Hotel.

"The Plaza? Isn't that place really fancy? Are we really going to open the vortex in their hotel?" Mia giggled.

"I thought it would be good to be near Central Park as the concrete jungle might be too much of a shock after all this time in paradise. And I figured we needed a suite, so we had plenty of room in case…Well, in case things get wild, which, given how it's been between us, I think it's pretty safe to say that they will."

"I trust your assessment and logistical strategy. Thank you for taking such good care of me." She hugged him and gave him a quick peck on the cheek.

"You are saving the world; it's the least I can do."

"It's getting late. I should go back to my room and get to bed since we have a big day tomorrow."

He looked at her and held her gaze. "Will you stay with me tonight?"

Mia hesitated.

"I just want to hold you in my arms. I promise I won't try anything. I learned my lesson. I know how much power you're packing so I won't do anything to turn you on."

Mia laughed. "Do you have an extra toothbrush?"

They fell asleep in each other's arms, feeling more at peace than they ever had. The contact with Mia's skin allowed Marco to finish integrating the energy download he had received on top of Mauna Kea.

23

Departure

———

"I can't believe you're flying to New York in a private jet. That is so cool," said Lori.

"I know. I feel silly but I'm kind of excited about it," said Mia.

"Perks of the job when the Universe is your employer," John joked.

"No kidding," said Nick. "Think I might need to upgrade my benefits package. Are you sure we can't all come with you?"

Dominique said, "Are you really asking that, given that we all know how they're going to turn on the vortex?" said Dominique.

Marco and Mia laughed standing in the lobby, waiting for the valet to pull their car around.

"So we'll touch base afterward and figure out what's next," Mia said to John.

"Yes," John replied. "We're going to head back to Maui later tonight if we can get a flight. And then fly back to Phoenix from there, then on to Sedona."

"What about you, Bree? I assume you'll be staying on Maui," asked Mia.

"Yes, Maui's home for now, but I could definitely use a trip to Sedona sometime soon," replied Bree.

"You know you're always welcome to stay with us," John answered.

Mia sighed, soaking up her last few minutes of island love. "It sure is hard to leave this place."

"Don't worry, my love. I told the concierge to make sure they stocked the jet with fresh pineapple," said Marco.

They all laughed. As the car pulled up, they all hugged each other goodbye.

"This is such a strange departure," said Lori. "I feel like I'm sending you off on your honeymoon, and yet really, you're going to save the planet."

"Well, love is always the answer," said John. He pulled Marco aside as they were walking to the car. "Are you sure you're ready for this? You need to stay vigilant. As soon as she's no longer cloaked, her new vibration will show up on their radar."

"I'm ready. I promise I'll keep her safe no matter what."

Mia held Marco's hand as the jet took off. Within seconds, they were high above the island, looking down at the turquoise water below.

"*Aloha Hawaii, mahalo* for everything. I hope we can return soon," said Mia.

"Are you sad we're leaving?" he asked.

"No, I'm not sad. I'm feeling a lot of things…excited about the mission, yet also concerned about how it's all going to play out. I'm excited to make love to you, yet also concerned about how that might also play out!" Mia giggled.

Marco picked up her hand and kissed it. "Me, too."

She leaned her head on his shoulder and sighed. "It feels like my entire life has been building to this moment, and now it's almost here."

"I felt that way as soon as I realized who you were."

When the plane reached cruising altitude, the flight attendant brought them water and a plate of snacks. "Hi, I'm Sasha. I'll be taking care of you today. We are well stocked with pineapple per your request. Please let me know if you need anything or how I can make your flight more comfortable."

"Thank you," replied Mia as she helped herself to the delicious fresh fruit.

"I love that you noticed my insatiable desire for pineapple and that you arranged to have it available."

"All I want is to make you happy," Marco replied.

"You do. And this jet, it's so luxurious, I feel so fancy. Although I am definitely underdressed." Mia looked down at her sneakers and tracksuit.

"You look beautiful and I think it's important to be dressed in something that'll be easy to move around in just in case we have to make a run for it at any point."

"Are you envisioning us being chased by entities down the streets of New York?"

"Haha, maybe!"

He pulled out his laptop from his leather satchel. "I need to check a few emails real quick, so please excuse me for a moment."

"Good idea. I haven't checked my email in weeks."

Mia turned to Sasha. "Would you mind getting my laptop from my bag, Sasha?" But she noticed that the woman, who had been friendly minutes earlier, now seemed annoyed by her request. *Maybe she's tired.* She had to make some kind of an excuse for the rude woman since all she did was stare and say nothing, certainly making no move to get up and retrieve the device for her. Mia decided to get up to get it herself as if she had said nothing.

"You're out of your league," Sasha said, out of nowhere.

"Excuse me?" asked Mia, denying to herself the words she had just heard.

"You're not used to flying private, are you?" Sasha gave Mia the once-over.

"Um, no, you're right. This is my first time." Why was Sasha being so unkind?

"You're not the kind of woman he usually travels with."

"How would you know that?" Mia asked, curious about where this was going.

"I've flown Marco before, and the rest of his family. We go way back. And you definitely don't belong here. Do you even know who he is? Who his father is?"

"No, I haven't met his family yet. But I don't see how that's any of your concern."

"He's one of the wealthiest men in Mexico. Clearly not people you belong with."

"I'm not sure why you're saying this to me," Mia replied. "Do you think I even care?"

"I just thought I should warn you that you won't be around for long. You're not wanted here."

Mia grabbed her bag and headed back to her seat.

"That was really weird," she said to Marco.

"Uh...just a second, my love. Let me finish with this email."

Mia opened her laptop and was surprised to see an email from Richard that had arrived just minutes ago. *Why is he emailing me? Do I even want to read this?*

Her curiosity got the best of her and she opened the message.

Mia,

Where are you? I've been looking everywhere for you. I have left my wife and am finally free to be with you, mind, body, and soul. Please come back to me. Let me love you the way I always should have, the way you deserve. I feel so much remorse, regret, and shame for how I handled us. I am so sorry for the way I treated you and all the pain I caused you.

I know now what's important, knowing that you are the love of my life, and I will love you until the day I die. I am in a safe place; please open your heart to me again.

I have forever learned from my many mistakes. Can you ever forgive me and allow me to give you all the love you deserve?

I love you,

Richard

Mia's solar plexus contracted. She knew very clearly that she wanted nothing to do with him, but she could feel his energy pulling on her, creating a sensation of pain in her body, as if she had just been punched in the gut. Mia closed the email and saw that another email had just arrived.

This one was from her sister.

Mia,

Where the hell are you? You haven't spoken to Mom and Dad for months; they are worried sick about you. You are so selfish and inconsiderate. How could you do this to them?

You better contact them right away or just consider yourself no longer welcome in our family.

Mia's stomach contracted even tighter, making her shoulders slump forward.

What the heck is happening?

Then she saw that there was an email from Amy too, deciding it was probably safe to open it since she was probably just bragging about her latest adventure as usual.

Mia,

I'm concerned about your mental health. I didn't say anything before, but I think it's completely delusional that you left your life to go on some ridiculous healing journey. I mean, let's be honest, you're not that deep. Those people you met in Sedona sound like total weirdos, like some sort of cult! You need to grow up and come back to reality.

What the heck? thought Mia. Her heart was aching and her body felt heavy. *Something weird is happening.* She glanced over at Marco but saw that he was still working on his email. *Ugh, I can feel their energy all over me.* She tried brushing it off, but it felt thick like sludge. *Maybe I need some water to wash it off.* She headed to the bathroom to rinse her hands and face.

The cool water felt good on her skin.

Ahh, yes, much better.

The lavender-scented hand cream was also helping. She tried to open the bathroom door but couldn't. *My hands must be too slippery from the lotion.*

She grabbed a paper towel and tried to turn the doorknob. That didn't work either.

So the only thing to do was to knock loudly. "I seem to have gotten myself stuck in here! Can you please open the door for me?" She had seen Sasha nearby as she entered the bathroom. *Surely Sasha will be able to hear me.* Mia waited, but there was no reply. She knocked louder and raised her voice. "Hello, I need some help in here, the door seems to be stuck."

She tried several more times to no avail.

Maybe she went up front and can't hear me after all? Is this door soundproof? She banged harder, looking around to see if there was any sort of intercom or "assistance needed" button, but didn't find one. She sat on the toilet and tried to send a telepathic message to Marco.

I'm stuck in the bathroom, come help me. I need help.

She repeated the message over and over, but he never came.

This is hilarious! I'm destined to save the world, but can't get out of the bathroom. Maybe Sasha was right; do people who get stuck in bathrooms even belong on private jets?

Mia laughed. "Hello, can anyone hear me? I can't get the door open." After several minutes, she tried knocking again. *Surely I've been here long enough for someone to wonder if I'm okay. Well, worst case, eventually someone else will need to use the restroom and will let me out.*

"You need to stop making so much noise," Sasha said through the door.

"Oh, thank goodness, you can hear me. The door is stuck, I need help opening it."

"No, you need to stay in there. You're not dressed appropriately for the cabin."

"What? Are you kidding me? This isn't even funny! You need to open the door."

Mia was getting annoyed.

"No. You don't belong here and you're not good enough to be with Marco."

"Please open it. You can't keep me in here. This is illegal. You're going to lose your job."

"It's my job to keep the passengers safe and that's what I'm doing."

Mia started to get nervous. *Something is really off here. This woman's acting crazy. Where the heck is Marco?* She wondered how unstable this woman was and if she was capable of hurting him. *Surely, I've been gone long enough that he would have checked on me by now.* Mia was too triggered to tune in and get any guidance. *I need to calm down. I can't panic. Breathe.*

She took several slow, deep breaths. *I can't worry about him right now, I need to stay focused on getting out of here. What is this energy coming at me? She's telling me I'm not good enough and don't belong. I need to show her I'm not a threat. I need to stop resisting her.*

"Thank you, Sasha. I know you're just trying to do your job. And you're right, I don't belong here," Mia said, making an effort to use a gentle tone. "You know this world so much better than I do. I don't come from this kind of wealth. Thank you for helping me see that."

"You never should have boarded this plane."

"You're right. I have no business being here. I appreciate you taking the time to let me know. I'm sorry for making your job harder."

Mia took her time, allowing her energy to soften so that she didn't feel like a threat. Somehow, she eventually convinced Sasha that she realized she was only trying to help her.

"Do you think I should ask them to let me off the jet when we reach California? Do you think they would be okay landing the jet in LA or San Francisco?"

"Maybe," Sasha replied.

"Can you ask them for me? Either Marco or the pilot?"

"Marco is sleeping and I don't want to disturb the pilot," Sasha replied.

"What if I tell Marco I've realized I shouldn't be here? Because I just shouldn't and I need to get off the flight for everyone's sake. Maybe I can convince him to let me off. He probably doesn't want me here either. He must have realized, like you, that I don't belong."

Mia heard a click and then the door slowly opened. "Thank you, Sasha. I really appreciate all your help." Mia smiled at her and meekly moved past.

She slowly returned to her seat, trying to keep calm although she was shaking inside.

"Marco, you need to wake up," she said gently. She placed her hand on his arm. "We have a situation we need to take care of."

Marco opened his eyes. "I didn't realize I'd fallen asleep; was I out for long? I just meant to close my eyes for a minute."

"I'm going to tell you something, but you need to remain calm," she whispered.

"*Que pasa, mi amor?*" Marco asked.

"I'm okay now, but Sasha had me locked in the bathroom for the past forty-five minutes. She seems to have lost her mind and is projecting all sorts of judgments onto me."

"What?" Marco sat up and looked toward the back of the plane.

"I think we should stay calm until we figure out what's happening. Something really weird's going on. When I checked my emails, it was nothing but messages from people who are mad at me or think I'm crazy, and one from my ex begging me to come back."

"May I look at them?" Mia nodded in agreement, and Marco picked up her computer.

He read through all the emails Mia pointed out.

"Whoa! These are crazy. Shit! This must be why John kept telling me I needed to stay vigilant and protect you. Are you okay? Did she hurt you?"

"I'm fine, thank you. I wasn't too worried as I figured someone would eventually need to pee and I'd get out. But she's seriously unstable, certainly not someone to be on a flight with! I convinced her that I agreed with you and that I'd ask to deboard in California. I don't feel safe flying all the way to NYC with her, though, and we don't have time to be delayed with travel changes, so we need to figure something out."

"This is terrible. I can't believe I fell asleep when you were locked in the bathroom. I'm so sorry, *mi amor*. And yeah, definitely something weird is happening. I've flown with Sasha before, and she's always been very professional."

"I know, she told me exactly that!"

"What else did she tell you?"

"Oh, that you're super wealthy and I'm not good enough to be with you." Mia smirked.

"That's utterly ridiculous. What has affluence to do with anything? We were literally made for one another. You didn't believe any of the things she said, did you?"

"No, nothing landed; it went in one ear, right out the other. I just played along to escape the bathroom. But I was worried she'd done something to you since you hadn't come to rescue me."

"I feel terrible about this. I'm already failing as your protector."

"I didn't see this coming either. Now we know we need to be on higher alert."

"It seems clear why this is happening. This all started once we left Hawaii, and these emails all came in after that as well. You're no longer cloaked, so the entities are starting to sense your energy. They've activated within the people who know you and those around you, and they're starting to attack you in attempts to lower your frequency. It's a damn good thing we took a private jet instead of a commercial flight. I can easily protect you from her, but don't know how well I would have done against two hundred other passengers."

Mia sighed. "I need to figure out how to get this energy off of me; it's really uncomfortable. We need to come up with a solution because it's only a matter of time before Sasha gets triggered again."

They glanced over. Sasha was scowling again, perhaps realizing Mia had tricked her.

Mia said, "Normally, I'd just go outside and ground into the earth or light some sage, but clearly, I can't do any of that now."

"Hold my hand and just know that you're safe now. See if that helps you tune in."

Marco took her hand in his.

She closed her eyes and tuned in to her heart, soon seeing all the bright colors of the rainbow flowing inside her. *Send their energy back to them.* Mia scanned her body, discovering the murky gray entity energy that had covered her solar plexus. *Transmute it with the rainbow ray.*

The colors swirled inside her body until there was no more gray energy.

She visualized it returning to Sasha, Amy, her sister, and Richard as a blessing. She placed her hands on her second chakra and asked her dragons to be on alert and to instantly transmute any negativity directed at her into love. Then she took a deep breath and let out a sigh, instantly feeling lighter. She opened her eyes and glanced at Sasha to see if it had worked.

Sasha was rubbing her head and seemed slightly disoriented. Mia guessed that it had hit her the hardest since she was so close.

"Whew! I feel a lot better," voiced Mia. "I need to stay in a place of compassion for them all as it's not really them attacking me; it's the entities that are controlling them at the moment."

"What about Richard? He wasn't attacking you. He was trying to win you back."

"No. Well, yes, maybe," she conceded, thinking deeply about Marco's words. "But I also see this black hole inside him, an insatiable need for the attention and adoration of so many women. He will never be satisfied and will always need more. It must be awful to live that way. For that, I can feel compassion for him too."

Suddenly, the plane jerked, and Mia tightened her grasp on Marco's hand to avoid falling out of her seat. Their water bottles fell off the table and spilled all over the floor.

The pilot's voice resounded from the overhead speaker, saying, "We've just encountered some unexpected turbulence, folks. Best to fasten your seatbelts until we're out of it. I'm going to increase our altitude and see if I can find some smoother air for us."

"Do you think it really is just turbulence, or are we being attacked?" asked Mia.

"I think the timing of it is pretty ominous," said Marco.

They fastened their seatbelts as the plane continued shaking violently.

"Looks like it's pretty thick. I'm going to do my best to get on top of it," said the pilot.

Mia squeezed Marco's hand. "Do you think we can make it all the way to New York? Would it be safer if we drove after getting to California?"

"I would think the entities will be able to sense you even more on the ground. Plus, I don't think we could get to New York fast enough to stop the hurricane from happening. I'm just hoping that as the pilot flies higher, they won't be able to sense you anymore."

"How high can these jets go?"

"This is a Gulfstream G650, so it can fly as high as fifty-one thousand feet."

"How high do regular planes fly?"

"Usually around thirty-six thousand feet."

"Okay," she said timidly. Mia felt vulnerable for the first time in a long while. She hadn't understood all the need for protection when she'd had the dragons and dolphins helping her. *I'm supposed to be invulnerable to attack. Why is this happening?*

She tuned inside again, searching for the answer, the face of her tiger appearing in her mind's eye. *You both have everything you need to complete the mission.*

You just haven't had the opportunity to train so you're having to learn to use your new gifts in the moment. Stay focused and keep your heart open.

Mia remembered what she had felt with him in Lemuria, knowing she had the power of the elements at her fingertips.

Talk to the wind.

Mia connected to the breath moving in and out of her body. *Thank you for sustaining my life, and thank you for always being here at each inhale. I humbly and respectfully ask for your assistance in getting us to our destination. Please blow away the turbulent energies attempting to sabotage us.* Mia envisioned a clear path all the way to New York.

Within seconds, the air outside was calm again.

"Sorry about that, folks," said the pilot. "I don't mind sharing that our turbulence was a little peculiar. It wasn't showing up on any of the instruments; it's as if it came out of nowhere. Looks like we're above it now, though, so we should be good for the rest of the flight."

"You did that, didn't you?" Marco asked.

Mia smiled and winked.

"And here I was, thinking I was supposed to be the one protecting you." He laughed.

"You already did by getting us on this jet and to our destination by the fastest means possible."

"Okay, I'll receive that acknowledgment," he nodded.

"You could also hold me and keep me safe that way." She smiled warmly.

"I can definitely do that as well," he said as he wrapped his arms around her.

"Don't let go," Mia whispered. She kissed him on the cheek and buried her head in his chest.

"I've got you, my love, and I'm never letting go," replied Marco.

Mia's body relaxed as she allowed herself to receive all the protection he was offering her. He reclined the seats and let her fall asleep in his arms, keeping his eye on Sasha until he was certain she didn't pose a threat. She seemed to be back to her friendly self as she brought them a blanket and pillows, also helping him further recline their seats so that they were completely horizontal.

After a few hours, Marco allowed himself to doze off, knowing he would need his strength and mental clarity for when they arrived in New York.

They awoke to the sound of the pilot's voice announcing their descent into JFK Airport.

"The northeastern seaboard is in for some rough weather this week, and we're just starting to see the beginning of it. Looks like we're in for a bit of a bumpy landing, but I'll do my best to get you on the ground as quickly as possible."

Marco brought the seats upright as they both yawned and stretched.

"Wow, that was fast. Can't believe I was able to fall asleep after our bumpy start," said Mia.

"Yes, it's a good thing we both got some rest. Now that we're landing, we'll need to be on alert. I won't be able to relax until I get you inside the hotel room."

"How are we getting to the hotel?"

"I arranged to have a car meet us as soon as we get off the plane."

Marco looked around to see if Sasha was acting weird again. She seemed to be occupied with getting ready for landing.

Mia connected to the wind again and asked for a smooth landing.

Within minutes, the jet was on the ground.

"Guess we got lucky. Whatever was showing up on the radar didn't have any effect on our landing," said the pilot over the intercom.

The aircraft proceeded to taxi to the hangar where the driver was waiting for them.

Mia put her sneakers back on and gathered her belongings. Now that she was on the ground, she felt a little disoriented. The jet door opened and they made their way to it. Mia paused at the top of the stairs to regain her balance, trying to take a deep breath, but the smell of jet fuel ruined the experience. Marco stood by her side with his hand on her lower back, waiting for her to disembark. "Are you okay?" he asked.

"Actually, I don't feel great. The energy's just really different than what I'm used to."

Mia was looking pallid and sweaty.

Marco took one look and said, "Let's get to the hotel right away, I don't like the way it feels either." They got off the plane and into the limo that was waiting for them.

"The Plaza Hotel, please," said Marco to the driver, then he raised the privacy window in hopes that the barrier could help Mia not feel so much. He then pulled her into his arms.

"Do your best to condense your energy right now; stay focused on your breath," said Marco.

"Okay." Mia imagined herself pulling back all her energy into a little ball in the back of her heart. *Help us get there quickly,* she said to the angels, knowing they were always watching over her.

She also imagined her dragons flying alongside the car on either side.

She rested her head on Marco's chest, focusing on arriving effortlessly at the hotel.

Marco called the hotel to expedite their check-in. "My fiancée isn't feeling well and she'll need to go directly to our suite," he reported. They agreed to have everything ready for the couple's arrival, not delaying by checking in; all this could be done by Marco after Mia was safely settled in their room. The driver sped through the city as quickly as he could.

Since it was early Sunday morning, thankfully, the traffic wasn't as awful as it usually was. However, other drivers were responding aggressively to the limo weaving in and out of traffic; they honked their horns and attempted to cut the driver off. The farther they drove into the city, the worse Mia felt. She could sense the darkness all around her.

Her nervous system was feeling agitated. It was such a sharp contrast to the energy in Hawaii. As they crossed over into Manhattan, her body started to shake.

"You're shaking, my love. Are you okay?" Marco asked.

"My body feels weird, as if I can feel the energy of everyone in the city. It's overwhelming."

"We'll be at the hotel soon. I so wish I could do something to make this better for you."

He held her tighter.

The driver made it in record time; thirty-five minutes after their flight had landed, they were in front of The Plaza. Marco tipped the driver $100, thanking him for getting them there so quickly; then he helped Mia out of the car as she was feeling weaker than before.

Taking her by the hand, he led her toward the entrance.

She needed more support, so he offered her his arm to hold

onto and walked a little slower. Marco walked up to the front desk and told them who he was. After a quick signature, he had the room key, and they headed upstairs to the Penthouse Suite on the twentieth floor.

Marco breathed a sigh of relief, closing and locking the door behind them; then he helped Mia over to the couch.

"Do you feel any better now we're inside?"

"Think I need to eat something," she replied.

"Good idea." He looked around for the room service menu, spotting it on the desk next to the telephone. "Do you want breakfast?"

"Yes, I'd love something hearty...Something like eggs and bacon."

"I'm beginning to think you love bacon as much as you love pineapple."

"That may be true, but don't worry, I love you the most."

He smiled and read her the list of choices from the menu.

"Eggs Benedict sounds amazing. What are you going to get?"

"The lobster omelet. Coffee or juice?"

"Both, please."

He placed the order and asked them to leave it on a cart outside the door.

"I do feel better now that we're here." She walked over to the window to look at Central Park. While the dark clouds in the distance looked ominous and the wind was starting to pick up, the treetop view gave Mia a feeling of peace. "This view is amazing."

"I'm really glad you're feeling better." Marco came up behind her and wrapped his arms around her waist.

"Oh, look, two red-tailed hawks."

Mia pointed to the birds as they circled in front of the window.

"Must be the Goddess acknowledging our safe arrival."

"Yes." Mia smiled.

"They said breakfast would take half an hour to forty-five minutes to arrive. Do you want to shower and change out of these clothes?"

"I do. Are you going to shower with me?"

"If you'll let me," he said and grinned.

"It's probably a good idea in case I get attacked in the shower," she said playfully.

"Of course, purely for safety reasons." He laughed. "Although we might cause the room to start spinning."

"We haven't experienced it since leaving Hawaii. Maybe it was just a way to keep us from making love before we were in the right location."

"Are you wanting to make love in the shower?" he asked.

"No, I think we should wait until after breakfast so we both have our strength back. I have a feeling we're going to need it," she said with a wink.

"Agreed. There's a fruit basket on the table; I actually need something now to tide me over until our food arrives. Can I grab you anything?"

"A banana sounds good."

Marco bit into an apple, grabbing a handful of fruit.

He followed Mia upstairs to the master bath.

Mia admired the 24-karat gold-plated fixtures as she turned on the shower, also noticing the exquisite detail of the gilded floral-tiled shower wall with its delicate motifs.

Marco set down the fruit on the counter, handing Mia the banana.

Taking her first bite, her body responded with joy.

"This is really good."

"As good as the pineapple on Hawaii?"

"Ha! Nothing's that good." Mia inhaled the strong aroma of the banana. "What else do you have in that pile of fruit?"

"I read somewhere that oranges are best enjoyed in the shower." He began to peel one, filling the room with the sweet scent of orange.

"Seems like the perfect time to test that theory."

The bathroom was now warm and steamy. Marco admired her as she slowly undressed.

He sighed. "You are really beautiful."

She smiled and stepped into the shower, the hot water feeling amazing on her skin.

She asked the water's spirit to cleanse and purify her energy field, imagining all the negative energy swirling down the drain.

Marco handed Mia the orange, quickly removing his clothes and following her inside. Mia fed him a piece of orange, following it up with a kiss. The sweet, tangy flavor on his tongue and the warmth of her lips was truly the best taste he had ever experienced. She bit into the orange and let the juices run down her chin, and then leaned her head back so the water from the shower would rinse the juice away. They finished off the orange between kisses.

"I'm going to have to agree that eating an orange in the shower is indeed the best way."

"Me too."

Mia traded places with him so he could be under the spray of water. She grabbed the soap and lathered up his chest, shoulders, and arms. He took it from her and did the same, moving his hands ever so slowly, then turned her around so he could wash her back. Mia filled her hands with shampoo and turned back around when he was done. She massaged his scalp with her fingernails as she lathered up his hair. He pulled her close and shut his eyes, savoring every sensation. As the water streamed the suds down his back, she followed with her hands, eventually cupping his buttocks once he was covered in bubbles.

"Do you want to wash my hair now?" she asked.

"I do." He rinsed the shampoo out of his hair and held out his palm for her to fill with shampoo. He tenderly washed her hair as if he might hurt her with his large hands.

"Mmm, your touch is so gentle," she murmured.

He kissed her on the mouth and shifted his hands to her waist so he could move her under the showerhead. Mia held onto his biceps as she leaned her head back. They both tried to ignore his erection, knowing they couldn't make love quite yet.

"Our food's probably arriving soon," Mia said.

"Good, because I don't know how much longer I can take you sliding your soapy body against mine," he exclaimed, laughing.

They allowed the water to rinse them clean and then turned off the water. Marco handed Mia a towel and grabbed one for himself. They put on the plush white robes that were hanging in the closet, then headed back downstairs and heard a knock at the door.

"Room service. I'll leave the cart here as you requested," said the waiter.

Marco waited a couple of minutes to make sure the waiter had left. He then wheeled in the cart and placed their breakfast on the table. Mia sat down as he poured her a cup of hot coffee.

"Ahh...I'm almost feeling fully human." She inhaled the aroma before taking her first sip.

"Well, you look like a Goddess, not at all like a human."

Mia smiled. "Even in a bathrobe and with wet hair?"

"Yes." He removed the cover from their entrees. "Voilà! Breakfast is served."

"Thank you, my love."

They were both so hungry, they ate without saying much. Once their bellies were full, Marco broke the silence.

"So you really haven't told me much about how this vortex activation will work."

"I really don't know any of the details, only that it happens after we merge our bodies, hearts, and energy fields."

"And then what happens?"

"I don't know."

"Really?"

"This has never been done before, so I'm not sure that they even know."

"They?"

"The Galactic Council."

"Oh, right."

"We should both meditate right now to see if there's any additional information we need before beginning."

Marco put the dishes back on the cart and rolled it out into the hallway. They positioned their chairs so they would be facing one another. Then they closed their eyes and focused inside.

They both clearly heard, *Go into the park.*

"Guess we need to go outside! Do you feel strong enough to make it down there?" Marco asked.

"Yes. Let me blow-dry my hair and put some clothes on and I'll be ready to go."

Mia sighed as she felt the energy of the twenty-six thousand trees in Central Park. Even though the wind was picking up and the scent of rain was in the air, the sun was still shining through the clouds. They found a quiet spot to sit on the grass under a large oak tree.

"Think you can delay the rain from falling?" Marco asked.

"I can definitely ask." Mia smiled and closed her eyes, crossing her hands over her chest. She connected with her heart and the earth and the trees, feeling her breath moving in and out of her lungs and giving gratitude for all of life. She released the thought that she was there to accomplish something, instead allowing herself to be fully present in this moment.

Her hands began to tingle and vibrate. She pointed her palms at the dark clouds gathering in the sky, respectfully asking for them to move in a different direction. Once she felt the acknowledgment from the Cloud Beings, she whispered, "Aho Mitakuye Oyasin."

With her eyes still closed, Mia asked for guidance about opening the vortex, seeing in her mind's eye the memory of the breathwork she had undertaken next to Oak Creek in Sedona. She remembered being told that the trees would help her with the new clear vortex.

She moved her body closer to the tree, placing her spine against the trunk.

"Marco, come sit next to me and let's ask the tree for help."

They held hands as they allowed their consciousness to travel down deep into the earth through the root system of the mighty oak. They experienced the interconnectedness of all the trees in the park, realizing the trees' incredible strength.

For over 165 years, these trees had been grounding the energy of the city. They were also the city's lungs, cleansing the air as fast as they could.

They stored the energy of the sun in their leaves as they reached toward the heavens. Mia and Marco felt their energy anchoring into the earth and knew they were being held with great care.

They felt the energy of the sun pour in through the crowns of their heads.

The wind swirled around them, promising to carry the energy

of the vortex as far as possible. They felt the Hudson River acknowledge its role as the cooling system for the vortex.

Two red-tailed hawks screeched as they flew overhead, causing Mia and Marco to open their eyes. A rainbow appeared in the sky, signaling that all the elements were now in place.

Marco squeezed Mia's hand and was about to speak when a blue swallowtail butterfly fluttered around them, coming to land on Mia's head.

"*Mi amor,* this is really turning into a Disney movie."

They both laughed.

"I guess it's time for the transformation to begin," said Mia.

They both felt their bodies begin to vibrate and energy swirl up their spines. The butterfly momentarily moved over to Marco's head before fluttering away. They soaked up more love from the earth, offering gratitude again. Marco helped Mia up and they headed back to the hotel.

They both changed back into their robes upon returning to the room. Marco waited as Mia took the extra pillows off the bed, then he pulled her into his arms and held her quietly for several minutes. His heart was beating loudly in his chest. He was feeling so many different feelings that he didn't quite know how to begin.

"Are you okay?" Mia asked, pulling back.

Marco sat down on the bed and took hold of her hands.

"The immensity of this moment is really hitting me right now. Searching for you for so many years, finally having you in my arms, yet knowing this moment is about so much more than us.

"That our souls came here to save the planet and help as many people as we can. I feel I've been preparing for this my whole life and yet had no idea what it would entail. I feel so grateful and humbled that I get to be the one to love you." Marco's eyes filled with tears as he allowed his heart to feel everything, increasing the energy flowing through him.

Mia smiled. She leaned in and kissed him deeply, causing their bodies to fall onto the bed.

"If you're not ready yet, I'm sure I can ask the Hurricane to give us more time," she said, pulling back.

"Don't you dare!" Marco responded, pulling her close again.

They were vibrating so strongly now that the bed was starting to shake.

"Well then, let's activate this vor—"

Before she could get the rest of the words out, he rolled on top of her and pressed his lips against hers. The kiss was long and deep, fueled by the sexual tension that had been building between them. She could feel his passion and desire for her. His lips were soft, yet so much power and force were being transmitted between them.

"*Mi amor*, I have always loved you," he whispered.

"And I, you," she replied.

They lay there holding each other, breathing one another's breath. Their chakras felt expanded and connected with one another's. Both were trembling from the energy coursing through them.

She giggled, adding, "Looks like this is going to be a wild ride."

"I think we've known that since Hawaii!"

"I don't know what my body's going to do, but I'm assuming you're going to be able to handle it, even if it gets weird—or should I say, weirder?"

"I can definitely handle all your weirdness and I wouldn't want it any other way."

As he kissed her neck and her breast, his lips began to buzz as he made contact with her skin.

A part of him desperately wanted to be inside her already, but everything about her was sacred to him now. He didn't want only to experience love and pleasure with her; he wanted to worship her with his body. His kisses traveled far below her belly button as he used his hands to spread her legs further apart. She sighed as she could feel the warmth of his breath between her legs.

He imagined himself at the entrance to the temple of the Goddess, the holiest place on Earth; he approached with reverence, asking permission to enter as his tongue licked her softly.

He could feel her vibrating as her lips became engorged, responding to his adoration, a force field of energy palpably emanating from her. The more he pleasured her, the larger the field became. He felt as though he was floating in a sea of golden honey.

Mia closed her eyes as she surrendered to the waves of pleasure moving through her. Suddenly, she felt herself slipping back through time and space, pulled into ancient Egypt, inside the pyramid. She tried to stay in her body and be present with him in that moment, but it was futile.

Her consciousness was in the center of the pyramid at the altar of Isis.

The room was filled with priestesses preparing to heal the men returning from war.

Yes, it has always been the Goddess who has healed mankind.

She saw the golden light of the temple activate within her.

Via the portal in her womb was how the Goddess would return.

Initiate him. Only then can the masculine on this planet evolve.

As the juices flowed from her sacred portal, his tongue began to vibrate. Now it was his turn to be transported. He saw himself connected to all of life, floating on the breath as the Goddess breathed him. He fell through the earth into the womb of the Cosmic Mother.

I exist in you as much as I exist in her. But your instinct to worship her, honor her, love her, please her, and celebrate her is correct, for it is the body of the feminine on your planet that must return to the realm of the sacred. As you love her, you will light the way for all men to follow.

Your love for her will heal the wounds the masculine has inflicted on the feminine. Loving her is your sacred mission. It is how you will become your fullest expression of self.

Like a falling star shooting through the night sky, he was catapulted back into the room in time to feel her nails digging into his shoulders. As orgasmic waves of ecstasy escaped from her lips, Earth's tectonic plates shifted, causing the building to shake, but neither of them noticed.

Once her grip on him had released, he moved up on the bed and lay next to her, desperate to be inside her but wanting to make sure she was ready for him. After what felt like an eternity, but was really more like sixty seconds, she opened her eyes and smiled at him.

Not able to wait any longer, he kissed her deeply and rolled on top of her.

She loved the feeling of his body weight on top of hers and she kissed him back, hungrily letting him know she was as ready as he was as she ran her hands down his back. He looked into her eyes, maintaining her gaze as he finally slid inside her. The electrical surge that bolted through both of them would have knocked them out if they hadn't been preparing for years for this moment. She grabbed hold of him tightly, pressing her nails into his back, trying to hold on.

He felt as though he was plugged into the Universe, stopping moving for a moment and gazing into her eyes again. Time stood still again as the two of them became one.

Motionless except for the throbbing created by him being inside her, he allowed himself to fully receive the truth of who he was. He felt the vastness of his soul, the power of his spirit, his greatness, his divinity, his value, his right to be here—here inside her, here on the planet, here in this body. He could feel the power of the entire cosmos flowing through him.

He felt as though they were God and Goddess, creating all of existence. That awareness caused his kundalini to bolt through his spine, thrusting him deeper into her.

He kissed her neck, biting her softly as their bodies moved rhythmically together, her hips rocking upward, allowing him to slide in deeper. He interlaced his fingers with hers, pinning her hands against the bed. The energy generated by their palms making contact forced his arms to straighten, lifting his chest off of hers. As he looked at her lying beneath him, he swore she was shapeshifting. She looked as if she was made of golden light, only it was denser than light, more like liquid gold. But her body still felt soft, juicy, and wet. He realized they weren't the only thing vibrating in the room; the bed was shaking, the clock on the night table fell off, and the lamp crashed to the floor. He decided it wasn't a good idea to have her pinned beneath him, so he grabbed her waist and rolled her on top of him.

Her back arched as the kundalini shot through her spine relentlessly, moving her body the way it needed it to. She ground her hips deeper into him as the golden light from her womb encased him. Her hair swished back and forth through the air as her spine whipped her forward and backward, the room starting to spin rapidly. He felt as though he was connected to a vortex.

He had never felt more alive, never before experienced so much energy moving through him. He felt expanded, connected to all of life. He felt like the spark that created all of life, that the Universe was straddling him, spinning, swirling, vibrating on top of his golden shaft of light.

He had never felt more powerful and yet more humbled. He was in awe of her. He wanted to give her everything he had, including his life. He was hers. Whatever she needed, he would do. He was filled with so much love for her, his body couldn't contain it any longer.

All of his masculine energy directed into her Goddess portal shifted Earth's gravitational pull. He fell out of his body into Earth's fiery core.

Like molten lava erupting from a volcano, he exploded into her. As the fire filled her body, it ignited orgasmic tsunami waves that propelled her out of her crown chakra into the cosmos.

As heaven and Earth connected through their bodies, the portal was opened and—just for a moment—time stood still. In that space of timelessness, Earth stopped spinning, the polarity on the planet neutralizing, and the Goddess returning from the shadowland.

Mia fell from heaven into Marco's arms.

She lay in his arms as their bodies recalibrated. Marco came to, still feeling a little dazed and disoriented. Everything felt different now, but he was still too groggy to discern what was going on. He tried to look and see what time it was, but the bedside clock was on the floor.

He kissed her softly on the shoulder and lightly rubbed her back.

"Mmm…" she purred.

"*Mi amor*, I have no words."

"Me neither." She opened her eyes and noticed the air in the room seemed iridescent.

"So what happens now? Is everything complete?"

"It doesn't feel like it. Seems like there's more to do." She rolled off of him, sitting up. "I suddenly have this intense pressure building inside me, like something wants to be released."

"Through where?"

"Through my heart." She placed her hand on her chest. "They are coming."

"Who?"

"I can feel the entities coming for me. Like a tidal wave of darkness."

"Oh shit!"

"No, it's a good thing."

"Are you sure? That doesn't sound like a good thing. You are glowing again, and the room feels really hot to me."

Mia remembered what John had told her: *When you activate a vortex of light, it stirs up all the unconscious energy in the area.*

"This vortex that we activated must be huge if it's drawing that big of a wave of darkness."

"So what do we do when it gets here?" he asked.

"Feel this." She placed his hand on her heart.

As his hand touched her heart, her touch instantly filled him with love and peace. His body relaxed, and a calmness overtook him.

"I have to go out on the terrace."

They put their robes back on, heading outside.

It had started to rain, the sky now turning black. Over the skyline and heading toward them was a huge swarm of dark energy that had assumed a physical form.

Like a heat-seeking missile locked onto its target, it prepared to take Mia out.

"*Ay, carajo!*" said Marco.

Mia stood her ground, opening her arms, leaving her heart exposed. "An undefended heart needs no protection." The wind picked up, beginning to swirl around her.

As the golden light radiated out of her, the darkness increased its speed. Everything she had been training for, preparing for, waiting for was happening NOW.

Marco felt completely vulnerable as he watched his beloved open her heart to all the darkness in the city. Just before the moment of impact, a wave of golden light shot out of her chest, expanding in all directions. As it propelled outward, it magnetized even more of the dark energy, pulling it into the center. It created a toroidal pattern, the dark being drawn in to be loved, to be transmuted into light, and then sent back out into the world. The new clear vortex of alchemy created a golden mushroom cloud over the city that could be seen for hundreds of miles.

Mia felt as though she was the eye of a hurricane with all the energies swirling around her. And with the force of a hurricane, the vortex in her heart transformed everything with which it came into contact. Everyone in the five boroughs felt the effects of this explosion of love.

Pain in their bodies disappeared, disease was neutralized, their hearts opened, and light within them multiplied as it replaced the spaces in which the unconscious energy had been residing.

Resistance was futile. There was no possibility for the darkness to escape; all places of contraction had been expanded, and all that had been hidden was brought to light.

The wave of love was experienced as a field of grace, compassion, and forgiveness, purifying the air and the rivers, restoring nature to balance in the few places it existed within the city.

Marco was hit hardest by the wave as he was the closest in proximity to her. If it hadn't been for the activation he had received from the dolphins, he would have been knocked out.

They had energetically calibrated his body to be in the field, all remaining negative thoughts in him dissolving.

His capacity to love expanded exponentially, restoring his body, reversing all signs of aging.

Neither of them knew how far the wave had expanded or how

much time had passed. An instantaneous flash also lasting several hours.

The rain stopped and the clouds blew back out to sea. Once the energy had dissipated, their minds were able to come back online. She turned and rested her wet body against the railing, gazing at him. She opened her mouth to speak, but no words came out.

Marco came to her as quickly as he could make his legs move.

She expected him to hug her, but once he reached her he fell to his knees and wrapped his arms around her hips. Tears of gratitude streamed down his face as he pressed his cheek into her stomach. "Gracias," he whispered, humbled by her power, by what had just happened. He was in awe of her and completely committed to living his life in service to her. What he had just seen and experienced would change the world, and he was honored to be a part of it, to be by her side.

She stood there looking down at him, not sure what to do.

His response surprised her. In her eyes he was her equal and his contribution had been essential. They were partners in this sacred mission. She placed her hands on his head and ran her fingers through his hair, loving the dark-brown color, wondering where the flecks of gray were that she had noticed yesterday. She didn't say anything as he seemed to be praying.

She looked at the skyline of the city and realized all she could feel coming from the people now was love. The hawks screeched several times as they flew in circles above them.

Where to next? she wondered.

She saw the image of a volcano erupting and heard, *Mexico City...*

Afterword from the Author

The seed of this book was planted during retreats in Sandia Park, New Mexico with David Elliott, the author of *Healing*, *The Reluctant Healer*, and *The Baptism*.

David believes that creative expression is key to our wellbeing; numerous times throughout my training with him, he turned to me and said, "Danielle, you've got a story to tell."

This story came through my healing journey with the pranayama breathwork.

This is the breathwork that David teaches in his trainings, an active meditation that quiets the mind, allowing the heart chakra to open. Breathing in this manner raises the frequency of our vibration to match that of our spirit/soul/higher self.

The messages and visions I received during the breathwork form the foundation of this book.

I first experienced the breathwork in a group setting in 2010, having such a profound experience I immediately asked the facilitator for a private session.

Toward the end of that session, I felt a powerfully uplifting, loving energy come into my body and I kept saying, "I'm home, I'm home." It was the most exquisite experience I had ever had up to that point in my life. I was 'all in,' instantly knowing I needed more of this for myself, also that I desired to facilitate this level of healing for my clients.

I completed all four levels of David's training in four months, but knew I wasn't done. Every time I attended a training or workshop, I found more things to let go of, experiencing an even deeper feeling of love and peace inside me. Once the majority of the painful memories became released, I started getting messages and visions about Earth.

My life became more magical and mystical with every breath.

This continued for several years and then the information slowed.

The next phase became more physical, my spirit beginning to merge with my body.

I don't know what will happen next, but I trust my breath, my heart, and my spirit to guide the way. Therefore, I write this for all those of you who are also seeking the way home to yourselves, for those of you looking to heal yourselves.

I write this, too, for all the Earth Healers who are here to help the planet, and for those who are here to help bring the Divine Feminine into balance with the Divine Masculine, both within themselves and on our beloved Mother Earth.

May we heal the world by healing ourselves.

A Note from David Elliott

I am honored and give my wholehearted blessing to Danielle and her wonderful book, *An Undefended Heart.* I have found very few people who are willing to live their story, whether they tell that story as fiction or autobiography. The greatest writers have the ability to lead you on a whimsical spiritual journey, and you can rarely detect what is their personal life and what is coming from the imagination—and that's why we call it art!

At least some of this story comes from situations that I have had close proximity to, and at times even thought maybe were a bit too close to home. Nevertheless, my encouragement to writers has always been, "Be personal, tell the story from what you know, and give yourself permission to stretch to get your point across—and that's what we call imagination!

So, I encourage you to lean into *An Undefended Heart*; it is chock-full of spiritual opportunities to inform your own life, and I am quite sure we will look back in the future and realize the important timing of Danielle's book. You don't need to be intuitive to realize there are some big revolutions evolving on Mother Earth, and in due time, I suspect we will recognize the Goddess has risen. We'll see you later on, down that road. Enjoy the ride!

David Elliott
Los Angeles

Danielle Hering, LMFT, is a psychotherapist and certified David Elliott breathwork practitioner specializing in healing trauma and sexual abuse.

Danielle also trains new breathwork facilitators and leads retreats around the country.

She found breathwork training in 2010 and it completely changed her life. The breathwork she learned there has proven so effective in helping clients heal more completely and feel better faster that it is now the main modality she uses. She undertakes it and teaches it as a spiritual practice that she has seen open up—for herself and her peers, students, and clients—all the kinds of experiences that Mia and others come to know in this book.

Danielle grew up in Lima, Peru, and now lives in San Diego County, California.

To learn more about Danielle and her work, trainings, and retreats please visit http://www.thrutheheart.com/